MW00945169

LET YOUR LOVE FLOW AGAIN

A BREATH WITHOUT LIFE NOVEL
- BOOK THREE -

AN INSPIRATIONAL ROMANCE STORY

Edited by Dr. Holly Smit

Cover design by P and N Graphics

Cowboy Model, Dr. Matthew Hooper

Cover cowboy pencil art by Joyce Geleynse

Book Layout by ebooklaunch.com

DEDICATION

This book is dedicated to the hard-working heroes that are our nation's smokejumpers.

As I researched everything I could lay my eyes on about smokejumpers, there was one thing every reference had in common. Though smokejumpers seem to bask in the risk and rush of their job, it is clear they have something more important in common: Heart. A heart to jump, extinguish, and ultimately save lives and property. Without this special group of people we would all have experienced much greater loss.

May God always bless the heroes of this world!

JANITH HOOPER

LET YOUR LOVE FLOW AGAIN

A BREATH WITHOUT LIFE NOVEL
- BOOK THREE -

AN INSPIRATIONAL ROMANCE STORY

Books by Janith Hooper

Harper Ranch Series:

Quaking Heart Novels

Ride With Me

Stay With Me

Fight For Me

Cooper Bar-6 Ranch Series:

Breath Without Life Novels

Let Your Heart Beat Again

Let Yourself Run Free Again

Let Your Love Flow Again

More to come…

PROLOGUE

August 1959
Fairbanks, Alaska

C lay Cooper seethed as he analyzed the backcountry blaze below. The fire had spread far beyond what it should have already. Dang the US Forest Service! They knew full well his smokejumpers were first responders; they were supposed to be called out at the first sign of smoke.

Ever since the Federal Bureau of Land Management established the current base in Fairbanks, Alaska, it had become a rival to the US Forest Service instead of an ally. It shouldn't be about who was best. It was about saving lives and protecting property. This conflict had to stop before smokejumpers lost their edge and became mere statistics.

Clay rose from the bench seat, having to hunch over a tad in the Grumman 21 Goose. He was too tall to be a smokejumper, yet employed as one anyway due to a shortage of men willing to put their lives on the line.

"Straighten up, Coop. Your pack's not right," Martin, Clay's best friend from school days, said at his back. Clay felt the sharp tug on his jumper's pack. This was part of the training. Getting others ready. Soon enough, Martin would be ready to make his debut jump.

"Where would you have me put my head? Through the roof?" Clay barked, then regretted it. He needed to remember Martin was fragile these days. He arrived in Alaska too soon after putting his wife in the ground. Martin never believed he was cut out for this job. But he'd come to be with his best friend and, like Clay, to rid his heart of pain. Two good reasons *not* to be a jumper.

Clay shifted from one foot to the other, anxious to get moving. With Martin's final yank to the strap at his chest, Clay drew in a deep breath, or tried to. The pack always kept him from it. Not so much from the strap, but from the reminder this was serious business and to keep his head in the game.

The plane circled then leveled over their target. Clay wanted to rage at the Forest Service for the red and orange licking lethally up through brown smoke. His group should have been called out when the smoke was white, still full of moisture. Now there was no time for extra thought. Just a race into more dangerous conditions and the hope it all went as planned.

Clay drummed on the window, unable to keep his fingers still. The ancient regret was there. Showing up as it always did just before a jump. Pushing his mind where it shouldn't go. Rule number one of the *do nots* of smokejumping. *Do not* let your mind go anywhere but on the fire, the jump, the team, the outcome.

But his mind never did heed that warning.

Peggy. If only he'd tried apologizing to her before he left Wyoming all those years ago. Now he could be making her a widow if he didn't survive today. Didn't matter she'd divorced him. She'd never remarried and neither had he. In his mind they were still 'one.'

Keep your head out of the past and on that blaze, he reprimanded himself.

"You're up next, Cooper!"

Flushing his destructive thoughts, Clay positioned himself at the doorless opening of the aircraft. He clicked his tail to the restraining line while his gaze landed on the jumpspot, his heart jumping madly in his chest. It always surprised him, the exhilaration and fear that mingled before a jump. Maybe not quite fear, more respect for what the beast could do.

After pulling his helmet on over his short-cropped hair, he strapped it in place, then pushed the screen down over his face. It reminded him. New gear was coming. Gear he'd pushed Cap to put in for. Bars instead of screens on their helmets were safer. Gave them better visuals.

Focus

His mind swirled back to the jump and his usual mantra. *Remember me, Peggy.*

Three, two, one... With a firm push, he sprang out the door. The airstream caught and yanked him hard against the stationery strap. The parachute released with a whoosh and a snap. It flapped in the slipstream until it finally swallowed enough air and opened into a white mushroom.

Everything roared—the wind, the fire below, the pulse in his ears. His legs stretched below him, as if he stood on the smoke-stained sky. The bite of acrid air hit his nostrils. Clay counted the seconds as he coasted toward the jumpspot. Toward his next collision with danger, landing with the extra hundred pounds on his back, chest, and calves. Hopefully with all his bones intact.

The clearing expanded as he drew near. Flicks of red and blue flame thrived within the smoke, a monster clawing its way through the haze to freedom. Way too hot, way too far gone for them to have been called in so late.

His inner fury rose, equaling the beast below.

The earth rushed toward him.

Clay's distraction was a crucial mistake. Regret and his right foot hit the ground at the same time. A sharp sting radiated from his heel up his calf as he tucked and rolled.

He ended in a heap of gear, howling with pain and rage at his own stupidity.

• • •

Twenty-five-hundred punishing steps later, with the help of his comrades, Clay found himself in the company of his frowning physician. He didn't have time for this. His crew was still out there, extinguishing the wildfire, while he and two other men he'd taken from the job gimped out of the Alaskan forestline to the stashed vehicles. One jumper went back to the front, the other drove him an hour away to the hospital in Fairbanks.

He'd acted like a dang rookie! Letting thoughts of his ex-wife distract him when by now she should be ancient history.

He was in no mood to be reminded he'd taken his mind off the jump. "Just get me back on my feet, *Dr. Cummings.*"

Samuel Cummings had been a friend of his since his first injury, two years ago. Since then he'd seen the doc for a dozen different injuries, all curable, all perfectly fine now—all preventable. Clay liked Sam, he did. But his nagging about being a daredevil was a moot argument for a darned smokejumper. He was getting tired of defending himself.

The doctor peered over his glasses at him. "You take too many risks, Clay. And you don't keep your mind on the jump. All your injuries are avoidable. You know that." The doctor took a breather while he seemed to be contemplating. He sighed. "I'm putting you on bed rest. I'll fill out the forms for your Commander."

"Just bandage me up. I need to get back to that blaze!"

Sam stepped forward and leaned in. "You're not going anywhere, Hotshot. Understand?"

"We're friends. Doesn't mean you can bully me. Get me back out there."

Doc leaned back on his heels and crammed his hands in his pockets. Not the professional now, but the friend. "Clay, you have a torn Achilles. Do you even know what that means?"

"I know what an Achilles is, Doc. I've injured it before, remember?"

"Yes, and that's my point. You do it again, and you could lose your ability to walk. To walk, Clay. Get it?"

Clay blew out a breath and braced his hands behind him, hearing the crinkle of the white paper covering the examining table. "That bad?"

"That bad." His look told Clay he was sympathetic but worried.

Clay studied the doc's face. Looked for a possible break in his resolve. Didn't see it. He worked at lowering his voice. "Okay. I won't go back out today. But I've got to go soon, Doc. This isn't just my job, it's my life."

Sam crossed his arms over his chest. "And why is that? Why no social life?"

"You know why."

"Your wife left you over four years ago. Too long to still be mourning what was."

Clay sat forward so fast he nearly slipped off the table and grabbed for the doc's lapel. Missed and banged his bad heel against the metal front. "Son-of-a—"

"Quiet down. I have other patients." Sam moved closer, dropped his voice. "What happened with you and Peggy? You never told me."

"That's because it's none of your business. Besides, like you said, I should be over it. I am over it."

Sam's eyes softened.

Ah, see. This is exactly why he didn't talk about it. "Don't start that pity bullcrap, Sam. I'm fine."

"Tell me what happened."

"What are you, a psychologist now too? It's not enough you get into my body parts, you gotta get into my head?"

The doctor stood silent with his arms crossed. Looked like he would wait all day. Clay cursed to himself. "Fine. I'll tell you, but then you gotta promise to leave it alone."

"I promise."

"We got married straight out of high school. Two dumb kids so wrapped up in each other, it was either get married or end up like my dad—in trouble and having to get married. We opted for the early marriage."

"What did your folks think?"

"Mom died in childbirth with the twins. Thought I told you that."

Doc shook his head, no.

"Dad was too busy to bother with any of us. So I doubt he cared one way or the other."

The look on doc's face said he didn't believe that, but it was how Clay remembered it.

"After we were married, I went off to make money the only way I knew how—rodeo circuit. Peg came with me for awhile. Then opted to stay home with Colt." That'd been the royal fist to the gut.

Shock brought a frown to doc's face. "What do you mean, stayed with Colt?"

"I mean she stopped coming with me. Colt was a bigger draw."

He shook his head. "I doubt any of your brothers would get in the way of your marriage."

Clay sighed, ran a hand down his face. "You'd be wrong. Colt did. It's what split us up." He jumped down off the table onto one foot and bounced a couple of times to gain his balance. "Enough talk. What do I need to do with this?" He pointed at the leg that was wrapped tight to mid-thigh.

"Time for you to make a decision. Are you going to comply? Or do I let your superiors know about your condition? Have them put you on permanent disability."

He glared. "You wouldn't."

"Don't test me. Now," Doc waited a few heartbeats. "What's it going to be?"

"I'll rest."

"For three weeks, at least. Preferably six."

Clay scrubbed a hand through his hair and grimaced. "I can't do that."

"You have to. What don't you understand about the possibility of not walking again?"

Clay dropped his head back, stared at the too bright lights overhead and sucked in breath after breath. Yes, he was breathing, but he'd stopped living long ago. What would be another few weeks? He straightened, met the doctor's gaze. "Fine. Three weeks. That's it. It'll be fine by then."

"We can only hope. Come back in then, and I'll check it for you. If the Achilles can't heal itself a second time, you'll need surgery to repair it." The doctor handed him a pair of crutches. The same ones he'd used several times before. The same ones he refused to keep, so the Doc kept for him.

"Fine, I'll be back." Clay crutched his way to the door and turned the knob.

"And Clay?" Doc said.

He glanced back over a shoulder.

"Give Colt a chance to tell you his side of the story."

• • •

June 1961

Peggy ran her fingertip down the graduation roster and grinned when she found her name, right at the top: Margaret Ann Cooper. In the top ten of her graduating class at Case Western Reserve, University of Cleveland.

She was officially a physiologist.

My, but that sounded important. More significantly, it *was* important. Not to give her boasting rights. No. She could care less about who she'd impress. It was to help people like her brother who never walked again after an accident because of a quack doctor and a backward philosophy. Her baby brother hadn't deserved to be bedridden for the rest of his short life. Now, he was gone, and she would do her best to keep others from that same fate if it was the only thing she accomplished from all her hard work.

She wanted to be one of the first house call physical therapists in the country. Help infirm patients right in their own homes. It would come to that. She'd be sure. But for now she was headed to Campbell County Memorial Hospital in Gillette to help open the Physical Therapy program as their first physiologist.

As soon as she found an apartment in Gillette, she'd relax a little. It was close enough to Sundance for brief visits home, but far enough away to ensure she didn't run into her ex-husband's family—the Coopers. At least Clay was in Alaska, last she'd heard. She frowned. He was doing what he loved best. Endangering his life. This time it was in the crazy pursuit of smoke-jumping. At least now he saved lives and property, instead of getting beat half to death on bucking broncs just to make a name for himself.

But becoming a smokejumper was just another excuse to be who he truly was—a daredevil. How typical of him to risk his life, panic those who loved him, and avoid responsibility through his single lifestyle.

Oh, people were only too determined to keep her informed about his bachelor ways. He liked women just fine, but he'd never remarried. Word was, he didn't want to be held up by any of them, or told what to do. She herself had found that out the hard way. Sorrow pressed her down, its weight familiar and suffocating. With monumental effort, she shook it off.

Once she got her career rolling in Gillette, she'd date again. But this time, she'd find a sweet-tempered man. Someone who knew better than to jump off the roof into a pile of hay, or wrap his hand in a rope tied to the back of a crazed bronc, or traipse around the country following a blaze and his own set of dreams.

Nope, she'd learned her lesson. Mild-mannered and accommodating it was. She'd never go for a lunatic again.

CHAPTER 1

End of November 1961

Ranch life. Clay couldn't adjust to it. Never had, never would. Too many people. Not enough real action.

He had a hard time wrapping his mind around the possibility that *rancher* might be his only title now. Ever since that second injury to his Achilles two years ago August, his leg had never been the same. The doctors knew it, his family knew it, but he couldn't quite come to grips with it—because it meant smokejumping was off the table. The ache that wrenched his chest the day the doctor had divulged that sorry piece of news was still there. Twisted in deeper than ever.

Now, he found himself at the Bar-6—asked to come here by his father—and it had been the worst decision of his life.

He glanced down at his casted leg. The re-injured Achilles. For the third time. This time from falling off a dang horse.

He cursed, and crutched his way across the drive-way and into the barn. No way could he live day to day as an invalid. He needed to do something—anything—to release the pressure building up inside.

"What are you doing out here?" The voice was Trevor's; the tone accusatory.

Clay tightened his grip on the crutches and turned a hair. Trevor walked out of the shadows to stand before Clay in a fighting stance—feet spread, weight balanced, head forward. One thing was certain, if he stayed much longer on the Bar-6, Clay would come to blows with his eldest brother.

He forced a response through clenched teeth. "Come to help."

Trev's retort showed on his face before he delivered it with a scoff. "Right. One-legged."

Lifting himself a mite on his crutches, Clay repositioned his good foot to hold him better. Trevor's gaze followed his movements. Anyone else would have been sympathetic. Not so this brother. No. He looked put out. One more *cowboy* unable to do his job, which put him farther behind the eight ball.

Clay stretched to his full height. "I came out to do what I can. Put me to work or don't. Your call. Just tryin' to make the old man happy."

Annoyance shifted to disgust on his brother's face. "Well, that's one thing we can agree on."

"You still fightin' the old man?"

"Coop and I don't see eye to eye most days. Not that he sticks around long enough to find out."

Clay clanked forward on his crutches, staring Trevor in the face. He was a tad shorter but had the same bulk, so he was one of the few people brave enough to do that. "Don't know about the last few years, but this time it couldn't be helped." Their dad had done the right thing by helping out his wife's family when Rebecca's dad had been seriously injured. They'd been in California ever since.

Trev sneered but didn't comment.

Clay sneered right back. "Yeah, we're all a mass of broken feelings, egos, and spirits. Waah, waah. Poor little Cooper boys, don't have a mom and their dad's never home."

A low growl came from deep in Trevor's throat, one side of his mouth rising in contempt before he took a step closer to Clay. Nearly nose to nose now, Clay wondered which one of them would throw the first punch.

"Knock it off you two," came a female voice from the barn opening. "You're wasting precious time with your pissing contest. And you're letting the cold in. What were you, born in this barn?"

They both jerked their heads in the direction of the voice behind them.

That'd be Betsy—or Rylee, now. Colt's nickname was going to stick for sure, seeing as how the two were engaged. Trev looked flatly at her, and stalked off. Of course it was her, offering her two cents. The crude language came from her years competing in rodeo. How strange that his peacemaker brother had chosen such a feisty, rough-edged woman. Then again, it was no skin off his back. Maybe the rest of his brothers would finally stand a chance with the swooning women of Crook County. Not Clay, though. He'd already had his chance, and wouldn't be looking for another.

Thinking of Colt brought on the same scowl he'd seen on Trevor's face at mention of their father. Calm or not, compliant or not, Colt still rubbed him wrong. The sod always wanted to do the right thing, even when gray lines were called for. The Goody Two Shoes nickname Clay used to call him growing up still applied. Colt could do no wrong. That is, until he'd played his part in breaking up Clay's marriage. Sure, he believed Colt now when he said he hadn't had an affair with Peggy. But he sure as heck had been there for her—too often. Listening. Sympathizing. And hugging. Those dad-blamed hugs.

"What do you want, Texas?" Clay asked Rylee.

"It's Wyoming to you, mister." She strolled over and gave him a poke in the arm.

"Not yet. I don't see a ring on that callused finger of yours yet."

She laughed, a throaty sound. "Yeah, maybe not but I'm not leaving Wyoming, or your brother, ever again." He found his mood lifting from the joy resonating off her. He missed female company. Never got much in Alaska. Not that he couldn't have if he'd searched it out. Too much trouble. And no point.

He couldn't help the small grin he gave her. "Happy?"

"Yeah, I'm happy. Colt and I just set our wedding date. Can't tell you yet." She giggled this time, her joy apparent.

Memories of long ago and another wedding socked him in the chest. The divorce had done the same, as completely and as painfully as the head of a bucking bronc. And a full breath had never returned to his lungs.

Rylee looked contemplative for a moment. "Say Clayton…don't you have a doctor's appointment for that foot?"

"Ahhh shoot! Forgot all about it." He turned, almost too fast to keep his crutches under him, but managed to put them in motion along with his one good leg. "Tell Trev I'll be back later to help," he hollered over one shoulder.

"Don't worry about it. I can do whatever he needs."

He'd wave a response but didn't dare take his hands off his crutches.

"Hey, wait a minute." Rylee was at his side in a flash. "You can't drive yourself. I'll let Trevor know I'll drive you there. Get yourself in the passenger side."

"No way you're driving my truck. She's an old girl. Can't take your abuse."

"Ha, men!" She jeered. "Get in my truck then. I'll be right back."

By the time she returned, Clay had barely lifted himself into the tall telephone truck Rylee drove. Crazy vehicle for such a petite woman.

She jumped in with no trouble at all and started it up. Clay had to admit, this girl could hold her own in any situation. Maybe Colt had the right idea after all.

She swung them around and headed down the long drive. "We'll be there in a jiffy."

Right about then the truck banged into one of their potholes and bounced them both up into the hard roof. "Ow! Criminy, why don't you guys fix this crappy road?"

Clay braced himself with one hand above him, the other on the dashboard. "Slow down, Texas! That might help."

"Are you finally going to call me Wyoming after Colt and I are married?"

"No."

She chuckled. "We going to the clinic?"

He did like how Rylee was always direct. Didn't hold back any truths. Peggy used to keep stuff from him. Made them argue over everything until they got to the bottom of things. If they talked at all.

His mind drifted to that marriage. Though it made him feel like a failure in so many ways, he missed the arguing—the bantering, as she used to call it.

"So, what's your plan, Clayton? You stickin' around now that you can't smokejump anymore?"

A small laugh burst from him. "Don't beat around the bush, do you?"

"Huh?" She shot him a confused expression.

"You just keep on rollin', no matter who you plow over."

She blew out a quick breath. "Did we miss an injury to your head? Don't know what the heck you're talkin' about. Or is this the way you keep the ladies from getting too interested? You baffle them."

He laughed again. "Keep up here, Rylee-girl. You don't pull any punches is all I mean."

Her face scrunched up. Could it really be she didn't understand the sayings? Nah, she was way too smart for that. He wasn't going to clear it up for her either. If it stopped her talking for thinking then maybe she'd quit digging around in his business and he'd get some peace and quiet.

It didn't take her long. "Oh. I get it. I'm being blunt. Asking about your plans. Too personal?"

The grunt he made let her know she was spot on.

"Well, too bad. You're going to be my brother soon, so get used to it." She laughed then, one of her raspy, throaty laughs, and he couldn't help but grin.

She was going to make an interesting sister-in-law. Might make the Bar-6 more tolerable in spite of his boycott against women. He guessed females in the family were okay. Safe. He hadn't met Rebecca yet. But if his dad chose her she had to be tough.

"Well?" she prompted.

Typical female. Never let up. "Don't know yet. We'll see what Doc says."

She glanced at him with sympathy written all over her face. "He's not going to tell you it's all right to go back to jumpin' out of airplanes, Clayton. You know that, right?"

Whenever he thought of it, he got even more depressed. How would he survive without the thrill of smokejumping? What could a broken daredevil do with his life?

He didn't answer Rylee, and was blessed by silence the rest of the way.

The over-large telephone truck rattled as Rylee maneuvered it into the parking lot for Dr. Trenton. By the time Clay got himself out, bouncing on one foot, Rylee was at his side, crutches in hand. At least she was helpful, if not reserved.

She helped him through the doors and pointed to a chair as she took it upon herself to check him in. Women! Treated men like little boys way too often. "Listen," he said when she sat down in a hard chair next to him. "I can handle this. You stay here." He gave her a stern glare and a rigid finger pointing at her chair.

"Nae. Don't think so. I was with you when you injured your Achilles—it was my fault, remember?—so I'll stay with you now."

There were others in the waiting room, so he lowered his voice. "Did you sabotage that saddle's cinch strap?"

She shook her head adamantly.

"It. Was. Not. Your fault. So you don't need to mother me."

"I'm not. I'm sistering you." She grinned, far too happy for the mood he was in. And it wasn't getting better any time soon.

A half hour passed while Rylee annoyed him with her humming. The nurse came through the door for the fourth time, and Clay decided if this wasn't for him, he was out of there. Of course, convincing Rylee of that made him curse under his breath.

"What did you say?" Rylee asked.

"Nothing."

"Clayton Cooper." The nurse said from the doorway.

"Finally," he mumbled. He pushed himself out of the chair and stood, wanting his little 'helper' to bring him his crutches, but she'd left his side to head toward the open door. Most likely to keep him from forcing her to stay in the waiting room.

He reached behind him, but before he could grab the metal contraptions, a young woman took hold of them at the same time another lady already had her hands on them. One a brunette, the other a blonde, both attractive enough, and both looking at him like he was their next meal.

He groaned. Bad time for Rylee to abandon him.

"I've got this, ladies." Neither heard him since they were currently fighting over who'd hand him his sticks. He tried to reach between them to get hold, but as soon as he grasped the darn things, one of the ladies yanked them away from the other—and from him. He was going over and there was no way to catch himself.

"Oh my gosh, grab him!" One of the women said.

"I've got him." The other said at the same time.

Clay spread his arms and caught himself on the women's shoulders. They all nearly ended up in a heap on the floor but for Rylee suddenly appearing, pushing them all back upright. Strong and meddling, that was his future sister-in-law. Pride seeped in, despite Clay's desire to keep all women at arm's length. The tally was in. This spunky redhead with the mouth that didn't quit had proven herself to him. She'd be a terrific sister and friend.

"Okay, ladies. I've got him." Rylee yanked the crutches from the two women in spite of the nasty remarks and scowls she received. Didn't faze her one bit. She carefully placed each crutch under his pits, flicked her hands at the interfering women, and made a path through the open door past the nurse.

Clay wanted to smirk at the two left behind, but decided a nod was the proper thing to do. Not that proper was his usual choice. But thanks to Rylee, he felt they'd had enough.

Once in the room, the nurse removed his cast, and wheeled him off to X-ray.

After re-settling himself in the room and onto the examining table, Clay's mood had shifted back to dark in time for the doctor's grand entrance. Thoughts of his future had invaded, leaving him utterly bereft. Thank goodness Rylee had picked this time to be silent in the corner. Likely hoping he wouldn't send her out. Which was what he should do. Still might.

Dr. Trenton came forward with his hand extended. As they shook hands, the doctor began his little speech. "How's the heel, Clay?"

"Haven't tested it yet, Doc. Should I?" He started to jump down, but the doctor stopped him with a hand to his knee.

"Let's talk first."

That didn't sound good. The expression on the doctor's face didn't bode well either.

"Well, the X-ray shows your Achilles has healed. There's a lot of scar tissue. The thing is, if you want full mobility, you're going to need physical therapy."

"How do you mean?"

"I mean I'm going to have someone come out to your home three days a week for several weeks to work on stretching and flexibility exercises with you."

"No need." He wasn't about to let anyone put their hands all over him. Not happening.

"Do you want to walk?"

He felt the blood drain from his face. "Are you saying that, without therapy, I won't walk? That I can't walk now?" He jumped off the table, careful to land on his good foot, and started to take a step.

Both the doctor and Rylee scrambled forward, and that was a good thing since his foot didn't flex when it was supposed to. With the doctor on one side and Rylee on the other, he hopped back and sat, a wave of nausea threatening to empty his stomach right there on the floor. After a few deep breaths he lifted his chin, looked the doctor in the eye. "You're serious. I can't walk."

"Clay, you will walk again, but you have to go about this properly. That's what the physiologist will help you with."

Bile came up his throat further this time. The doctor back in Alaska had warned him not to take this foot for granted after the first injury. After the second…well, he should have listened back then. Maybe he wouldn't be in this predicament if he'd just get out of his own way.

"Okay, Doc. I'm listening. I'll do whatever you say. If I do, will I be mobile again? Fully?"

The doctor eyed him with the same warning look he'd seen many times before. "I know you, Clayton. Been seeing you your whole life, every time one of your stunts broke or strained or tore something. But this time, it can change your whole life. No more stunts; no bronc riding, no jumping off bridges or horses, and *no smokejumping*."

Both the doctor and Rylee stilled at the fatal words, watching for his reaction. What could he say, other than, "I hear you, Doctor."

"All right, you hear me, but will you do as I say?" The physician knew him well.

Clay ran a hand through thick hair that needed cutting. Ran that same hand over his face, feeling a several-days-old beard that had already grown soft to the touch. Like *he* would soon be—soft. His life had gone to cow dung and there wasn't a dang thing he could do about it.

Since his breakfast was still in his throat, he just nodded his agreement.

"We're good, Doc. Thank you. I'll just take him home now," Rylee said in a whirl. "Can he use his foot yet or should he keep using the crutches and wait for the physio—waddaya call it?"

"Crutches and wait for the physiologist, or physical therapist. Same difference. I'll send her out on Monday. Since this is Friday, that gives you a few days to get used to the idea. Take it easy, my boy." He patted Clay on the shoulder and turned to exit the room.

"Doc?"

The doctor turned, waited.

"Why a woman? Don't you have any male therapists?"

"No. And even if I did, Sally is the best."

Sally? "Sally Wagoner, by chance?"

The doctor's eyes lit up and a smile Clay couldn't remember ever seeing on him crossed his face. "Yes, do you know, Sally?"

Clay nodded.

"Good. That should help you relax about it. Sally's one of the good ones—good person, I mean. She'll see you Monday after her normal hours. Probably around 6:00 PM. Will that work for you?"

"We'll be watching for her," Rylee answered for him. "She can join us for supper."

The doctor nodded one last time and vacated the room.

Once alone again, Rylee asked him, "Who's Sally to you?"

"You get right down to the nitty-gritty, don't you, girl?"

"Yeah, yeah. I'm blunt. Who's Sally to you?"

Clay took the crutches that Rylee was holding and placed them under his arms. "Grab my sock, will you?" He clomped on his good foot and the crutches toward the door and waited for Rylee to open it.

"Sally?"

"Tell you in the truck."

By the time they got him settled back in the too-tall truck and they were on their way home, Clay was exhausted.

"So. Sally?" Rylee asked as she rounded the corner for home.

"No one to me, Texas. She was this tall, shy thing in school. Stayed in the background."

That seemed to appease Rylee, but didn't soothe him. The thought of Sally coming to his house for physical therapy ate at him. He hadn't let a woman put her hands on him since Peggy had left. No one knew that. His bachelor reputation gave everyone a different impression. He'd never worked at correcting it. It never mattered.

But now, the thought of having a woman touch him awakened something in him besides what it should. The very real possibility of opening old wounds.

CHAPTER 2

C olt stood at the barn door, arms akimbo, a scowl riding his face. Clay shook his head. Looked like he was going to get a good old-fashioned scolding from his big brother. He chuckled at the ridiculousness of it.

"What's so funny. We're both in trouble," Rylee said with a frown that matched her fiancé's. "I hate disappointing him."

Colt tromped forward the minute the telephone truck parked in its usual place next to the barn. He had Rylee's door flung open and her in his arms before Clay could even open his door. *Not disappointed then*, he scoffed to himself.

Not one word was spoken, but a glance told Clay their lip-lock might last awhile. Seeing their intimacy made Clay's smirk vanish. He'd had that once; affection, connection, love. It was rare to let himself go back there in his mind, but seeing Rylee and Colt every day was changing that. As soon as his dad and Rebecca were back home, his discomfort would double. He'd seen affectionate couples before, but there was something about it coming from family that made all that lovey-dovey stuff tougher to stomach.

He had to figure out how to get off the Bar-6 as soon as possible. Once his foot was functional, he was gone.

Clay struggled to get himself on the ground, then reached behind the seat for his crutches. Just as he turned to put them in place, Colt was in his face. "Taking off with my woman, huh? Couldn't give me a heads up?"

Rylee was at his back, patting him. "My fault, Blue Eyes. I insisted on driving him, he was late, and I told Trevor. Didn't he tell you?" Her voice was light, calming.

Colt glanced over his shoulder at her, his face instantly softening. "Trevor? You're joshing, right? He doesn't tell us squat—ever."

"Oh. Didn't know that. Sorry, Hon. Come on, I'll help you feed the animals." Rylee took his hand and turned him as easily as a brand new calf. And then they were off, holding hands and smiling at each other like they were the only two people left on Mother Earth. Clay growled. *It's okay, Clay. Not your fault.* Colt could have said that, but hadn't bothered.

Dad-gum, he had to get out of here.

He looked over the large ranch house with its many rectangular windows, all lit up for the evening. This was the place where six sons had tried to grow up with a father who had only been there half the time, and a housekeeper—the only mother figure they'd had—who'd tried her best until her own family needed her back in Mexico. Clay figured his upbringing was likely why his own marriage failed. What did he know about women?

A slam brought his attention to the back door and an emerging Brand. Great, another brother getting in the middle of Clay's life. Made him want to rant.

"Hey, Big Daddy. What's going on?"

"Nothing. I'm going in."

Brand turned to accompany him to the back door. "What'd the doc say?"

He debated whether or not to fill Brand in, but the truth was, Brand would be available. And without his obnoxious twin, Bronc, he might actually be helpful. "I start physical therapy on Monday."

"Physical therapy? What's that do?"

His crutches were beginning to make his armpits sore. He knew better than to use them that way, but he was tired and his arm muscles had had enough. "Help me to the sofa and I'll fill you in."

Brand took one of Clay's crutches in hand and swung a shoulder under his arm. They made it easily to the couch, where Clay flopped down and tossed the other crutch aside. He was sick of being injured. Had done it too many times in his life. And now a physical therapist…

He groaned, his mood growing darker.

"What's the groan for, brother?"

"I don't want some woman in here rubbing on my leg for the next six weeks."

"If that's what the doctor says has to be done, you need to do it. I'll help."

That gave Clay an idea. "Maybe you can. You can watch her do her job, then you can take over. We'll get rid of her."

Brand beamed. Good ole Brand. The only brother wanting to please everyone all the time. Especially when his twin wasn't around. This might work out just fine.

• • •

The weekend had proved to be even more annoying. More and more, Clay yearned to go back to Alaska. At least there everyone left him alone. Here everyone bugged him. *Do you want anything? Can I help you to the table? Let me help you with your shower.* That last one came from Rylee, and he found himself wanting to take her up on it. Strip down, shock her to the core, then laugh his fool head off. Rub it in Colt's face. See how he liked having a brother spend time with his woman. Time that should be reserved for husband and wife only.

Yeah, Colt had tried to explain. *Peggy just talked to me. Told me things I thought she was telling you. She was unhappy. It was you who should have been listening.*

The whole debacle turned his gut over again.

And why was Peggy still in his thoughts? "Because I'm stuck in one spot with nothin' to do but hark back to memories better left in the trash!"

"What?" Brand hollered from the kitchen. He came out a few seconds later with a tray of lemonade and cookies. Looked like Rylee'd been at it again. He was gonna get fat on top of dying from boredom.

"Wasn't talkin' to you. Why are you bringing this stuff out?"

"Cuz your therapist is going to be here any minute now. Thought it would be the kind thing to do since Rylee had to pass on making supper."

Clay rubbed his hand across his mouth and the week old beard growing on his face. "Geez, Brand. You're becoming a girl."

Brand clanked the tray down the last few inches, nearly spilling the lemonade, and straightened. "What the heck, Clay! Just because I want to make things easier for you doesn't mean you have to go all nasty-brother on me. Get your own darn snacks from now on!" He turned on his heel and stormed toward the kitchen.

Shoot. He always had to apologize. "Hold on."

Brand slammed on his brakes and turned. The look on his face was comical. So offended…and young. Clay needed to remember Brand was only twenty. And had a personality that didn't benefit a man. As in, sensitive to the point of wimpy. Poor guy. If he hadn't also had the Cooper good looks, he'd be sunk with the ladies. Ha! While Clay was here, he'd have to toughen him up.

"Thank you, little brother. It was *nice* of you to make snacks." Crap, just using the word *nice* made Clay's hair stand up on end.

A car door closed outside. Both brothers looked at the front door. "I didn't even hear a car roll in," Clay said.

"I'll go see." Brand launched toward the door, helpful as always, and swung the door open just as a tall brown-haired girl was about to knock. They both laughed as she introduced herself.

"Hi, I'm Sally Wagoner, here to see Clayton Cooper."

Clay leaned forward, trying to see around Brand but couldn't quite. The boy had really gained some girth over the past four years.

"I'm his brother, Brand. Good to see you again. I think I met you at one of Clay's games, or maybe it was the rodeo. Can't remember where, but I remember you. You're a tall one, aren't you?"

She sighed. "Yeah." There was acceptance in her voice along with disappointment. "I'm almost six foot. Too tall."

"Not for me," Brand said and gave her one of the smiles the ladies loved. It was true. All of the Cooper men were well over six foot. Sally should feel comfortable here.

Brand backed a step and swung his hand in the direction of the family room, and Clay. "He's right in there."

He had to give Brand points for good manners and courtesy.

She smiled prettily back at Brand, then moved past him and into the room. Brand nearly skipped along behind. Seeing the suitcase for the first time, his brother reached for it. "Here, let me get that for you."

Sally turned her head and smiled at Brand again. "No need. I'm used to it. It's like one of my appendages now." She laughed, a sweet sound that had his brother swooning.

Clay wanted to laugh at his brother, but his own sour mood at having to do this therapy thing kept him from it. He wanted this over with. The sooner the better.

Sally set the suitcase down without a sound and stuck her hand out to Clay. "How are you, Clay? It's been a long time."

Clay leaned forward enough to grasp her hand and give it a quick shake.

"I have some snacks for you two. Would you like a lemonade?" Brand asked her. His face beamed with interest and joy.

Too dang happy for Clay's mood. "Enough. We see it. We'll get it if we want some."

Sally frowned at him, then swung another sweet smile at Brand's downtrodden face. "Thank you, Brand. I do believe a lemonade would be very nice right about now." When she looked back at Clay, she puckered her lips in disapproval.

Good going, Clayton, old boy. Great way to start off the dang sessions on a bad note. But that wasn't unusual for him. He was known in all circles as the bad-tempered hothead and showoff.

Brand smiled and poured Sally a glass of lemonade. Handed it to her. She took such a small sip, Clay knew it was only to appease Brand. All right, fine. He was an asshole. He knew it. Everyone else needed to get used to it. It was about to worsen. "Let's get on with this. What do I do?"

Sally's head popped over to him, the drink halfway to her mouth. "Oh. Okay. We'll get started." She carefully set her lemonade on a coaster on an end table then hefted her suitcase to the end of the sofa. Once opened, she removed some sort of liniment. "We'll start with a good rub-down, then we'll stretch."

He stiffened at the inevitable *touching*. "Are you doing this too?"

Confusion marred her expression. "What? No. Just you."

"Then say *you* not *we*."

"Oh, I'm sorry. Of course."

"Stop it, Clay!" Brand barked. "Be nice."

Nice. There was that word again. Not part of his vocabulary. He ignored his brother and kept his glare on the woman, waiting for her next move.

She perched on the edge of the coffee table in front of him, then stood again. She looked to Brand. "Would you mind pushing this back a bit for me?"

"Be glad to." He jumped forward and shoved the heavy table back a foot. "That enough?"

She smiled sweetly and perched again. Her attention back on Clay, she said, "Okay. Put your leg right on my lap."

Sally wore a white nurse's uniform and white tights. Her dress hung modestly past her knees when she sat. Clay was sure she worked in this uniform all the time, but to put his dirty ole foot on her pristine lap? Wasn't happening. "No."

"Excuse me?"

"Not putting my grimy foot on your dress."

She sighed in relief and laughed a bit. "Oh that. Don't worry. I'm used to this. This is my work uniform."

"Still not gonna do it."

"Oh for cryin' out loud, brother. Do it or this is gonna take all day," Brand barked.

He had a point. While debating the request, Clay watched the expression on her face turn fearful, and her hands began to shake. Who had the doctor sent to him? He had to remember who Sally was from school. Always in the background, never said much. Meek, shy, a push-over. He groaned to himself. Nothing seemed worse to him than a weak woman he would run all over.

"Fine. Here." He lifted his leg and tried to set it carefully on her lap.

"Oh. Heavy," she tittered on an exhale.

He started to lift it off, but she held tight to his foot. "It's fine. Leave it. I'm just going to remove your sock."

"What?" He jerked more upright in the sofa, which pulled his heel heavily against her thigh.

She gave out a tortured sound, her eyes growing wide. He yanked his leg off this time.

"I'll get the foot stool," Brand said. Smart boy. Once he had the stool in place right next to Sally's knees, Clay positioned his foot on it. Brand stood over him for a few seconds until Clay glowered up at him. "I'll…uh…just take this tray of goodies back to the kitchen."

Sally gave Clay a tight smile. "This should work. Now, I'm going to remove your sock."

"Why?"

"Remember, I told you we have to massage the leg first."

"You and who?"

Her dark brows creased down the middle. "Just me."

"Then say, '*I* have to massage your leg.'"

Yeah, she was getting angry. He could see it clearly, still she'd yet to bark a thing back at him. He'd always thought his ex-wife was annoying with her talkativeness, or the way she ignored his ultimatums, or reacted to his demands, but at least she stood up to him.

This filly…

Man, he detested women he could trounce so easily.

He really shouldn't goad her, but he couldn't help himself. It was too easy. Didn't find this sort of woman in Alaska. Well, he didn't find many women at all in Alaska. Another reason he wanted back there.

"Yes, sir. I'll do better. What *I* need to do now is massage this leg first before we attempt stretching exercises."

"Why don't you just show me what to do and I'll do it. No need to waste your time."

"No, we need to—"

This time he gave her a look she instantly read. "I mean, *I* need to do the deep massage. There's a particular way it's done."

Brand sauntered back into the room.

"Teach Brand here what to do."

Her mouth tightened in response. "No. Mr. Cooper, you must let me do this. Dr. Trenton wants me to do this."

"You still giving her a bad time?" Brand said. "Just let her do her job."

He glared at Brand but it didn't seem to intimidate him in the slightest. Funny how Brand never let anyone bully him when his twin was such a bully, and more easily intimidated than Brand ever was.

"Fine," Clay said. "Don't linger."

Her lips pursed into a tight ball. Reminded him of his old maid high school English teacher, Miss Steward. Sally pulled his sock off by the toes and pushed his pant leg up. He guessed he should have worn shorts. He reached down and tugged on the pant leg, trying to help, but it wouldn't go past his knee.

She huffed, frustrated with the task, or with him… or both.

Finally, leaving the pants where they were, she poured a hefty quantity of liniment into her hands and rubbed them together for a few seconds. Though a large-boned woman, her hands wouldn't be able to encircle his calf muscle, and he wondered what good they'd do. She surprised him though. With a strong, vice-like grip, she grasped his calf.

He jerked and stiffened. Had to consciously stifle a need to use his other foot to shove her away. He didn't want her touch. His forehead and upper lip dampened. How was he going to get through this?

She peeked up at him as she slipped her hands down his leg to the ankle, massaging the muscles in his calf as she went. Her fingertips dug in hard, taking his mind off her touch and onto the pain she was creating.

His eyes were glued to her task, as if she might deviate and touch him elsewhere. The dark hair on his legs matted with each swipe down and stuck out in all directions on her slide back up. That time it tickled a little. If he told her that, would she huff at him again? The thought almost amused him. Almost.

Clay thumped his head onto the sofa back and tried to relax. The massage began to feel good except for the pressure on the Achilles. It was still tight and painful. Hadn't Doc said it had healed?

When Sally slid her hands down for a fourth time, he raised his head and glared. "Are you trying to torture me?"

"It's where the tendon tore," she said while massaging. "Not once, but three times. It will take a long while for it to heal properly so you can walk without pain and without the fear of tearing it again. We'll stretch it—"

He shot upright. "What do you mean tearing it again?"

"I mean, *Mr. Cooper*, you have injured your Achilles, which is the tendon that travels along the bottom of your foot up past your heel to—"

"I know what the Achilles is, Sally. You saying the chances are good I'll tear it again?"

"Yes. If you don't let it heal completely, and if you don't let me do my job."

"I was in a dang cast for a month! Are you telling me physical therapy is the only thing that will save it? I'm not buying that."

Sally pressed a little harder, making him jerk. "Physical therapy is only one of the things you need to do. There are other things."

"Like what?"

"Like eating right, getting enough sleep, walking— the proper way—then eventually bringing in more physical activities. But for now, we have to take it slow. Very slow."

When she began rubbing the back of his heel and pushing his toes toward him, he hollered and cursed, yanking his foot away. She let him. Swinging his whole leg to the right, he rested it on the sofa, away from digging hands. "No more."

"Okay. If that's what you want. We'll be done for the day."

He started to call her on the 'we' thing again, but she jumped back in to correct herself. "*I'm* done for the day."

Clay lowered his brows, showing her he meant business. "I can handle what you did today. Or Brand can. If not Brand then someone else. There's no reason for you to come all the way back out here. Thanks anyway, Sally. Good to see you. Take care now."

He hoped she got the message because he sure as heck wasn't repeating himself.

She swallowed hard and blinked. So help him, if she started to cry he'd really give it to her but good. He couldn't stand it when women cried. It broke him somehow. That all started the day his wife told him she was through being married to him. But did she say it and go? No. She said it through a slew of tears that flooded the beautiful pale blue eyes he had spent hours drowning in. The tears had streamed down the soft cheeks he'd showered with countless kisses. It had crippled him. Then hardened him. In more ways than he'd yet to face.

Clay softened his voice. "Just go on, now. I'll be fine. Tell Doc I'll be in touch."

Without another word, Sally boxed up her gear in that huge suitcase and practically loped to the door.

Brand was there to see her out. He walked out behind her and closed the door.

Clay let his head thud back onto the cushion and closed his eyes. This had been far more painful than the injury alone. Being touched by a woman had rubbed all the raw pieces of his heart into a big ugly glob.

The front door banged open and Brand stormed through, slamming it in his wake. "What in Hades is wrong with you? Do you always have to be a son-of-a-bitch?"

Here it came. The same wrath he got from everyone each time he couldn't be decent. Maybe one of these days he'd learn to keep his trap shut—or more likely one day he'd head out and become a hermit, never to be seen by anyone again. "Calm down."

"Calm down. *Calm down?* Is that what you always say when you've stirred the pot and added jalapeno peppers to it? And cayenne pepper? And chili pepper. And—"

"All right, all right, I get it. Go away, Nilla. Leave me be."

"You're not gonna distract me with that stupid nickname. Not gonna happen this time, *Hot Dog*. You hurt that girl. There was no need for you to be such a jerk. We all know you are and put up with you anyway. But why her? She didn't deserve it!"

Why *had* he grown into such a jackass? Life had been hard on him but so what? Plenty of people had it tough but didn't give into bad attitudes and unforgiveable behavior. He hadn't been whole since Peggy, and by the looks of it, he was rotting from the inside out, clueless how to stop the decay.

CHAPTER 3

"I won't do it, Doc. I can't."

Dr. Trenton stood up then crossed in front of his desk, his eyes sympathetic. He leaned his backside against the solid wood and crossed his arms. The next thing out of his mouth wasn't going to be pleasant. "Margaret, you're the only one in the area who's trained and available."

I knew it. "I'm not available. I'm searching for housing all while setting up the Physical Therapy Department at the Campbell County Hospital, and Dr. Jordan—"

"—has offered your help to us."

Peggy swallowed hard and blinked up at him. It was good she was sitting, otherwise her legs would have been spaghetti. She already felt the tingle of nerves dashing up and down her spine. She hadn't felt that sensation since the last time she'd been near Clay. The day she'd said goodbye. "Why would he do that? We've only just begun setting everything up. I'm sure I'll have a patient soon."

"That's just it, you don't have any patients right now. And you haven't moved yet. You're close and available."

She needed to remain professional in front of Dr. Trenton, but couldn't quite muster the willpower. He knew her situation. How could he expect this of her? Her hands came up to cradle her face. She rubbed up and down to stop the threat of tears.

"It won't be that bad, Margaret. It's been years since you and Clay were married. You've both moved on."

Has he? Her heart nearly stopped at the thought. Since she hadn't, she figured he hadn't either. She'd certainly moved on education-wise and was very proud of her accomplishments in academics. But personally? Not a day went by that something didn't remind her of the wildly outlandish man she'd been married to.

How was she to touch that remarkable body of his three days a week and manage to survive?

It wasn't fair.

She wouldn't do it! She jumped to her feet. "No, Dr. Trenton. You'll have to find someone else."

"Sit down, Margaret."

Obedience to superiors came naturally. She sat.

Dr. Trenton dropped his arms and gripped the desk at his sides. His expression relaxed, the frown and look of sympathy deepening. "I'm sorry, Peggy. It's already been decided. You need to head out to the Cooper Ranch today at 5:30. Take your gear with you."

She started to argue that she didn't have her gear, but now that the art of physical therapy had become more mobile, the doctor knew she carried the bag of needed paraphernalia everywhere she went.

Possible scenarios tumbled around her mind. She needed to quiet her brain before she sprained it.

Hadn't she decided she wanted to help people? Who needed it more than her ex-husband? The man was a bonafide poster child for the benefits of physical therapy. He'd broken more bones and torn more muscles than anyone in all her studies.

Okay. So she would go. She'd be fine. Really.

• • •

"This is the last time I bring you supper. Do you hear me?" Brand shouted to Clay from a few feet away.

Brand had repeated that very statement at the beginning of each meal for two days now, and Clay was about ready to knock his block off. "I didn't ask for the dang food. I'll get my own."

"Rylee asked me to take care of you since she and Colt are busy with that rescue stallion. He won't eat unless they hand feed him. They've been keeping a close eye on him—sleeping out there even."

"You sure it's the stallion they're keeping an eye on?" Clay waggled his brows.

Brand crammed his hands on his hips. "The horse is in trouble. Have some compassion and stop the lewd remarks. If Dad were here he'd—"

"He'd what? Spank me? Ground me?"

Brand cursed.

Clay inhaled a calming breath. His intention wasn't to irritate the kid, his only true ally on the ranch. "Tell them to float the old boy's teeth. If he's having difficulty eating, he might have dental points cutting into his cheek or tongue. I bet his teeth were neglected long before he was abandoned."

Brand glanced away and stared, as if in thought. "You know, you may be right. I remember Rylee mentioning to Colt she saw blood once, in his hay."

Brand turned for the kitchen but stopped and jerked his head in the direction of the front door. "Hear that?"

"Hearing things again, little brother?"

"Shut up. Don't you hear that? Someone just drove in." He loped to the door, swung it open, and stuck his head out. "Some woman. In a blue Valiant," he said over his shoulder.

Clay's heart somersaulted and kept tumbling. Couldn't be. "What year?"

Brand scoffed, glancing briefly back at Clay. "Heck if I know. I'll find out who she is. Don't worry."

Such a helpful squirt. But what he wanted Brand to do was send the woman away. He had a bad feeling about this. There was a very real possibility he'd be meaner yet this time around.

Brand jerked his head to look over his shoulder. Caught Clay's gaze, his eyes wide. "It's...it's...you're not going to believe this, Clay."

He was afraid he would. "Send her away." A knot was forming in his throat.

Brand turned back, stuck his head out the opening with one hand on the door, the other on the door jamb. He popped his head back in. "It's Peggy. *Your* Peggy." Turned back. "She's going to her trunk, lifting a satchel out of it."

Not his Peggy anymore. "Crap!"

"Yeah, crap!" Brand agreed.

"It can't be she's replacing Sally. She can't be a physiologist. Can she?" The last words were practically whispered. Had all his thoughts of her lately actually conjured her up?

"She's coming."

Clay suddenly felt seventeen again. He sat up straighter, ran his hands through his hair, pushed the rolled sleeves farther up his arms, scrubbed at the beard on his face. He blew a breath in his hand and smelled it. Shrugged. He gave a quick sniff at his armpit. No help for that. Or for the wrinkled clothes he'd spent two days in.

"Peggy," Clay heard Brand say in an almost wistful voice.

"Hi, Brand. How are you?" The sound of her voice ran like pure honey over his battered soul, already soothing the frayed edges of it.

Peggy stood on the porch with the satchel hanging from her hand, waiting.

"How'd you know it was me?" Brand responded.

"Always did," she said with a smile in her voice. "You and Bronc are very different."

"Huh. Everyone else says we look the same."

"Look *mostly* the same. But your mannerisms give you away."

"Let her in, you moron," Clay barked, then regretted how those would be the first words his ex-wife would hear from him in years.

Brand jumped to the side. "Sorry. Come in."

"Thank you."

"Why are you here?" Brand asked. Man, sometimes his brother's manners were as bad as his own. Still, he didn't correct him.

Clay was pleased he wasn't affected, seeing Peggy stand there almost regally with her spine straight and shoulders back. But when she turned and her gaze traveled the room looking for him, his first impression went out the window. The instant the splash of baby blue caught and hooked him, it was the first day of science class all over again. He couldn't breathe. He fought not to pass out from the thunder of his heart. All he was able to do was stare, absorb, then drown in her eyes as he'd always done.

His lungs seized as she took in her own stiff breath. So, he still affected her. Good. Same boat. But, since his own pulse was still galloping, he feared his boat was a whole lot bigger.

She stood for the longest time in one spot, those eyes wide against the same translucent skin, playing havoc with his shredded heart. He forced his gaze from her more mature but still perfect face to the rest of her. Sam Hill, she'd filled out her skinny frame and was more stunning than he remembered. All straight-laced in a gray nurse's uniform with white cuffs and collar and sensible lace-up white shoes. She had her blonde hair trapped in some kind of tight bun at her nape, and looked petite and fragile.

No, on second glance, that same underlying strength she hid well was still there. She'd always looked breakable, but she was anything but.

"I'm here for Clay."

Those sweet words he'd yearned to hear four years ago and every day since dug at his heart, effectively popping open the old wound like it was a ripe cherry. Now he felt vulnerable—exposed and hurting all over again. How would he endure this first sentence, let alone a whole conversation?

Couldn't happen. He'd never survive it. "Turn yourself right around there, missy, and head back to that Valiant of yours."

She hissed in a breath, and for a split second pain registered on that pretty face. But then it was gone as she dropped the satchel with a thump and planted her hands on her more noticeably curvy hips. He swallowed, hard.

"Clayton Cooper, you are as rude as ever!"

"Not rude, sweetheart. Sensible. You and I in the same room? A smart man would avoid that like hoof-and-mouth disease. And I'm a smart man." He thrust a finger at the door. "Out!"

Indignant or rattled? He wasn't sure what he'd call the look she was trying to hide now. Her lips pressed together, her nostrils flared, she blinked several times, and then her gaze left him for elsewhere.

He drew in a quick breath to fortify himself.

He'd always had a love-hate relationship with upsetting her. One side worried it would hurt her, but the other? Dang but she looked beautiful when she was irritated. Always had. The memories of pestering her just for the fun of it came flooding back.

He really was a jerk.

But as Clay studied her, threads of pain shot one by one through him, impaling him with every memory they'd made together. High school days when all they could think about was each other; his proposal as they leaned against the corral fence under the stars, her face tilted up to his with the hope of a life together shining out from her glistening eyes; their wedding day in the little chapel in Sundance where he'd given himself to her and laid their lives at God's feet; their wedding night and every night thereafter when he'd been privileged to touch his bride as he'd only dreamt of before.

And then the day she'd walked out on him...the day he'd taken his life back from God, never to trust Him again.

Sharp eyes stopped wandering the room and landed back on him. She'd gathered herself. He forced his mind away from memories and onto what would spill from her lips. The anticipation was like a gulp of fresh air off freshly fallen snow. He felt so alive in that moment, he wondered where he'd been for half a decade.

She sucked in a breath.

He pressed his lips together to keep from grinning in delight.

"Now see here, *Mr. Cooper*, I've come to help you recuperate."

He could think of a few ways she could help him with that, though he didn't dare dwell on them. Had enough trouble with those thoughts on nights he couldn't sleep.

Her hands remained planted on those hips as she took a few steps toward him. Still, she maintained enough distance between them to keep him from taking hold of her wrist and pulling her to his lap, where he'd kiss the tar out of her as he used to all those years ago. "And what do you think you can do to help me *recuperate*, Miss Sassman?"

"Actually, it's Mrs. Cooper." Then she froze, as if this was how she usually corrected people but had forgotten who she was talking to.

That set his mind and emotions jumbling together in an unsteady mix of toxic sensations. Ones he hadn't felt since she'd closed the door the day she walked out on him.

He held himself still. Panted the next few breaths as he gained control, trapping hurt against one side of his brain and failure against the other. A few more breaths and he was steady.

She was clearly unnerved. "Well, I...I'm going to...you see...Stop looking at me like that." What did she see? His devastation, or his rage? She stomped a foot and clenched her hands at her sides.

Gad, he'd forgotten how he loved to egg her on. How they interacted. How she gave just as good as she got. Which to him was more fun than getting along.

Yeah, anytime now. He smirked at her, suddenly feeling more alive than when he'd made his last jump.

She blinked, flustered.

Maybe this wasn't going to be so bad after all.

She sighed heavily, unfisted her hands. Drat, was she giving up? She went back for her bag. Hefting it to the other side of the sofa, she plopped it down and unzipped it. Brought out a bottle of liniment and a towel, then went after the footstool she must have remembered they had.

Once it was positioned in front of him, sweat popped out on his forehead. Then his spine. Then every crevice on his body. This couldn't happen. If he thought it was bad with Sally...He'd be a puddle of goo before this session was over. "Listen up, Margaret—" He'd never called her that before—ever. "We are not doing this. Brand will walk you out." He'd kept his voice low, but even he heard the tremor in it. He cleared his throat. "You can tell Dr. Trenton to send Sally back. I'll behave."

The hurt that ran across her face surprised him. His mouth dropped open slightly to draw a better draft of air. She couldn't want to be here. Must be something else. If he was sure of one thing, it was that Margaret Ann Cooper didn't want to be in the same county as ex-husband Clayton William Cooper.

Not four years ago. Not now.

Her breaths were short, and she flutter-blinked. He recognized that reaction. The night he'd finally limped home after three weeks on the road as a rodeo star, she'd come to him in the barn while he put up his horse. Instead of throwing herself in his arms and congratulating him, she'd teetered before him, her breath clipped and ragged just before delivering the words that tore out his heart and left it for dead. The ones that told him they were through. And then came the torrents of tears.

So many tears...and no redemption.

He'd been so stunned he couldn't say a word. So, like a stupe, he'd stood and forced a glare so he wouldn't break down like a baby and join her with sobs of his own.

Now, it was happening all over again. He had to stop her before she broke down this time. He barely survived it last time. This time it would destroy him. "Get out! Now!" Rolling to his feet, he hop-jumped out of the room and down the hall to his bedroom on the first floor.

Once he banged the door closed behind him, his breath hitched in his throat and he knew the next would be a wail unless he stopped it. He hopped to the bed and plopped down. Smashed his face into his hands and rubbed like crazy. He worked his palms into his chin, cheeks, forehead, and back again until the emotions shifted from raw pain to anger.

How dare she come into this house and rip him up again? Had he invited her? No. Had he needed her? No. Did he want her? Silence invaded his mind. He wasn't about to answer that question, even to himself.

He heard the front door slam, rattling the hinges. So loud Clay knew Brand would be back in to rake him over the coals again.

He needed to get out of here!

With much difficulty, Clay managed to skirt his way into the mudroom and tug on his socks and one boot. He grabbed the dang crutches. At least that would make escape a little faster.

He made it all the way out the back door and half-way to the barn when Brand caught up to him, and yanked one of his crutches out from under him. Clay windmilled his free arm until the next step took him down. He hit the ground like a fallen pine, barely catching himself with an elbow and a knee.

And there he lay like the miserable wretch he was. His back was tweaked, he'd probably sliced his knee and elbow, and the dark dread of regret loomed over him.

"Oh sh—" Brand cursed. "Are you all right?"

Clay didn't want sympathy from Brand. He deserved the flaying he'd been about to receive, not this. "Go away," Clay grunted, his face planted in the scree and grime of the road.

Brand cursed again. "Come on, you belligerent reprobate. Grab onto me." Brand pulled on the arm that Clay had twisted around the now bent crutch. Guess Brand figured it was the least injured. He'd be right about that.

Clay let Brand lift him to his one foot. Blood trickled down his forearm and off his fingers, while he felt the same warm tickle of blood crawling down his leg from knee to sock.

"Ah, crap. I'm so sorry, Hot Dog. I never meant to hurt you more. I'm just so stinkin' mad at you." Brand's own words seemed to remind him that he was angry. He swung Clay's arm around his shoulder and clamped onto his hand. Hard.

Clay grimaced as Brand continued to the barn. "Nah. Take me back to the house. I'm gonna need to clean up." He flicked his hand, spattering blood in all directions.

"Dang. I'm an idiot." Brand loosened his grip on Clay's hand, anger dissipating. So the sympathy act was working. Good. He couldn't stand the thought of being reprimanded any longer. Not by Brand. Not by anyone. He was tired, injured, and more defeated than ever.

Once Brand got him in the house and helped wash his arm, Clay faced his little brother—and saw in the boy a better man than he was. "I'm going to head to the shower, then go to bed."

"*What?* Shoot, you aren't okay, are you? It's only 6:30, Clay. Too early for sleep. Come on, I'll have supper ready soon. You'll be fine. It's all gonna be fine."

"No. It isn't. It hasn't been fine for years."

CHAPTER 4

"She's back," Brand said to the window at the kitchen sink.

Clay's soup spoon hovered an inch from his mouth as he shifted mental gears from what Trevor would let him do to help today to what Brand just said. "Who's back?"

"Peggy."

Clay sucked in air and soup at the same time, and launched into a fit of coughing.

Brand whirled around and whacked Clay on the back, making him cough harder.

"Stop," Clay choked out.

It had been two days since he'd sent his ex-wife away. Relief and disappointment had lived with him since.

Finally, his voice returned, though it sounded pinched. "Why is she back? What did you say to her?"

Brand wouldn't look at him.

Oh boy. Guilty as all heck. "What. Did. You. Say. to her?"

"Nothin'." Brand twisted back to the window, tensed, then jogged off toward the front door. He opened it before Peggy could knock.

"Go on in to the family room," Clay heard Brand say. "We'll be right with you."

When he wandered back into the kitchen, Clay glared at Brand.

"Hey," Brand whispered. "I know you don't want her here. But you hurt her feelings last time, so I told her you were in pain and didn't mean what you said. Told her you'd be better by Wednesday." He beamed then, using his charming smile on Clay. "And, how 'bout that. Today's Wednesday. So, when you're ready, come on in." Brand's smile fell off and a frown twisted his brows. "But be nice!"

Brand shot out of the kitchen before Clay could grab him and beat the stuffing out of him. He ran a hand down his face and over the scruff that was still growing. He groaned quietly before deciding he didn't have a choice. Though he had fallen asleep on the couch last night, he'd at least thrown on a clean shirt this morning. *Deep down, had you expected her to come?*

He hefted himself out of the kitchen chair. Grabbing the crutches Brand had worked all last evening to repair, he placed them under his armpits and took a slow *thump, slide, shuffle* across the floor out of the kitchen and toward the couch.

Peggy, her back to him, had on her same nurse's uniform. He told himself not to look her over, to keep his hankering in check, but since when did his brain obey him? Or his body? Instead, he let his gaze linger with melancholy on her hourglass figure, slender calves, and blond hair tied loosely in that same knot with wisps sticking out from it against her neck. Looked like she'd had a day already.

Guilt tapped at his mind. Time to be *nice*. When he drew near, she turned and smiled. The same smile he remembered that used to take his breath away. Still did.

"Evening, Clay. How are you today?"

Her manner was too chipper, voice too lofty. She was trying hard to be professional. He guessed the short time he'd have with her would work out fine. Yet, the thought of her hands on him scared the bejeezus right out of him. "Peggy," he greeted.

"Sit down right over here." She gestured to the end of the sofa where she had the stool set up and her equipment bag resting on the floor, unzipped.

He sat.

She took his crutches and leaned them against the wall behind her before returning, looking a tad nervous. "That's perfect. Okay, just put your foot right up here." She patted the stool.

He complied. But when she slid those long-fingered hands under the hem of his pants and pushed, he nearly climbed out of the seat.

Her eyes jerked to his. "You all right? Did I touch a painful spot?"

"No."

She let out a shaky sigh. "Okay."

Clay gritted his teeth as she slid his pant leg up over his calf and to the knee. She talked while she worked, her eyes on what she was doing. He didn't know if it was to relax him or her. "Next time, shorts would work better. These probably won't go up as high as I need them to be."

She looked up to see if he was listening. He wasn't. Not really. All he could think about was how good she smelled and her soft palms against his hairy legs…and whether or not he was about to embarrass himself.

"Clay?"

He swallowed, then blinked until his eyes rested on hers. "Got it. Shorts next time."

When she dropped her gaze back to his pant leg, he grabbed a pillow and plopped it in his lap.

She glanced up in question, so he rested his forearms on the pillow and leaned in, pretending interest in what she was doing. Thank goodness for Rebecca's introduction of throw pillows to their masculine world.

Peggy gave one final push at the denim and gasped. "What happened here? There's dried blood everywhere. And I noticed your elbow is bandaged. What happened, Clay? Did you try walking? Did your heel give out?"

Her distress gave him pause. Suddenly every incident where he'd been scraped, broken, or gored flew into his mind, along with Peggy's concern and the nurturing that followed. He'd nearly forgotten how kind and caring she'd been. Never berating him until he was fixed up. Then…yeah, then she gave it to him like a blast from a shotgun. He almost chuckled out loud. She was a bossy little thing when it mattered. She'd been right to scold him. He'd always taken too many risks. Still did. The difference now was he recognized it.

"Don't worry, Twinkie." The old nickname fell out of his mouth so naturally it surprised him. He'd forgotten it until now.

She frowned. Had always hated being called that. She thought it made her sound brainless or self-indulgent. He'd named her that years ago so she'd fit in with his family's crazy food nicknames. Not only did she love Twinkies back then, but they were a blond treat, just like her. He had to admit, he'd used it too often when he was angry or wanted to derail her.

He'd been mad at her for so long, today it fit. But, if he wanted to get along now, he'd be wise to use the nickname she liked since it reminded them both of her smile—*Sunbeam*. Trouble was, the name seemed too intimate to use anymore.

All he wanted now was for her to leave him alone. Get out of his life for good. After all, that's what she'd wanted, to leave him. She should have stayed gone.

"I'm the one who did it," came Brand's voice from the doorway of the kitchen. Had he been watching to make sure Clay treated Peggy right? The thought made him clench his teeth to keep from lashing out at the kid. Brand had always been the tattle-tale. Even telling on himself. Most of the time that gave him a lesser punishment, charmer that he was—and manipulator. But not with Clay. Or Peggy. Maybe he'd forgotten that Peggy had been trained to ignore Brand's charms by Clay himself.

Peggy's head wrenched around to see Brand standing in the doorway with a tray in his hands. Suspicion marred her lovely face. "You did what?"

Brand came forward and set the tray of drinks and two heaping plates of food down on the far end of the coffee table. Steak and potatoes and beans on one, steak and salad and fruit on the other. Impressive the kid remembered how she liked her supper. Where was this spread when Clay had rummaged the shelves and landed on soup for dinner, anyway?

"Food for two. I'm sure you haven't had time to eat yet." Brand's sweet look at Peggy just made Clay madder. He'd always flirted with Peggy, even when she was his wife. Though back then he was a harmless kid. Now he was a man, and his charm wasn't harmless. What did he think? That she was free game now?

"Leave it and go," Clay barked.

Brand's brilliant smile shifted to a smirk. "What's the matter, big brother?" *Jealous?* seemed to be the word that lingered in his eyes.

Clay growled deep in his throat. "Get out!"

Peggy glared at Clay. "Goodness. Have you learned no manners in all these years?" She turned her gaze back to Brand and smiled apologetically. Dang, he hated when people felt the need to apologize for his behavior. "You're always so helpful. And you remembered how I like my supper. That's remarkable, Brand. Thank you." Then her smile vanished as if it had never been there. "Now, what did you do?"

"What do you mean?"

Clay wanted to throw his head back and laugh at the *oh no* look on Brand's face. Yeah, the look that said he now remembered who he was talking to. Peggy had always been a smart one. No one was able to pull the wool over her eyes, least of all Brand.

"You're being awfully nice, bringing us supper and all. You said you were 'the one who did it.' Is there something you need to confess?"

Peggy always could get the truth out of him. He didn't even hesitate. "Uh…yeah, I uh…" He dropped his head, looked like he might cry.

So Brand was going through with it, hoping the sympathy angle got him out of it. Bold move.

His lip quivered. "I was upset with Clay for how poorly he treated you...and Sally—" Brand threw a quick glance his way, but Clay's scowl at Brand for divulging this information didn't deter the brat. "So I kinda yanked one of his crutches away while he was walking."

Clay scoffed. "So, that's what you're going with? How do you *kinda yanked* a crutch away, kid?"

Brand had the good grace to look sheepish, but used it to his benefit. He turned to Peggy while she focused solely on him and his explanation. "Well...like I said...he was really mean to Sally and you."

Clay slammed a fist to the couch. "You already covered that!"

Peggy turned those baby blues back on Clay. "What *did* you do to Sally? She said she wouldn't come back, so I figured you refused her help, not that you were mean to her. Not that I'm surprised to find that out."

"What's that supposed to mean?" The moment Clay muttered those words, he regretted them.

"You know exactly what I mean." Clay was instantly unnerved by Peggy's quiet delivery. Where had the emotional, screaming girl of the past gone? *Replaced by a woman, Cooper. Can't you see that?* "You can be a mean son-of-a-gun, and you know it. I've seen plenty of that side of you."

She had no idea how much worse he had gotten.

He forced a one-sided smile that always got to her. "So you remember the other side of me, eh, sweet thing? Which side is your favorite?"

Her eyes widened and she gasped. Loudly. Then stood and huffed. "Clayton Cooper, behave yourself!"

He leaned farther over the pillow on his lap and caught her gaze fully in his. "You want me to behave?" he said with a bigger smile. The one he used to seduce her in the first place. The same one he'd used every time he'd wanted his way with her.

While she stood there all indignant-like, he shifted gears, remembering exactly how he used to throw her off during their arguments. Except the need to win wasn't there anymore. Only sadness remained. And the memory of how she'd obliterated him. "You don't have any say anymore—about my life, my injuries, or my behavior. Why don't I have Brand package up your dinner, then show you out?"

Hurt—plain and agonizing—flooded her face, piercing his resolve. Had she truly expected a happy reception from him? Not likely.

He'd been an irascible character long before she'd ripped his heart out. After?…well, his behavior was mostly intolerable, and he had no reason to change it. But, hurting her? No, he didn't have the stomach for that. Never had. "I'm tired. The leg hurts. Think I'll go lie down."

A delighted expression replaced the defeat on her lovely face. "Oh. I can help with the leg pain. Hold on. The liniment will help a lot."

He cursed under his breath. See, this was what happened whenever he went soft. Got himself in deeper. "Nah, another time, Twinkie."

She flinched but ignored his comment. "Brand, why don't you take the food back to the kitchen for now, and get me a warm, wet washcloth. I want to clean his leg of the dried blood before I massage it."

The word massage struck Clay's brain with force. He didn't want her touching him, reminding him of the bond they once had. Or the injury he'd foolishly courted...again. He flopped his head back and squeezed his eyes shut.

Brand was back before Clay opened his eyes.

"Okay, you just rest like you're doing and I'll take care of your leg," Peggy said. "You'll see. It'll feel so much better." The purr of her sweet voice couldn't override the anticipation of her touch. How was he going to bear it?

A warm, wet cloth slapped against his shin, followed by two petite hands. His eyes flew open as he choked in a breath, nearly coming off the couch. Peggy began pushing the cloth up and down, cleaning off dried blood—and a sheen of new sweat. Efficiently, she drew the warm cloth over his calf and shin and on up, pushing against his jeans. She slowed, leaned in, and peered at the wound.

She asked something, but Clay didn't hear it over the whoosh of his pulse. Her nearness made him wild and soothed all at once. Memories flooded his brain— all the times she'd stroked his wounded ego, repaired his battered body, soothed his unsettled mind.

She'd always been there for whatever he needed, whenever he needed it.

"Clay?"

"Hmm?"

"This hurt?"

"Hurt?"

Her eyes narrowed as she assessed his expression, which probably showed his awakened, confused state. Maybe she wouldn't notice. After all, she hadn't been around him all these years. The years he'd had to live without her and her ability to quiet his spirit. Without her, he'd learned another way to live. Angry, closed off, unresponsive.

"This." She poked her finger right in the center of the gouge made by a rock and got his complete attention.

"Yes, that hurts! What the heck?" She'd always done that when they were married; poked bruises, scabs, scrapes, broken bones, strained muscles, you name it, anytime she wanted his attention, or was furious with him for being reckless. Dang it, her proximity had always befuddled him. "It wasn't my fault."

She pulled her mouth in disbelief. "That's debatable."

He opened his mouth, ready to defend himself as he always had with her, but she was right. He'd found long ago, trying to defend his own bad behavior was futile. He was rash. He was a jackass. And he was needing her gone. Best way to do that was to agree with her; be still, let her finish and go.

When he didn't answer, her eyes found his and her eyebrows lifted. "No argument?"

"No. Just finish what you're doing." He dropped his head back and crushed his eyes closed again. Every time his tone was mean, hurt crossed her face. He couldn't take that. Didn't have to anymore.

"Good," she said, then quietly went to work.

Time moved like garden snails. Clay found himself wondering if she planned to come back to do this again. Part of him hoped so. The other part, the one that would win, worked madly against it.

When she removed the washcloth from his leg, he mistakenly thought she was done and breathed a sigh of relief. No such luck. If he'd thought the washcloth was bad, those hands of hers, warm with liniment that she rubbed up and down his shin, calf, and heel, shot his equilibrium off the charts. He gripped the pillow on his lap with such force it threatened to burst its stuffing.

"My goodness, Clay. You have to relax. The calf muscle keeps contracting."

He felt her fingers over one of his hands, unhooking his grip from the pillow. "Why are you so tense?" He stiffened more as his eyes opened to her slender fingers pulling at his bear paws. "I don't want to hurt you."

Those same words he'd said to her on their wedding night sailed uninvited into his conscious mind from the black hole he'd stuffed those memories into. His head spun. "Enough!" The emotions and recollections swirling around his brain were more than he could take.

Say it nicely. "Listen. Peggy. Uh…I have to take a— use the facilities. Let me up." Escaping her was vital.

Thankfully she believed him. She jumped up and went for his crutches.

"Thanks." He pushed up on his good leg, the pillow dropping to the floor. He stuffed the sticks under his pits and scrambled clumsily around the corner of the sofa and on toward the downstairs bathroom.

Once he'd shut the door, he threw the crutches against the tub and sat heavily on the side, stuffing his face in his hands. Never once, in all the years they'd been apart, did he think he'd be expected to face her again. And he certainly never expected her hands on him again.

Somehow he would think of a way to stop these sessions before he went insane. Send her on her way without hurting her feelings. Maybe it meant he needed to escape the Bar-6 sooner rather than later. Far enough away so their paths would never cross again.

CHAPTER 5

Peggy waited for a good ten minutes before she moseyed into the kitchen toward a nosey Brand.

"Not back out yet, eh?" Brand said as he poured himself a cup of coffee. "Don't think you'll see him again tonight."

His back was to her, but from what little she saw of his profile, he had a smirk riding his mouth. Brand always had liked it when Clay couldn't keep a tight grip on himself. In fact, all the brothers felt that way. They really needed to back off him. Clay couldn't help who he was.

Peggy pushed the damp curls from around her face back into her hairline, exhausted by far more than her work day. Clay was still too much man for her. "I should talk Sally into coming back." Pulling a chair out, she sat heavily, nearly missing the chair. She squeaked, righted herself, and watched as Brand swung around at her distress. Coffee swished over the side of the cup and onto his hand.

"Yow." He flicked his hand, then, seeing she was okay, shook his head. "Even if Sally were willing to come back—which she isn't—she's not going to work out, Peg, and you know it."

She nodded. "No. I suppose not. She's pretty fragile, and Clay is…difficult."

Brand snorted. "That's an understatement. He's the worst. Everyone thinks Bronc is the tough one, but he's a pussycat in comparison."

She knew what he meant. Clay had the strongest will of all the brothers—even Trevor. At least Trevor had the sense to back down when the odds were against him. Clay was impulsive on top of a temperament of iron. A lethal combination. One she'd sadly learned she couldn't live with.

If only he'd grow out of one or the other, then maybe…

No! She couldn't think that way. He still appealed to her way too much for her to flirt with possibilities. Giving him physical therapy was already pushing her limits. But for now, thanks to Dr. Trenton, she was stuck here.

"You've got the upper hand, Peg. Don't let him buffalo you."

She laughed. "Really, Brand? This from the brother who gets bossed around by him daily?"

Brand grinned, showing his signature Cooper smile. Too bad the Coopers weren't all as perfect as their handsome faces depicted. Such a deception.

Brand sobered, making him look older than his twenty years. "You'd be surprised what I can handle around here. You need help, you come to me."

"My, but you've grown up." Her half-smile snuck out. Brand was a cutie—and a con artist. She knew to watch him closely. Still, he seemed so mature at this moment.

"You think I haven't been involved all along?" His hurt look surprised her.

She thought about that for a minute. "You were only, what? Sixteen when I left? Still a kid, trying to keep his twin out of trouble. I don't know what you've been doing since, but back then you were young...and preoccupied."

Brand pulled out a chair next to hers, set his mug down, and looked into her eyes in that deep Cooper way. Then his expression shifted. He looked sad all of the sudden. "Why'd you leave him, Peg? You broke him. In a million ways. He's never recovered. I worry he never will."

Her next breath caught in her throat. *Unflappable Clay?* She'd seen him broken physically in dozens of ways. But emotionally? She didn't remember any emotional weakness from him. Except maybe passion. She cocked her head in thought. Was passion an emotion or just a reaction to an emotion? Hmm.

"Peg?"

"Yes?" The sincerity in his voice captured her complete attention.

"Why did you leave?"

The reasons rushed her in a blur of jagged pain. She jumped up out of her chair, then grasped the back to keep it from tumbling over. "You're right, I should leave."

Brand rose beside her. "Wait. That's not what I said."

"Will you tell Clay goodbye for me?" Should she make plans to come back? Dr. Trenton's words slid into her mind. *I'm sorry, Peggy. It's already been decided...'*

Yeah, for now, she had to endure this. For now. "…and that I'll see him on Friday."

Brand got it. Didn't even mention the supper she and Clay hadn't touched.

He nodded. It showed her just how grown up he was. Things had changed in the Cooper realm. Now, if she could just get her job done and leave them to handle their business, she might survive with her sanity intact.

• • •

Clay thump-swished into the kitchen, shirtless. He'd needed a cold shower after he'd quit the room. And right about now, he didn't feel like talking to anyone, much less Brand. "What are you, the chief cook and bottle washer around here? Don't you have some horses to feed, stalls to muck, damsels to save, or something?"

"Rylee's doing it since she and Colt are in the barn so much lately. Said we should swap jobs for now."

"So you're the lady of the house, eh? Suits you."

Brand scowled. Yeah, Clay could always get under the twins' skin. Didn't seem quite fair anymore but he was in the perfect mood to bite someone in half.

"Do you always have to be mean?"

"Waah, waah. Toughen up, little boy."

"Why don't you sit down so I can punch you? Don't want to knock the sissy over and hurt him again."

"That's the best you can do?" He took a crutched step toward Brand and puffed up. He might be injured but he was still the tougher brother. "Give it your best shot, baby brother."

Clay was bigger and broader, yet Brand didn't back down. Not one bit. They stared each other down.

"You gonna scare her away again?" Brand asked, his breath warm on Clay's chin.

Clay recoiled. Neither of them said a word for ten heartbeats. Brand always could wait out the best of them. As a small boy, he'd learned the hard lesson of 'the first one who speaks loses.' Finally, Clay turned, clomped back to the table, and sat.

Brand delivered his crutches to the far corner of the kitchen, then returned to sit with him. "Talk to me."

This kid. When had he grown up? And become so wise? Reminded Clay of the way Colt was all those years ago…before their falling out. Dare he share any thoughts with him? He sure could use a voice of reason right about now. "Probably."

"Probably what? You're *probably* going to scare her off?"

"Did it before. Just like you said."

Brand scrubbed a hand down his face. "Ah, darn it, Clay. She left you. I figured it was your fault. Wasn't it?"

"Truth?"

Brand nodded.

"It broadsided me when she left. Never felt such pain."

Brand studied him, unblinking. Clay scanned Brand's face. His features were more angular now. Forehead more square, cheekbones more prominent. He looked more like a man now than the kid Clay remembered. And right now deep lines of concern split his brows.

"You didn't see it comin'? At all?"

Clay huffed out a breath, dropped his head back, and gazed up. Looked like the kitchen could use a coat of paint. He let his gaze wander back to Brand. "Ah, I don't know. I guess. I knew she wasn't happy."

"What did you do to help that?"

"Didn't know what to do. I was barely an adult myself back then. It made me uncomfortable, so I just worked harder."

"At rodeo."

"Yeah, at rodeo. It's all I knew to do. I was good at it, so I made money. Figured that was my part in the marriage. Earn the money."

"She ever tell you she was unhappy?"

Clay pressed his lips together. Yeah, she'd told him. But since he didn't know how to fix it, he'd stopped listening. Colt had listened, though. That soured his stomach all over again. Made him want to punch Colt in the mouth, though he knew it wasn't his fault. It was Clay's. Plain and simple.

"Seems reasonable," Brand went on, ignoring his own question. "Someone had to bring home the bacon. Ha! That should be Trevor's job. You know, his nickname and all. Bacon. Right, Hot Dog?"

And there was the kid again. Clay was done going down memory lane anyway. "Get my crutches. I'm going to bed."

"No way! It's too early to go to bed. Besides, I saved your supper for you."

"Lost my appetite."

Brand studied him, then sighed. "Fine. I have one last question for you."

"Make it fast."

"What's this?" Brand leaned forward and poked the tattoo over Clay's heart.

Clay dropped his head and stared at the initials on his chest as if he'd forgotten they were there. "Long story."

Brand sat back at a tilt, hooked an arm around the back of his own chair, and seized Clay's gaze. "I've got all night."

For some reason, Brand had a way of pulling information from him. Always had, though he'd had less finesse in his youth. It had been no less effective. "Initials."

"I see that. Whose?"

"A buddy's."

"It'd be easier if you'd just tell me the story."

Clay was tired of fighting the world. Brand's calm voice snaked in and unraveled his tightly coiled secrets. "I suppose you'll sit there 'til morning if I don't spill."

Brand tilted his head in a half nod of agreement. Waited some more.

Clay cursed. "I'll try to make this short."

"Those aren't Peggy's initials?" Brand gave it a shot. "M.T.S. I know her name is Margaret Sassman but don't know her middle name."

"Nope. Her middle name is Ann. This was Martin Travis Smith. You were probably too young to remember him. My best buddy all the way through school. He eventually followed me to Alaska. Joined my team. We jumped together dozens of times before we lost him." Clay swallowed hard, caught off guard by the swelling emotion, and the reminder the initials *did* double for Peggy: Margaret 'Twinkie' Sassman. Once he realized he could use her nickname for the middle initial, he'd gone straight to the tattoo artist that day, knowing it would fool everyone. It was still one of his best kept secrets: a tattoo that reminded of the two moments that had impacted him most: the death of his best friend and the death of his marriage. Nobody knew. Only him.

"What happened?"

Brand's words popped him out of the dark space and into the here and now. "He wouldn't jump. I'm the one who coaxed him to go. We jumped late, he landed straight in the flames." The memory crashed over him like a burning pine. He remembered how he'd wanted to beat his commander to a pulp. The boss on the ground had commanded two other guys to hold Clay back from running into the blaze. It saved his life. But he wasn't grateful. Not even a little bit. While restraining him, they'd all watched Martin perish into ash.

He'd been at odds with life ever since. Between his dad, Peggy, and Martin, Clay had finally learned the lesson that to love was to lose.

Clay stared at the stick man he'd carved into the kitchen table as a kid. Got put on stall mucking duties for a month after that. Every time he felt inadequate or frustrated he'd wanted to add another stick man. It was all he could do to not pull out his pocket knife right now.

"Dang, Clay. I'm sorry. Still hurts?" Brand's voice was low, soothing.

Clay brought his eyes up to Brand's, saw the glistening. "Every day."

Brand bit his lower lip, glanced out the window and then back at Clay. "I have to take Trevor, Colt, and Rylee some food. Wait for me. We'll talk some more."

"Thanks anyway. Bring me my crutches. I'll see you in the morning."

He must have looked like he could use the space. Brand didn't say another word. Just nodded and brought him his sticks.

Clay needed solitude. Now more than ever. The ache in his chest was back with a vengeance.

Time to devise a plan to escape the Bar-6. Get away from the bad memories and the people who wanted to drag them out of him 'for his own good.' For now he'd have to survive Peggy's visits. But once his leg was good to go, he'd be good and gone.

CHAPTER 6

C lay stood in front of the bank of windows in the formal living room, gazing toward the road. From his dad he'd learned this room was one his mother had decorated. All in white. Who decorated with white in a ranch house, especially with six boys under foot? His mother must have either been a bit looney or oblivious to simple logic.

Yeah, maybe that was his problem too. Simple logic escaped him. All Clay needed to do was sit still and let a physiologist work his injured leg. Didn't matter that the physiologist happened to be the one woman who'd shared his life for over a year…well, realistically more like four months total, beings he was gone the rest of the time. Still, how in Sam Hill was he to brush aside the pain and longing she stirred in him?

He groaned when he saw the little Valiant bouncing up the road toward the house. *Buck up, tough guy. Think of the leg. Forget who she is.*

He turned toward the front door and waited until she was halfway up the walk before he opened it, wishing like crazy Brand wasn't out in the south pasture with Trevor today.

"Afternoon, Peggy."

"Good afternoon, Clay."

No words could be more stilted, but Clay had decided to paste on a smile and shelve his snide remarks today. Worse than having to endure her touch was having to see tears swimming in her eyes over something he'd said. So he'd behave if he had to grind his teeth flat…with his tongue trapped between them.

Clay gestured toward her satchel. "I'd offer to get that for you, but…" He shrugged and glanced down at his crutches.

Peggy smiled, a genuine Sunbeam smile. "No problem. I can see your hands are full."

He thumped back out of her way and then closed the door, following her into the family room.

She plunked the satchel down on one end of the sofa while he settled on the other end.

Peggy looked him over for the first time, surprise evident on her face. Yeah, so he'd showered, shaved, and combed his hair. Oh, and most importantly, he'd dressed in cut-off jeans. Never let it be said that Clayton Cooper couldn't cooperate. He knew how to, just didn't want to most days.

"Thank you for wearing shorts. It'll be a lot easier."

"Sure."

She reached up with both hands to push the hair from her face back to her bun. Clay's breath log-jammed in his throat, and he quickly dropped his eyes to the stool. His resolve to not think of who she'd been to him was already weakening.

Before he allowed his brain to take him on a journey, he forced back errant thoughts. "So, what got you interested in Physiology?"

She busied herself taking her gear out of the bag. "You remember my brother, Kenny?"

Clay certainly did remember the boy who'd sat in the wheelchair parked in the center aisle at church the day Clay married Peggy. "Is he getting around better these days?"

She looked surprised, then sad. "You never heard? He passed away three years ago."

"Oh, Peg." Clay floundered for words. "I'm sorry. He was a good kid."

"Yeah, he was." She swallowed hard, her eyes peering down at him. "Pneumonia. He should never have been bedridden. I believe if someone like me had been around to help him right after the accident, he'd be alive today. I could have helped him walk. Then he wouldn't have been lying in that bed so long." Her words ended on a sob. "What a waste of a beautiful life." Anger laced her words. He couldn't blame her. The doctors had been no help back then.

Her eyes glassed over, and he wanted so badly to hold her, comfort her. But she'd taken that right away from him long ago.

Rather than let past hurts dictate his behavior, Clay forced his resolve back to the forefront. He'd make it through therapy without conflict. He still didn't know how he'd brave her treatments three times a week, but now he knew her true motivation. To heal. That was clear enough. And if she could endure their closeness, he sure as heck could. "Why don't we get started? Want my foot on the stool?"

Peggy jerked her head up and blinked. Was it so hard to believe he could cooperate? He could almost hear his brothers shout out, 'Yes!'

Okay, okay, so he was a bad patient. He was changing that, as of now.

"That would be great. Thank you."

Clay smiled. Peggy smiled back—*the* smile. It brightened the room. He didn't want to remember that smile had once been offered to him alone. *Just get through this.*

"I aim to please," he said, his smile faltering.

She snort-laughed, which made him laugh. It felt good to let loose and relive a moment out of their better days.

"All right, so I'm not always cooperative. But I've decided to be, so let's get this over with before I change my mind."

"Sounds good," she said on a lingering chuckle. "Just give me a minute to warm up the liniment."

She started to rise, he assumed to go to the kitchen.

"Not necessary. Your hands on my leg will warm it soon enough."

"If you're sure."

He nodded.

She sat, poured some in one hand, then rubbed both together. When she positioned her palms on his calf, he jumped and gasped. His mind started racing, trying to come up with ways to ignore her touch.

"Too cold still?"

"Yeah, but it's getting better." The lie came out gruff.

Before he knew it, Peggy's hands were rubbing up and down his calf muscle, soft at first—which was torture—then hard, which distracted him enough to save him.

"This hurt?"

"It's fine."

Up and down she rubbed, digging her fingertips into the muscle of his calf as she went. Then she slowed, her hands warm against his leg as she slid up past his knee then stroked back down to his foot. He recalled the time she massaged his shoulder like this once, after getting tossed around on a particularly twisty bronc. She'd kneaded and massaged until he'd fallen asleep, then curled up next to him. It was days like those he'd had the hardest time trying to forget. The days when just being together had packed them clean full of contentment.

He was just drifting off when pain shot through him. "Ow. Now that hurts," he barked, then glared.

She made a dismissive sound. "You're fine. Think about something else." Any other person would have shied away at his bark. Not his tough girl.

His tough girl. All of a sudden all humor was gone. He'd promised himself long ago he'd never let a woman get under his skin again. And certainly not this one.

He reached down and shoved her hands off him.

"What?" She stammered.

"Gotta go."

"Where?"

"To take a leak. I think we're done for the day."

Peggy jumped to her feet and smacked both palms to his chest, knocking him back into the sofa. "Oh no you don't. I'm not playing this game with you, Clayton Cooper. I get this is uncomfortable for you. I get there is a current arcing so hard between us, we'll likely *both* get scorched. I get that you don't want me here. But too bad. Live with it. I'm here by Dr. Trenton's orders, and you'll never walk right if your leg doesn't heal. Not on my watch. Not if I can do something to prevent it. So, live with the discomfort! Sit there, and shut up!"

Behind Peggy a loud, slow clap began. A second joined it, then a third.

Peggy turned. Clay leaned to see past her. Brand, Trevor, Colt, and Rylee were grouped just inside the doorway from the kitchen. The three men were clapping. Rylee looked downright ready to smack them for it. Well, at least he had one ally.

Peggy pointed toward the doorway. "Out!"

He jolted at Peggy's shout. Surprised she didn't use their support to control him. "All of you. Out of here. This is not a circus. Clay is not the clown. So get out and don't come back for at least half an hour." Peggy stabbed her finger at them and held it there.

Rylee grinned. The men stopped clapping. Looking a bit shame-faced, Brand turned away. Colt followed, with Rylee giving him a good wallop on his behind.

Trevor was the last to leave. His expression was a glare, but that was nothing new. Peggy didn't look away or give in. Without a word, he turned into the kitchen and disappeared.

Clay had never been so moved.

He could hear his family arguing in the kitchen through the open doorway, but soon Brand toed the rock that held it open out of the way. The door swung back and forth, back and forth, until it finally stood still. Only then did Peggy turn back to Clay.

She didn't say a word, though she was visibly shaken. With unsteady fingers, she pulled the stool over, sat, and lifted his foot to her lap, right on top of the skirt of her starched gray uniform. She began working the back of his heel. Stopped, poured more liniment in her hand, then began again. She never once looked up.

Clay wondered if he should say something to her. But what would he say? 'Hey, way to ream out my meddling family' or, 'Nice job being my champion.' No. She'd just tell him to sit there and shut up again.

One thing had changed for the good. His reaction to Peggy had shifted from pathetic nostalgia with a splash of ardor to all-consuming pain. "Should it still hurt this bad?"

"For now I'll work your foot and stretch the Achilles for you. In the future you can do some exercises yourself. I'll teach you. And, to answer your question, yes, in your case where you've injured it more than once, it can be excruciating."

Clay winced, then rolled his eyes.

She caught it. "What we want is to regain flexibility and strength. Otherwise you could lose your ability to walk correctly or reinjure it again. The doctor already told you that."

Peggy stared right into his eyes, the message clear. Do it right or be a cripple. "Okay. I get it. Enough of the lecture."

Her puff of exhaled breath and small nod showed she wasn't quite convinced he'd gotten it but would let it go for now. *For now* was typical of Peggy. She never gave up on anything she deemed important unless she'd exhausted herself in the effort. He'd learned that lesson good and well when she gave up on their broken marriage. In her mind, she'd been the only one who cared to save it. She'd been wrong, of course. But when she left, he'd made the mistake of letting her go.

That regret haunted him still. What a fool he'd been, to lose the best thing that would ever happen to him because he was too blind to see they might not make it.

Nothing for it now but to move on. He knew cattle and horses. He knew hay farming. But most importantly, he knew smokejumping. He warmed to this train of thought. It was more than a momentary distraction. Somewhere in here was the answer he'd been searching for. He couldn't jump anymore, no. But he sure as heck could teach it.

Did he *want* to teach it? His heart sagged a little, until another jolt of pain from Peggy's hands sped his thoughts forward the only direction they could go now.

There was a smokejumping facility in West Yellowstone, Montana, at the old airport just west of town. He'd visited twice before. Both times to recruit a trainer for the Alaskan program. Both times they'd declined due to the shortage of trainers nationwide.

A particularly sharp prod brought his attention back to the here and now. "What are you doing, woman? That can't be good for it." He squirmed but didn't yank his foot away. Had to show her he wasn't a pansy.

"Hold still. I told you it would be painful at first. We have to stretch the Achilles or you could snap it in half next time."

Clay's eyes widened. "It could do that?"

Peggy stopped her ministrations, her hands wrapped loosely around his foot as she brought her eyes to his.

He stared down at those delicate, strong hands against his skin, remembering how she'd used them to explore his body. He swallowed hard and squeezed the throw pillow in his lap. He should never have tested Sally. She hadn't affected him like this. Now he not only had to be in pain but was sure to embarrass himself every session. *Brilliant move, Clay.*

Peggy pulled her lower lip into her mouth, trying not to smirk. Yeah, she knew what was going on, and that made him all the more peeved. "Get on with it then," he barked.

She shook her head and sighed. He knew that sound, that exasperation that usually ended in silent treatment. But this time she surprised him by catching his eye. As soon as he focused on her, she lowered her head. *"Lord, help us today. Help me to help Clay with this serious injury. Help him understand if he doesn't have this therapy, he may never walk again correctly. You know our history. Please help us tolerate each other."*

Tolerate each other? *Tolerate?* Hardly. She needed to pray for him to refrain from tossing her over his shoulder and carting her off to bed. That's what she should pray for.

CHAPTER 7

The last two weeks crawled by as Peggy visited her irascible patient every other day. She'd rejoiced when the second weekend approached, knowing she'd have time to recover and get all prayed up for the week to come. Still, Monday arrived, and she wasn't even close to ready.

Clay had improved daily. He was a lot of things not so pleasant, but determined was not on his list of failings. Hardworking, focused, organized, logical, brave—those were his strengths. Where he failed? Impatience, recklessness, and relationships.

Peggy stepped out of her Valiant and glanced at the sky. It was overcast and dreary, just like her flagging spirit. Being around Clay's mulish personality drained her, as she'd expected. What she hadn't expected was how involved her heart had become.

"Lord, here goes another day with Clay. With your help, please let my fingers heal his Achilles, sooner rather than later. And please keep my heart from sliding into his."

She prayed this prayer every time she came, yet as she walked through his door, it was as if he clicked a tether to her heart, attaching the other end to his.

Unawares, he'd been reeling her slowly toward him. She wondered, did he feel the same?

Once she'd unloaded her paraphernalia from the Valiant's trunk, she pulled her white cardigan closed at the front and patted her hair to make sure all the strands were in place. Bending down, she curled her fingers around the satchel handle.

Right about then the front door to the house crashed open, and Brand raced toward her. "Don't you touch that, Nurse Peggy. You know that's my job!"

Funny that this younger brother had been named Brand, since he had a particular *brand* of charm. She couldn't help but smile at his over-the-top chivalry.

She waited as he jogged toward her, snatched the satchel up with one hand, slammed the trunk with the other, and then ushered her toward the house. "I have a cup of hot Bosco ready for you. Or, you hungry?"

She hadn't had hot chocolate since she was a little girl. But boy did it sound good and warm on such a blustery day. "I'm not hungry, but the cocoa sounds great. Thank you."

"Don't thank me. It's the least I can do to make up for you having to deal with my bear of a brother. Be careful." Brand gave her a sidelong glance. "He's particularly grizzly today."

They were nearly to the door when she halted and put her hand on Brand's arm to stop him. "Is he in pain?"

"I think so. But it's more than that. I think it's the prayer you always start with. You know he blames God for a ton of stuff in his life. You might want to forego poking him with a stick today."

So, he'd complained to Brand. *Father God, I don't plan to stop praying over him first, so help me here. Please.*

Peggy shook her head, and Brand groaned. "Then I'll give you your cocoa and make myself scarce. Good luck."

Brand opened the front door and let her in. She shivered as she crossed the threshold, both from the chill and a sense of foreboding. Clay was a strong-minded creature, rarely agreeable and addicted to quarreling. She'd never understood why someone like him attracted her so much. For sure she'd thought when she matured, things would have changed. They hadn't.

"Evening, Clay," she said as she marched toward him. It was a good thing she'd prayed in the car on the way here, because with just one look at his face, her resolve started to falter.

With his good foot, he pushed up from the floor to sit straighter and grunted.

"That good, huh?" She purposefully kept her voice light and cheery even though it seemed to grate on him.

"You can by-pass the dang prayer."

"No can do. Without God's healing power, how good do you think this heel can get?" She smiled, though it was strained.

"It'll heal just fine. Let's get on with it."

Peggy locked her knees to keep them from trembling and planted her hands on her hips. "Who's in charge here?"

By the stormy look on his face, maybe she should have chosen her words better. But they were already out there, so she lifted her chin to wait him out. Before he could speak again, her legs weakened. She sat heavily on the stool and took hold of his ankle to stave off argument. He helped her lift his foot to her lap.

Using both hands to hold it in place, she lowered her head.

"I said forego the prayer." His voice was stern, thick with warning.

She ignored his statement, held faster to his foot, and began, "*Lord, please help my hands to bring healing to Clay's whole leg. I'll do my part but only you can heal him. Make it better than ever. Thank you, Lord.*" Instant perspiration broke out at the hollow of her neck. She didn't know why she'd prayed for a three-time injury to be better than ever, but she'd felt compelled to say it. Trepidation shot up her spine at what that meant. It was practically impossible to expect such a lofty goal.

Clay huffed and grinned, making it known he'd paid close attention to her prayer. "Well now, if that happens, I can go back to smokejumping. Good plan, Twinkie. I'll expect that prayer every day now. And the results."

Blood drained from her face. That couldn't have been God's plan. To give Clay hope for a future in smokejumping when the doctor had forbidden it? A knot of dread formed in her stomach. *What have I done?* How could she have placed God in such a position in front of an unbeliever? She wasn't David advancing on Goliath to save the Israelites; or Shadrach, Meshach and Abednego thrown into a fiery furnace because they refused to bow down to an earthy king. How could she expect God to answer such a prayer? *It was foolish of me. I'm so sorry, Lord.*

But peace came over her. The kind of peace she only felt when she'd truly left her life in God's hands. She didn't understand it, but she vowed to go along with it.

Gathering much needed courage, Peggy looked up and lifted her chin a notch. Clay sported a half smile that looked more like a smirk. His smile faltered a bit when he saw the confidence on her face. She didn't feel it, but was determined to pray between sessions until it came.

Pouring the liniment in her hands, she rubbed them together. *Give my hands healing power, Lord.*

She encircled the top of his calf with her effective fingers. A glance up told her Clay had lost the arrogant expression and seemed to be fighting pain. But, no… She stared for a moment. If she didn't know better, she'd swear that expression meant pleasure. She bore down, furrowing her brows in concentration. The thought was too disconcerting.

But, as she massaged, her eyes remained on his face. Clay squeezed his already shut eyes and rolled in his bottom lip, biting down hard. His nostrils flared.

A current shot up her arms and went straight to her face with a scalding heat. She'd seen that look on this man's face countless times before. Always in intimate settings.

She gasped and threw off his foot so fast she lost her balance.

Clay's eyes flew open. He shot out an arm to steady her. "Whoa, Sunbeam. You okay there, darlin'?" He hadn't even noticed what an awkward pretzel he'd made of his own body trying to save hers. Or what he'd said.

Peggy could only stare. This was the first true glimpse of the man he'd been. Concern for her was etched on his handsome face. It brought a stab of yearning so painful, she feared a torrent of tears would follow.

Just then the back door banged open, rattling the windows from two rooms away. Whoever it was stayed in the kitchen.

Peggy watched as Clay came back to himself and shook his head imperceptibly. The grim line was back on his mouth as he flopped back to the couch and sighed, looking heavenward. Then he let his eyelids drift closed.

Peggy wondered what he was thinking. That he'd slipped up and shown his true feelings? That he'd given her a glimpse of the man who'd once loved her? That *that* man might still exist?

For the first time in over four years, hope entered Peggy's heart. Hope for the future she'd once believed in and wished she'd never closed the door on. She breathed in and could almost fill her lungs again.

Her gaze roamed over the beautifully rugged face that had given her joy for such a brief interlude. As his eyes remained closed, she drank her fill; from the messy dark hair streaked from the sun, longer than he'd ever worn it; to the sculpted forehead, long straight nose, thick brows riding low on his deep-set eyes; and the Adam's apple in his whiskered neck, so prominent as he lay back. He'd matured. She could see it in the new lines that webbed the corners of his eyes and bracketed his mouth. They didn't look like laugh lines, more like the marks of a man who'd been wrestling hardships and sadness through defeat. Though she knew it wasn't all from her, her heart stuttered in her chest for every agony he'd endured.

After many long seconds, Clay jerked his head up, startling her out of her admiration. He gave her a sharp glare. "You going to keep me here all night?"

And just like that, hope was vanquished…cast out of her heart on the next beat. She pulled his foot back into her lap. *What is it, Lord? Why has Clay remained such an angry creature?*

And then the answer was there. She could see it clearly now. This wasn't about his injury, or the loss of smokejumping, or even their divorce. It was about Clay's prior brokenness. About being raised by a father who was rarely available to a young boy who grew more reckless to draw his attention. About the motherless youth who married young for affection, only to find he'd married a girl incapable of staying at his side no matter the circumstances.

And hadn't she heard he'd lost his best friend to an Alaskan wilderness fire?

This was about crushing, soul deep loss. And she was in no position to fix that.

He'd needed God.

He still did.

"Hey, Twinkie. Ignoring me now?" He pulled his foot off her lap and sat up. "Time to end this thing."

Her stomach bottomed out. *End this thing.* She'd already done that once. No way she'd be the one to walk out that door—to end anything of theirs again. A shiver ran through her. "No. No, we're not done." She was sure he'd hear the panic in her voice. She cleared her throat, forced it to sound calmer. "Sit back. We have a lot to do." That was her professional voice. Thank goodness.

A loud curse came from the kitchen. Her gaze met Clay's. "That sounded like Colt." Odd. She'd never heard him curse before...in front of his fiancée, no less. "What's got your brother so upset?"

She started to rise out of curiosity and to see if she could help, but Clay bent forward and pushed at her stomach, forcing her back in place.

She gawked at him.

"Sit down and stay out of it."

She frowned but couldn't let it drop. "What's going on do you think?"

Clay snorted. "Nothing changes around here. Probably one of Colt's admirers. They bother him all the time. If it were me, I'd tell them to get lost."

She sneered. "Of course you would."

Clay opened his mouth as if to argue the point but changed his mind. Then his mouth twisted in disgust. "Why don't you go to him, Twinkie. It's what you want to do. It's what you've always done." He mumbled the last words but she caught them.

We're back there again? Reliving the pain of their marriage...the *misunderstandings* of their marriage? Had they neither one grown up at all?

"Now hear this, Mr. Cooper. Colt and I became friends when I was married to you. Nothing more. Why do you insist on making more of it than it was?" She'd never confronted him on this before, having been too scared to provoke his wrath. Funny how maturity changed that sort of thing.

Clay clamped his mouth shut and glared right through her. Then his face softened, and he sat back. Another look came over him. One she'd grown quite fond of back in the day…*mischief*. He was about to shock her…or try to. She braced herself. "Are you going to do something with my leg tonight or shall we just make out?"

Peggy blinked. Well, he'd done quite well in the shock department. She felt heat rise up her throat as another flood of recollections came at her. Making out with Clay everywhere: the house, the barn, his pickup truck, beneath the rodeo grandstands. The list went on and on—each time better than the last.

Her eyes dropped to his hard mouth, the mouth that had hovered over hers thousands of times before, taking it with a hunger so profound she'd never attempted to find the same ardor with anyone else.

It finally sank in that Clay had probably been reliving pieces of their marriage too as she'd kneaded her fingers into his calf, with every rub of liniment matting the dark hair. No wonder he was struggling with so many emotions.

She swallowed hard. How could she get this job done without impaling them both on their past?

Loud, angry voices arose in the next room before the back door slammed again. Peggy couldn't stand not knowing. Clay had always told her she butted in way too much. It was one of the reasons she'd stopped going on the rodeo circuit with him. She'd given her youthful opinion one too many times, to Clay and anyone else she thought could use her wisdom. It annoyed Clay to the point he'd started avoiding her, then stopped talking to her altogether. That, she couldn't live with. Add Clay's rodeo buddies' relentless flirtations and it had been the beginning of the end of their marriage. "Go ahead, Margaret. You're dying to know what's happening with your *buddy*."

Margaret. He knew her mother only spoke her proper name when she was in trouble, and that she hated it. He'd never wanted to hurt her before. Now it seemed that's all he wanted to do. Was he after vengeance? Or was she just reaping what she'd sown?

She wasn't going to convince Clay she only wanted to help Colt because he still felt like family to her, so she didn't try. Instead, she rose and departed the room, leaving Clay to wonder after her.

CHAPTER 8

Two days passed. Peggy thumbed through the closet of her childhood bedroom for a sweater, girding herself for another visit to the Bar-6. She groaned inwardly. After leaving his side to go see about Colt, Clay hadn't been the same when she'd returned to him. Not even close.

The sad part was, Colt and Trevor had only been arguing about how Colt's latest scavenger—who was sitting out front in her brand new Corvette—should be handled, so there hadn't been much she could do to help. If only that had prompted her to keep her mouth shut. Oh no, not her. The look on Trevor's face when she'd told him how thankful he should be Colt was such a sweetheart was still burned on the backs of her eyelids. Adding that he should be grateful Colt didn't go around making enemies was an inference Trevor hadn't missed. When he turned on his heels and hit the back door, Colt treated her to a glare of his own before following. She'd managed to upset three Cooper men in twenty short minutes, and felt guilty ever since. She had no right to stick her nose in Cooper business. Not anymore.

Going back today would be a much bigger challenge.

"Peg," her mother hollered from the entry hall. "You have a visitor."

Peggy tugged a blue sweater off the hanger and groaned again to herself. How much longer until she found an apartment in Gillette and could live on her own? Her mom and dad were good people, but her mom doted on her way too much. Fat chance her mom would leave her be at the door without inserting herself into the conversation.

Peggy glanced at her watch and hurried to the door, with its lavish Christmas garlands and strands of lights. "Mom, you don't have to yell," she whispered as she breezed past her to the open door. The stocky man with dark blond hair and a smirk on his handsome face was as familiar to her as her roommates had been. "Larry. How did you find me?"

"Hey, beautiful, is that how you greet an old friend? How about, 'It's great to see you, handsome,' or 'Welcome, give me a gigantic hug.'"

"Welcome, give me a hug," she complied. Sort of.

He stepped over the threshold and enveloped her in a crushing hug. "Now that's better." He turned to her mom. "And who is this? Your sister?"

Her mom tittered, and the grim line on her mouth morphed into a blushing smile. "Oh, you're a charmer." She held out her hand for him to shake. But he didn't. Instead he grabbed her up in his arms as he'd done Peggy and gave her a careful hug.

"Oh my. Who is this young man?" she asked when she'd collected herself and her gaze landed on Peggy.

"My study partner at Case Western. I told you about him."

Larry took it upon himself to close the door and scoot them both toward the kitchen. "Oh, so you told her about me? That's coolio, Leggie-Meggie. Got any coffee?"

Ugh. Peggy'd forgotten all about Larry, and the hated nickname he'd given her. Though a good study partner, not much else appealed to her about him.

"Yes, we have coffee. Why have you come?" Peggy couldn't usher him out fast enough.

"Margaret Sassman, that's rude."

"*Cooper*, Mom. It's Margaret Cooper. I shouldn't have to remind you of that anymore."

"Well," she huffed. "You should change it back. That man wasn't worth your time, let alone leaving you stuck with his name."

"I'm not stuck—" She stopped herself. Her mom had never liked Clay, so what was the point of going over this futile argument again? Especially in front of Larry. Time to distract. "Larry, would you like a slice of my mother's Christmas fruit cake with that coffee?"

Peggy gestured toward a kitchen chair at their round table. "You still like your coffee with milk and sugar?"

"You remembered! Yep. Listen, Megs," There was another nickname she didn't like. "One of the reasons I looked you up is I brought the photo album of us."

One of the reasons? "Of *us*?" There'd never been an *us*.

"Yeah. Trish made it of the three of us."

Oh, Trish. Another study buddy Peggy had mixed feelings about. Between Trish's garish clothes and capricious personality and Larry's manipulations, studying had always been a challenge. At least until they got the shenanigans out of their systems and buckled down. Then they'd been so helpful, she stopped toying with the idea of finding other study partners.

"I haven't talked to her since I first moved back. How is dear Trish?"

"A little sarcasm there?" He laughed. "She's Trish. You know. Not much changes there. I left the album in the car." He gestured toward the window at his beat-up junker of a Chevy. "I'll give it to you when I leave."

The fruit cake and coffee were placed in front of him, and then she went to pour a cup for herself. "You want coffee, Mom?"

"No thanks, honey. You have a nice visit. I have things to do upstairs." She gave her daughter a wink and left before Peggy could object.

Her mom picked now to make herself scarce? Peggy planted a glare at her mom's back until she disappeared up the stairs, then turned back to Larry. She lowered herself into a chair across from him. "How have you been?"

"Everything's fab. How about you?" It took all Peggy's willpower not to roll her eyes. Larry seemed to be locked into the same vernacular of their college days, when most of the words he used then should have been left back in high school. Such a kid. Larry's levity used to be entertaining, breaking up the monotony of tough classes. Now it was downright grating.

"I'm fine. Been working hard. In fact, I have to get rolling," she said. "I have an appointment."

"Oh? Is that at the hospital in Gillette?"

Peggy blinked. "How did you know?"

Larry's lips parted into his charming grin. He paused, letting his eyes roam over her face, then slide down her throat and beyond. "It's really good to see you, squirt. I've missed our study sessions."

She crossed her arms. "You didn't answer my question. How did you know about my job at the hospital in Gillette? In fact, how did you even find out where I live?" The fact he knew all this began to concern her. If Trish told him, she was going to have words with that girl. Peggy had warned her not to tell Larry anything about her.

He waved a hand. "Trish knows everything."

"She did it."

"What?"

Darn, the meddling scamp. Never could keep things to herself. Peggy didn't mind keeping up with Trish, but Larry had begun to get clingy as they approached graduation. Leaving school behind had been a relief in that respect.

Standing, she swept Larry's empty plate and cup up and headed for the sink. "It was nice seeing you, but I need to get going."

Peggy hurried to the front door and stood by to wait for Larry to catch up. Thankfully, he followed. "You take care now."

Larry looked puzzled but stepped through the doorway. She closed it behind him and scooted to the back door to gather her satchel and keys. Keeping an eye on his car, she waited until he drove off before she got in her own car.

As Peggy bounced up the long drive to the Bar-6, she breathed a heavy sigh. This felt like home. Even the gaping potholes they still hadn't fixed in all these years were calming to her spirit if not to her chassis.

She only had a couple of weeks left with Clay. Though he'd been a stinker most of the days of his therapy, he hadn't been able to hide his good heart from her. She'd been one of the few people in his life who saw it—and it was still there. He kept it carefully hidden behind walls of stone, but she could see through stone. Thinking of himself as a jackass was preferable to being seen as tender. Clay didn't know how to live with the decent side of himself. He was so used to being wild and making waves that anything else seemed foreign to him. It had only gotten worse in the years since she'd seen him last.

But, to Peggy? She remembered the evenings when the rugged man would come into their small trailer after being slammed and tossed by broncos all day. Once showered in the tiny stall to wash away the grime, he'd shower attention on her next. Brush her hair back from her face, kiss her gently, love her all night long…

Every tender moment was emblazoned on her mind. So much so now that she wondered who that person was who'd shut the door to a life with such a man.

Someone young and foolish and crazy insane, that's who.

Now that she was more mature, she looked back and clearly saw the insecure girl she was. What she wouldn't give to go back there as the person she was now and start again.

But no, hadn't she promised herself the next time around she'd fall for a mild-mannered guy like Clark Kent? Not the flying, leaping, fearless superhero?

It didn't matter what she thought now, anyway. The Clay she knew would never go back. Once anything in his life broke, he never fixed it. He just walked away, on to the next adventure, never to return to the same spot twice.

Then again, he *had* returned to Cooper Ranch. Someone *had* convinced him to come back here.

Hope bloomed. Could she convince him to open the gate to them again?

Her Valiant thumped into a particularly large pothole, jarring her out the cloud of hope she'd submerged herself in. The house was in view, making her heart skip then speed. Clay was in there, waiting. And while she could, she would drink in her fill.

• • •

Why had he done it? Why had he come home?

Because Dad asked you to, the voice in Clay's head reminded him. He scoffed at that voice. Still trying to please the old man. As if he was really needed. He hadn't helped Colt or Rylee one bit with her traumatized barrel racing horse, and only managed to reinjure his Achilles in the process. Plus he sure as heck hadn't helped Trevor on the ranch once he'd come up lame. So why was he staying?

His ex-wife belonged here more than he did.

"Peggy will be here in a few minutes." Brand stood over him, looking down into Clay's neglected, sleep-deprived face with a grimace on his own perfect mug.

Clay stared up into eyes the same shade as his but with a sparkle he never remembered having in his own. "How much longer you think this dang heel needs?"

Brand looked down at Clay's naked leg, his bare foot resting on the stool. "Last I saw her…" Brand scrunched his face and looked to be calculating in his head. "I think Peggy said two weeks." He gestured to Clay's foot. "She been walking you around yet?"

"Yeah, she's working me pretty good. Still hurts, which has her concerned. Says it needs more stretching. She has some ideas."

Clay scrubbed a hand down his face. He was coming to the end of his patience, seeing his ex-wife's pretty face every other day and sitting on his useless ass the rest of the time. He needed out of here before Christmas—less than a week from now. Though you'd never know it to look at this gloomy place. He couldn't remember the last time they'd actually celebrated a Christmas together. "I plan on asking her today when I can get back to work."

Brand's head came up as he cocked an ear. "She's here." Geez, he had the hearing of Dash, Trev's dog.

Clay's dang heart thumped hard in anticipation. Traitorous organ. Would this reaction to her never end? He sat up straighter, ran both damp palms over his hair, and tried to calm his pulse. Even standing in the open door of the Goose, their smokejumping plane, never spiked his blood pressure like this.

Brand ushered Peggy in. "Hey there, beautiful. Good to see you again."

Clay rolled his eyes. It was good this brother hadn't been older when Clay dated Peggy or the outcome might have been different. If Brand had married her, Clay had no doubt they'd still be married. At least Clay had found out early on he was no good at the marriage scene. One less thing to waste time on.

"Come in, come in. Would you like hot cocoa? Coffee? Hot cider?"

When had he made hot cider? Brand was about the only one who liked this time of year. Clay coughed, trying to loosen the knot in his throat. "Why you trying to impress her, Brandon?" As usual, he couldn't keep his dratted mouth shut.

Peggy had half-shrugged out of her blue sweater when both she and Brand swung their heads in his direction and glared hard enough to burn a hole through him. He didn't care. He needed her out of here and himself gone. His heel didn't feel right yet, but it would survive. He'd smokejumped in worse shape than this before. Maybe instead of teaching, he'd ignore his doctor's assessment and slip back to Alaska, to the work that needed him and truly called his name.

Yep. After his therapy session, he'd call his boss. Tell him he was 100% and able to return. He breathed a sigh of relief, feeling a calm he hadn't felt in weeks coming over him.

Peggy strode over to him with—by the smell of it—a steamy mug of cider in her hands. She set the cup on the end table then dropped her gaze to his leg. "Have you been doing the exercises I gave you?"

That would be a 'no.' Bracing his toes against the wall and stretching forward hurt like hell. He *had* practiced walking though. He'd even jogged a bit in spite of her warning against it. He'd done it with a slight limp, but he'd needed some sort of progress. "Sure."

"*Sure?* I know you, Clay. You did what you wanted to do. *What* did you do exactly?"

I know you, Clay. The words sent another zinger straight to his severed heart. She did know him. Better than anyone ever had. At first, he'd fought that with everything in him. Having someone else inside his head was so suffocating, he'd avoided spending time with her. But by the time he'd adjusted to—even loved— how she knew him, she'd up and called it quits. So long pardner. She may as well have said, 'Now that I know you, I don't want you.'

The memory brought a grimace to his face and the knot back to his throat.

Peggy's hands fell to her sides as she leaned in to study his expression. "Are you in pain this morning?" The look of concern on her face made him madder. She had no right to feel anything toward him anymore.

What's it to you, he wanted to spout. Instead he took a steadying breath, then another. He'd done enough sniping at her during these visits. "No. Not in pain." *That was a lie.*

Her mouth pulled to one side in disbelief as she eyed the crutches propped in the corner. "Really. Show me." She reached for both his hands. Tugged. "Up we go."

A shot of awareness traveled through his arms straight into his head, making him fuzzy. A deep inhalation steadied him.

Focus on the leg, he reprimanded himself.

Carefully, he lowered his injured foot to the ground and let her haul him up. Once he gained his feet, the fact he towered over her petite frame brought more memories on a painful surge—some good, some bad. So many times he'd used his size to dominate her, to make her feel small. To get his way.

Funny how he wasn't that man anymore.

Too bad she wouldn't remember him any other way.

But then, there were other memories. The ones where he smoothed the blond wisps from her silky cheeks then lowered his mouth to connect to hers. Some kisses were slow and tender, others wild and impassioned. All were memorable. Every. Single. One.

But you can't trust her anymore. He tugged his hands away.

She gazed up into his eyes with fondness in hers, lacerating him slowly.

With his head tilted down and hers up, he felt an overpowering urge to remind himself how soft her lips were. How could he betray himself so easily?

"What now?" His words were brusque and gravelly.

She cleared her throat, rubbing her hands down her skirt as if it needed straightening. "Walk around the room for me—heel, toe. Don't limp."

Easier said… He looked around, charted his course, then began. With every step the pain shot up his heel into his calf. It felt as if the tendon would snap at any second. But if he let her know that, his escape to Alaska and a job he needed more than air was out the window.

Heel. Toe. Heel. Toe, he repeated in his head to blot out the pain. Sweat popped out on his forehead. He swiped at it with the back of his hand before she noticed. Managed to make it around the room without giving his agony away. Or so he thought.

"Sit. We have work to do."

Drat! More touching, stretching, touching, massaging, *touching*. It flabbergasted him he hadn't gone crazy yet.

Finding his place back on the sofa, he huffed, agitated.

"Stop growling. You want to walk without pain, don't you?"

He plopped his foot back on the stool, grimacing from his carelessness. How did she know he was in pain? The one skill he had developed from his years in rodeo was a blank expression.

"You don't think I noticed you sweating?" She adjusted her voice. "I'm not the enemy here."

The smooth, tender sound soothed his battered soul and, since it was her, tore it up all at the same time.

"I want you to walk correctly someday, stubborn man. Don't you want that?" She took advantage of his sitting position to make her point, stepping between his legs to look down at him with balled fists. "Don't you?"

Clenching his jaw, he fisted his own hands while staring up, rattled. It was only a matter of time now until he caught her hand and hauled her into his lap. He couldn't be held responsible for what happened next when she stepped into his orbit like this.

He forced his thoughts back to the day she'd left him. "What do I have to do to be done with this? Tell me. I'll do it. I'm going back to work."

She reared back, nearly tripping over her own two feet. "You're what? No! It's too soon." Her reaction stunned him. If he didn't know better, he'd think she wanted him to stay. For her.

"It's time."

Her breathing increased, and her face flushed. Flustered, she reached up and pushed at hair that wasn't a bit out of place. "Listen, Clay. If I've been too strict, just tell me. You can't go yet. I have to…*we* have to get you well. It will kill you to not be mobile."

So that was it? She was worried he couldn't be wild anymore? Figured it would end him? Well, she was probably right. Still knew him well. "If I have to slow down some, I will."

"You won't."

"I will."

She sighed, shook her head. "Clay, hear me. If we don't do this correctly now, your heel might seize up. If it does, you'll lose your mobility. That doesn't just mean you can't do crazy stunts anymore. It means you may never walk right again. Or, God forbid, at all." Her eyes widened, tearing. The look of horror on her face softened his approach.

"It's okay, Peg. It'll be fine, I promise."

"Promise? If you're going to promise anything, promise me you'll stay long enough to finish with me."

It crossed his mind to yell she'd already finished with him. But that wasn't what she meant, and he knew it. He had to stay reasonable in order to end this. "You've done well, Twinkie. You've fixed me." That was a lie straight from hell.

A heavy knock sounded at the front door.

Brand materialized from the kitchen, jogged to the door, and opened it. "Howdy."

A deep voice resonated from the porch. "Hello. Is Megs—I mean, Margaret here?"

Who in the world would be here for Peggy? And who calls her Megs? "Let the man in," Clay hollered from his position on the sofa.

The man took a step, then two, into the house, a large book in one hand against his side. By the decorative cover, it looked like a photo album.

The man's eyes glanced around then searched out who'd given him permission to enter. When he saw Clay he waved, then shifted his gaze to Peggy.

His smile and wink had Clay's pulse shooting up. "And you are?" The question was a little late, but Clay needed to know who had the nerve to ask for his wife here, ex or not.

A tender touch alighted on his forearm. "It's okay, Clay. I know him. I'll take care of this."

Stunned to be so annoyed, Clay could only observe as she paced to the man, took the album out of his hand, and set it on the end table. Then took his hand and tugged him toward the kitchen.

Clay sat motionless, his eyes following where their hands were joined together until they disappeared through the doorway. He'd never thought to ask if she had a boyfriend. The lead in his gut told him that possibility was distinctly not okay.

"Huh. Who do you suppose that is?" Brand said, just as puzzled as Clay.

"Don't know. None of my business." Though the need to punch the fellow in his smiling mouth felt very much like his business.

The plastic cover on the album caught the light when Clay repositioned himself on the couch. He shifted to rise up on his good foot, then limped over to it. Flipped the cover open.

"Thought it was none of your business," Brand said.

"Shut up, pest."

The first page of photos was enough to floor him. Every picture had Peggy in it. The first two were of this strange man with his arm slung around her shoulders. Both were dressed in casual clothes as they stood against a wall of books. A library, maybe? The last two showed a third person between them. A female. Cute, brunette, also in jeans and an outrageously designed top.

Clay flipped through a few pages of the album and found all were taken on some college campus. Probably the University of Cleveland, Peggy's alma mater. A flip to the next page confirmed his guess. The three stood behind a big sign with the college's name, each with an elbow or arm propped on it.

Clay felt the churn of jealousy in his gut. The same jealousy he'd felt dozens of times when he arrived home from rodeo to find his wife holed up in the barn, talking to Colt.

He wasn't going through this again.

Peggy re-entered the living room and caught him flipping through the album. Instead of the reprimand he expected, she turned back to the man. "Larry, this is the Cooper home. This is Brand." She gestured to him. "And Clay's the one looking through what's not his."

Clay gave a curt nod but didn't shake the man's hand and didn't stop his snooping. Brand reached out immediately, of course. "Hey there. Good to meet'cha. Any friend of Peg's is a friend of ours." He glanced over. "Right, Clay?"

Peggy ushered Larry to the front door. "Thanks for bringing me the album, Larry. It was good to see you. Now I have to get back to work. Take care." She opened the door and patted him on the back in a way that gave Larry the hint to go through it.

Pride and relief swelled within Clay. At least now he knew Larry wasn't important to her, and that she could take care of herself in this big, unpredictable world. Larry found himself on the other side of a closed door before he had a chance to protest.

Clay grinned.

When Peggy strode back to Clay, she stopped in front of him and frowned. "What's so funny?"

Since she was now in front of him with her sweet face tilted up and his mood altered for the better, that curiosity he'd had about her lips crept in, steering his thoughts in an unsafe direction. Before he could think any more about it, he leaned down and brushed his lips across hers, the barest of contacts. He swallowed the whispering hitch of her gasp. Though the kiss was fairly chaste, her soft lips were everything he remembered, and more.

When he straightened back to full height, her eyes caught his. Her look of confusion scraped over him like a rake caught on overgrown underbrush. What had he been thinking? Reawakened emotions scattered everywhere until he wanted to holler with latent pain. This was the woman who'd told him goodbye. She didn't want him. No matter how soft her lips were. No matter how much his body wanted hers, this could go nowhere. No. Where.

The shock in her now darkening eyes was the last thing he saw before he turned and limped away.

CHAPTER 9

The following day passed at a crawl as Peggy's thoughts revisited the kiss. By the time Friday arrived, she felt like a kid on Christmas morning as she drove down the lane toward the Bar-6. She shook her head at herself for the sweaty palms against the cold steering wheel in the dead of winter, and the small smile that kept creeping back to her mouth.

At the dip of the final pothole, her heart fluttered in anticipation.

The house stood majestically against the bluster of a wind-driven storm. Light spilled from each window, radiating warmth and splendor.

He was in there. Open one door and she'd see him again. *For his session*, she reminded herself. *To help his heel. Only that.*

She shuddered a sigh, then another, trying to gain her equilibrium. Little did Clay know, he'd always done this to her. Her heart would race each time she was about to lay eyes on the most compelling man she'd ever known. He was handsome, powerful, ardent...the list grew in her head.

Amazing how quickly the deep affection she still held for him had come flooding back and nearly submerged her. *That kiss*—that brief, tender touch—unlocked every passion and pleasure of marriage that she had caged behind the bars of her heart in order to survive. With the slightest pressure of his lips, the door to her heart burst wide open in a flood of escaping feelings and refused to swing closed. She'd yet to collect the elusive emotions and push them back inside. She doubted she ever could again.

Finding herself standing at the front door, she wondered how long she'd been there. A shiver reminded her to pull her coat tighter around her. Strands of hair that had been caught tight in a bun at her nape had torn loose and were flying about her face as she rapped on the door.

It took quite awhile before the door opened. Rylee stood on the other side. "Peggy!" There was surprise on her face. "Come in, come in. It's a cold one tonight."

Peggy hurried through, and they both pushed the door closed against the wind.

"Whew. It's going to snow soon," Rylee said.

"You think so? I thought maybe rain." Peggy rubbed her palms together.

Rylee grinned. "Well, you'd know better than me. I'm a Texan. Your weather is way more unpredictable than ours. 'Course, I gotta get used to Wyoming weather now, don't I?" Her face softened with an I'm-in-love-so-it-doesn't-matter kind of grin. "Watcha doin' here? Come to see Brand?"

Brand? "No. I'm here for Clay. His therapy?" She gave Rylee a look like she'd lost her mind.

Rylee's face fell, her smile gone. "Um…why don't I go get Brand."

"Brand, no—" But she'd already turned and rushed off.

Less than a minute later, Brand skidded into the room. "Hi, Peg. What's up?"

She frowned. "I'm here for Clay's therapy."

Brand's face whitened, emphasizing the dark whiskers on his young man's jaw. "Can I get you some hot chocolate? It sure is cold tonight. Probably'll snow soon. I've got to—"

"Brand! Tell me what's going on."

Brand squirmed, a worm on a hook. "Uh…well." He scrubbed a hand down his face. "Didn't Clay tell you?"

"Tell me what?"

"That…oh shoot. Sorry, Peg. Clay's gone."

Gone? Why? But she couldn't quite spit the words out over a heart that had leapt to her throat.

"H-he talked to his boss after you left Wednesday night. Apparently, Doc Trenton had already called his employer in Alaska and told him straight up not to let Clay back on the jumper squad. He knows Clay. Knew he'd ignore being told he couldn't smokejump anymore. Clay was furious. Packed up and stormed outta here the next morning."

"And you let him go? He's not done with his therapy. He shouldn't drive angry. What were you all thinking?" Peggy wanted to slap Brand, then line up the rest of them for the same punishment.

Brand backed a step, as if he'd read her mind. Smart man. "He borrowed my 4 x 4 truck. At least he's not flying his plane, it being winter and all."

"He has a plane? When did that happen?" She shook her head to get back on track. "Never mind that now. Where? Where did he go? Or do you even know?" Her voice squeaked the last question.

Brand smiled then. "Oh sure. 'Course we wouldn't have let him just go off not knowing where he went. Don't worry."

"Don't worry? *Don't worry?*" she squeaked again. She stepped forward and pressed a fingertip to his chest with every word. "Where. Did. He. Go?"

He looked confused. "He'll be fine, Peg. You should be glad to be done with him."

"You think I'm going to let him go without making sure his heel is all right?" She threw her hands in the air, built up steam to rant harder at Brand. But in a flash she realized what that would give away. *Stay calm, Peggy.* She lowered her voice. "I want to finish my job. Just tell me where he went, okay?" She managed a strained smile.

"Went to Montana."

"*Montana?* Why, Montana?"

"Smokejumper training camp. Once his boss cooled him down a mite, he told him a special job listing had just been posted to teach there. I never took Clay for the teacher-type, but life's got a way of changing your mind, you know?"

She did know. Wished life had a reset button. "Do you have the address of the training camp?"

"You plannin' on going there? Chasing after Clay?"

Chasing? She didn't like the sound of that. But in essence he was right. "I need to do my job. *Doc Trenton* expects me to do my job. I will finish with Clay's leg whether he likes it or not. Now give me the darned address."

"Whoa, easy now. No need to get all riled up." Brand turned and ambled back to the kitchen. She wanted to shoo him into a run with a cattle prod. Peggy planned to leave tonight before her folks got home from an evening at her aunt's. She was too old to have to explain her actions. Seemed like, since coming home from college, that was all she'd done.

Instead of Brand, it was Colt who strode back into the room. So, Brand had gotten reinforcements. "Hi. How've you been?" he asked with a sweet smile. Same old Colt.

"Just dandy, Colt. You?" She'd seen the way he looked at Rylee, so she already knew how he was.

He chuckled at her testiness. "Been great. What's this about you chasing after Clay?"

She huffed. "Oh for pity's sake. Those are Brand's words. I am going to Montana to finish my job. That's all."

"Peg—"

"No. Don't you say it. I'm not chasing Clay. I'm following my patient where he decided to run off to. To. Finish. My. Job."

Colt's deep blue eyes saddened. "We both know how deeply you feel about him, Peg. I was there, remember?"

Did he have to bring that up? "That was over four years ago." Though those feelings had never lessened—they'd only withered some. Sure, Colt knew why she'd called off the marriage. Knew she'd still been in love with Clay when she did it. Also knew her young self had figured Clay would stop his dangerous and elusive life to chase her back home. Fight for her.

He'd called her bluff and showed her his back. She'd watched as he walked away, waiting for him to at least glance over his shoulder one last time. It never happened. Not once.

The sympathy on Colt's face was crushing. How had she stood that all those years ago? "Give me Clay's address, Colt. I'm leaving tonight."

He shook his head. "No, you're not."

"Let her go, Blue Eyes."

Colt swung around to Rylee coming up behind him.

She stretched her arms around him, so petite her hands barely met at his other side. Her green eyes flashed with adoration as she peered up at him. "She needs to go," she said with a quiet voice. "Don't you see that?"

They had this all wrong, but if Rylee could convince Colt, maybe Peggy could finally get the stinking address! She rolled her lips in and bit down. The less she said the better.

Colt's shoulders hunched as his arms came around his fiancée. He nestled his face in her thick red hair and breathed in.

"Please, Colt," Rylee said into his chest.

He nodded. Neither moved, so Peggy did. "Is the address in here?" She pointed to the kitchen as she set out across the living room.

As soon as she banged through the kitchen's swinging door, Brand handed her a slip of paper.

A glance at it told her it was what she needed. "Thanks. I'll be fine."

"You make sure you are. It's stormy tonight, but tomorrow promises snow so you'd better get at least halfway there tonight. If you leave within the hour you can get to Billings by 11:00 PM. From there it's a little less than four hours under normal conditions. I'll call Clint and let him know you'll stay with the Harpers like Clay is doing."

"What? Oh no. No. I'll stay in West Yellowstone. They have a hotel there. I don't want you to warn Clay I'm coming. He may escape somewhere else."

Brand searched her face, making it heat with a blush.

She hadn't intended to tell Brand that. But if anyone would understand, it was this particular Cooper. He cared deeply about people. Always had.

Soon he nodded and grinned. "Have it your way. I won't warn him." His smile fell off and an expression of concern replaced it. "Promise me you'll be careful. Clay's not an easy one."

Peggy gave Brand a smile back and reached for a hug. He tucked her under his chin and wrapped her up tight. When had he grown so tall? And so wise?

"I will," she finally said.

Releasing her, Brand stepped back and handed her a second slip of paper. "Directions to Harper Ranch in Montana. They're good people. Family. Stay with them. They'll love it."

She narrowed her eyes at him then smiled. "I'll think about it."

He leaned down, kissed her on the cheek, and walked her to the door. "Be safe."

• • •

Clint Wilkins entered the guest room and grabbed Clay up in a robust hug, patting him on the back a couple of times. "Good to see you, old man. When did you get back to our neck of the woods?"

Clay had rolled into Harper Ranch just before sunset as the snow began to fall again. He'd been stuck in Billings overnight due to this early storm. According to the weather man, it hadn't been expected until the dang weekend. Since arriving, nearly snow blind and grumpy as all heck, Mabel had stuffed him so full of beef stew and homemade bread that he could barely walk, much less survive a bear hug. "Just—an hour—ago—" Clay managed to grunt back.

"Come back down to the kitchen. Mabel made her specialty dessert—tapioca pudding. Best in the state. I have someone I want you to meet."

He'd pop if he ate anymore. "I met Jessica. Years ago."

"When she was twelve?" Clint laughed. "Please. I haven't seen you in years. Come meet her again…and someone else."

Clay was tired. Not just fall-into-bed-with-your-clothes-on bushed, but drained, defeated. He needed to be left alone, not trip downstairs to face more people under bright decorations hanging from every dratted shelf and deer antler. But Clint was his host while Roy was away, so there was nothing to do but follow him into the mix. Trying his best not to limp to avoid questions, he took his time going down the stairs.

Entering the kitchen, he heard two kinds of giggles. One from an adult, and one from a small child. At first glance he caught Mabel making funny faces at a toddler in a wooden highchair. The youngster giggled, and Mabel copied. The elation was catchy, and he found himself smiling in spite of his exhaustion and bad mood.

Clint motioned toward the woman standing at the sink. "Little one?"

She turned, dried her hands on a kitchen towel, and smiled at Clay. "Hello, Clay. Good to see you again."

He tilted his head in confusion. "You remember me?"

Jessica laughed. "Of course I do. When you're twelve, you don't forget meeting a dashing young cowboy you've decided should be yours."

Clay's jaw dropped as he glanced at Clint.

Her husband laughed right along with her. "Not worried, Clay, if that's why you look like a deer caught in a cougar's sights." Clint swept Jessica into a bone-melting kiss right in front of Clay. Why had he decided to stay with these people? Tomorrow he'd head to West Yellowstone, try to line up some lodging at the training center.

"Come closer," Clint gestured Clay over to the high chair. "Come meet our newest addition 'round here. God blessed us with our sweet little Molly."

"Da da," she screeched on cue.

"She'll be a year old in a little over a month—February 7th. Molly, wave at Mr. Cooper." Clint waved and so did she, then she giggled. "Da da," she said, pointing a finger at Clay. Clint grinned so hard Clay thought he might split his face open.

"Is she done with her snack?" Clint asked Mabel.

"As done as she's gonna be. Time for a bath and bed." Mabel cleaned her up and tugged her out of her highchair. "Go to yer Papa, sweet girl."

Mabel handed her over. Clint kissed her head and immediately shoved her into Clay's arms. "Here. Give you something to strive for. About time you started your own herd, don't you think?"

The last of Clay's good mood bled out over that comment. How could he tell Clint he wouldn't be having any kids? Had to have a wife first, and he'd never try that again.

Wispy-haired, turquoise-eyed Molly grinned a four-tooth grin at him, twisting his heart into a pretzel. "Cute," was all he could muster.

Jessica scampered over and pulled Molly out of his arms. "You're scaring him, Clint-honey."

Clay shook his head. "It's just, I haven't had much sleep lately. Think I'll join Miss Molly here and hit the hay."

Clint took Molly out of Jessica's hands and held her to him in one beefy arm. The baby stuck a figure in Clint's mouth and jabbered. He talked around it. "You headin' into West Yellowstone in the morning?"

Clay shrugged. "Not due there until Tuesday, but if it's not snowing, I'll go in tomorrow. I've already been held up an extra day by the storm, so thought I'd be smart and beat the next round of snow. Don't wait on me for meals. Don't know when or if I'll be back."

"What do you mean, *if*? Thought you were planning to stay with us for a spell."

"I was, until this dad-blamed storm."

Clint nodded. "Makes sense. Well, listen, don't worry about lettin' us know. We feed a crew around here. One more doesn't matter much."

"Thanks. 'Night."

"Goodnight, Clay," Jessica said while Mabel and Clint chimed in.

Clay climbed the stairs, feeling like a shell of a man. In the last few months he'd managed to lose his job, his buddies, his Alaskan home, and the wall he'd erected to try to forget Peggy. With his next step, he leaned heavily on the stair rail, which twisted his Achilles. A strip of pain blazed up his leg. He pushed off the railing, wanting instead to shove it through the blasted wall, and continued his list of losses. The brand new Piper Comanche plane he'd flown into Gillette. The old rattletrap ranch truck he'd learned to drive in, which couldn't handle winter roads. Nothing here was his. Certainly not his life.

Loneliness smothered him as he lay atop the covers, fully clothed but for his boots. Watching Clint give Jessica the kind of heart-stopping kiss he used to give his own wife had nearly shut down his pulverized organ all together. What did he have to look forward to? Work and more work and pain.

That was the sum total of his existence.

God blessed us with our sweet little Molly. Did Clint really believe that? That God had blessed them? God. It had been a long time since he'd thought about God in any way but as a curse. Yet, lately when he'd talked to

Colt, or even his dad and Rebecca on the phone, they'd always brought God into the picture. Even Rylee had begun to throw out the name with reverence.

"So, God," Clay said to the ceiling. "It's quite the mess you've given to Clayton Cooper, third son of a father who couldn't be bothered and a mother you took home too early. Guess I didn't qualify for your blessings, eh? Haven't quite measured up. Well, if you truly exist, how about bringing me something worth living for?"

He sneered, huffed a doubting breath, and turned over to give sleep another chance.

CHAPTER 10

Peggy felt like she had driven for days, not just hours. The Valiant's windshield wipers beat a steady rhythm against snowflakes attempting to land, all while her head pounded its own tempo. *"It has to be coming up soon. Right, Lord? You won't let me be stranded, will you? Even though I was crazy to take this trip and didn't bother to ask you first."*

She'd left Billings this morning as soon as there was a break in the weather, and it had taken her six hours to get to Hwy 191 toward West Yellowstone instead of just under four as promised. The minutes ran together as she strained to see past the snow to the road. Somewhere along the frozen and hazardous tundra-like path, she'd decided stopping at Harper's was the better choice after all. Thank God Brand had insisted on handing her those directions.

"The turn-off is supposed to be here somewhere. Anytime now—there! Turn!" She hollered at her car as if it were alive, thankful she didn't slide when she swung left onto the small road. "Whew, that was close."

She fought to control her small car through the slush and mud. Trying to keep a constant speed as her dad had taught her, she splattered her way up to the Harper ranch house.

The big two story, white with green trim, loomed out of the falling snow. *Thank you, God, for getting me here safely.* Glancing at her watch, she realized she'd been on the road for over seven hours now. It was already getting dark, and she hadn't dared to stop to call anyone.

As she let herself out her car door, the front door to the house slammed opened and a familiar body dashed madly down the steps toward her. Her heart tumbled all over itself. *Clay.* His tense stature and grim mouth told her he was fuming. Even the snowflakes melted instantly in his heat except for the ones on his hair, shoulders, and eyelashes. He shifted into an awkward walk to close the distance between them. "What the hell do you think you're doing, *Margaret*? Trying to get yourself killed?"

She winced at the name and the force of his words.

Before she could give him a plausible explanation, a large man in a cowboy hat and sheepskin-collared coat scooted past Clay toward her. When he got closer he grinned, nearly knocking her off balance. This had to be the foreman. She'd heard he was a looker, but…wow.

"Hello, young lady. Welcome to Harper Ranch. I'm Clint Wilkins, and who might you be looking for?"

She glanced over Clint's shoulder, and he followed her gaze. "This guy?" He turned his gaze back on her. "You looking for this guy?" He hiked his thumb back at Clay and smirked.

Clay must have spouted some royal profanities when he'd spotted her Valiant out the window for this man to tease him.

Pursing her lips together, she debated what to say. "Might you invite me in?" She glanced at the well-lit house and the colorful Christmas tree in the window, feeling a little melancholy she wouldn't be back in time for Christmas with her family.

He laughed. "Of course. Where are my manners? Come in. We'll get your things."

Clint grinned again, took hold of her arm above the elbow, and guided her up the front steps. Clay had pulled up halfway to her car, his weight shifted off his bad leg after taking a bad step on ice. When they came even with him, Clint gave him an open-handed thump on the chest, let out another glorious laugh, and kept on going until he'd safely delivered her into the warmth of the house with greetings from two women-folk. He snugged the door closed behind her and headed back out.

"Oh my goodness, you're brave to be driving in this mess," a woman with a toddler in her arms said, concern written all over her face.

An older lady with a tight gray bun stood behind her. "Outta my way, Jessica." The woman elbowed the duo to the side. "This young one's shiverin'. Go get the teapot on."

Who was this woman, with her easy grasp of command, and an apron that looked to have tonight's supper speckled all over it? Grandma, possibly?

"I'm Mabel. Cook 'round here. And a whole lotta other stuff."

Well, that answered that. "I'm Peggy. I'm…uh…I'm here for Clay." Peggy couldn't help but look behind her, waiting for him to burst through the door like an angry bear.

"Peggy? Clay's Peggy? I heared when you married up with him. What? Five, six years ago now?" She pointed toward the stairs. "His room's the first on yer right up the stairs. I'll have the fellas put your things in there."

Peggy clasped her collar together at her neck as if that would protect her against the emotion this evoked. "No, I—"

"It's fine, Missy. The fellas 'round here are pretty good 'bout helpin' out. Here, gimme yer coat. It's wet, so won't be keepin' you warm no more anyways." Her chubby arm flew over in a gesture toward the dining area adjacent to the kitchen. "Go on in there, and Jessica'll get ya some hot tea, warm yer bones. Keys." Mabel stuck her hand out and waited.

There was something about this woman that compelled obedience. Peggy reached into her coat pocket and retrieved her keys, handing them to Mabel.

"Be right back." Mabel darted off toward the door.

"No, Mabel, wait."

"Don't bother," said a masculine voice beside her.

Peggy jumped at the sound and turned. A burly man stood at her elbow, fresh from outside. He plucked off his snow-dusted hat and strode to the back door to hang it on a hook. "Mabel doesn't really listen too good. Not when she decides to do somethin' that's on her mind, you know? Who are you?"

"Pete, for goodness sake." Jessica handed him the baby, who'd already started screeching happy sounds and leaning toward the man. "This is Clay's wife, Peggy. Peggy, this is Pete, one of the crew. I'm Jessica, Clint's wife, and this little cutie is Molly." She grinned at her daughter as Pete bounced her in his arms.

They had this all wrong. "No, I'm not—"

"Good to meet'cha," Pete said, his words running over the top of hers. "First time I met Clay too. He's Cord's kid, right?"

"Yes, but I'm—" Peggy started again.

But it was too late. Pete had already turned toward a stuffed horse with a big red bow around its neck by the tree with baby Molly sticking her little finger in his ear and giggling. "Oh you think that's funny, huh, Moll-baby?" Pete said, then plopped the little girl on the rocking horse and squatted down next to it.

Okay, well, looked like no one was listening to her about *not* being Clay's wife. Didn't matter, she guessed. She was worn out and dreading her conversation with Clay. She'd let him handle the misunderstandings around here.

Just then, Clay and Clint and Mabel and two other men she'd yet to meet entered the front door and banged it closed behind them. "Whew, storm's collectin' strength," Mabel said as she dusted herself off. She pointed to the stairs and turned to the two men. "First door on the right."

Clay was too busy dusting the last of the snow off his shoulders with his gaze fixed on Peggy to notice what the other two men were up to. By the clenched jaw and sizzling glare, he was livid. No doubt because she'd followed him here, not because of the weather as he'd like everyone to think.

She lifted her chin a notch and stared back. She had a job to do and she planned to do it.

Clint gave Clay a smack on the back. "My wife and I are staying here at the main house while Roy and Mary are out-of-town, so why don't you and Peg use our place. Fairly new little house down by the turn in the crick." He grinned knowingly. Peggy had the sneaking suspicion Clint knew all about how she and Clay were divorced. Stinker. But then, wouldn't that give her a chance to be alone with Clay in order to explain herself in private and then get the chance to work on his heel? Might be considered inappropriate by some, but they were a long way from home and, frankly, she didn't care what anyone thought.

"That's a great idea," Jessica said. "It will give you some alone time." With a wide smile she gave her husband a quick glance. He winked at her and threw out that heart-halting grin of his. *Whew, how does she manage to live with that?*

In a sudden fit of conscience, she blurted, "That won't work—"

"Sounds perfect," Clay said over the top of her.

Of course, Clint only had ears for Clay. He dropped a set of keys in Clay's hand and pointed him in the direction of the old three-quarter ton truck resting under the overhang of the barn across the lane. "Leave your pickup. I'll have Pete gas it up." He nodded toward his own truck. "Old girl won't have a problem gettin' you there in this snowfall."

Clint winked, which only amped up Peggy's nerves. What was Clay going to do when he had her alone behind closed doors? If they were still married, the thought would excite her. But divorced with an angry man…

She shuddered.

Maybe it would be best if she explained everything. She strode up to Clint. "You see, Clay and I aren't—"

Clint glanced over her head at the big clock she'd noticed upon arrival. "Oh, look at that. Past Molly's bedtime." He glanced briefly at Peggy. The twinkle in his eye told her the whole story. "See you two whenever the snow stops. Clay tells me he's not due at the training camp until Tuesday. Have fun!" With that he shot past her to Pete and Molly in the corner, grabbed up his daughter off the toy horse as she squealed in glee, and headed for the staircase.

Jessica followed behind her husband. As she climbed the stairs, she said, "Good night, you two. Be careful out in this muck."

As if Clint and Jessica's exit had pulled a plug on the rest of the crew, everyone scurried around until they had all dispersed out the back door.

Two minutes later, Clint showed up with two suitcases—one Clay's, the other hers—took two steps at a time going down the staircase, plunked the cases down at the bottom, then took the same two steps at a time going back up. "Night, now."

Peggy blinked at where Clint had disappeared, amazed at the efficiency of the group in scuttling them off to a separate location and then disappearing.

Clay literally growled his next words. "We need to get going before this storm decides to strand us."

Peggy allowed her gaze to seek his for the first time since his glare. "You're okay with this? Shouldn't we tell them we're—"

"No, we shouldn't. Let's go."

Peggy slapped her hands on her hips. "I'm getting pretty sick of everyone cutting me off—"

"Are you going to talk all night, or are you coming?" Clay marched over to the suitcases, grabbed them up, and swung to the front door.

Peggy huffed a breath. Criminy, had everyone gone loco around here? Fine, she would go with him to the little house by the stream, but she'd be darned if she'd let him scold her the rest of the night.

CHAPTER 11

"What were you thinking, *Margaret Ann*?"

With a decided limp, he paced across a thick Aubusson rug—a surprising feature for a Montana country home. Peggy decided to ignore Clay a little longer by turning a circle and pretending fascination with the décor of the little cabin by the stream. When she could feel him pacing, about to blow a gasket behind her, she took a breath and swiveled back around to face him.

His wet jeans and flannel shirt clung to his strong thighs and wide shoulders. A swath of damp hair curled at his forehead. The fury in his eyes kept her from distinguishing their color. They almost looked black from here, though she knew intimately they were a spun green. Muscles flexed with every step he took, and it was all Peggy could do not to tune out everything else and just watch the show.

He jabbed his finger toward the window in a rage. "Do you even know how dangerous these roads are in a truck, let alone a squirrely little car like yours?"

Still going with the weather argument? Surprised, she cocked an eyebrow. He cussed, not one, but four blasphemous words in a row. Anger reared up and painted her vision red. Determined to stay calm, Peggy perched on the edge of Jessica's new Harcourt Chesterfield and crossed her legs, her ankle bobbing in time with her pulse.

Clay glowered at her foot. "You always were impulsive. You could have been killed out there."

"You don't get to chew me out, Clay Cooper. You're the one who took off without a word in the middle of your physical therapy."

"*That's* why you followed me here? This is about my damn foot?"

She stopped swinging her foot, then shot off the sofa. "Why else would I be here?"

He sneered, looking so absolutely disgusted, she felt her resolve wither. Then his expression faltered into knit brows and an expression of naked disappointment. "I thought you came..." He paused. "It really was because of my heel?" Fury returned, narrowing his gaze. "To torment me?"

"I see you limping. It still hurts, doesn't it? This is important, Clay. Be honest with me."

He ran a hand down his face. He looked haggard, disillusioned, upset...she didn't know what all. When he reached the leather chair, he plopped down. Hard. "It hurts, all right. Nothing to be done."

Peggy dragged up a smaller chair and sat right in front of Clay. She put her hand on his knee. "Yes, there is. I can do something for it. Please, let me help you."

Clay leaned forward, dropped his forearms to his spread thighs, face so near hers, she saw how dilated his eyes were. He studied her, as if he'd find answers. "This is really why you came?"

Was he digging for the real answer? Could he see it on her face? She held her breath, wishing with all her might to hide the truth, hoping with all her heart he'd know it. She quivered inside. Did she need to come out and say it?

He grasped both her wrists and took the decision away from her. One yank and she was in his lap. His hands cupped her face and then his lips were on hers.

The shock was so great she gasped, giving him the opening to deepen the kiss. Desire filled her. She let her eyes drift closed.

She was in dangerous territory here. Fog filled her mind. The more Clay beckoned her lips, the more she wanted to throttle caution and answer with a fervor all her own.

This was Clay.

This was familiar and right and so delicious.

This was home.

He was home.

Before her brain shut down completely and let her body rule, Clay broke the connection and pressed her head away from him.

Her eyes popped open.

His expression floored her. He was angry; she could see it in the dip of his brows, the flash of his eyes, the twist of his mouth. "Why did you have to follow me here?"

He practically dumped her off his lap as he stood, barely righting her before he quit the room and banged a bedroom door behind himself.

Still winded from the kiss, Peggy melted into the small chair until her breathing evened out. Twenty minutes went by. Then thirty. No Clay. No sounds from the bedroom even. Her head spun with what had happened. The kiss was his doing, but had she prompted it by sitting so close, resting a hand on his leg? Guilt seeped in.

Pushing her attraction aside, she forced her thoughts toward safe territory. His heel. If she didn't get his Achilles stretched, she may as well put a bullet in his head. He would self-destruct. She knew it in her bones. He'd already lost so much.

Fueled by conviction, she stood and headed toward the bedroom door. *For his leg*, she told herself. Love, desire, longing, passion—the emotions he'd reawakened in her writhed into a knot at her core. She pushed it down and clawed with all her might toward higher ground. *Lord, keep my motives pure.*

With a knuckle, she rapped softly on the door. "Clay? Let me work on that leg. Give you a running chance at getting better. Please come out."

She listened for any sounds. He had to be awake. "Clay?" Nothing. "Clay, may I come in?" Still nothing. "Okay, I'm coming in...you stubborn..." She mumbled a colorful word under her breath.

"I heard that." His voice was a rumble deep in his chest.

She pictured him lying on his back on the bed with an arm slung over his eyes—just like he'd done after the Fort Worth rodeo, six months into their marriage. Peggy set her hand on the door knob, but couldn't turn it. Clay had been thrown from the only bronc known for an easy ride, and within three seconds at that. No matter his aching body, it was his pride that was wounded most. After he'd holed up in their trailer bedroom for over an hour, Peggy had lost her patience and launched herself through the door. Found him still fully clothed, lying on his back on their bed with an arm thrown over his face. It was the first time she'd seen him, all muscle and smudged dirt and hurt silence, as vulnerable. He'd never been more appealing.

She'd coaxed him out of his funk with a particularly jarring ride of her own, which left him smiling for days. The memory nearly put a smile on her face now.

If only things weren't so dismal between them.

Shaken by the memory, she cracked the door open and took a step in. The room was dark but for the bulb he'd left on in the closet, and the strip of light it cast across the bed and his body. Sure enough. On his back, arm slung over his eyes. Her heart took a leap.

"If you know what's good for you, you'll get out." Though his voice was low and unthreatening, she knew what he was about.

Her heart raced. Dare she push him when she was no longer in a position to use her feminine wiles? Unsettled and unsure, she stayed in the doorway. "Come out, Clay. All I want is to work on your leg. Shall I do that in here?"

Clay whisked his arm away from his face and thumped it on the bed. He glared in her direction. The light from the closet caught in his eyes, showing his feral gleam. "You risk too much. Get out. Now!"

Every cell in her body wanted to go to him. Wanted a repeat of that night in Fort Worth. To help him get past his feeling of defeat and remind him what they'd once had together.

Be smart. Remember your true goal. Words of wisdom poured into her head, beating hard against the petition from her body. This was about Clay. About helping him be whole.

But she could see tonight was not the night. "You win. I'll see you in the morning. 'Night, Clay."

Hoping he'd stop her, she hesitated in the doorway.

He said nothing.

CHAPTER 12

When Peggy awoke, she peered out the window Jessica had yet to curtain in the little guest bedroom. The sky was gray, but the snow had stopped falling. The gloom matched her mood and the heaviness in her limbs. She hadn't slept well last night. Every time she thought she'd drift off, the image of Clay lying on the bed with his arm slung over his eyes tormented her.

Rolling to her side, she tugged the blankets up to her chin. She wanted Clay back in her life, realized that the first day she'd seen him again. Had never stopped loving the man. But four and a half years was a long time to let a Cooper stew about anything bad, and divorce topped the list.

And back then, when she'd confronted him about their ended marriage, by the devastation on his face she knew Clay would never forgive and certainly never forget. By now that image would be cemented in his soul.

But didn't she owe him more than simply quitting again? Was she willing to put the time and effort into what it would take to repair the damage she'd caused?

She flipped the blankets off her, a sudden surge of elation filling her. *Yes.* He was worth every single second she'd suffer for it. In fact, she deserved every bit of agony it caused.

She dressed in a hurry and raced out of the small bedroom to the other end of the house. Since it was just after dawn, she expected Clay would be in the kitchen brewing coffee. He'd always been an early riser, just as she was, so she was astounded when she arrived and took a whiff. No coffee had been made. No breakfast either. Because there was no Clay.

"He's still in bed?" she whispered to herself, her heart speeding at the thought of waking him.

Grinning, she headed to his bedroom door and rapped. "Clay? I'm about to make some breakfast." She had yet to peruse the cupboards or the refrigerator, but she figured Jessica had supplies enough to feed her family. "Any requests?"

She felt giddy. Like the new bride she once was, about to offer her new husband an early meal.

No answer.

Another *tap tap tap*. "Clay? I'm coming in."

She knew she shouldn't. He wasn't hers anymore. She had no rights to him. Yet he'd kissed her last night. That opened a door to hope, and she was walking through it.

Her pulse thrummed in her ears. "Clay?" Turning the knob, she pushed her way into the dark bedroom. As her eyes adjusted to the gloom, she saw an empty bed and dark bathroom.

Gone? He's gone? Anger replaced euphoria. How could he leave without telling her?

When had he left?

The old familiar feeling of abandonment came over her. A heavy, cloying blanket. Clay had often done this very thing while they were on the road. She'd understood that his dedication to rodeo had been linked to their income, but the fact he never woke her, told her his plans for the day before leaving their bed always bothered her. In spite of asking him for a morning kiss time and again, he never gave it. That slight became just another on a long list of blunders that convinced her to leave him.

In retrospect, she'd begun to blame her own immaturity for shutting him out. But the way she felt now? Maybe she had been justified.

Slogging back down the hallway to the kitchen, she looked around in the silence, overwhelmed by a desperate sort of roiling in her stomach. Nothing for it but to bundle up and walk back to the main house. No doubt Clay had taken the truck.

When she finally made both beds and closed up the house, she stepped out into an icy wind. Snow flurries circled her boots, then whipped straight up her legs and under her coat. Wrapping the warmth tightly around her, she pressed forward to the pickup that was still parked beside the house. Chivalry wasn't dead after all. Fancy that.

Still, hurt simmered just below the surface as Peggy drove herself to the main house, parked, then raced up the steps through the gathering storm. She tapped on the front door.

Jessica swung the door wide and grinned a welcome. Her eyes shot past Peggy to the squall outside. Grabbing Peggy's arm, she pulled her in. "Whew. It's brewing something out there. I hope you're planning to be here for a spell. Have you had breakfast? Clay's already come and gone. He said he let you sleep in." Jessica's expression showed she still didn't realize they weren't a couple. Maybe now was the time to enlighten her.

She opened her mouth to speak…and found that she didn't have the spirit to face it. Instead, she put her attention on removing her coat.

"I hope you like bacon and eggs and biscuits. That's our menu for breakfast."

"Get back to work, girly," Mabel spouted into the pan of bacon she was frying. "Ya think this food is gonna cook itself?"

Jessica smiled, rolled her eyes, and practically flounced away. Peggy recognized that jubilance. She'd once had it for almost a year.

After washing her hands, donning an apron, and grabbing a blob of dough to roll for biscuits, she asked, "Where is Clay?"

Jessica glanced Peggy's way. "Gone to West Yellowstone."

A lump formed in her throat. "Why?"

"He didn't tell you?" Jessica's look of sympathy gutted her. Yeah, any wife would know where her husband went. "He went to the Smokejumper Training Center at the edge of town. By the airport."

She was already humiliated, so she may as well get all Jessica knew. "Now? He told me he wasn't expected there until Tuesday. This is only Sunday."

"Shame on him for not telling you about the phone call before leaving. Men!"

Peggy frowned, tired of being the only one left in the dark. "What phone call?"

Jessica hesitated, mid-egg-crack, to look at her. "Oh, it was just about twenty minutes ago. Clint took the call. A man there said he'd come to see Clay. A Bruce Smith."

Bruce Smith. Why did that name sound familiar? Peggy had made a point to keep up with Clay's life, in whatever way she could. She knew about the many awards he'd earned for saving lives. Right along with the reprimands he'd publicly received for taking too many risks. There was a scrapbook in her bottom dresser drawer at home containing all things Clay Cooper. On the days she felt particularly melancholy, she'd take it out, look through each page, and have a good cry. Then back it would go for another week.

Jessica sidled up next to her and bumped her hip with hers. "You okay there, Twinkie?"

Peggy jerked her head toward Jessica and gaped.

Jessica took the kitchen towel from her shoulder and wiped at Peggy's cheek. "Got a little flour here."

"Oh." Peggy swiped at her face with her forearm, distracted.

"Seriously, are you all right? You seem a bit... downtrodden."

"Clay told you my nickname?" He'd never told anyone else before. Suddenly a sense of belonging filled her. For the first time, the nickname she'd chafed at for years made her feel like family.

"We all got a good laugh when he explained it to us."

Peggy raised her eyebrows. "Explained it?"

"Yeah. First he told us his dad gave all his sons food nicknames when they were boys. So when he married you, he gifted you with the name Twinkie, because you were a golden blonde on the outside and all sweet and gooey on the inside. Gave us a good laugh this morning." She laughed all over again.

Her genuine delight made Peggy smile. "He told you that this morning? How in the world did the subject come up?"

Jessica resumed cracking eggs. "He asked if we'd be serving pancakes this morning. When I said no, he looked so disappointed, I joked that he must have a monster of a sweet tooth. 'Nah,' he said. 'Just the wife.'"

Peggy froze with a wad of biscuit dough in her hands.

"Funny, Clint's brows shot up like that surprised him. Shouldn't have," Jessica said with a wink.

Peggy felt her face burn with heat. Clay had said that? As if they were still married? And Clint played along?

The last of Jessica's conversation died off without Peggy catching a single word. But the other woman was grinning as if whatever she'd just said had earned her something.

It earned her something, all right. One less helper. "Excuse me a minute." Peggy wiped her hands on her apron and dashed off for the bathroom.

With the door shut behind her, she worked at getting her breathing back in rhythm. Why wouldn't Clay have told them the truth this morning? Was it just easier for him this way? Was he waiting for her to do it?

She nodded to herself. Of course, that was it. Clay was as dominant as they came, capable of skinning anyone with his words. But when it came to issues of the heart, he rarely confronted them head on. Instead, he evaded, escaped, and dodged.

A jolt of clarity blasted her anger to pieces. That was why he never fought back when she told him their marriage had come to an end. He never had it in him.

She'd read it wrong when he didn't bother fighting for them. All along she'd thought he didn't care enough about her, when in fact, she now realized, the opposite was true. He cared too much.

Wilting inside, she let herself out of the bathroom for the kitchen, wanting only to find Clay and cry out for his forgiveness. But he was gone. To meet *Bruce Smith*. She rifled through her memories again, and hit home. Of course. He was the older brother of Clay's best friend in high school.

A shudder tore up her spine. Because now she remembered everything.

Peggy glanced over at Jessica, who was laying large plates out on the rectangular tables in the dining area. With her heart in her throat, Peggy asked, "Did this Bruce Smith guy say what he wanted with Clay?"

Jessica glanced at her with arched eyebrows, then at Clint, who had just come through the door dusted in snow. "Big storm we've been watching for's here," he said to the room at large, as he hung up his coat and hat. "Supposed to have 30 mph winds. Four feet of snow expected in the next two days." Clint caught Peggy's anxious inhale and went on. "Clay'll be fine. He's used to snow."

But Peggy's worry only doubled.

Clint caught her gaze and lifted his chin. "Clay said Smith was the brother of the man he partnered up with for jumps. Looked forward to seeing him."

"Uh huh." Peggy swallowed hard. "Did he say specifically why he wanted to see Clay?"

Clint squeezed Jessica's hand on his way across the room, then leaned his backside into the counter beside Peggy. "All Clay said was he owed this guy some time."

Peggy pivoted toward him, fully aware Clint would see the tears in her eyes. "He said that? *Owed* him time?"

Clint's brows scrunched in the middle. "This concerns you. Why?"

Should she tell this stranger? Would that help or hurt? In the next heartbeat, something in her shouted to trust him…now!

"This *Bruce* guy is the brother of the man who *died* on a jump with Clay. From what I've read, Bruce and his family blame Clay entirely for Martin's death. This—" Peggy shook her head, her fears piling into her throat. "Nothing good can—" She searched the kitchen frantically for answers she couldn't find. "I need to go!"

Clint cursed and pushed off the counter. "There was something in that voice…" His words trailed off but Peggy could see the wheels turning. Clint turned to Jessica. "I'm going after him, babe."

Peggy tugged on his arm. "What? Wait. I'm going too." She reached around to untie her apron.

Clint stopped her hands at her back. "No. Too dangerous. You stay with the ladies."

Determined, she twisted away from Clint and his strong hands, untied the apron, and threw it off. "I don't care how you feel about it. I don't even know you. But I know my husband…"

She choked on the word *husband*. The lie began to turn sour in her mouth. "He will try to do right by this man, but all Bruce wants is vengeance. Believe me. The articles written about the incident never looked good for Clay. They made it sound like the flawed jump had been Clay's fault. Really, Clint. I think he's walking into a trap!"

Another curse flew from Clint's mouth as he took two steps to his wife, kissed her on the cheek as she murmured a 'be careful' next to his ear, and headed back for his coat and hat.

Peggy raced after him and grabbed her own.

"Peggy, no!" Jessica said, scrambling to her.

Peggy held up her hand and gave Jessica a look that said no one would stop her from helping her man. Jessica stared at her resolute face, then nodded, wringing her hands at her waist. "I understand. Be careful, you two. Maybe you should take Pete along."

Clint gave one last glance to his wife as he opened the front door and a gust of snow-filled wind blew in. "Give Molly a kiss for me. I'll be back, little one. Just pray."

Peggy wondered if she could be as brave as Jessica to let her husband go out in a snowstorm to help in a dangerous situation. Then again, they were prayerful people.

"Oh, you know I will," Jessica said sternly, then blew him a kiss.

Peggy nodded, silently agreeing she would be praying too—for safety, for speed, and for a second chance at love.

Chapter 13

"I haven't been in this kind of whiteout in a long time. Can you even see the road?" Peggy asked Clint.

The man had a death grip on the steering wheel and a cobra stare on the road immediately beyond the hood. The truck they were in was old, but heavy enough to plow through the drifts and high enough to afford the best visibility possible. Clint chose well. The wipers thumped hard, practically setting the pace of her heart.

Clint cleared his throat. "Not how I'd hoped it would be. We'll make it, though. Sit back, try not to worry."

"How far is the training camp from here?"

"Half hour from our place. We should be there in ten, fifteen minutes now."

"Good." Peggy slumped into the seat, trying to force herself to relax, her eyes glued to the horizontal snow outside. A deep foreboding settled in her chest, and with it a renewed sense of danger. "Why are you doing this?"

"What? Going after Clay?"

"It's not like you know Clay well. Why risk the storm and whatever might happen with this Bruce person?"

"I'm the one who took the call."

So that made him responsible? Peggy frowned. Anyone could have taken that call. Did they really make men this noble anymore? The question took her aback. Fact was, she had married a man just like this. Sure he'd been untamed, inexperienced, immature, the opposite of mild-mannered, but so what? He was principled, honorable, had a good heart. Had loved her.

Regret flooded her. She had been a fool. Such a fool!

She clasped her hands in her lap, trying not to think about losing Clay again…this time in a much more permanent way.

"So…" Clint's jaw clenched, and his hands gripped the wheel tighter. "Fill me in. How'd this guy's brother die?"

"I only know what the papers said." She sucked in a quick breath, knowing how that must have sounded. "Uh…Clay wouldn't talk about it." That was true enough. Before Clint could question her statement, she went on. "Clay and Martin were on a jump with a half dozen other men. Martin was still considered a rookie. He and Clay were the last two in the plane. Martin balked…got scared. Clay urged him forward so they wouldn't jump late and land in the fire. But that's exactly what happened. A wind gust caught them both, pulled Martin into the flames. He burned to death right in front of Clay, the captain, and some of the crew."

Clint winced, letting out a heavy breath.

"Worse yet, a reporter from an Alaskan newspaper—I don't remember which—was on the jump with them. First time they'd allowed such a thing. It was '59, the year Alaska received its statehood, and the reporters were having a bonanza on all things Alaska. This reporter got it all on film, from Martin landing in the fire to Clay being held back by his captain and crew to keep him from running into the fire and trying to save his friend. Only, the reporter made it sound like Clay had pushed Martin out of the airplane without his permission, and the pictures made it look like Clay was holding the crew back from trying to save him, not the other way around."

Clint grunted in disbelief. "How's that possible?"

"The men had grabbed Clay's arms as he tried to run toward the fire. The reporter's angle made it look like Clay had stretched his arms to keep them back. Ultimately, he was painted the villain in all of it. From what I heard through the Sundance grapevine, it destroyed Clay. The loss of his best friend, the decision to make Martin jump, the newspaper's accounting…" It hadn't helped she'd already destroyed him by divorcing him a couple of years prior.

"Peggy…"

She'd nearly flunked out of school that semester worrying over what she'd read about her husband…ex-husband…and whether or not he'd climb out of the depression.

"Peggy…"

Her head snapped up and over to Clint. "Yes?"

"I know you and Clay are divorced. If I'd had any doubt, you just confirmed it."

Her head dropped. On an inhale of breath, she said, "Yeah."

"What happened?"

"Rodeo. Irresponsibility. Immaturity."

Clint turned his head enough to grace her with an empathetic half-smile. "Startin' to sound like the cowboys with one word answers. Care to elaborate?"

"No…look!" She pointed, relieved to see a building swirling in the gusts of snowfall. Then runway lights and a row of hangars. "That has to be the training center."

"It is." Clint aimed the truck toward what looked like the main gate.

Peggy bounced forward on the seat and pointed again. "Clay's truck." It was parked beside two other trucks at a main entrance. Okay, so if Bruce was here already, maybe Clay wasn't alone. Maybe this third fellow would be a buffer between the two. *Please, God, let that be the case.*

No sooner did Clint throw the gear shifter into park beside Clay's truck than Peggy made out the silhouette of a man with a thick coat and ski mask sprinting toward the far truck. Through the streaming snow, she saw something long and dark in his hand. It glinted briefly in their headlights, and she knew, beyond doubt, what it was.

"No!" Peggy launched herself into the storm and screamed. "He's got a crowbar!"

The man slammed into the far truck, cranked the ignition, and fishtailed out of the parking lot.

"Clay!" Peggy pounded toward the entrance. Clint reached it first and flung the heavy door open. They both sped through. "*Clay!*" A shiver turned her guts to water.

Peggy followed Clint through a large open room and then on down an empty hallway. She slipped, glanced down. The linoleum was worn to a fine polish under her wet boots. She reached for the handle of the first closed door she came upon. Cold seeped into her fingers, matching her frigid fear. She opened it. *A blasted broom closet.*

A knot grew in her throat, so heavy it restricted her voice. She tried to clear it and shouted Clay's name again. No answer. She opened the next door, and the next.

"Clay?" Clint's voice echoed from a ways down the hall. Still nothing.

"Oh, Lord, please let him be okay," she prayed aloud as they searched.

More doors. More empty rooms.

The thump of Clint's boots came toward her. She jerked her head up, catching the worry in his eyes. Panic rose in her throat. "Where is he?"

Clint shook his head. "Keep going down that hallway." He pointed. "I'll go out back."

She watched as Clint ran, sliding every few steps, back the way they'd come.

The jarring bang of the metal entry door rang out as he left the building.

She carried on. Another door. Closed. Had she already checked this one? Didn't matter. She thrust it open. A musty odor poured out. Not used, and no Clay.

She came to the end of the hallway. *No! It can't be the end.* Where was Clay? She turned back, her shoulders slumping, her mouth dry.

The metal entry door banged back open ahead.

"Peggy!" Clint's voice sounded distressed.

No, God! Don't let it be…

Taking off at a slippery run, she steered her way down the hall and back into the open space of the main room. Clint looked over his shoulder at her as he backstepped deeper into the room. "Peggy," he said, out of breath. Beyond him, she glimpsed a man in a tan janitorial jumpsuit laboring forward with stilted steps. The two finally shuffled sideways enough for her to see the burden they carried.

"Dear God," she whispered as a cry for help.

Clay was unconscious, soaking wet and dripping blood.

"Please be okay, please be okay," she chanted again and again.

"Over there," the janitor said, tipping his head toward the wall.

The men laid Clay down across four chairs. The three of them scrambled to find the source of the blood.

"Here," the janitor said as his hand came up sticky and red. "Left side of his head. He's been clobbered pretty good. We've got to get him over to the med clinic. What kind of vehicle do you have?"

Clint's eyes widened with what looked like sudden inspiration. "Peggy, search Clay's pockets for his keys."

His voice snapped her out of her panic. She began to rummage

Clint tilted his head toward Clay, then addressed the janitor. "He's got four-wheel drive on that truck of his. The snow's gettin' thick. We'll need it."

Peggy stilled the jarring tremor in her hands and closed her fingers around Clay's keys.

"Get out there and open it up," Clint said.

Peggy rose to obey, then rocked back, clarity reawakened in her. "He needs to stay horizontal, head and shoulders barely elevated. That means the truck bed. With me."

The janitor accepted her authority without so much as a blink. "I'll find a blanket and compression bandage." He sped away.

"What's your name?" Clint called after the man.

"Jerry," he yelled back.

Within minutes, Peggy found herself in the truck bed beside Clay, blanket hauled over them with one hand and compression bandage clutched with the other.

The wind howled, banking snow against the bumper and rear wheels of the truck. *Get us out, Lord. Safely.* Snow pelted Peggy's bare neck from under the blanket's edge. *Please.*

Clint threw the gear shift into reverse. The truck shuddered, wheels slipping briefly until they caught traction and clawed into the snow drift. Peggy jounced forward and backward again, trying to keep her balance as the truck lurched to a stop and then cut a labored arc forward onto the road. Jerry followed in his smaller truck, close behind.

The wind chill was brutal on Peggy's exposed skin as she fought to keep the blanket over her head and the bandage against Clay's matted hair. By the time they reached the medical clinic, she shook all over, from cold and fear and the terrible weight of the sodden blanket.

The Lord wouldn't bring Clay back into her life just to rip him away from her again, would He?

Please heal him, Lord. Give him the life he deserves, not the one so many of us have stolen from him. Her fury rose as she remembered the dark, skulking figure in the snow, and the crowbar he'd used to bash Clay's skull. The fury flipped inside her. With sharp pain in her heart, she added, *But I'm the worst offender.* It seemed a lifetime ago that another horrible creature of the dark had crushed his heart. It made her sick to the marrow to know that creature had been her.

She would make it up to him. In every way she could.

Please let him live, Lord, and I promise, if he wants me there, I'll never leave his side again.

CHAPTER 14

After being questioned by the police, Peggy sat stiffly in the lone chair in the sterile room, waiting for the doctor to return with Clay from x-ray. Down the hall in the waiting room, Clint and Jerry were now giving their statements.

Clay's wheeled bed squeaked around the corner. Peggy jumped as if bitten. She was instantly at the doctor's side to help steer the bed to its proper place by the wall.

Clay. A thick white bandage covered the entire left side of his head. She peered into his face, so magnificent even in repose, yet so still and ashen. Her heart ached in a way only fear could make it. She couldn't lose him…she just couldn't.

Her nose burned sharply. She told herself it was the tang of antiseptic, but she knew better.

The doctor motioned for her to sit and rolled his stool around the foot of the bed to face her. His solemn expression sent acid sloshing from her stomach up into her chest. Clint and Jerry appeared in the doorway, away from the circle of Clay's bed, the doctor, and Peggy. She hadn't told the doctor she was no longer Clay's wife, and Clint was tight lipped as well.

They both knew this was the only way they would get the information they needed.

"I'm sorry to say, Clay's injury is extensive, Mrs. Cooper. His skull is badly fractured. What did you say it was? A crowbar?"

She nodded bleakly. "What is the prognosis, Dr. Barnes? W-will he wake up? Will he even be…all there when he does?" Peggy stopped short, her entire body trembling.

The doctor's face was grim, his lips pressed together. He shook his head in an 'I don't know' way, and Peggy's heart thudded heavily. Despair swelled in her chest until she had only a sip of air left in her lungs.

The doctor cleared his throat. "Let's not get ahead of ourselves. As soon as this storm blows over, he needs to go to a trauma center. I recommend St. Patrick's in Missoula. It's about four or five hours from here if the weather cooperates."

Peggy sucked in a frozen breath. *Trauma center?* "Before he wakes up? Why?" Something inside her refused to grasp what she already knew to be true.

"There's a high probability of brain damage."

She barely kept her moan locked inside.

"I don't know to what extent," the doctor said. "He needs to be in a facility where he'll get the best care for whatever happens next. He's stable at the moment. His vitals are good. I don't have the equipment needed to decipher what degree of injury we're talking about here. He'll get the best care in Missoula."

"How will we get him there without causing more injury? Five hours on the road. Isn't that better done in an ambulance?"

The doctor shook his head. "We don't have an ambulance near, I'm afraid. Closest one is over two hours away, and it would come from a hospital we don't want him to go to. Do you see the dilemma?"

Clint approached and placed a calming hand on her shoulder. She jerked at his touch. She was panicking, she felt it. Looking up at Clint, she saw sympathy in his eyes—and grim resolve. "We'll get him there as soon as the weather breaks, Peggy."

"How?"

The doctor looked over at Clint and Jerry. "Do you have a vehicle that can get him to Missoula? The snow will be a problem."

Clint jingled the truck keys in his pocket. "Got it covered."

The doctor shook his head. "There's no way he can be in that truck bed for five or six hours. He'll be fine here until you find another form of transportation. I'm able to put him on an IV for fluids and set him up with a catheter, but I'm not equipped to sustain him long-term. A few days won't be a problem."

"What if we laid Clay across Clint and I in the cab of the truck? We could put his head on my lap and his feet on Clint's. Would that work? I know he's big, but what else can we do?"

"No. I don't suggest that. He'll be fine here for the next two days. You should find another type of vehicle. The minute the weather breaks, be ready."

"But, if you think he should be there, shouldn't we go now? We shouldn't wait, should we?" Peggy could hear the rising worry in her voice. Next up, hysteria.

She inhaled a deep breath, forcing herself to calm the heck down.

Clint tilted his head to catch Peggy's eye. "We don't have a choice but to wait out the storm, sweetheart."

The endearment did nothing to comfort her. But it did remind her she was a professional and she needed to pull herself together.

"We'll be ready to take off the minute we can." Clint shifted his focus to the doctor. "Can I use your phone, Doc? I need to let my wife know what's happening."

"Of course. Help yourself. You too, Jerry."

Clint left the room, and Jerry followed.

Peggy's gaze wandered to the window beside Clay. It cast a white glare into the room from the mid-morning snowscape beyond. Was it only Sunday morning still? The exhaustion she felt was beyond words.

When Clint came back through the door, hat in hand, he looked ready to leave. "Jerry's gone back to lock up the facility then on home. I'm going to head back to the spread. The storm isn't over by any stretch. But there's a break. Christmas is in two days. I need to be with my family for as long as I can be. I'll look into another vehicle for us. Will you be all right if I leave you here with Clay? Or you can come home with me. We'll come back when the weather clears."

The thought of leaving Clay caused her to shake her head overhard. "No. I won't leave him. You go."

Clint nodded, though she could see the worry on his face. Clay wasn't hers anymore to take care of—she knew it, he knew it. But he didn't say a word about it, to her or anyone else. She took it as tacit permission to keep playing the part.

So, for the rest of the day, she sat beside Clay, scooting out of the way only when Dr. Barnes retook vitals or changed IV fluid bags. The growing cramp in her stomach finally forced her to scrounge for food. All she could find was a tiny packet of saltine crackers and an apology from Dr. Barnes. She nibbled the crackers slowly; the cramp only worsened.

Come evening, Dr. Barnes gave her his home phone number and backed out of Clay's room, bidding her farewell until morning. He cut the hall lights to half power, then thunked the deadbolt to the front door closed. She was alone now, with just the faint buzz of overhead lights and the steady sound of Clay's breathing for company.

Please, God, let Clay survive this tragedy. She dared not ask for him to be hers again. For now, if he woke up with his mind intact, that would be enough. The thought soothed her as she laid her cheek on Clay's bicep and fell into a shallow sleep.

Peggy jarred awake. Something had roused her but she didn't know what. Silence pressed in. In two heartbeats, she knew. His breathing had stopped. "*Clay?*"

She was on her feet without a thought. "Clay? *Clay!*" She shook his shoulders, then leaned over to listen. No sound came from his nose, but she felt a flutter of air against her cheek. Then another, and another.

She laid both palms against his solid jaw. "Why so shallow, my sweet man?" Should she call the doctor? But what could he do? She pressed Clay's fingernail until it blanched and watched it pink back up. The fluids were running, Clay's temperature was normal, and he appeared comfortable. Had she imagined he'd stopped breathing? One of her own full breaths slowed her heart some, keeping her from a panic attack. "I must have dreamt it."

Satisfied he was in no immediate danger, Peggy glanced at the clock. Midnight. Her lonely vigil would continue for another eight hours until the doctor returned the next morning. She rubbed her cheek, cherishing the warmth of Clay's arm under her head when she'd dozed off. Well, she was awake now, and intended to fill Clay's unconscious mind as she had the last seventeen hours, with as many terms of endearment and shared stories as she could remember.

It was bittersweet, this one-sided exchange in which she could get her fill of him without his snide remarks, lewd comments, angry outbursts, severe glares…

Oh, how she'd missed him. She hadn't known just how much until now. "My sweet stud," she said as she stroked his cheek, then grinned at the memory of calling him *stud* and the irony of the tribute, *sweet*. No one knew he had a kind heart. Oh, how enraged he'd be to even hear the word. But sweet he was, and his sweetness she would always cherish.

She sat silently, staring at Clay, regathering her wits, resettling her heart until the need to talk with her God came over her. *"Lord, only you can sustain Clay. None of us has that kind of power. Please watch over him, Father. I pray for a break in the weather in the morning, and for You to get us to Missoula safely. Please help the specialists cure him. Bring him back to us. Whole."*

• • •

The gray light of morning shone into Clay's room, surprising Peggy with its suddenness despite the interminable hours before it. Snow still fell lightly outside the small window. Couldn't those darn white flakes stop? They needed to get Clay to Missoula.

"Good morning, little lady," came a deep voice from the entrance. She jumped a little, and turned toward the sound, trying to shake fatigue from her fuzzy mind.

A large figure filled the doorway. Peering through scratchy eyes, she took in the man's appearance: tall with wide shoulders, neatly combed dark hair, and the most vivid sapphire eyes. At first she thought it was Colt, but a double take told her this man was Cooper-rugged, all right, but more striking, in an angular, sophisticated sort of way. Like, he could pull off a cowboy hat or a white lab coat equally well.

Of course! "Hunter!"

Peggy leaped to her feet and threw herself at the man, relieved another Cooper had arrived. He caught her in his arms and squeezed before setting her down and stepping back. She hadn't laid eyes on Hunter since he'd come to see Clay ride broncs on their sweep through Colorado, over five years ago. Back then he'd set his sights on entering veterinary school in Fort Collins. Now he was in his last year there.

"What are you doing here?" She grimaced at how rude that sounded. "I mean, aren't you missing classes?"

One side of his mouth tipped up, deepening the crease in his cheek, before he swung his eyes to Clay. "How is he?"

"Not good. How did you find out about this?" She gestured toward the bed.

"Clint started the grapevine, Colt called me, and I figured I'd save Colt a trip out since I was heading home for Christmas anyway. Just veered a little more west."

Her hand came to her mouth. "For five more hours…and through a snowstorm no less. That's crazy, Hunter."

"I only traveled one hour more than Colt would have had to, and the conditions would have been worse for him. I got about an hour of light snowfall. No big deal in my Suburban. Four-wheel drive, you know. Besides, Clay and I have always been closer than he ever was with Colt…" He stopped, rolled his gaze away from her.

Yeah, she knew she was the cause of plenty of Cooper family grief.

He brought his gaze back, looking a bit snappish. "Didn't mean to bring up bad blood. Clay and Colt never did get along, even before…" His finger twirled in the air to vaguely indicate the chaos of her marriage.

She swallowed hard, taking no comfort from the hard eyes behind the gesture.

In the silence, Hunter stepped farther into the room, shed his heavy sheepskin-lined coat, and grabbed the rolling stool she'd just vacated to sit next to Clay. "Tell me about my brother."

She scowled at his filching of her chair, but let it go, coming to stand at Clay's head. "He got hit with"—she swallowed, the image of the attack burned in her mind—"it was a crowbar, Hunter." She started to stroke Clay's head but thought better of it, clasping her hands instead, trying to hide the shake in them. "He has a fractured skull, and possible brain—" Her voice broke. *No, Peggy. You will not cry.*

Hunter's expression softened as he waited for her to finish.

She swallowed down the fear of what the future held and continued in a pinched tone. "Possible brain damage."

Hunter nodded, looking contemplative rather than alarmed. Peggy shouldn't have been surprised. Of course veterinary school would have changed him, taught him to think clinically rather than reactively.

"Colt said we're taking Clay to Missoula. I think we can manage that fine today. It's not supposed to storm again until tomorrow."

"Oh, Hunter! That would be great. Clint can stay with his family and we can take Clay in your vehicle. Oh my goodness, that will work out splendidly." She silently clapped her hands together. "We were trying to figure out how to transport him horizontally in the cab of his truck." She blew out a breath and looked skyward. "Thank you, Lord."

"That right there will not happen on this drive."

Peggy's knees nearly buckled at Hunter's rebuke. His face darkened, and his eyes looked stormy. "What won't happen?"

"No praying. No God talk, period!"

What was with the Cooper men and their hostility toward God? But on second thought, this reaction of his was raw. Current. She rested her hand on Hunter's. He jerked it away, centering his attention on Clay. Even from the side, she could see his eyes blazing.

"What happened, Hunter? Something recent, I can tell."

He swung his gaze back to hers and narrowed his eyes. "There will be no discussion about this or about God. Do you understand?"

Her eyebrows shot up. "This isn't like you. What's wrong?"

"How would you know what isn't like me, Peggy? You haven't seen me for years."

A chill trickled down Peggy's spine. Well, this would be a long and interesting day indeed.

CHAPTER 15

"Take it easy, you two. The roads could still be thick with snow," Dr. Barnes said before he handed a large manila envelope to Peggy. "Give this to the trauma doctor. It's Clay's X-ray and my evaluation."

Peggy waved a hand, unable to speak past the lump in her throat, and tried to smile at the doctor.

"Be careful," he said, then shut the passenger door of Hunter's Suburban.

They had spent the last hour prepping Clay for transport, arranging him in the back of the Suburban once the men removed the rear bench seat. Peggy glanced back, feeling equal parts relieved for the progress and fearful of any complications that could arise while they were on the road. At least Clay wouldn't be awake to feel any pain.

Heading north, Hunter wound his way slowly through West Yellowstone, then turned west onto Highway 287. The snow plows had done a great job here. Peggy prayed the roads would be just as clear all the way to Missoula.

After more than thirty minutes of silence as Hunter concentrated on their route, Peggy finally said, "So tell me, how've you been?"

He readjusted his grip on the steering wheel, his skin blanching at his knuckles. "How have *you* been? I hear after you divorced my brother, you went to school to become a what? Nurse?"

Peggy could hear quite well the tightly held anger in Hunter's voice. So this was how the drive was going to go. She tried to get her armor on. "Actually, I'm a physiologist."

"Ah, a physical therapist. I see. Is that why you left him? To become a career woman?"

Plenty of derision there. His mood matched the gray skies overhead. "What is it, *Dr. Cooper*? Do you not like women in the world of medicine, or is it just me?" She always saw red when men pigeon-holed women. She'd had plenty of that in the last five years.

"I don't have an opinion about any of it."

"Well, that's obviously a lie. Your horns are showing."

"My horns—what are we, in grammar school?"

"Don't try to change the subject. You're obviously furious with me. Just spill it. We have plenty of time to hash this out."

Hunter groaned loudly.

She laughed. "What? A little mad at yourself for letting the cat outta the bag too early? Couldn't quite keep the fury under wraps, eh?"

"You always did needle. Clay hated how you constantly nagged about what you wanted. Never gave one hoot about his needs."

His dagger hit home. Tears stung the backs of her eyes. It took her a minute to recover her breath from the impact. "Are you saying Clay told you about our personal lives? He wouldn't have done that. You're lying, Hunter." She hated that her voice cracked on that last statement. Hated even more that Clay may have complained to his brother about her.

The car's back end slipped as Hunter took a turn a little too fast for the conditions. He gripped the wheel like it was their lifeline...which it was...and let off the gas a mite. "Black ice." With expertise, he completed the curve, then kept his speed more contained and his attention more riveted.

Silence reigned for the next twenty-five miles as Peggy willed her heart to slow. Highway markers whipped by in a blur, mesmerizing her until she at last focused in on the snow depth they tallied. Four-foot banks stood on either side of the highway. She gulped, recognizing for the first time how dangerous this was. She knew Hunter was used to driving in all conditions, but what a responsibility...to get Clay to Missoula safely, along with himself and his *favorite* passenger.

One glance at the side of Hunter's face, and she knew he intended to give her the silent treatment the rest of the way. No way was she going to let that stand. They still had four hours to go, and she had lots of words left. "I know I'm the one who officially ended our marriage, but from what you're saying, Clay was glad I did."

A muscle in Hunter's jaw bulged. She saw his struggle to keep his thoughts to himself. Probably had already said more than he knew Clay would want. "I never said that."

No, she guessed he hadn't. But the thought it could be true had gripped her hard. A sudden compulsion to check on Clay had her stretching around to feel his cool forehead and brush stray hairs off his handsome face. He seemed to be resting okay. His chest rose and fell, shallow but steady. To anyone looking on, he just looked like a fella sleeping off a bender.

If only that were the case…

She glanced at Hunter just as he took his eyes off her and refocused on the road. "You still look like a woman in love." His voice was harsh, laced with false pity.

A breath of agitation huffed out as she faced forward again. "How would you know anything about love? From what your brothers tell me, you play the field at school. You've run through all the single women there, haven't you?"

He choked out a laugh. "Who told you that?"

No one, actually. She just wanted to hurt him back.

Another glance her way and he chuckled. "Thought so." He sighed. "I don't want to fight with you anymore. I get it. It takes two to tango, right? I'm sure he gave as much as he got. We all know he's not an easy man to love."

"Yet you do," she said.

"And you."

"I did."

"Did? Come on, Peggy. There's no one else in the car. May as well admit the truth."

"So you can tell him later all that you found out?" Her words were barely out of her mouth when their meaning caught her in the chest. Her next breath came in choppy, on a sob. *Oh Lord, please, please give Hunter the chance to tell Clay all he found out. Let Clay survive this!*

Hunter placed his hand over hers. "He's going to be okay, Peggy. He'll wake up soon and give us both hell for not handling things the way he thought we should."

Peggy studied the tenuous smile on Hunter's mouth and tried to breathe through the constriction in her chest. "I hope you're right."

"I'm right."

She nodded, wishing her agreement would make it so.

"How do you like being a physical therapist?"

Her mind stuttered before she caught on to the change of subject. "I like it so far. Love it, in fact. Clay is my current patient."

"Clay is?" Hunter's brows pulled down in confusion. "But he just got hurt."

"No. Not for this, of course. For his Achilles. He injured it for the third time falling off a horse he was training for Rylee. Dr. Trenton sent me to the ranch to work with him."

"Whoa, whoa, whoa. For the third time? And who's Rylee?"

"Haven't you been in contact with your own family at all? Goodness. A lot is going on there. Don't you ever call home?"

He sighed again. "No lecture. Just fill me in. First about Rylee."

"Rylee is Colt's fiancée."

"Fiancée? Colt?"

"Yes, Colt. I guess they haven't known each other that long, but he asked her to marry him. They've picked a date but haven't told anyone yet. They want to tell your dad and Rebecca first, and they're out-of-town."

Hunter huffed another breath, obviously feeling out of the loop. "Where are they?"

"When *was* the last time you talked to them? Goodness, Hunter." Before he could yell at her for judging him, she jumped back in. "They're in California at Harper West. Jessica's dad fell off his tractor onto the disc." Hunter let out a strangled sound. Yeah, she agreed that sounded bad. "He'll recover, but they went to help with the harvest and to winterize the place, though California's so mild, I don't know what they had to do for that. Then stayed for Christmas. Her folks really needed them."

"Huh, figures."

"What do you mean?"

"Dad's always figured ways to escape his own sons. You remember."

"No, I don't. Your dad has done the best he could trying to raise six sons without their mother. I've never understood your attitudes."

"You weren't the one who needed a parent. You have two. We had none."

Were all the Cooper sons' spirits crushed by their upbringing? "Sorry. I won't judge. It just looked like he was overworked and tried his hardest."

"Yeah, that's how it looked. Why do you think I left for school?"

"To become a veterinarian, of course."

"Yeah, that's how it looked."

Now she was confused. Wasn't that what he wanted?

"I'm not going back."

She swung her head in his direction and saw the determination on his face. "To school?"

He pressed his lips together, nodded.

"You can't be serious. What are you thinking? You'll be a veterinarian come June."

He was silent for several beats. Much longer than she wanted for his answer.

"So," he finally said. "My big brother's getting married. How 'bout that?"

If only she could shake the truth from him, but the change of subject seemed final. For now. She nodded verification of Colt's nuptials and waited to see where Hunter steered the conversation next.

"Okay, back to the Achilles. I knew Clay injured it smokejumping, but you said three times."

"Twice smokejumping. The third time, a horse bucked him off."

"Yeah, but that's happened a million times before."

Peggy shrugged. There was no disagreeing with that. "This time the saddle came off with him. You can't exactly tuck and roll with that between your legs."

"Do you like Rylee?"

"I do. She's spunky." Peggy laughed. "Typical redhead, for sure."

"Ah, a redhead. Now it makes sense."

"What do you mean?"

"He and I saw *Journey to the Center of the Earth* with Arlene Dahl a couple of years ago. Colt fell madly

in love. Thought we'd have to leave him at the theatre."
He laughed. A bold, rich rumble. Sounded nice right
about now. "Doesn't surprise me another redhead
would sweep him off his boots."

Peggy giggled. "You know, I think Rylee looks a
little like Arlene Dahl."

They both roared then. When was the last time
she'd felt like laughing?

When they finally settled back to silence, he said,
"Back to Clay."

She had hoped it would be back to Hunter's
troubles, but she'd go with the flow. "I came to the
ranch and started work on his Achilles over a month
ago. It's been…" She struggled to pick the right word,
gauging how truthful she could afford to be. But if
Hunter could drop that vet school bomb on her, she
could at least be genuine. "It's been really, really hard."

He glanced at her. Yep, her cheeks burned all right.
All or nothing now. She chose All. "To start, Dr.
Trenton sent Sally first. Do you remember Sally
Wagoner?"

"The big, mousy-brown-haired chick who was
painfully shy in Clay's class?"

"Well, that's not very flattering, but yes. That's
Sally."

"Go on."

"Clay was so mean to her, she told Doc she
wouldn't go back."

Hunter didn't look the least surprised by that bit of
information.

"So he sent me."

"Wow. That seems like a lack of judgment on Doc Trenton's part. He knows your history."

"Right? I argued the point, but he said there was no one else and it was decided. Period." She fumed at the memory.

"Was Clay mean to you, too?"

"Of course he was." She blew a breath through her lips, making them flap with a funny noise.

"But you rose above it."

"How'd you know?"

"I've seen you with Clay. It's one of the reasons he fell in love with you. You don't take any crap from him."

It was the first compliment Hunter had paid her, maybe ever, but Peggy sagged at the thought of Clay never giving her a hard time…ever again.

CHAPTER 16

Bruce Smith quietly tiptoed through the door to his foster mother's home in Sundance. It was 5:00 AM, two days after he'd killed Clayton Cooper, but relief had yet to wash over him. Maybe it just needed a nudge, like getting Martin's fat life insurance check this so-called mother had promised him. And it wouldn't hurt to see the joy on her face when he told her the news.

"Who's out there?" the gruff smoker's voice came from the back bedroom.

"It's me, Ma," he hollered before she could pick up that shotgun of hers. "I'm back."

The woman he'd called mother for over two decades came around the corner in her tattered robe and slippers. This woman and her husband had fostered him when he was ten and then proceeded to forget about him when she got pregnant with his little 'brother.' But if it hadn't been for Martin, Bruce would have been forgotten altogether. Yeah, he'd overheard that conversation between his two *parents*. The one where they had another place all picked out for him. Until Martin intervened. Begged and cried until his mother gave in. As she always did for Martin.

He owed Martin. He'd have been shipped off to that other foster home. The one where all the boys worked like slaves until they got kicked out at eighteen, skinny and calloused. He'd seen it with his own eyes. Yep, when Martin perished in that fire, his mother lost the only person she'd ever cared about and Bruce lost his only real advocate.

Nowadays, Bruce only lived in the periphery of his mother's world. While growing up, despite fair grades and winning nationals in baseball, she'd only had praise for Martin. Then, as an adult, the steady job that helped their income didn't warrant her pride either. He'd learned to hate the only mother he knew, and hate even more his compulsion to please her. Weak, that's what he was, weak.

This should do it now. She'd be proud, for sure.

"It's about time yer home. So, did you do it?" Yeah, revenge was all she lived for now.

He tried to smile, knew it was strained. "Yes, ma'am. Done."

She smiled, and it made his heart flip. He smiled back. Maybe she'd finally accept him.

"Tell me how you did it. I want to know every detail. Don't leave nothin' out."

His pulse sped at the memory of the night, at the thought of being the center of her attention. He shivered, at the cold or the anticipation of raising her hopes in him, he wasn't sure. "Can I get a cup of coffee first? Get you one?"

She waved him off. "Sure, sure. Go do it. I'll wait in the livin' room."

He joined her with two steaming cups in hand, practicing what he'd say. Handed her one, took a sip of the other. He plunked it down and stood before her like a student ready to give a speech. "I found out from his little brother he'd gone off to the West Yellowstone Smokejumper Base. When I called there lookin' for him, my speech was so believable, the guy told me he was bunkin' at Harper Ranch." He grinned. "So I called there next—"

"Yeah, yeah," his ma said, waving him off. "Get to the good part."

Bruce scowled, angry his sleuthing wasn't earning any praise. "Got him to meet me at the base."

She leaned forward, looking excited and proud. He was sure that look was pride. "How'd you get him to come?"

"Told him I needed to talk with him…about unfinished business Martin had with his best friend." Her face fell at her dead son's name, so he hurried on. "Cooper mumbled something about owing me his time, so he came." He beamed then. Certain his mother would praise him. She did look pleased.

"Well, keep goin'…"

"So, when he got there, I took him out back for 'privacy.' We talked some 'bout old times. Cut it short cuz a storm was pickin' up. I told him I had some stuff in my truck to give to him from Martin and waved him back toward the building. He turned to go ahead of me. That's when I clobbered him upside the head with that crowbar Pa kept in the bed of the truck."

"So, he's dead."

"Yep. I heard the crunch. There was blood all over the place. It spilt real fast then. I got out just as another truck drove up."

His ma sat back, her eyes hard. "So, you know he's dead."

Dread started to seep in. "Yeah, Ma. I mean, I had to bug out in a hurry, what with the people in the truck. One of 'em was that Wilkins fella from Harper Ranch. But I wore a ski mask." He was sure she'd praise him now for using his head.

"So, you checked to make sure he was dead."

"Gad, Ma. He was bleedin' everywhere and still as a broken baby bird."

"You leaned over and what? Felt for a pulse? Listened for a heartbeat? Put yer ear by his mouth to feel for breath?"

"Ma! I had to get outta there. Like I told you, there was people comin'—"

Ma jumped to her feet, her robe catching underfoot to reveal her flannel nightgown. She yanked at it. "Are you tellin' me you didn't check to see if he was dead?"

"I told you—"

"I know what you said! But if you didn't check, you didn't do your job! Idiot!"

Acid hit his gut so hard he thought he'd throw up. "Don't call me that."

"You are an idiot." She stepped forward and poked him in the chest. "You've always been dumb. Martin was the smart one. Smart and good lookin'. And sweet. You're nothin' but the kid of a whore—"

That was it! He grabbed the finger poking him and shoved it at her own chest.

She took another step forward. "Don't you dare touch me like that, you ignorant...mule!"

Shaking with rage, he pushed her away.

She tottered backwards but caught herself. "What the—? We was crazy to take you in all those years ago. I wish every day it'd been you and not Martin who died in that damn fire!"

The heat of hurt and fury filled his head, propelling him forward. He palmed the top of her head, his fingertips pressed into her paper-thin hair, and gave her forehead a hard shove with the heel of his hand. Her neck snapped back, and fear filled her eyes. The satisfaction of that look was worth everything that came after.

She flailed backward. Her skull cracked against the corner of the end table. The lamp careened off, crashing and splintering against the hardwood floor.

His gaze shifted from the shattered porcelain to the crumpled woman. He'd heard the crunch. There was blood everywhere. His lips rose at one corner. Surprised that he felt elated instead of horrified, he grinned some more. "Wha'dya think, Ma? Should I check for a pulse? Listen for your breath?" His laughter rang out before he clamped a hand over his mouth. He shouldn't feel this happy, should he?

He tittered, backing a step to avoid the advancing pool of blood on the floor. "You're not worth the bother," he said, an airy euphoria settling into his mind.

He could get away with this. No one expected him to be in Sundance. No one saw him come in, and he could dang well make sure no one saw him leave. When they found her body, the authorities would assume she slipped in her shabby slippers and created her own mess. Ha! Couldn't have happened to a more deserving person.

He was free of her. Finally free!

He carted the coffee cups back to the kitchen, washed and towel dried them, and returned them to the cupboard. There. Evidence erased. He peered out the side yard window. The sky was still dark, the neighbors still asleep.

Asleep. His skin crawled with sudden doubt. He crept back to the living room. Nah. His ma's lips were parted, eyes fixed, skin blanched. But the doubt in his head only leaped to a different target. He didn't get the chance to see death on Clay's face this same way.

His hands curled into fists. Maybe the woman had a point after all.

CHAPTER 17

A warm hand nudged Peggy's shoulder, jolting her awake.

"Wake up, Peggy Sue."

In her groggy state, the nickname struck a raw cord. The new Buddy Holly song had been playing on Clay's truck radio the day she'd met him outside the Bar-6 gate to give him his set of divorce papers with her signature on the dotted line, and instructions for him to finish the job; to sign and send them in to the state. He'd signed her copy and thrown them at her even as he mumbled something about how he hated that she'd been 'lumped together with a dang girl in a song.' She'd beamed with pride, despite the sadness. If she'd thought he would have agreed, she would have called the whole thing off right then. But one look into the eyes she'd always loved and she had her answer. He loathed her.

Icy air and a few snowflakes flurried in through the open passenger door. "We're here," Hunter said. "Gotta get Clay into the hospital. I already alerted them to get a gurney."

Peggy stiffened her spine, instantly awake. "Oh! Sorry to leave you to drive alone."

He chuckled. "Hey, a little silence goes a long way."

"Very funny. I'll help you get Clay ready." She jumped out of the warmth and into the light snowfall.

Two burly men raced out of the hospital doors, pushing a gurney between them, only slowing when they reached the open back door of the vehicle.

With Clay now headed through the front doors, Hunter veered off to find the ER doctor on shift, or someone he could hand the X-rays off to.

Peggy stayed with Clay, using the nurses' assumptions to her benefit. The twinge of guilt she'd felt back in West Yellowstone with Dr. Barnes had long since left her. She *was* Clay's wife. In heart and mind and soul, if not law. She wasn't going anywhere, and that resolve made her oddly content.

Clay was given a hospital room, a hospital gown, and an ER doctor who handed him off to the head trauma doctor on call—a Dr. Harris. Ushered out so the doctor could give him a thorough examination, Peggy plopped down in a folding chair outside his door, bent on staying close.

The crack of boot heels against floor tile brought her head up to see Hunter approaching, two styrofoam cups dwarfed in one long-fingered hand. As he strode toward her, Peggy took in the whole man. All Cooper men were muscular and good-looking. But there was something that made Hunter stand out in a crowd. Could be his lean stature with those extra wide shoulders, or the too-long dark hair that had a mind of its own—on anyone else it would look unkempt, but on him it lent a harried-professor sort of appeal. Or maybe the jewel-colored eyes that seemed to flash about like bright blue pinwheels. He was striking, and as he passed each woman on the floor, it became apparent he was one of a kind.

Too bad Peggy's heart couldn't beat for a man like Hunter—a doctor of medicine with a steady temperament and solid future plans. But no, she had to fall in love with the unruly, crazy, impulsive, passionate Cooper. She sighed. Oh, so passionate.

"…you even listening?" Hunter knuckled her arm softly.

He had sat down next to her and was trying to hand her one of the cups. Taking it by rote, she looked down into it. Coffee, looked like. She took a sip. Yep, coffee.

"You all right?"

She shook her head, forcing the tears back, afraid to look into Hunter's concerned eyes for fear the last of her reserves would whoosh out of her. Soon she would have the verdict on Clay. She needed energy to battle the news, but had none. Her eyes burned, she blinked. She could barely sit upright, waiting for the prognosis. Bitter fear and gnawing grief struck her hard from the inside. Numbness. Sorrow. So much sorrow. If he never woke up again, she'd be gutted. If he woke up and didn't recognize her, she'd be demolished. If he woke up and didn't want her…

She swallowed past the lump growing in her throat. Whatever happened next, she had to prepare herself.

But how?

Prayer. She hadn't prayed since they'd arrived at the hospital. Knowing how Hunter felt about prayer, she closed her eyes, rested her head against the cold wall, and prayed in her mind. *Lord, please wake Clay soon. Let him heal; his body, his mind…his heart. Let him remember everything and everyone. Let me have the chance to show him how much I still love him. Please. Oh, and Lord? Whatever happened to cause Hunter's hostility toward you, I'm here to help him if you want to use me. I know you will provide the strength for that difficult task. Please let me draw the energy from you to receive the words from the doctor about Clay. Let them not be arrows to the heart.*

The next thing she knew, Hunter's voice woke her. "Whoa, hang on." He grabbed her cup before it toppled to the floor, still half full with coffee. "We need to find you a place to lie down."

She stiffened, the back of her head sliding back up the wall. "No. I got plenty of sleep on the drive here. I'm fine. What about you? You're the one who needs a bed."

Hunter shook his head, though the shadows under his eyes gave away his fatigue. This was one heck of a way to spend Christmas. For both of them.

The door next to her clicked open. She jumped, then reprimanded her jangled nerves.

The trauma doctor stepped out and motioned for her to rise.

The coffee in her stomach churned.

No emotions showed on his face, but he stared at her longer than was comfortable. Did he have really bad news? Notice her paleness? "Mrs. Cooper, let's go to my office. Follow me."

Hunter got to his feet and followed.

The doctor proceeded to a door a short ways from Clay's room, gesturing for her to go in before him.

Dr. Harris stopped Hunter. "And you are?"

Hunter offered his hand. "Hunter Cooper, Clay's brother."

With a small nod of his head, he brushed past Hunter's hand and took a seat at his desk. "Get the door," he said to Hunter.

The door clicked. Peggy wrung her hands. Hunter took a seat beside her and clasped his hand over both of hers with a squeeze.

"Clayton has a fractured skull. There is cerebral edema, which we're concerned about. As his brain swells, it puts pressure against his skull. Our biggest concern is something called ICP, or intracranial pressure. This pressure can prevent blood from flowing to his brain, which deprives it of the oxygen it needs to function."

Peggy's grip on Hunter's hand tightened. A glance his way showed deep concern, but also concentration. They both understood more of what the doctor was explaining than the common layperson. Which only made it worse. Much worse.

Dr. Harris continued, "Right now he's in a coma, but we have tested him for 'awareness.' He has a degree of it, which means he reacts to certain stimuli. Pain, to be exact."

She pulled in another deep breath and closed her eyes to gather her courage before asking, "Did he perceive the pain, or was it just a reflex?" she asked.

"We don't know just yet. He had his eyes open at one point, but there was no eye contact or response to our calling his name."

Her own eyes widened with hope. No, no. She had to stay realistic. She'd heard of other head trauma patients who opened their eyes but progressed no further.

"What is his prognosis?" Hunter asked just as she was about to.

For the first time emotion, maybe worry, showed on the doctor's face. "Thankfully, Clayton is young. Twenty-four, I'm told."

Both Hunter and Peggy nodded.

"Our first course of action is the hardest, I'm afraid. We wait. Watch. Hope the swelling goes down on its own so the brain can begin to heal. The skull was fractured, but it was the best case scenario—a closed, linear fracture—which means the bone didn't penetrate the skin or the brain and the fracture runs along one line. He's a fortunate young man. He has a hard skull. The damage to his brain is the biggest concern. We'll watch him carefully through the night. The fact he made it through his first night already is to his advantage. My regards to Dr. Barnes. He's got a fine reputation. All alone there in West Yellowstone without a hospital facility nearby is not a situation I envy."

The doctor got to his feet. "I'll talk to you more tomorrow. You may as well go get some sleep."

Peggy shook her head. "I'm staying. I hope you have a bed or chair you can bring in for me."

"I'll let the nurses know. Try to rest. You're going to need it for when he wakes up."

With that he swept around his desk and let himself out the door. Rude and efficient. Better than personable and inept, she thought. At least he said, 'when he wakes up,' so he expected it. Or, at least was thinking positively. Thank goodness.

Hunter followed the doctor out and held the door for her. She entered Clay's room on feet that seemed detached from her body. It wasn't until she clasped one of his work-worn hands that she became grounded again. The warmth of his skin soaked into her. Hunter took up vigil at the foot of the bed, but Peggy had eyes only for Clay. Reaching up, she smoothed his hair back and let her gaze roam his face. There were no signs of the usual impatience that generally lined his forehead and bracketed his mouth. Not that he was less appealing that way. Just the opposite. His intensity was one of the things she loved most about him. He simply seemed more at peace now. She wanted that for him. When was the last time this poor man knew peace?

"Peg?"

"Mm hum?" she answered, only half listening.

"I'm going down to the cafeteria before it closes. I'll bring you back some food." Without taking her eyes off Clay, she nodded. Soon she heard the hard soles of Hunter's boots against the floor as he let himself out of the room.

Glad to be alone for a spell, she pulled the small chair closer and bowed her head. *"Father-God, thank you for getting us to Missoula safely. Thank you for Dr. Harris and his expertise. I lift Clay up to you now. Please heal his brain and his skull and wake him soon. Help Hunter and me to be patient and wait for your perfect timing. In Jesus' name I pray. Amen."*

"Amen," came a whispered sound.

Her eyes flew open, her head whipped up, and her gaze landed on Clay's mouth. Had he really spoken or had she willed herself to hear it? "Clay?" She stood, leaned over until her face was a hair's breadth away from his mouth. His warm breath slid in and out steadily. "Clay?"

Nothing.

She had imagined it then. On legs as weak as a brand new foal's, she collapsed back to the chair. And then the dam broke.

This was familiar, the sobs, the keening pressure in her chest, the tears that spilled down her cheeks past tightly shut eyes. She had shed so many since making the sickening choice to leave Clay that they were almost her only comfort anymore.

"Don't cry…" another whisper came.

She gasped and looked up. Stopped up any sound at her throat so she could listen. The deep convulsions continued to rack her chest but she held her breath anyway. Watched and listened.

Nothing.

"Clay? Did you say something?"

He lay so still she couldn't imagine any words could have escaped him. Had that been the Holy Spirit trying to comfort her? Or maybe trying to quiet her so she could hear Clay when he did speak? That had to be it. *Stop thinking of yourself, Peggy. Concentrate on Clay.*

Pulling in a deep, purging breath, she swiped the tears off her cheeks and just breathed. *Only breathe. Worry about living later.*

CHAPTER 18

T he door to Clay's room swung inward on a slow
arc. Hunter backed in and turned, both arms full
of foil-covered plates and bowls. Looked like he was
ready to feed the whole floor.

She giggled. "What have you done?"

"Bought out the remainder of the food. There
wasn't much left so I negotiated for the rest for one
price."

He grinned. She stared. When was the last time
she'd seen Hunter smile… Maybe never? It changed his
face from stunningly attractive to downright superb. All
she could think was, he'd better keep that under wraps
or the women would be drawn to him like dogs to a
Galton's whistle.

"You okay?" His smile slid off his face as he flashed
his gaze to Clay. "Is he all right? What's happened?"

With that beacon of a smile gone, Peggy came back
to herself. "Nothing. Here, let me help you with those
before you decorate the floor. Hold on."

The two of them settled the dishes on the various
tables throughout the room. Peggy was amazed at how
much he'd managed to carry. "Wow. You must be
hungry."

"You should be too. We haven't eaten since before we left West Yellowstone. Dig in."

Peggy didn't bother to mention her skimpy saltine feast from the day before. She grabbed a fork, and her stomach rumbled loudly. They both laughed.

After several minutes of scarfing down food, Peggy's mind finally cleared. Conviction burgeoned inside her. She took a sip of water to clear the way. "I could have sworn Clay said a couple of words."

Hunter had just shoved the remainder of a dried-out hamburger into his mouth. "Wha—?" he choked out around the bite. With a big gulp of a bottled soda, he tried again. "Are you saying he woke up?"

"No." She shook her head as she studied Clay anew.

"Well, what did he say? Come on. Did he open his eyes?" Hunter dropped his rumpled plate onto the table behind him, then went to Clay's side. "Clay?" He rested a hand on Clay's shoulder and gave it a little squeeze. "Brother? Can you hear me?" He took Clay's hand and held it loosely. "Squeeze my hand if you can hear me."

They both waited with anticipation.

Nothing happened.

Peggy's newfound clarity cracked. Maybe she'd hallucinated the whole thing, gone crazy with the raw want of it all. Insane, looney tunes, deserved her own bed in the brain trauma ward… Wiping her mouth, she sat back and rested her head against the chair as she watched Hunter try to rouse Clay through slitted eyes.

After several minutes of trying, Hunter gave up and went after the second chair in the corner of the room. He dragged it over to Peggy. "You're losing it, sis."

Though she appreciated the endearment, Peggy elbowed him. "Knock it off, I'm serious. I heard words and they didn't come from me." She couldn't tell him she thought the Lord might have made them loud and clear in her mind. He'd never understand that. Hmmm. Maybe now was the time to approach this.

"Well, if Clay said them, it had to be in his unconscious state. He's still totally out."

"I guess so. Listen, Hunter…"

Hunter stretched out his long legs and crossed them at the ankle. "No."

"No, what? I haven't said anything yet." She turned in her seat and frowned at him.

"Nothing good comes from that start."

Peggy whacked him on the arm. "That's not fair."

"Ow. Keep your hands to yourself."

"Oh, ha ha. A big, strong guy like you is really a sissy?"

He straightened, puffed out his chest. "No sissies in this room. Including you."

"Ah, aren't you sweet."

"No. And no to whatever you were going to ask. You haven't distracted me."

"Come on, Hunter. It's been a long day. Humor me."

He crossed his arms over his chest and gave her a side glance. "One humor."

She chuckled. He did have a way about him. "About what happened to you back at school."

"Nothing happened."

"Don't make me call you a liar, tough guy."

His gaze left her and wandered over to Clay. With a forlorn expression, he stared at his brother for so long Peggy figured he was shutting her out. Until finally he answered, "I'm not going back, so it's a moot point."

"Obviously something happened. Tell me. Maybe I can help."

He scowled at her. "How can you help? By praying to a God who doesn't give a rip?"

She sighed. "Did this attitude about God come from what just happened, or from long ago?"

He leapt to his feet and strode over to the window. It was dark and snowy outside, but the lights from the city gave the view a sort of ethereal charm. He stared out at the silent night.

Peggy prayed in her head for wisdom, and waited for Hunter to speak first. He didn't.

"So…when you get your degree, will you work at the ranch? Or in Sundance with Dr. Willows?"

"Knock it off. I just told you I'm not finishing."

"It's Christmas time, Hunter. Merry Christmas Eve, by the way. So, you only have, what? A little over five months to go? You'd be foolish not to finish."

"Yep. That describes it perfectly. I'm a fool."

"What. Happened?" Her voice demanded he tell her. She hoped it didn't make him rebel. It's just, she'd lost her tolerance for wasted moments. You never knew when you'd run through them all until it was too late.

Hunter glared at her as he found his place in the chair again. He huffed a breath. "Fine. May as well tell you, then you'll be the first one to talk me out of finishing."

"Not likely." She patted the hand he had on the chair arm, ready to wait him out.

He scrubbed a hand down his face, leaned his forearms on his thighs, and slumped his shoulders. "Kind of a long story."

She crossed her right leg over the left, bringing herself closer to him. "Do you see me going anywhere?"

A weak smile twitched at his lips briefly. He stared at Clay's feet and at last tried to take a full breath. It was stifled by a hitch and something that sounded a bit like a sob. She didn't dwell on how badly this *something* had affected him. Just waited and listened until she noticed his breathing evening out.

"I've been an arrogant S.O.B. all four years of school, you have to understand. Good grades—no, great grades. Highest in the class mostly. My clinical rotations have gone exceptionally well."

Sounded good so far, but she knew the bomb would drop soon.

"At school, we work on animals from all walks of life. We see a fair number of patients from local ranchers who want to support the program, but we also get champion bulls and prize-winning roping horses who truck in from several states away to get cutting edge care. And sometimes we get people who love their animals entirely too much." He looked askance at Peggy.

Peggy lifted an eyebrow on cue. "How so?"

Hunter shifted his gaze back to his empty hands. "I think…well, there was this woman client who came in with her sick mare. The horse wasn't a barrel racer or anything, just a lawn ornament with pneumonia that this lady was crazy over." He ran his palms over his thighs and took a breath. "She didn't have kids. Or a husband. It was just her and this horse. And she didn't have much money either, but she came to the vet school for the best care she could find."

Peggy knew what was coming, and she already hurt for Hunter. He slumped a little farther in his seat, and she almost wished she hadn't made him speak of it. Except she knew God could heal, and the Lord was exactly who Hunter needed right now.

"She got me instead. Oh, I assured her we would take good care of her treasured partner. So she left the mare in my hands. The orders were for the horse to get Pen G—that's a type of penicillin—in the muscle every eight hours. It gets to be painful for the horse. Pen G stings…and you have to give a lot of it. I don't blame the horses, but they can start to act out when they see you coming with that 60-cc syringe. They shy and swivel, and sometimes they haul off and kick…" Hunter shook his head. "Like I said, it's not exactly the horse's fault, but it's dangerous for the people giving the shots. So sometimes you just have to—" He scratched his nose. "You just have to get it in. You know?"

His gaze wandered, his mind back in time somewhere. Peggy hardly breathed.

"I jabbed that needle in and pushed that plunger down as fast as I could. You're supposed to aspirate"— his eyes flitted to hers to gauge her comprehension— "you know, pull back on the plunger to make sure the needle's not in an artery or vein. But I didn't. I just gave it. All. And that mare dropped dead of anaphylactic shock before I even crossed off the treatment on her chart."

A tear slid down Hunter's cheek. Peggy ached for him. *Lord,* she prayed, *grace me with the right words to say.*

"I killed that animal, Peggy Sue. As sure as if I'd put a gun to her head. I—I can't get the sound of that lady's wail out of my head when I had to…" He ran his hand through his hair again. "I'm not going back."

Peggy placed light fingertips on Hunter's back. He didn't flinch away. "Hunter." She stroked his back. "I'm so sorry." *And I don't know what to say.*

As she fumbled for encouragement in her head, a gravelly masculine voice answered from the head of the hospital bed instead.

"Get over it…"

Peggy buzzed from her scalp to her toes. *Clay?*

Hunter launched to Clay's side. "Clay? Brother?" He swiped at his wet cheeks. "It's me, Hunter. Open your eyes."

"So you heard that too, right?" Peggy said, standing at his side now.

"Yes. He's not responsive, though."

"How's it possible for him to respond to something we're saying but not be awake?"

Hunter shrugged, his expression a perfect mix of bafflement and hope.

They coaxed Clay to open his eyes for another half hour before giving up and settling back in their chairs, Peggy leaning back, Hunter slumped again on his forearms.

"You have to go back, Hunter."

He peered at her over one shoulder, his eyebrows drawn together and lips pressed tight.

"It was an accident, what you did. You're brand new at this. Do you expect to be an expert already?"

"No. But I expect to not kill my patients. I can't go through that again, don't you see?"

She faced him and grabbed one of his hands, forcing him to sit up straight. "So you learn from this. You never do it again. Next time you aspirate. And that horse will get better. And you'll save lives. Don't you think Dr. Willows has lost a few patients in the past? You can't save them all, but you can sure make a difference. I know you'll always do your best."

"That's just it. I've been so sure of myself. How can I be that now?"

She squeezed his hand. "You can't. And that's good. A humble doctor, one who doesn't think he knows it all, will do a far better job than the arrogant schmuck."

His lips twitched. "Schmuck, huh?"

"Yes. Schmuck. During my schooling I met plenty. You don't want to be one of those. You'll be a better doctor because of what happened to you, not the other way around."

He blinked, and it felt like an answer to prayer.

CHAPTER 19

Christmas day arrived with only a skeleton crew manning the hospital and no further movement from Clay. Peggy watched the nurses with growing compassion, certain they all would have preferred to be home with their families. She felt a little melancholy after making a call to her parents, but with her fingers entwined with Clay's, she knew she was exactly where she wanted to be.

When Hunter returned from his calls to family, the two of them worked together to handle Clay's daily ritual. They exercised his Achilles and calf muscle for thirty minutes, then massaged the muscles of the other three limbs. They gave him a sponge bath, and even cleaned his teeth with a minty sponge on a stick before changing out his hospital gown for a fresh one. Then thumbed through the magazines they had scrounged to tab a fresh article to read to Clay out loud. When it was meal time, they rotated through the cafeteria, spicing up lunch and dinner with Christmas cookies and red-and-green-sprinkled cupcakes. Other than that, the day passed like any other, except the small talk they shared carried an undercurrent of growing friendship.

The next morning, with a kink in her neck and a sleep-sogged mind, she began her morning prayer aloud, as she had since their arrival.

Knowing what was coming, Hunter rose from his chair, stretched exaggeratedly, and excused himself as he had the last two days. Peggy blinked after him, disappointed but unsurprised as the door closed between them.

She turned back to Clay, perched on the edge of the chair, and bowed her head. *"Dear Lord, thank you for another morning where Clay is still breathing, still healing, and for giving us hope."*

The door clicked open and closed again behind her. Her head popped up. Maybe Hunter wanted to hear after all—

Her eyes landed on Dr. Harris instead, standing with clipboard in hand and an odd expression, not quite a smile, on his face. "Don't stop on my account."

She smiled back, elated by his forbearance. With a small nod, she bowed her head again. *"Guide the doctor's hands, give him your wisdom, and heal Clay's brain. I would love to have you wake him, Lord, but not in my timing. In yours alone. In the name of Jesus, Amen."*

He strode closer. "In all my years of handling trauma patients, I've never once had a family member leave their loved one's waking to God's timing. Extraordinary."

"With all due respect, Doctor, you don't know what they pray silently."

His brows shot up, at the same time his lips tilted up ever so slightly. Yeah, she guessed people weren't bold with this man often…if at all.

Then he grinned. A big glorious grin that took the grim reaper look away and gave him a younger appearance. "Well, can't argue with that logic." He turned his focus to Clay and the grin changed back to the usual impassive manner. "How's our patient doing?"

"I wish Hunter were here, but I'll try my best to describe what's happened."

The doctor's brows lowered as if his nurses had neglected to fill him in on something important.

"Oh, we didn't tell anyone else. We waited to tell you."

He nodded. "Go on."

Peggy took the next few minutes explaining the three times Clay had talked to her and Hunter. Words that made sense and were a part of the conversation.

Another smile lifted the corners of Dr. Harris's mouth. "Well, now. That is good news. Let me examine him and we'll talk about it. Why don't you go ahead and step out. Wait for me in my office. Maybe your brother-in-law will be back by then and can join us."

Her head spun with the reminder that the doctor thought she and Hunter were family. Collecting herself, she said, "Okay. Thank you, Dr. Harris."

He nodded, and she exited.

Hunter hadn't gone far. He was just outside the door with his upper back planted against the wall, his long legs crossed at the ankle. Peggy watched as one nurse after the next walked slowly by him, looking up and giving him a smile, nearly losing her stride as she passed. He'd nod to each and graced a few with his Cooper grin. At least he seemed better than yesterday when he confessed his grief over the mare. She was glad for him.

She tapped him on his arm. "Come. The doctor wants us in his office."

They waited only a few minutes before the doctor came in, the same wide grin he'd shown in Clay's room splitting his face. Relief flooded her.

"He woke up briefly."

"What? I've got to go to him." Peggy jumped to her feet but was stopped by the doc's next words.

"You mind sitting back down, Mrs. Cooper?"

Mrs. Cooper. She dropped back in the chair, her legs weak and stomach aflutter. Yet another reminder she wasn't Mrs. Cooper anymore. How would Clay react when he woke up for good? She shivered.

"We used pain stimuli on him again and this time he opened his eyes and pushed us away." When Hunter smiled, he held up a hand. "I want you to be forewarned. It was only briefly. But the fact he woke up and perceived the cause of the pain for even a moment is positive. Be patient. Time is on our side. I'll be back to see him tomorrow. Spend time with him, watch for any more wakefulness."

Hunter rose first and reached a hand across the desk. "Thank you, Dr. Harris."

The man nodded at Peggy, ignored Hunter's hand, and left the room.

Peggy looked at Hunter and rolled her eyes. "At least he seems to know his stuff."

"It's a good thing or I'd give him his own head trauma."

"Hunter!" She struggled to keep a grin off her face. "Maybe God's giving you a glimpse of the doctor you're *not* to be."

Hunter's jaw ticked as he clenched. "It's not like my patients will need a good bedside manner. And I told you, I don't want to talk about God."

"No, but their owners will. I guarantee you."

He turned to go out the door, but Peggy tugged at his sleeve. "Hold on. You're not blaming God for the death of that mare, are you?"

He drilled his glare into her. She felt that blue-eyed stare clear down to her toes. "He sure as heck could have prevented it from happening."

Yes, she agreed He could have, but God was not required to do what people thought best or even to fill them in on His plans. Creation had no cause to question the actions of The Creator. She hoped she could get Hunter to understand that. "We don't know God's ways. Don't try to figure them out. Just know He does what is best for you when you trust Him with your life."

Hunter's lips pressed to a blanched, thin line.

Peggy sighed. Course change. "Come on. Let's go see if Clay's awake."

Hunter's expression softened as he gestured her toward the hall.

Peggy opened the door to Clay's room so slowly, she startled when Hunter reached above her head to push harder. "This isn't a nursery, Pegs. Go on in," he said peevishly.

Clay's eyes were closed as they approached.

"Clay?" Peggy asked quietly, but didn't touch him.

No response.

"Hey, brother." Hunter squeezed Clay's shoulder, then knuckled his sternum. It looked like a half-hearted effort, but Peggy figured that was the pain stimulus the doctor had used.

Clay remained still.

Hunter's shoulders slumped. She felt the same way. This was a waiting game. She knew her prayers had been answered the moment she'd prayed them, and that this time, the answer was "wait." God was in control, and wait she would. But not in silence.

Peggy walked around the bed and put a hand on Hunter's back. "It may be a long haul, Hunter, but like you said before, we have to believe he'll be all right. You should go back to school now. You'll regret it otherwise. There's no need having us both waiting here. Finish your schooling, then go home and show everyone in Sundance you're the best veterinarian in the state of Wyoming."

Hunter patted the blue hospital gown where it stretched tight over Clay's too wide shoulder. Several seconds passed as he studied his brother as if he might never see him again, then lifted his chin to stare out the window. He rubbed his fingertips together, faced her. "How will you get back if I leave?"

He's going! She wanted to squeal for delight, but knew to play it cool for fear he'd reverse course again. She hitched a shoulder. "We'll work it out. It could be weeks, even months before Clay is ready to leave."

Hunter pulled in a chestful of air and blew it out slowly. "I'll go back. If for no other reason than to gather my stuff." His gaze swung back to the window.

There was thick cloud cover, but it hadn't snowed all morning. "The weather looks to have taken a little respite. I'll leave tomorrow if it sticks."

Elation filled her. It was a start, and it was enough. The ranchers in Crook County needed him. Dr. Willows needed him. Being the only veterinarian for the county for the last decade had prematurely aged the poor man.

By early the next morning, Hunter was packed up and ready to go.

Before he left, he helped Peggy one more time with Clay's daily ritual. This time a change of sheets followed. When they checked off all their tasks, they tucked Clay back in, fresh and ready for another day of waiting.

Hunter stood beside his suitcase, his eyes on Peggy and hand in his back pocket. He withdrew his wallet and flipped it open. "I want you to take some—"

"Nonsense." Peggy lifted her hands. "I've got a bit of money saved up, and—"

Hunter pressed a wad of bills into her palm. "For Clay's care." He stooped to make direct eye contact. "I insist."

His earnestness disarmed Peggy. She saw that he would not leave unless she accepted. "Th-thank you." She tucked the money in her purse, then faced him again, palms against her pants, feeling oddly shy.

Hunter's head bobbed. She reached up to give him a hug. He bowed down into it, then gave her shoulder a squeeze. Straightening, he gazed at Clay, swallowed, and said to the air in the room, "Take care of him."

He glanced at Peggy with a pained smile and ducked through the doorway.

The sound of Hunter's footsteps grew softer. "Take care of him," Peggy murmured softly in turn. She faced Clay, feeling vaguely unbalanced—and then utterly free. Taking Clay's hand in her own, she pressed her lips to his warm skin. *"Lord God, take care of them both."*

CHAPTER 20

"It's about time you showed up."

Bruce Smith's spine went rigid at the gruff voice coming from the dark corner of the room. Bar room chatter buzzed one wall away. He blinked into the darkness ahead of him, wishing the patch of light from the hallway extended farther in. "Who are you?"

He'd been summoned by a note under the door of the motel where he'd gone into hiding. He decided not to ask too many questions about how a stranger knew where to find him. Despite his best plans, his name was all over the news in conjunction with Clayton Cooper. There was even a warrant issued for his arrest. No way could he show up for work. And no way could he hunker down at his old home.

His mother's death played in his head again. Her rage, her wide eyes, her sticky blood clotting on the rug by her head. He shook the vision away. Would the police connect the dots? Any reasonable person would empathize with why he'd pushed her. Problem was, juries weren't made up of reasonable people.

"Come farther into the room."

He took a tentative step, then another. While holed up in his fleapit of a motel room, he'd learned from the radio that Clayton Cooper was still alive and had been taken to Missoula for head trauma treatment. If he hadn't been a Cooper, he would never have made the six o'clock news. Rich, entitled, lucky bastard. Now that Bruce had lost the life insurance money, the house, and freedom, the bottom of a whiskey glass was all he cared about.

Down to his last dollar, he'd come at the request of some unknown stranger offering him a covert job. Ha! What did they want? For him to hit a baseball out of the park? Do their taxes?

"What do you want?"

Rowdy bar customers broke into a chorus of profanity and laughter.

"Close the door," the voice in the shadows said.

"I won't be able to see anything."

"Flip on the light."

Did he *want* to see this stranger's face? But what choice did he have? He eased the door closed and clicked on the light. "You!"

"Yeah, me."

Bruce snorted a laugh. "*You* have a job for *me*?" With what this person did for a living, it wouldn't be a job he'd know how to do.

"You won't think it funny when I tell you you'll make twelve thousand dollars. That's two years' salary for you."

Bruce's eyes grew wide. "Why me?"

A raspy laugh filled the room. "You tried to kill Clayton Cooper, Mr. Smith. That will serve you well with me. You're broke. Lying low." The disgraceful creature leaned forward, templing slender fingers. "And your mother's dead. By your hand?"

Bruce stiffened. No one knew that.

Another menacing laugh made his gut flip. "That's a yes. You're the perfect candidate."

Bruce tried to swallow, wishing he had another whiskey to burn the dryness away. "What do you want me to do?"

"I'll pay you three thousand now—so you can get by—and the rest when it's over."

He was irritated now, and a whole lot scared. "To do what?"

"Come summer, you're going to burn the Cooper Bar-6 Ranch down to the ground. The whole blasted place."

CHAPTER 21

The landscape outside Clay's hospital window had shed its winter coat for a much thinner version of itself; swatches of brown peeked through the frozen ground; rivulets of once solid ice streamed down gutters through grates, disappearing into the earth. Nature was plodding on resplendently into April while Peggy remained in a vortex of worry and Clay withered away.

Her life revolved around eight-hour physical therapy shifts at the hospital bracketed by a few hours with Clay morning and evening, and a few more hours of sleep at a former classmate's house. She was grateful to Mary for the job and the empty bed. Really. But looking at Clay's inert body day after day drained her joy.

The sadness of the past months reared up in her today. Words needed to be said. Words she had locked away for when Clay awoke…but which she couldn't keep inside any longer.

Turning away from the window, her gaze landed back on the man she feared was slipping away from her more each day. Dear Clay, the man who had long ago captured her heart and directed her course.

Crossing over to the cold, stark bed, she took her time looking him over. She stood silently, mere inches from his left arm. It lay on top of the sheet, motionless and unresponsive. The hospital gown stretched tight across his shoulders; underneath only thinning flesh covered bone. Her eyes trailed down his biceps to his forearms. Muscles and veins, surprisingly still visible, were only a remnant of his once magnificent strength.

A swallow caught in her throat. Would she ever be held by those arms again? Even if he were to awaken—and yes, she'd begun to doubt it—would he even want to hold her again?

Her gaze found his precious face next, the classically handsome features now protruding so prominently from neglect. Peggy longed to nurture health back into Clay, to pour herself in and fill the holes she had cleaved. To witness the swirls of autumn color in his eyes as they again peered so intensely into her own.

With a deep sigh, Peggy reached down and stroked the back of his hand. She'd always loved his hands. So broad, long-fingered, large. Ceaseless in their work, gentle in their loving, and she could only imagine how they'd be relentless in their ferocity to dig trenches and extinguish fires.

She bit down on her lower lip, a tear trailing down her cheek.

Threading their fingers together, she ticked open the door to her heart. "Clay…my complicated, passionate man. I miss you. Please come back to me."

The ancient ache welled up in her. "Forgive me, sweet man. I was such a fool." She stroked her thumb over his skin. "If God would grant me just one wish, I'd go back to our marriage in a heartbeat. Not only would I not have left you, I would have been a better wife. I know I broke you when I left. Believe it or not, it broke me too. But you…are so gentle, so vulnerable. You never let anyone see that sensitive heart of yours, did you? But I knew it was there. I knew it, and I didn't protect it." She sucked in a ragged breath on a sob. Another one escaped before she could stop it with the back of her hand.

Wiping the moisture from her nose and face, she went on. "Do you remember that time after we'd been married a year, when we thought we might be pregnant? Of course you do. I wasn't even two days late and you knew. I hadn't realized before that day that you kept such close track of my monthlies. You beamed at me when you told me that you thought we were with child. You told *me*!" She laughed, then choked out another sob. Pressure swelled within her head, shutting out all noise but the whimper in her throat. Slowly it eased—and the beep of the monitor, the low murmur of nurses in the hallway encroached back in.

Her mind snuggled into the wonderful memory for several long minutes. "It wasn't to be, as we found out later that night. I remember that haunted look on your face. That look, Clay…that sad, broken, tortured look. It broke my heart. It was almost as if you knew a child would save us. Things had already started to disintegrate. After that, I didn't see that much of you. You drowned yourself in beer and bronc riding and anything and everything but me. Did you know then, Clay? Did you know we wouldn't survive?"

She crawled up onto the bed. It squeaked its displeasure but she ignored it. Pulling his hand into her lap, she continued. "Do you ever wonder where we'd be today if I hadn't thrown in the towel?" The familiar guilt rose up. "Would we have a couple of kids? Still be riding the circuit? Be ranching with your brothers? Be loving each other? Oh, Clay…" She sobbed in another sorrowful breath. "Forgive me. I was young, immature, had no business being married to someone like you. Certainly didn't deserve you. What a force of nature you were—a vibrant, passionate hurricane of life, you crazy, wild daredevil. I loved every minute. I really did. I loved you. So why did I leave you?"

She swallowed past her raw throat. Let the truth seep into her mouth so she could deliver it, wishing he were awake to hear it. "It's simple really. I lost my faith. In us…and in a great God who, if given the chance, could have fixed us. If I'd only let Him."

A knock sounded at the door. She slid off the bed and let Clay's hand slip out of hers. Without energy or heart, Peggy turned to see Dr. Harris enter. He was all smiles and restless energy. She wanted to wilt. Instead she locked her knees to stay standing.

"How's our patient this afternoon?" Dr. Harris said, too cheerfully.

She wished he'd go back to the morose grump she met back in December. Bad bedside manner or not, that man had been believable. This man was playing a part his personality couldn't carry off, too eager by half to convince her Clay had a chance.

"No change," Peggy said blandly…for the second time today.

"Come now, Margaret." First names were used by doctors when too much time had passed. She knew it. He knew it. The whole situation had become unbearable. *Where are you, God? Why haven't you awoken him?*

She hadn't helped the situation by deceiving everyone at the hospital about who she was—or wasn't. Only Mary knew the truth, and even she had been disappointed in Peggy's deception. Come to find out, Mary had always admired Peggy's faith. Her ability to pray over anything and everything. The way she trusted God in all things, and left Him to handle not just the big things, but the minor ones too. Now Peggy felt responsible for causing Mary to stumble in her own neophyte faith.

"Clayton has opened his eyes several times in the last few months. Sometimes for several minutes," the doctor said.

"I know." She sighed. "But why won't he wake up for good?" The whine in her voice irritated her as much as it must have Dr. Harris. He only knew what a human could know. She knew who was in charge. Her own deception had caused this gap in her prayer life. It was no one's fault but her own. But it was too late to change it now.

Dr. Harris came closer. She had noticed he'd been doing that more lately. Sticking around to comfort her. Did he do that with his other patients' families? When he swung an arm around her shoulders and squeezed, she knew the answer was no.

She sidestepped.

He dropped his arm but ducked down to look in her eyes. "Don't lose heart." He smiled now, and she knew he was about to change the subject. Had she gotten to know him that well? "The hospital administration appreciates you, Margaret. You're a very good physical therapist. It shows in the work you've done here. Including the mobility Clay has regained in his leg. I'm sure he'll appreciate that when he's awake and walking."

His brandy-colored eyes seemed to glitter with appreciation, and something else she was afraid to name.

"Thank you, Dr. Harris."

"I've told you before. Call me Daniel."

"I'm afraid I can't do that, Doctor. Not the protocol around here." Before he could try to convince her otherwise, she pressed on. "What brings you to Clay's room this evening?"

"I'd like to take you to supper."

She jolted. She was a married woman. Or at least he thought she was. How dare he become too familiar with her.

He must have seen the disgust on her face. "As friends, Margaret. Only friends. You've been stuck here for months. You need a break. It's a beautiful evening out. As your doctor, I prescribe some fresh air and a thick steak." He grinned a wide, attractive grin. Not for the first time she wondered why the man wasn't already hitched. He was easy on the eyes, successful, professional, and didn't seem to be the kind of doctor who blew through all the nurses and staff because he could. In fact, in all the months she'd been here, she'd never seen him cozy up to anyone.

"Oh, I don't know. It doesn't seem appropriate, friend or not. And you're not my doctor, you're *my husband's* doctor." She rubbed in.

He had the good graces to look abashed as he brushed a glance at Clay. When he looked back at her, the confidence was back. "I really think you need a change of scenery. When I came in this evening, the look on your face could have convinced me we'd lost Clayton. That's not good for you. That's not good for him. You know it and I know it and so do all the nurses, candy stripers, and your friend, Mary."

Her eyes widened. "Mary? She's in on this? What did she say?" She'd better not have told Dr. Harris—Daniel—about her status as an ex-wife.

"Mary is most definitely 'in on it.' When I asked her if she thought you'd go, she actually squealed and clapped. She thinks you should go. So do I." He watched her for only a moment before he jumped back in. "It's only supper."

She teetered inside. Going to supper sounded heavenly. But she'd rather it was with Clay. Tears welled at the hopelessness of it all. *Please wake him, Lord.*

The doctor must have seen her willpower breaking down. "I got Mary's address from her. I'll pick you up there in two hours. Dress up. It'll be good for you."

She rolled her eyes, and he chuckled. "Perfect. See you then." He dashed away before she could clarify…what?

This was getting way too complicated. Guilt squeezed the living breath out of her. She felt as if she were cheating on Clay. Ex-husband or not, in her mind she'd never stopped being Mrs. Clayton Cooper. But Clay wasn't ranting or pacing or ramming his fist into a wall over Dr. Harris's invitation. No, he was silent, inert, and utterly beyond her reach.

• • •

Dr. Harris was more than prompt for the supper date. He was at Mary's home fifteen minutes early, and Peggy had barely finished wrapping her hair in a tight, low bun. She'd dressed in a simple black shift and low matching pumps. Pearls were her only adornment, along with a cropped black-and-white-striped jacket with three big black buttons down the front. She grabbed her clutch and answered the three sharp raps on the door.

When she swung the door open, Dr. Harris stood before her, tall and neat in a dark gray suit with a thin black tie. Put together, as always.

"Good evening, Doctor. You're looking dapper."

The good doctor brushed his gaze down and back up Peggy until their eyes met. "You're beautiful, Margaret."

A deep blush started at her chest and rose into her cheeks. This was a bad idea. "Look, Dr. Harris, this is…I think maybe we…"

He shifted his head down a notch and pinned her with his dark stare. "Daniel. And, like I said, it's supper. Just supper. Take a deep breath. You need it." His bossiness reminded her of Clay.

Let's just get this over with. She breezed past him, closing the door behind her. She didn't dare invite him in, especially because this was the night Mary stayed with her folks across town.

As Peggy's heels clipped down the sidewalk toward his sleek, black Corvette, she felt his hand at the small of her back. Granted, the walkway was a little uneven, so she allowed it. Grudgingly.

The drive to the swanky restaurant was pleasant enough. Come to find out, Dr. Harris was a decent conversationalist. Peggy relaxed into talk of the weather, small town politics, the latest Tony Curtis movie.

The maître d' recognized the doctor as soon as they entered, and ushered them past the line and to a table in the rear. The man offered the wine menu. Dr. Harris waved it off. "I'll have the '57 Bordeaux reserved for me in the cellar."

"I'm not much of a drinker," Peggy said.

"It's fine. You'll enjoy this wine. It's smooth and flavorful, and it'll help you relax."

Peggy arched her eyebrows, annoyed.

Dr. Harris didn't seem to notice. He nodded once to the maître d', who whisked away.

Peggy pressed her fingertips into the tablecloth. "I'll have one glass is all."

He shrugged. "Just wait 'til you try it."

She glared, he grinned. Irritating man.

Once he'd poured the wine for them both, he settled back in his chair, his long fingers stroking the stem of the glass. "So, tell me about Clay's family."

Ah. Safe ground. She felt foolish for thinking the doctor would grill her on her own life. Warming to the subject, she was about to sit back herself when she realized she would have nothing much to say about

Clay's last four years. Well, she wasn't going to lie. She'd done enough of that for a lifetime.

"Clay's dad, new stepmother, and youngest brother are in California."

Dr. Harris seemed to be sincerely interested. He cocked his head and frowned, then asked, "Why there? Don't the Coopers live in Wyoming?"

"They do, but Rebecca's dad was badly injured and needed help. They've been there a few months." She thought so anyway. "I'm sure they'll get back home once he's fully recovered."

"Doesn't Clay have five brothers?"

The waitress strode up to their table, bringing her pad to her chest. "What can I get you, Dr. Harris?" She smiled at him like she'd known him awhile.

He smiled back and then turned to Peggy. "We haven't looked at the menu, yet. Why don't I order for you? Do you like steak?"

"Certainly. Medium well."

His gaze met the young brunette's. "We'll have two filet mignons, your fresh vegetables, and baked potatoes with everything on them. We'll let you know about dessert later."

"Medium rare for you?" the young woman asked through a smile.

"Yes. Thank you."

Once she left, Peggy continued. "Yes. Clay has five brothers."

"He used to be a rodeo star, correct?"

He didn't miss a beat. She nodded. "Saddle bronc riding."

"What's he done in the last few years?"

"Smokejumping."

"In Alaska."

She didn't like how this conversation was going. "Why don't you tell me what you know of Clay, and I'll try to fill in the blanks." Did her voice sound as peeved as she felt? It was like he already knew the answers and was testing her. Was she just paranoid? She admonished herself. He was likely just a doctor interested in his patient.

"The Coopers own a cattle ranch in Sundance, right?"

She nodded and took a small sip of wine.

"He has past injuries…many past injuries…" He leaned forward and caught the hand she had resting on the table, squeezed. That crossed the line. She started to pull away when he finished his statement. "…according to his doctor."

She froze, felt the blood drain from her face. "Oh, you've been in touch with Dr. Trenton."

He nodded slowly.

"What—" She stopped, cleared her throat over the threatening lump. "What exactly did he tell you?"

A charged pause had her shifting in her seat, her hand still trapped in his firm grip. He finally released it and sat back. An amused smile lifted the corners of his mouth. He knew. He knew her secret. The little bit of wine in her stomach made her light-headed.

They stared into each other's eyes for too long. "What did he tell you, Dr. Harris?"

"Daniel." He took a drink from his glass, finishing off half the wine in it. "I know you're not married to

Clayton anymore, Margaret. When were you going to tell me? Tell the hospital?"

Would he fire her now and kick her out of Clay's room as well? "Uh…I can explain…"

He didn't move, just stared, his eyes turning dark brown in their severity. Like no one else, ever, he waited for her to explain. Would her explanation get her absolution? With the doctor? With the hospital? With God?

She sighed, sat back in her chair, and took a big gulp of her wine. "Fine. How much do you want to know?"

"Might start back where you and Clay divorced."

"You seem to already know all of that. Dr. Trenton told you I am Clay's physical therapist for his injured Achilles?"

He nodded.

"And that we ended up in West Yellowstone where he was assaulted." She didn't think it was any of Dr. Harris's business that she had followed Clay there, uninvited.

The smirk told her he knew already. The rat. He nodded again. "Go on."

"That's it. I said I was his wife because I am… I was, and I knew you wouldn't let me help with decisions if I wasn't a relative. His dad and the rest of the brothers didn't come because they didn't need to." Her voice was growing louder. She took a breath. Waited a few heartbeats. "Not when they knew I was already here."

This time it was his turn to pull in a breath and let it out slowly. "I understand, but you deceived me...the hospital. We'll need to evaluate the current decisions."

"Oh, for crying out loud!"

A patron two tables away looked at her.

Chagrined, she whispered, "Just let it go. I'm not going anywhere. Go ahead and fire me, but you're not kicking me out of his room."

Shocked and amused, Dr. Harris stared into her eyes for a long time, obviously mulling through his options of what to do with her.

"Please, Dr. Harris—Daniel—let me stay and help." Honey. That's how you got what you wanted. Not with vinegar, she reminded herself. Shifting in her seat and squaring her shoulders, she began again. "I want to be there when he wakes up. Logically, I am his physical therapist, though it's through Dr. Trenton, but that should be easy enough to transfer to you. Do I need to get permission from his father? He'll give it, you know."

Dr. Harris softened his eyes. "To tell you the truth, I've already given this a lot of thought. I've known for quite some time now. You've managed to complicate my life."

That statement had her nerves on edge, and her humility in check. Her shoulders slumped. "I'm sorry about that. If I had trusted God more, let Him handle Clay's care, not lied...I wouldn't be in this predicament. And you wouldn't have to figure out how to handle Clay's future at the hospital. I'm truly sorry."

The doctor waited so long to speak she thought he'd get up and walk out. "I think we can work it out.

Put you in charge of his physical therapy. You're right. His Achilles has needed the treatment. Your diligence has restored the range of motion. And, like I said, when he wakes up, he'll appreciate it."

She sighed in relief, dropped her chin to her chest. *"If he wakes up…"* she said to herself. She lifted her gaze back to his. "I'm so sorry."

The right side of his mouth lifted in a half-smile that lit his eyes as well. "I never said your complicating my life was a bad thing, Margaret."

Their food arrived, and she sighed inwardly that she had a little more time to figure out what Dr. Harris planned to do with her. Both she and the doctor were quiet through the meal. When she declined dessert, he paid and they were on their way.

At Mary's house, he walked her to the door and stood near as she unlocked it. "It looks dark in there. Where's Mary?"

"She…uh…is at her folks. Well, thank you for the wonderful food, Dr. Harris. I'm not sure what our next step is…" There was a question in her voice.

"How about a night cap and we can continue conversing about it?"

"I don't think that's wise. Thank you for the evening. Maybe a conversation in the morning in Clay's room?" She tilted her head and waited.

He chuckled, then leaned down. She tensed, but he just kissed her on the cheek. "Goodnight, Maggie. See you in the morning."

She raised her chin and stared, wide-eyed, at his familiarity.

He let out a startled laugh at her expression, then turned for his vehicle. The laugh continued on down the walkway. Hardy and masculine and delightful to her ears. She jumped across the threshold and closed the door behind her, back pressed to the wood, shaking all over.

CHAPTER 22

Weeks passed without so much as a whisper of Dr. Harris firing her, so Peggy relaxed into a somewhat unsettled but stable daily rhythm. April slid into May, and with it a long visit from Clay's dad and wife before they returned to where they were still needed in California. Then May slid into June with a surprise visit from Colt, Rylee, and Brand. They'd retrieved Brand's truck and Peggy's car from Harper Ranch and left Brand's truck with her in Missoula. When she was ready to drive Clay home, they explained, she'd need the more reliable vehicle.

Since then, only telephone calls kept the family apprised.

Dr. Harris still insisted Peggy escape Clay's room for 'fresh air' and 'sanity' time. She acquiesced, mostly because she did need fresh air every now and then. But she guarded her heart—through many a dinner and park picnic—until temptation no longer held sway. She could allow that Dr. Daniel Harris was cordial, intelligent, and surprisingly funny. If Clay weren't in the picture, she would certainly have given the good doctor a serious look. But her love for the belligerent Clayton Cooper had only grown in the past months.

Just gazing on him, and intimately caring for his unresponsive body, reminded her how she'd given her whole heart to him years ago, and had never gotten it back.

A quick knock sounded from the right side of the doorframe. The usual spot. Peggy turned. Dr. Harris stood leaning against the door in green scrubs, arms crossed, fresh out of surgery. He did cut a fine image.

"Good afternoon, Dr. Harris." She grinned, unable to help herself. "How are you today?"

His smile was brilliant. Where had it been when they'd first met the man? Hunter would be shocked. "Fine as frog's feathers, Miss Maggie."

She giggled. She'd gotten used to his odd sense of humor, and had even begun to like the nickname. Funny, how he'd tunneled under her skin somehow. "Why are you here?"

He grinned. "Well, now, I came to see you."

"Shouldn't it be Clay you've come to see?"

"I saw Mr. Cooper this morning, if you'll remember."

She did remember, only too well. He'd performed a sternal rub, and Clay had opened his eyes for a few seconds before falling back into a coma. They'd all hoped it had been sleep instead of coma. But after hours of inactivity, doubt set in, and Peggy's heart broke all over again.

"I'd like to take you to supper tonight, Margaret."

She sighed and strode up to him so no one else could hear. Lowered her voice "I know you say you're concerned for my well-being. But, I've really been wondering. Why me? Why have I never seen you date anyone else?"

The sad smile he gave her was so genuine, it made her heart hurt for him and she didn't even know why.

"I had a girl once. She was nothing like you. I've seen you sit with a comatose man for months on end, never leaving his side except to work and sleep. You are faithful. Loyal. Even though you have no idea how he will feel about you when he wakes up. Yet, here you stay."

He tugged the surgical cap off his head and bunched it into a ball with both hands. "My girl and I…" He shook his head, at a loss. "I was gone for a week-long medical conference and came back to find her with another man. That's the kind of woman I picked in the past, Maggie. Couldn't quite trust another…until now."

Peggy was so stunned, she couldn't find the words.

"So…" He smiled sheepishly, waiting.

"So…" Peggy murmured, mind racing now.

"Supper?"

She'd already promised herself an evening of Bible reading and prayer for Clay tonight. Just her and God. She didn't want to hurt the man, but… "I'm sorry, Dr. Harris."

He blinked, as if coming out of a trance of past pain. "No matter what you're doing, you have to eat." Sadness lingered in his eyes. This was exactly the reason she couldn't go now…or ever again. She'd been giving him false hope.

She tore her gaze away from Dr. Harris to look over at her poor Clay, alone in that bed, shrinking in size daily, needing an advocate to plead his case to a merciful God, not romp around Missoula enjoying filet mignon with a handsome physician. Especially not now. She hated to do it to the man, but it was time to end these outings. "I'm sorry, *Daniel*. I can't go with you. Not tonight. Not again."

The man looked stunned. She didn't blame him. She'd been a fool, and now she had to own up to it.

"I'll not take no for an answer," he said. Though he'd sounded jovial about it, deep down he really meant it. "You can eat, then I'll bring you right back for whatever it is you think is so important tonight."

Whoa. Now that gave her pause. Was this a genuine glimpse into his true nature? Whatever it was, it sent her hackles up.

A second look showed her the tired lines in his face. Suddenly, she felt horrible for thinking he intended anything more sinister other than to take care of her. But it was time he saw that she wasn't letting go of Clay. No matter what the outcome. Maybe he knew more than he was telling her. That thought spiked her blood pressure. *Don't borrow trouble*, she heard in her head. "Thank you for the invitation and your concern, Dr. Harris. But I really have to decline. I'll see you tomorrow?"

His eyes softened. "I'm concerned about you. How about I bring you something."

"No. Really. I just want to be alone with Clay tonight."

He finally nodded, but didn't look convinced. "We'll see. Try to get some rest, Maggie." She could see in his eyes that his concern was genuine. As impossible as this situation was, he didn't seem likely to give up. He'd be back.

She sighed.

He gave her a sweet smile, then departed. As she stared after him, a revelation came to her, sharp and clear, as if God had spoken it straight to her soul. She could never choose a mild-mannered man like the good doctor to be her soul mate. Not when God had built her for a man like Clay.

Not a man *like* Clay. For Clay. Only Clay.

A supernatural peace came over her, filling her with hope for a future with the man she loved.

If only he'd wake up.

She tugged at her scrub shirt, feeling dingy from the day's work. Thank goodness for the hospital policy of scrubs for the PTs instead of nurses' uniforms. She set a blanket, pillow, and her Bible on the chair by Clay's head, then made her way to the therapy room to grab pajamas, otherwise known as a second set of blue scrubs, out of her locker. With her night's attire wadded in her hands, she let herself back into Clay's room and swung his door closed. With a quick glance Clay's way, Peggy dropped the locker key onto the table with a loud clunk.

• • •

Clay jolted. Acute awareness hit, then fear.

He wedged his eyes open. Blinked into blurriness. Blinked again and again.

Vision began to clear. His gaze moved around the room. Nothing held still.

He'd been forced to open his eyes before. The terror grew worse with each rousing.

Thoughts of one injury after the next assaulted him. Broken bones and twisted ligaments; his legs, ankles, wrists, ribs, knees, groin. Each memory set fire to his nerve endings until he wanted to scream in agony.

Sink back into the darkness.

Usually he would, but this time the person who made the sound won out. Who was with him?

Prying his eyes open further, he tried to focus. Blinked. Tried again.

A woman. At the end of...his bed? He was in a bed. She was...standing near his feet. His gaze drifted. The room spun. Nausea began in his gut. Just like before. Pain roared through him like a devouring lion. *Close your eyes. Sleep. It's easier.*

But the woman drew him, extinguishing the torment. Disconnecting the raw pain.

Something was familiar.

He squinted. The room was too bright. A new pain pulsed in his head...especially the left side. *What happened to me this time? The bronc? The fall?*

A flash of fabric caught his attention. What was the woman doing? Looked like...removing clothes? He squinted harder. His heart sped. He knew that sweet body. Knew it by sight. Knew it by feel. Knew her. Of course she'd be here.

Where is here?

He looked past her. To catch his bearings. White walls. So much white.

Why couldn't he move? *Try.* The left hand worked. The right didn't move on command. *What's going on?*

"Wire?" he rasped on too dry a throat. No sound emerged. That word wasn't right. "Wry. Are…" No. No. Why wasn't his mouth working? Pursing his lips just so, he took a bigger breath and tried again. "Where?"

The woman gasped and swung toward him, eyes gawking. "Clay! Thank you, Jesus! Clay. You're awake."

Yeah. Awake.

She lifted her arms. Something slipped down over her. A shirt? Then she was suddenly at his side, hitching a hip into the mattress. She leaned over him, posted her other arm on his opposite side. Close but not touching. He could see blue. Her eyes. So blue. He knew those eyes.

Her free hand touched his hand, then his cheek. Words came from her mouth, sounding so foreign. "It's a miracle you're awake, Clay. Thank you, God!"

A miracle. Yes, something God does.

She leaned back. He could see her eyes and nose and mouth…

Her hands cupped his face. Rubbed. Soothingly. Up and down.

Memories flooded him. Of this woman. Another memory came. Of her edging up the bed to him. Smiling brightly. So happy.

Sleep beckoned. He fought against it.

"Clay! Stay awake. Please. I don't want you to slip back into a coma. Please, stay with me."

Yes. He blinked. Felt his eyes cross.

"Oh! I'm too close, aren't I?" The bed moved. Her face moved away. "There. Better? Can you understand me?"

He wanted to say 'yes,' but 'sah' was what came out.

"You're trying to talk, aren't you? That's wonderful." The bed moved again. She sat next to him, grabbed something, and put it to his mouth. A straw. In his mouth. *Suck,* he told himself. He tried. Needed a bigger breath. He did it. Sipped. That felt good. Cool, wet.

She set the water down and reached past him for something. A button. Pressed it.

Another lady padded in and came into view. "Oh! Mr. Cooper, you're awake. Thank God!"

God again. A miracle.

Then two more ladies. One wore a hat. Nurses?

Returning the water to the table, the first lady—pretty, blond, blue eyes—took his hand. Squeezed. "Talk to me, Clay. Do you know who I am?"

Yes. No.

"When the doctor calls in, I'll let him know right away," the hat lady said. "He said he wouldn't be home tonight or I'd call him there."

"Uh…I think his plans changed. Please try him," the pretty blonde said, looking…something. Guilty?

A redheaded nurse bobbed into view. "There are tests he'll want to do."

"In the meantime, I'll stay close and try to keep him awake." The blonde again.

He watched each lady leave the room, except for the blonde he knew well.

She came close, grasped his hand in both of hers. "Do you know who I am?" All her teeth showed. He liked it when she did that.

His mouth didn't work, but his thoughts seemed to. He pushed his lips out but only air escaped them.

"It's okay. Rest. We'll try again later. I'll talk to you, how about that?" This woman of his. She was his. He was sure of it. So alive. So full of joy. "You probably want to know where you are."

His eyes widened.

"Oh, was that a yes? Do that again when you want 'yes.' Narrow your eyes if 'no.' Okay?"

Smart lady. That worked. He widened his eyes again.

"You were at the Harper Ranch in West Yellowstone. Do you remember that?"

His eyes narrowed.

"I see. You don't remember…"

Suddenly, she looked unsure.

He waited.

"I hate to be the one to tell you this. You were assaulted, Clay. Hit with a crowbar on the left side of your head." She touched his head tenderly.

So that was the injury this time. He opened his mouth to ask 'who' but nothing emerged.

Thankfully, she got it. "You want to know who did it to you."

His eyes widened.

"Bruce Smith."

Who?

"From your frown I'm guessing you don't remember him. He's Martin's brother. Do you remember Martin?"

Martin. That was…Yes. He went to school with a Martin. There was more about him he couldn't quite remember…

"Listen, I'm probably saying more than I should. I'll talk to your doctor and get his advice about how to proceed now that you're awake." She squeezed his hand again. Her touch felt good, right. "I'll be right back. Don't go back to sleep."

• • •

Clay opened his eyes. He blinked, hoping the same phantom pains didn't flash through his body.

The pretty blonde stood near him. He looked at her shirt. Blue. Like her eyes. He stared at it.

"Clay." Her tone was wispy, relieved. Her eyes were teary. "I'm so glad you're awake. You've been asleep for hours."

Asleep? *Weren't we just talking?*

Her face lit up with a smile. That was it. When showing teeth…called a smile.

"Can you talk?"

Yes. But no words arrived.

"Try saying Peggy."

When she smiled like that, he couldn't deny her. "Pig…"

She laughed. "No. Not Piggy. Okay. Maybe try Twinkie. It's a nickname you used to call me. Try that…Twink-ie."

"Wink—"

"That's close. Twa-ink…twa-ink-ie. Try again."

He studied her face. So beautiful. "Wife," he said, matter-of-factly.

Right before his eyes, her face paled. White as the walls. His eyes could focus better this time. So much so he could see she was lost in thought. Then, as if agreeing with herself, she nodded, her silky blond hair sliding across her now rosy cheeks.

"Yes. Wife," she finally said, her face growing pinker.

Somehow, he'd known it. She was too familiar. Too right. His wife. Yet, why couldn't he remember much about her?

What did he recall? A wedding seemed to come to mind. Bronc riding. Traveling. Living in a trailer. Wrapped in each other's arms in their narrow bed.

So why had he been in West Yellowstone at Harper's? Something Roy needed?

"Do you want to sit up a bit? Maybe try to eat a little something?"

He didn't want to move, just sleep. But she looked so hopeful, he nodded.

She got to work adjusting something. The bed clunked into place, sending a shock of pain through his head. He winced.

"Sorry. That wasn't supposed to happen. Let me get the other side." She rushed around the foot of his bed to the other side and adjusted something there. The jarring didn't hurt as bad this time.

More upright now, the room began to spin. He squeezed his eyes shut.

"Give it a minute. The doctor says dizziness is common with change of position. Especially since you've been lying flat for months. It should subside. Try opening your eyes slowly."

He felt her stuff a pillow behind him. Leaned his head back against it and slowly pried his eyes back open. Better. Eventually the room settled.

Twinkie touched his hand. Without moving his head, he rolled his gaze to her. Her hair caught the shine from the lights overhead. He saw gold shimmers and a bright smile.

Sunbeam. The nickname he'd given her that she liked. He remembered now. She hadn't liked Twinkie. Made her believe he only thought of her as fluff. Not so, but he had used it against her many a time when she acted ditzy, or he was mad at her. Why had he done that to her? Used a name she hated? And why did she want him to use it now?

"You look deep in thought. Or are you trying to control a dizzy spell?"

He tried to smile. Give her something back. He didn't remember much, but he had a hunch he hadn't been kind to this wife of his. He shifted his attention away from her, troubled by the strange thought of regret.

"Um…Clay?"

He brought his attention back to her.

"Do you remember your Achilles was injured recently?"

Pressing his lips together in concentration, he pondered what he knew. A broken wrist came to mind. That bronc in Texas had thrown him high and wide. He'd landed hard on his left side. He should have a cast…on his left hand.

The confusion on his face must have alerted her. "What are you remembering? When you last broke your wrist?"

Last? That's right. He'd broken it more than once. He managed a nod.

"That was years ago, Clay." She looked unsure again. "Listen. I'll be right back. I pressed the button but the nurses may be still trying to track down your doctor. I'll go check."

Before she could bounce away from him, he grabbed her hand. She'd touched him a time or two since he woke up, but had yet to kiss him. He needed that kiss more than answers right now, yearning for the softness of those rosy lips against his parched ones. His wife was reserved in public places, but he only wanted a quick kiss and there was no one else in the room at the moment.

With a tentative tug he brought her closer. Her eyelids widened and her pupils dilated. Looked more like fear than arousal. Maybe she was more shy than he remembered. She did mention he'd been lying here for months. *How many months?* He'd take it slow. He released her hand to slide his fingers into that glorious hair. He shivered with the feel of it, the joy he still remembered from touching it. Ever so carefully, he tugged her to him. When his lips met hers, warm and wet, he sank into her sweetness, struck with a sense of coming home.

He tasted mint on her tongue.

Then felt everything about her tighten and withdraw.

CHAPTER 23

Peggy broke the kiss and pulled back.

Clay's hand dropped to his lap, his brows drawn together, confusion clear in his expression.

Her breath had seized entirely. As she struggled to take in air, she stared into the swirls of green that were Clay's eyes, one pupil still slightly larger than the other. When was the last time Clay had kissed her like that? It had been over four years ago. His more recent kisses had been tentative or rife with tension.

This one. Goodness, this one. It was real. Brought back every nuance of their intimacy as a couple. Made her ache for what they'd had.

He thinks you're his wife.

The flush of her deception rose up her neck, shouting her guilt. How could she do this? For someone who professed to love the Lord, she was such a fraud.

She backed up a few paces, put her hand to her lips, and felt the tingle still there, quickening the pace of her heart. He'd never forgive her once he figured out the truth. Yet, she knew once he remembered everything—and he was soon to do that—he would push her so far away she may as well live in Timbuktu.

Enjoy this short time with him then, the wrong voice shouted in her head.

The still, small voice of God tried to gain her attention from under the sin of deceit. He was there, a subtle pressure instead of the sledge hammer she needed right now.

"I—I'll go get the doctor."

Clay's expression collapsed into hurt. He reached out his hand. Peggy tore her eyes away. He didn't understand, but he would. Oh would he...

She stepped up to the nurse's station on shaky legs. Pulling in a ragged breath, she waited until she knew her voice wouldn't betray her. "Has Dr. Harris arrived yet?"

The pretty brunette who worked the weekend day shift looked up from her paperwork. "We finally reached him. He's on his way."

"While we wait, maybe you could give me some advice?"

The nurse set her pen down and gave Peggy her full attention. "I can try."

"My...husband"—she hoped the doctor hadn't told anyone different—"is in room 352, right down the hall. Clayton Cooper?"

"Of course. I know of his case."

Peggy chewed her lip for a minute, trying to wait out the lump forming from her ongoing lie. "I just wondered. How much should I fill in when he doesn't remember something? Should I be waiting for him to remember it naturally? Or tell him everything I happen to know?" All of a sudden she realized what a corner she'd just painted herself into. She hadn't been around

Clay or known of his activities for years now. How was she to fill in the gaps? She should just excuse herself and forget the whole idea.

"Oh, I can help you with that," the nurse said. "It's fine to fill in or show pictures, but we find family members will often overwhelm the patient. You might want to wait until he requests knowledge. For instance, instead of just rambling on about everything that's happened in his life that he doesn't remember, it's better to wait until he says something like, 'Who is that person?' or 'Remember the last time we went to the Red Bird for supper? When was that?' or 'Is Eisenhower still president?' That sort of thing. Do you see what I'm saying?"

"I think so. He seems to think we're back a few years ago. He remembers when he broke his wrist. Thought it had just happened."

"That's common. Short-term memory is often the last to recover. And even if he does remember something, or you remind him of something, he could forget it again, multiple times. Don't get discouraged. Take it as slow as he needs to. Much of it will come back in time. Some things won't and may never. I'm sorry. Just be there for him. Seeing your face every day will help him considerably."

Peggy wished that were the case. Fear slid in. One day soon, Clay would realize her face was the last one he wanted to see. If only she could pray for God's help in this, but how would she pray it? Um, God, please help Clay to continue seeing me as his wife? Or, how about: Oh, Lord, please keep Clay from finding out I'm deceiving him. Pfft.

Her only hope was to come clean. She had to tell Clay the truth.

But it could wait until tomorrow. Or maybe the next day.

God would understand. She was sure of it. Didn't it say in the book of Romans, *All have sinned and fall short of the glory of God?* God already knew she was a sinner. Not to mention, it would complicate things with the hospital if she confessed she wasn't his wife. That would only hurt Clay in the long run. She would not do that to him. He needed her right now.

With a nod and a squaring of her shoulders, her mind was made up. For Clay's sake, she would remain his wife.

Abruptly, her heart tipped into freefall. How would she keep Dr. Harris from telling Clay?

He's a professional, Peggy. He'll keep it to himself.

Would he?

"Thank you for your help. I should get back to him." Peggy's smile was a bit starched, but the nurse didn't seem to notice.

She smiled back. "You're welcome. I'll send the doctor in when he arrives."

A niggling of warning tried to find entrance, but Peggy shoved it out repeatedly until she didn't hear from it anymore.

Determined to be the wife Clay always deserved, she strode back into his room, finding him sitting on the edge of the bed, his catheter lying on the floor and his fingernails peeling back his IV tape. "Clay!" She rushed to his side. "Stop. Don't do that. Get back in bed."

He stopped peeling and hunched over, his big hands gripping the bed's edge. He looked weak but determined to stay put.

When she came close he swung his head up to look at her, and what she saw tore at her heart. His eyes were bleak, his dark brows low and scrunched in the middle. She had done that. Caused his confusion and hurt. When they'd been married, as difficult as so much of their lives had been, she'd never rejected his physical advances. Pulling away from him had pummeled his already clouded brain.

She softened her expression and gave him a tender smile. Stroked a hand down his bristly, gaunt face. "Are you okay?"

He laid his hand shakily over hers and pressed it to his cheek. She loved his big hands. Always had.

"Wife," he said, as if the word covered it all. And it did.

She smiled. "Husband." The word had always come so naturally. Today a whole bucketful of guilt came with it. But she ignored it. "What's troubling you? Can you put it into words?"

Instead of trying to speak, he lifted her hand from his face, kissed her palm, then used it to tug her closer. His arms wrapped around her middle and dragged her between his legs, pulling her in for a deep hug. He shuddered a sigh into her that warmed her heart clear through. Tears burned her eyes as she blinked to keep them from careening down her cheeks. Love and guilt and loneliness, but mostly love, wrapped her within his hold.

He drew back and looked into her eyes, using a knuckle to wipe the tears off her cheeks. When he opened his mouth to speak, nothing came out. But his stare was enough, for within it swirled depths of love she had forgotten were possible.

As his eyes roamed over her face, her heart soared at the adoration she saw there, just before a look of hunger took over. Before she could say a thing, he swooped in and took her lips for a second time. She closed her eyes and didn't allow herself to think, or worry, or regret. *Get your fill of him before it's too late.*

A man cleared his throat in the doorway behind her. She knew who it was without even a glance in his direction.

Peggy broke the kiss but kept her eyes on Clay. The heat of a blush rose up her neck. She cleared her throat, bracing herself. "Hello, Dr. Harris. How are you this evening?"

Clay never moved his gaze from hers. After several heated seconds, she shifted her attention to the doctor, her eyes pleading with him not to tell Clay the truth. She knew he understood by his flattened lips and the disapproval in his eyes. But then again, that expression could have stemmed from her rejection earlier.

"Excuse the interruption," Dr. Harris finally said. "I see our patient has decided to join the living."

Peggy frowned, furious at the phrasing.

The doctor's smile was a bit stilted as he ventured forward, a metal clipboard in his hand.

Peggy stepped between Clay and the doctor, feeling like she needed to protect him. "I was just trying to get Clay back into bed. He's weak."

The doctor cocked an eyebrow in disbelief.

Finding it impossible to look the man in the eye, Peggy shifted her gaze to the stethoscope around his neck. "I guess he was trying to get out of bed while I was at the nurse's station. He pulled out his catheter."

The doctor stepped into her space. To get closer to Clay, she realized.

She backed up and came around to Clay's other side. "He hasn't said much. A word here and there. But his actions seem less confused."

"Does he know who you are?" the doctor asked nonchalantly, though she knew it was anything but.

"My wife," Clay said as clear as day, his hazy gaze sharpening as it drilled into the doctor.

Pride swelled. Clay always was a man who'd rise to the defense of his loved ones. He'd been many things not so proper, but taking care of his own when needed was not one of them.

The doctor smirked at Peggy, making her wish she'd never taken up with him, even as friends. She didn't want Clay's care to be compromised.

Dr. Harris shifted closer yet to Clay and began an examination—shining a small flashlight in his eyes, one at a time; listening to his heart and lungs; checking his reflexes.

"His right side is a bit slow, as is his speech, but he's come out of the coma nicely. I'd like to put him in therapy right away to get his brain and body back in sync. I'll relocate him to acute care on the second floor for that. Men tend to be more impatient when it comes to the kinesis portion of therapy, so we'll get started tomorrow. He'll need it for a few weeks, maybe even months."

Months? Was he dragging out the time because of her? The sooner they were out of this hospital and away from the doctor, the better. "I'll take care of him for his physical therapy."

"I don't think that's wise, *Mrs. Cooper.* You're too close to the case. I'll put Mary on his recovery."

Her friend? The one who knew Peggy's entire history? Including how she'd divorced her rodeo-star husband over four years ago? She loved Mary, but she'd never been able to keep a secret in school. If she worked closely with Clay, she quite accidentally might spill the beans.

"I'd really like to be there, Dr. Harris. Don't you think you can arrange it?"

"Yes...please..." Clay said.

Peggy could see the doctor didn't like the idea. If she hadn't gone out with him in the first place, this conflict of interest wouldn't be an issue right now. She knew she should pray about it, but her own deceit kept her from wanting to pray.

Dr. Harris squeezed the bridge of his nose, closed his eyes a brief moment, then nodded. "All right. We'll try it, Margaret. But if I find it's not working, then Mary will take over. Is that agreeable?"

She wanted to argue. Ask what he would consider 'not working,' but in the end, she nodded. "Yes."

"Thanks," came the pinched word from Clay.

The doctor held out his right hand. Clay looked down at it. The expression on his face clearly showed he knew what he was supposed to do with it. He frowned with intense concentration, lifted the correct hand from his grip on the bed, and reached out. It fell short. The doctor grasped it before it could fall away and tilt him off balance. He squeezed slightly and pumped once. "Can you squeeze back?"

Clay's gaze met the doctor's, then dropped back to their hands. Nothing happened. Clay pressed his lips together tightly, but still…nothing.

The physician released Clay's hand. "It's okay, Clayton. You'll get there. There's no need for you to worry. Understand?"

Peggy watched as he gave the doctor a Clay Cooper Stare of Intensity, but remained silent.

"That look means he's comprehending you, doctor," Peggy said. "I know it well. It doesn't mean he necessarily agrees."

Clay's eyes shifted to her and softened. She nearly melted at his obvious affection. She hadn't seen that look since their first few months of marriage. Hadn't known how much she'd missed it until now.

Unable to help herself, she reached up and stroked his cheek. She felt rather than saw the doctor looking on. Observing Clay's ability to interact, or stewing with jealousy?

The corners of Clay's mouth curled up ever so slightly. Maybe not enough for the doctor to notice, but she did. She grinned back.

"Sunbo," he said.

"Sunbo?" the doctor repeated from over her shoulder.

Peggy shook her head, her eyes still glued to the man she loved. "Sunbeam. My favorite nickname."

The yearning in Clay's eyes made her want to burst into happy tears. She wanted this man back in the worst way. This man right here. The one who wanted her, loved her, only remembered the good.

How could she keep him from remembering the bad, or bring them through it back to this?

"I see," Dr. Harris said, dragging her back to the moment.

One look at the doctor and she knew this was going to become complicated. It seemed he was struggling with Clay being awake at all. Not a good reaction for his doctor to have. *Oh, Peggy, what have you done?*

"I'll see you tomorrow, on the second floor. The nurses will tell you what room."

Peggy had a hard time peering into the doctor's eyes. Seeing a man who was hurting yet still carried the weight of responsibility. "We'll see you tomorrow. Thank you."

When the doctor left the room, he pulled the door shut behind him.

Before she had even turned fully back to Clay, his left hand slid back into her hair. He held her head in his big paw and perused her whole face. Drank her in like she was the sustenance he'd been missing all these months. The subtle tug on her hair tilted her head down enough so his lips could take hers. His mouth slanted over hers and sank in, erasing the loneliness of the past four years as if they'd never happened.

"Need you..." He spoke almost perfectly against her lips.

If he was well and they'd been alone, she'd too easily have been persuaded to take him up on his offer. She certainly hadn't thought this through. It was logical for a husband to want his wife. But she hadn't predicted it would happen so soon after he awoke. How was she to turn him down without making him feel rejected, make him regress in his recovery?

Perspiration popped out in the suprasternal notch between her collar bones. She almost laughed aloud at the clinical vocabulary her nervousness brought forth. *Think, Peggy. Think.*

The problem was, she wanted to *feel* instead of think. She wanted to enjoy her husband again. To the fullest. Forget about the past, move into the future. With this man only.

"Clay," she whispered as she pulled away. "Stop. This isn't good for you." But at least she knew his body was functioning as it should. And so quickly after awaking from a long-term coma was a miracle on its own. Everything pointed to his quick recovery. But that also meant her secret had to be revealed, and soon.

He pulled her closer, closed his eyes and pressed his forehead into hers. "My Sunbo…"

Yes, your Sunbo. They stayed that way for several long minutes. At last pulling back, she looked into his eyes, resisting the urge to sink back down into them. He tried to tug her back, but she placed a hand to his chest to stave him off. "Clay, I love that you want to get close. I do too. But, the doctor says you have to heal before…" It was another lie heaped on the first. She gave him a flirty smile. "Once you're healed, I promise." Another lie. This time with a promise attached.

Goodness, what was she doing? Once he was healed, he'd remember and never forgive her.

"Please?" Clay said clearer than ever, the plea clear in his eyes. He slipped his arms around her waist and tried to secure her to him, but his right arm was still not working right and she was able to spin out of his hold. Men could care less about their own health when it came to loving their wives. She had to come up with something better.

She stood a few feet away but leaned her head toward him. She whispered, "It's not a good time...you know...of the month."

Disappointment clouded Clay's expression. His mind was tracking every conversation now, even if his speech wasn't there yet, or the mobility of his right side.

Still, he was well on his way toward recovery. She was thrilled—and terrified.

CHAPTER 24

"Hold onto me. It's fine," Peggy said.

Clay wobbled, but not as badly as he had a week ago when he first came to.

His growl turned into a chuckle. He was so darn cheerful these days, even when his pride was on the line. Had the injury obliterated the obstinate, cantankerous part of his brain? Or was he just happy to be alive? "I'll crush you, Sunbo. Not my plan."

She giggled, then poked him in the ribs. He wiggled but just chuckled again. Who was this man?

Holding him with one of her arms slung around his waist and his own draped over her shoulder, she smiled up at him. "I'll get you to the parallel bars, then you can support your own weight while you walk back and forth. Deal?"

His answering smile nearly made her lose her footing, her knees had gone so rubbery. Being this close to this man never failed to speed her heart, weaken her legs, and want for more. If only his memories could start from this day forward, she'd be set for life. Except, of course, for the small problem of no more marriage license.

This will end badly. The thought harried her. She smiled her way through it with teeth clenched until it buzzed into the background noise of her mind again.

"Here we are." Leading him up to the bars, Clay grasped hold of either side and began his walk to the end. She watched him in his sweatpants and sleeveless undershirt while he took his first few steps. Try as she might, she couldn't take her eyes off the beautiful physique Clay still had, even if he was a good thirty pounds lighter.

His right foot caught her attention. He half lifted, half dragged it into position with each step. It concerned her, but not too much. She knew it wasn't the Achilles. The mobility of that tendon was good. This was from the head trauma. The left side of the brain controlled the right side of the body. His brain would re-process and eventually re-route his walking pattern. It was an amazing feat of electrical engineering. Only something a Master-Creator could do.

Clay cantilevered himself to the end of the bars and slowly made his way back to her. After a few steps, he looked up, caught her gaze with shining eyes. He lifted one side of his mouth before following it with a wink. She melted. Would she ever get used to this version of Clay? And yet, would she have fallen in love with the man if he had been this way all those years ago?

• • •

"When's therapy?" Clay asked as he exited the bathroom, walking stiffly but without his prior limp.

The last three weeks had passed in a blur. Clay could dress himself now. He had moved beyond the parallel bars to a walker, a cane, and now only an occasional hand for balance. Not that he always knew to ask for it. Peggy sidled up beside him in case he toppled over. "Not until 2 PM."

He glanced at her, a glimmer of teasing in his eye. Oh, the man was incorrigible. The stronger he got, the more intimacy he wanted. If he could walk correctly, he might have already chased her down and dragged her off to a closet somewhere. She yearned for him, but would never use him in that way. Not with her personal day of reckoning looming so darkly ahead.

They reached the big square armchair in his second floor room. She looked at the side table. "Do you want a new magazine? I think you've worn the pages off that "JFK: Man of the Year" edition of *Time*. It's pretty tattered. I'll get you a new one."

"No need, Twinkie. Reading slower these days." Once his calves backed into the chair, he sat. "I need my morning kiss." He grinned up at her with all those teeth flashing. The tease. He'd rarely done that in his happiest moments in the past.

She couldn't help but smile back, and bend down to give him a peck on the lips. Instead, he caught her wrist and gave her a tug down onto his lap.

She squeaked. He laughed, the rumbling sound rolling through her. His arms came around to embrace her.

Equal strength on both sides, she thought with heady joy, then jolting dread. He was recovering by leaps and bounds.

Yes, this would end badly.

She groaned inwardly. Every time she tried to tell the truth, the words in her head flitted away. But the stress of the unknown was killing her.

He freed his hands and brought them to the sides of her face. Those eyes with their swirls of green and brown, were lit with happiness. If she could capture this expression of love, she'd bottle it for later. She'd need every ounce.

She was no longer needed for big decisions; she could visit him daily without having to be his wife. There were no more excuses left. Today had to be the day.

Her heart hammered against her chest, in equal parts anticipation and fear. "Clay…I need to tell you something."

She tried to sit up straighter. He didn't let her. "Uh-huh?"

"Clay. Let me up. Really, this is important." She was going to do this, really and truly.

"No, Sunbo. Kiss me." He leaned in just as a soft rap on the door startled them both. Their heads swung toward the door in unison.

"Excuse me," the nurse said with a shy smile. "Time to take your blood pressure, Mr. Cooper. And your lunch will be here soon. Can you hop on the bed for me, please?"

Clay growled his frustration, but allowed Peggy to remove herself from his lap. He gave her a final slap on the rear. She yelped and scurried away, too distraught by the interruption to admonish Clay.

Peggy watched as he headed to the bed and settled himself, fully clothed in soft denims and a V-neck pullover sweater, on top of the blanket. While she could, she drank in the sight of him. He'd shaved just yesterday for the first time since he'd awoken. Told her he remembered how his beard bothered her skin, so insisted he had to do it no matter how long it took. It took him over half an hour. She'd watched him uncover the lines and planes of his splendid face, falling more deeply in love with him with each swipe and grin and wink he gave her. When he was done, he smiled like he had on the day he'd given her the diamond engagement ring—the one he'd scrimped and saved for—the same one she had hidden away in her bottom drawer back in Sundance.

"Okay, there you go," the nurse said. "All's good. You can have your lunch now, then head to therapy. Busy day." She patted Clay on the hand, then ducked her head like a smitten school girl caught stealing her first touch, before she scuttled out.

Clay smirked as he grasped Peggy's hand and pulled her closer. "Now you can give me that proper kiss."

"Clay. I really do have something to say."

"So you said." In the next moment his smile fell off. He cocked his head to the side, his eyes looking off in the distance.

"What is it? What's wrong?"

"A memory—a woman..." Clay brought his eyes back to hers. A deep line formed between his brows. "Is Colt married?"

"No," she said too swiftly. 'Not yet' would have been the correct answer but she wanted to avoid a drawn out explanation. "Listen. Please."

He ignored her. Snapped his fingers. "He's engaged. To a redhead." He looked to her for confirmation. "Do you know who?"

She inhaled a hardy breath and nodded. "Yes. You're right. Her name is Betsy…or Rylee, as Colt calls her."

He beamed. "Right. Feisty little thing. Fought with me over a horse." An expression that looked a lot like anger took over his features, or maybe it was just confusion. "Why don't I remember you there?"

Okay, now was the time.

"Lunch time," came the sparkling voice from behind a rolling cart. A cute little candy striper came through the door, a sandwich and a pickle slice on a plate in front of her. "I hope you like egg salad sandwiches, Mr. Cooper. We also have jello and fruit. Ooooh, and apple pie for dessert."

Clay never took his eyes from Peggy, studying her as if he'd never seen her before. Peggy jumped into action. "Here, let me help you." The candy striper lifted the tray and placed it on Clay's lap.

Clay bounced his knee, deep in thought, and almost dumped the tray. Peggy steadied it with wilting strength. "Thank you. We'll take it from here."

The little candy striper hustled out the door. "Bye now. See you tomorrow."

"Peggy?"

"Eat, Clay. Then we'll talk." The last thing she wanted was for him to forego food for an impossible conversation. After seeing the change in his disposition from a single confusing memory, Peggy found herself wanting to leap back into the safety of the unsaid. But the small voice in her head reminded her the truth was long overdue.

Clay's focus shifted from that distant inward gaze to the sandwich. He picked it up and took a monstrous bite. His mouth was jam-packed when Dr. Harris decided to show up at the door. He knocked on the frame before walking straight in. "Looks like eating isn't a problem for you."

Clay just stared at the doctor and chewed on the giant lump in his mouth.

"Everything else all right?"

No word or nod from Clay, so Peggy answered. "Just fine, Doctor. We're heading for therapy right after lunch."

"Good," he said and gave a stiff smile. His eyes shifted back to Clay. "We have good news, Clayton. I plan to discharge you by the end of the week. That will give you plenty of time to set up a ride. You can have one of your brothers or your father pick you up."

Clay frowned and turned his head to search Peggy's face. She was sure guilt was plastered all over it. He looked back and pierced the doctor with an intense stare, swallowed the last of the bite. "Why would I need that? My wife will drive me home."

"You do realize, Margaret is an employee of St. Patrick's Hospital now. You'll have to find your own ride back to Sundance."

"Dr. Harris, Daniel—" Peggy started.

Clay yanked the tray from his lap and swung it back as if he intended to hit the doctor. Peggy grabbed it before all the food tumbled off. He tried to jump off the bed but lost his balance. Peggy had to practically slam into him to keep him from falling, then shoved him back onto the bed. He stood right back up and maneuvered around the bed, his hands crawling along the edge all the way around to keep him stable. This was exactly why he had recovered so quickly. Clayton Cooper had the tenacity of a bulldog.

He rose to full height once he reached the doctor. Had at least four inches on him, and though thinner, had a lot more girth. "I'm a little tired of your interest in my wife. Think I haven't noticed? That the common sense was bashed out of me?"

"Now listen here, Mr. Cooper. Settle down. We don't want you raising your blood pressure."

"I'll raise more than my blood pressure if you don't back off." Clay lifted a fist.

Peggy knew Clay wouldn't hit the doctor. Didn't think so, anyway. At least, the old Clay wouldn't have without more provocation. How had he noticed the doctor's interest in her?

Dr. Harris's face went crimson. "Don't you think it's time to let her go—"

Peggy gasped. "Oh, look at that—" She was suddenly in the middle of the two men without knowing how she got there. "It's nearly 1:00 PM, Dr. Harris. You must be hungry for lunch." She laid her palm on his chest and pushed. When she got nowhere, she gave him a full-strength shove.

The good doctor glanced down at her as he rocked back two steps. What she saw in his eyes worried her. He had no plans to back down. Sure enough, he lifted his eyes back to Clay. The two men glared at each other over the top of her head. This was not how she wanted Clay to find out. She needed help.

Daring to extricate herself from between them, she ran to the nurse's button on Clay's bed and jammed her thumb into it.

But it was too late…

"What are you talking about, 'Let her go,'" Clay barked.

Peggy pulled on his arm from behind. "Uh, Clay, I need to talk to you."

He didn't seem to hear her.

"She lives in Missoula now. Works at this hospital. You live and work in Wyoming. Come Friday you'll be discharged. You can go home."

Clay twisted around to face her. "What the hell is he talking about?"

Acid, instant and nauseating, hit her stomach, and she thought she'd throw up right here. "Let's send the doctor on his way, and you and I can talk. I need to tell you—"

With a glare, Clay held up his hand to stopper her words. This was the first glare he'd directed her way since waking. Normally she wasn't fazed. She'd seen glares aplenty when they'd been married, but this one broke her heart. Because she knew what was coming next.

Clay turned back slowly to the doctor. "Looks like you have something to get off your chest."

The doctor puffed up, all professionalism gone straight down the toilet. "That's right. I am interested in Margaret. Have been since the first day I met her. But that's when you were still in a coma. I wasn't going to get in the way of that. I do believe I will now that I'm discharging you."

Peggy's legs wobbled. Wasn't there any way to stop the inevitable?

Clay stood stock still, the blood slowly leaving his face. "Are you saying…"

Forcing her flagging legs to move, Peggy came around to face him. But he only shoved her behind him, his focus remaining on the doctor.

"That she is a single woman. Yes," the doctor said, then glanced at her. His hard eyes seemed to finally see her, and his bravado deflated. He blinked sheepishly at her. It was the first sign he'd realized what he'd done. "You have to understand. She didn't feel she should tell you yet. That it would hinder your healing. I agreed with her…"

He droned on and on, but the damage was done. Sickened, she watched as Clay absorbed every word and didn't move one muscle to defend against it.

When Dr. Harris ceased talking, the silence thickened around them.

No one moved until Clay stepped forward with one foot, then the other. Barefoot and stiff-legged, he walked out the door and disappeared down the hallway.

CHAPTER 25

"How dare you tell him before I could!" Peggy could barely breathe through her outrage.

The doctor's expression was grim but firm. "Why haven't you told him already?"

"That is none of your business. Now, I don't think it's my place to go after him. You need to make sure he's safe and gets back to bed. You haven't discharged him yet."

A muscle bulged in the doctor's jaw, a retort on his tongue, she was sure. But he was wise enough not to say anything more. "I'll take care of it."

He moved forward and caught her forearm in his hand. "Maggie, I—"

"No." She tugged her arm away. "I don't have anything to say to you right now. I'll tell you this much: if Clay lets me, I'll be driving him home." She wanted to rail at him more, but she couldn't. This was her fault, not his. She should have told Clay weeks ago. The doctor had been right about that. The Holy Spirit had nudged her enough. Yet she'd ignored what was right for what she wanted. Now she'd have to live with the consequences.

The doctor studied her face for a few seconds more before deciding she was closed to him. Smart man. Spinning around, he strode to the door. He started to step out but turned back. "This isn't done, Maggie. I may not have handled this correctly, but I want you to stay—at St. Patrick's, in Missoula, with me. Just think about it." And then he was gone.

Her legs gave out the minute she was alone. Plopping down on Clay's bed, she gripped the edge, trying to curb her emotions. She didn't have time to sit here and blubber; she needed a plan. One that would land her beside Clay on his way back to Sundance. Because she needed time to convince him she did what she did out of her bottomless love for him, not her duplicity.

• • •

The doctor and nursing staff frantically searched for Clay in the block-long hospital, scouring stairwells and restrooms and all six floors of the hospital's Broadway Building. After one hour stretched to five, Peggy's fear grew frantic. Could the man have up and walked out? Surely not in his condition. She glanced out the windows every so often, gauging how much the heat was affecting the passersby. No, he had to be inside.

But where?

She spun in place, then came to a full stop in mind and body. Her skin tingled as if hit by a bucketful of cold water. Nobody knew Clay like she did. She walked on stilted legs to the elevator bay, staring at the directory. Who had Clay been during their marriage? Not the agnostic he made himself out to be, but the quiet observer who had seen her lean on God, love Him, put Him first in her life over friendships and teenage gossip and bad behavior, back when they were only kids. He used to ask her to pray for him every time he got on a bronc, every time he had an injury. She'd seen his love for God grow, until the divorce cut him at his knees and shattered his faith in God.

She pushed the elevator button, rode the car down, and headed for the chapel. *Please.*

With a shuddering breath, she nudged the door open.

There Clay sat, in the front row, opposite the cross with Jesus still nailed to it. Her tightly coiled muscles relaxed. Clay's head was bowed, his hands folded in his lap. She slipped into the silent room, her gaze rising from Clay back to the cross.

Jesus.

Once again her skin tingled, but this time she may as well have been thrown into an arctic lake for the shock of it. The Holy Spirit was talking, and she was caught dead to rights. She wouldn't make the mistake of not listening this time.

Jesus had died for sinners, for her sin—her selfishness, deception, and greed. Every mistake of her last four years had been piled onto that tortured body two thousand years ago and taken to the grave.

Even if Peggy had been the only one to save, Christ still would have endured the horror of that death for her—and risen victorious.

The truth slayed her. *He set me free.* Her attention fluttered back to Clay, bowed and broken and wronged.

And that is what I did with my freedom. Her heart retreated into a tight, cramped ball in her chest.

Weak and humbled, she moved up behind Clay and sat in the pew behind him.

It was time she asked forgiveness for her part in Clay's torment, this blow to his heart and mind and faith.

She bowed her head, praying in her mind. *Please forgive me, Lord. How can I share my faith with others when I am such a bad example? I haven't prayed since I started this farce. The fault is mine and mine alone. Please help Clay to regain his health, his faith in you, his faith in me. I don't know how I can even ask this, but I ask that you bring his heart back to you, then back to me, Lord. You know I love him. Please give me a chance to prove my love to him. Help him to trust me again. In Your name, Jesus, I pray.*

When she raised her head with tears welling in her eyes, Clay had turned in his seat. The look in his eyes was stark and hate-filled. His hours in the chapel hadn't softened his feelings toward her one bit.

"What are you doing here?" The words were punitive, an arrow to the heart. Just what she deserved.

"I've come to find you. Bring you back to your room. The doctor and nurses have all been looking."

He scoffed. "The doctor. Your doctor, not mine."

She searched for words that could possibly work. "Come back with me, Clay. You must be hungry, tired. It's nearly supper-time now."

"I remember a wedding. A honeymoon on the rodeo circuit. You were with me. We are...were married, weren't we?"

"Yes. We were married." She didn't want to rehash their painful past. He would just hate her more. But he deserved the truth, and he'd get it.

"So, when did it happen? The divorce?"

She swallowed hard, wished she had water with her. Rising from the pew behind Clay, she scooted into his pew, sitting next to him.

He slid backwards a bit, slashing her heart. She knew it wouldn't be the only time during this conversation. Squaring her shoulders, she began. "We were married right out of high school. Had a year and a half together. It was blissful for that first year. Going into the second, not so much. We'll talk about that another time. By the end of the rodeo season in '57..." She wasn't ready to tell him she'd been the one to ask for a divorce. It hurt too much. "We got a divorce."

"*1957?* This is 1962, Peggy." Uncertainty washed over his face. "Isn't it?"

"Yes, we're in July of 1962."

"We've been divorced for *five years?*"

"Four...and a half," Peggy said meekly.

"And you're here acting as my wife?" He ran a hand through his too long hair. "Why?" He slid back a bit farther. "No wonder you didn't want me to touch you, kiss you. You let me embarrass myself."

Had she done that? *Oh, Lord, help me.* But even as she prayed that prayer she knew she didn't deserve God's help. "Clay, listen..."

"No." He jumped up and bashed his knees on the front pew from his sheer size. He only winced, then backed out of the pew all together. "I can't believe a word you're saying. Why, Peggy? Why did you act like my wife if you aren't?"

His question ignited anger inside her. No, fury. "I am your wife. In my mind, I still am. Don't say I'm just acting."

"You are acting. We've been divorced for five years, *Margaret*."

The name turned her stomach.

"Why would you do this?"

The hate in his eyes and the disgust twisting his mouth made her want to wail.

Feeling deboned, she nonetheless rose and threaded her way toward him. "You were hurt. Clint and I found you, took you directly to the clinic in West Yellowstone. To Dr. Barnes. We had to get you here where you could be treated for head trauma. I wanted to help you, Clay. Help you!"

He looked about ready to fall down, he was so weak. This was way too much activity for him yet. She tentatively reached for him with one hand. "Let's get you back to bed. You need rest."

"I'm not done. I want to know what happened. Why you were there. Where you've been all these years." He ran a hand down his face. "Wait a minute. You weren't just helping me as my wife, were you?"

She shook her head.

"Are you an actual physical therapist like Mary, not just her assistant?"

"Yes. I went to school right after we divorced. You're my patient."

He backed a little farther. Looked ready to escape all together. "For the head trauma? That doesn't make sense."

"No. You tore your Achilles…again. I came to the ranch to give it therapy…give you therapy."

"None of this is making any sense to me, Peggy. I need you to start from the beginning."

Should she placate him by continuing this conversation? He needed rest. "Why did you come to the chapel, Clay?"

He looked taken aback by the change of topic. When she thought he wouldn't answer, he finally did. "I figured I'd get answers here."

"You prayed?"

He looked away from her probing stare. Shook his head.

She felt her rising frustration morph into anger. "What? Did you think you'd get answers just from sitting here? By osmosis?"

Angry eyes slid back to hers. "I'm a country bumpkin, Peggy Sue." This was colossal scorn. "I don't know what 'osmosis' means."

Yeah, playing the 'stupid cowboy' was his usual default. "You're full of you-know-what, Clayton Cooper. You do know what 'osmosis' means. I'm going back to your room. Maybe you should try actually praying this time, before you return."

Mustering up her courage to actually walk out, she made it to the door and pulled it open. Couldn't quite walk through without turning back. "I truly wanted to help you, Clay. The hospital wouldn't have let me stay with you or make decisions for your care if they thought I wasn't a relative. That's why I did it." He didn't need to know she longed to play the part for a lifetime.

The strength he'd used to remain standing, to fight back, bled out of him. He plunked back down on one pew and rested his arms on the back of another. Just before closing the door, she saw him plant his forehead on his arms. She left him to wrestle with his demons. She had her own.

• • •

Clay's mind rifled through tangled memories, trying to connect the dots. For better or worse, Peggy had just unlocked a great gate in his mind, and entire chunks of his past life were tumbling in.

He'd been captivated by Margaret Ann Sassman since the first moment he laid eyes on her, her first day as a Sundance High School senior. She was so alive and gentle, a perfect friend, grounded in her love for God. She thought he hated that about her, when all the while it was the thing he loved most about her. Her passion for Christ had always surpassed everything else in her life. And she'd had plenty of passions—for learning, for giving, for healing, for him.

She was the first person to make him *feel* clear through. Before that he'd only ever been the daredevil, the one likely to die young from one of his stupid escapades. They'd been drawn to each other, him and her. He needed to be loved and nurtured. She needed a taste of the unpredictable and rush of excitement.

And now, here she was. With him. Again.

He rubbed his temples, trying to force memories into their proper places within his damaged mind. After high school, who had they become? His passion for her never changed. His heart told him that. They had continued to be a couple. He remembered their wedding, a honeymoon, days upon days of travel…with the rodeo. What he didn't remember was what had happened to them. Why had they divorced? No matter how hard he worked at it, he couldn't get his brain to snap that puzzle piece into place.

Had their marriage only been a sham of needs and passions? Because he knew those emotions were still alive and well. The last few weeks had shown him that. Obviously they were still drawn together, inescapably so.

Was Peggy right? Should he pray? It seemed to him he'd always left that part to his wife.

He shifted his backside on the hard bench, threaded his fingers together. But that posture didn't feel right. Finally, full of nerves and awkwardness, he sighed and planted his head in his hands, elbows drilling holes in his knees. *Dear God. I'm Clay.* Well, that was dumb. Of course the Almighty would know who he was.

Maybe he should be more reverent. He rose from the pew and swayed up to the pulpit just under the cross. Dropped to his knees. Pain shot up when his kneecaps hit the wood, too hard. He winced, sloughed it off, then stared up at the image before him. Tried to summon the facts Peggy had told him about Jesus.

He is God's son.

He is God and man.

He died on the cross when he could have called down a legion of Angels to save Him. Clay remembered that part. Had looked up how many a legion was—six thousand.

He rose from the dead—the grave—after three days.

He is seated at the right hand of God the Father.

He intercedes for the saints—those who receive His offered gift of Eternal Life.

Seemed simple, yet the Bible said it confounded the wise. Not that Clay was wise. No. The way he'd lived… Each new memory confirmed just how unwise he was.

He bowed his head again. *Dear God. As I begin to remember my past, I realize I have blundered my way through life. Made a mess of most things. Help me to live right. Thank you for my second chance. Now, about Peggy…*

Nope. He couldn't put anything into words with the fury still radiating within him. Or was it hurt? Embarrassment? All of the above?

Time might help. He doubted it. Best thing to do was thank her for her help all these months and leave her behind. The doctor had said she lived in Missoula now. Worked here. She had a life here.

So leave her behind he would.

CHAPTER 26

B ruce opened the creaking back door to the abandoned bunkhouse on the old Peterson spread. He didn't have to wonder why he'd been summoned to this property. It bordered the Cooper Bar-6 Ranch.

Batting away spider webs, he made his way toward the back room as instructed, to the man with the voice. That ominous voice on the other side of his motel room door.

Beside him, a torn sheet of plastic trembled over a broken window, then pivoted into the room and reached for him with streaming fingers. He jumped, the breeze hot on his skin, a shiver racing clear down to his toes. Yeah. Okay, he was spooked—by the haunted feel of this place, by the company he now kept, by the warrant on his head for his mother's murder, by the clock ticking down until Clayton Cooper positively ID'd him in a court of law.

Dim sunlight sliced between old boards that made up the walls around him. He moved forward at a snail's pace toward the far corner, a thin white light showing under the back room's door.

He halted in front of the door. Raised a trembling fist. Knocked.

The same voice bade him enter.

He reached for the door knob, turned it. The door opened silently on well-oiled hinges. He blinked against light that nearly blinded him from overhead fluorescents. Made him wonder why he'd had to swim through cobwebs when this room was so immaculately clean. The burly man sat behind a big mahogany desk. The same voice, the same face. This time dressed in a gray power suit, rigid back, and air of inborn confidence giving him an air of kingship.

"Sit down, Mr. Smith." The man gestured toward the swivel chair in front of the desk. The door at the man's back explained how he'd gotten in here without even one web lingering on his lapel.

He sat forward, linked his fingers. "We're having a particularly dry summer this year, don't you agree?"

Just at the mention of it, Bruce's throat went dry. He swallowed painfully, then nodded as his gaze drifted from the valuable portraits on the walls to the Ficus tree in the corner to the standing globe next to the desk.

"Do you have your plans in place?"

Bruce was so startled by the question he nearly missed the .45 revolver sitting with the barrel facing him only half a foot away from his employer's right hand. Without moving his head, he shifted his gaze to the man's. His hard stare made him fidget. "Uh…I have the plans you gave me."

"What's the matter, Mr. Smith. Worried you can't pull it off?"

Yeah, he worried about that, and so much more. He'd fumbled the Clayton Cooper job and only killed his mother on accident. This man's plan was an atomic explosion compared to his fizzled little firecrackers.

There was no backing out now. Not with this guy—or he was sure to end up burning in Hell earlier than expected, like a good many other of the scoundrel's minions. Which he had become. Oh, how he longed to go back to his dead-end job with nothing to show for his life.

"Nah, I got this." He gulped. Wished he'd been offered a glass of water.

"Excellent. Mr. Cooper's coming home."

Bruce's eyes about bugged out of his head. "Wha—?"

The man shrugged. "I have people"—he twirled his finger—"everywhere. I'll let you know what day to expect him." The man's laughter rang out so loud it made Bruce jump.

Clayton Cooper was coming home? He had another shot at putting him down.

The man flashed a Cheshire grin. "That's right. Cooper's coming home to roost. Briefly. Right?"

Bruce nodded, but only weakly, suddenly overwhelmed. He wasn't cut out for this.

The man laughed. "Don't worry. You won't have to go after him mano a mano."

Was he so easy to read?

"You just have to snatch up his woman and lure him directly into that fire you're going to set. I'm sure he's missed the heat."

The last round of laughter had Bruce on his feet and out the door.

• • •

Peggy flipped the pages of her magazine too fast. One tore out. Whoops. She hadn't even remembered reading that page. She stuffed the page back in. It had already been fifteen minutes. She was sure Clay would have skipped the prayer and left the chapel right on her heels.

Flip. Another page of nondescript blather.

She stewed in the excruciating netherworld of rationalization and regret. The typeset blurred under her stare. *Flip. Flip.*

She looked at the clock again. Thirty minutes. Would he return at all? Or leave the hospital and hitch a ride back home?

Her crossed leg swung back and forth. She pushed her hair out of her face. Flipped another couple of pages. Gad she was exhausted. The months of playing this part of *wife* had worn her down. The real problem was, her heart was on her sleeve, and Clay had rubbed it raw.

Another glance at the clock told her forty minutes had passed. Uncrossing her leg, she slammed her foot back to the floor. She was going to have to go get him. He needed rest. She heaved a breath, then shot to her feet. *Here we go.*

The door pushed open. Peggy sucked in a quick breath. Clay or a nurse?

Clay entered.

Relief and trepidation took turns. At least he seemed calmer.

"Hello, Clay. It's nice to have you back." Definitely meek. Un-Peggy-like.

"Nice." He scoffed. "Such a bland word for you."

He was after banter, she knew that. Whenever he was frustrated or angry, he'd always sparred with her verbally. Now wasn't the time for that.

She waited until he came near, then took hold of his arms and turned him toward the bed. "Have a rest. We'll talk later."

Surprisingly, he didn't argue, but instead planted one knee on the bed and fell face first on top of the blanket. His breathing deepened instantly.

One problem solved. Now for the bigger one: who was going to drive Clay home? With a quick glance at Clay to confirm he was fast asleep, she tiptoed quietly out of the room.

Part of her wanted to manipulate her way into the driver's seat. But her conscience, so recently restored by the Lord, bade her submit to the natural course of things, no matter what. Unsettled and shamefully undecided, she banged out the front door of the hospital to stand under the sunshine, but only choked on the thick July air. Unusual though humidity was for Missoula, she couldn't wait to get back to her hot and dry hometown, one way or another.

The telephone booth by the street was unoccupied. She slipped in, leaving the door open so as not to suffocate. The operator connected her to Brand.

"Hey, sis. How's my brother doin'?"

Sis. He couldn't know how good that sounded to her. "Dr. Harris is discharging him in two days."

"What? Already? He just woke up a few weeks ago. He's doing that good?"

"That's what the doctor says." She anxiously wrapped the cord around her fingers, then shook it off remembering where she was. "Listen, I know we have your truck here so I can drive him home, but it's gotten complicated."

"Complicated, how?"

"Well." She hesitated. Decision time. Manipulate or submit? She teetered on the brink, then slid into calm resolve. She told Brand everything. It took quite a few minutes and twenty more coins, but when she ended her story, she waited for a response.

Nothing.

Oh no, had the connection dropped while she was spilling her guts? "Brand? You still there?"

"You lied the whole time? Didn't think you had it in you." His voice was low and carried a distinct tone of disappointment.

She sighed. Great example of a person who loved God, wasn't she? *I'm so sorry, Lord.* "I know. I was wrong." Sadly, if she had to do it again, she still wasn't certain she'd be strong enough to let God handle it entirely. What did that say about her? And her faith?

"Brand?"

He breathed on the other end of the line, processing.

Rats, now she wanted to cry. God would have worked out something else for Clay. And it would have turned out better, as only the Almighty could accomplish. When would she learn to stop getting in the way of God's design?

Finally Brand said, "I wish I were available to come and get him."

Peggy dared to hope a little.

"The problem is," Brand continued, "without Dad and Rebecca and Bronc, we're swamped over here. He'll just have to make do with you."

Make do with you. She got her wish, but Brand's words scraped all the way down her spine like broken glass.

"Do you think you can get his discharge papers here all right, so we can study them? We need to know how to take care of him from here on out."

She swallowed. Didn't help. "Of course. I'm sorry, Brand. I didn't know what else to do."

"You didn't, huh?" Brand exhaled into the phone. "I'll get in touch with Clint. Make sure he knows not to drive Clay if he calls. No need for him to get involved with our family business anymore. He's done enough."

When did this boy get so wise...or so wounding?

She wanted to hang up on him, but knew whatever he dished out, she deserved. "We'll leave by Saturday, likely, so if we're not home by Tuesday at the latest, better come find us. We'll take the northern route, of course."

The operator came on the line. "Deposit another ten cents."

"Bye, Brand," she said instead and hung up.

Taking a detour to the cafeteria for supper, Peggy moseyed into the large room of milling people. Most wore white coats or scrubs. She pushed her tray down the line, setting a bowl of hot stew, bread and butter, and then a cup of coffee on it. Finally, she nestled into a corner table where she could lick her wounds. She pushed the stew around in the bowl. Her stomach seemed to reject what little she actually ate.

In two days, she and Clay would be on their way home. Until then, would Clay kick her out of his room, make her hole up at Mary's in the meantime? But that was minor. The bigger question was, would she be welcome at Cooper Ranch?

"May I join you?"

The familiar voice of Dr. Harris brought her eyes up from the steaming bowl of food she'd only been staring at while her mind waded through her hopeless options.

Pressing her lips together, she decided to be the bigger person. She gestured to the chair across from her.

He chose the one next to her instead.

Putting his hand over hers, he said, "Maggie, I need to talk to you."

She pulled her hand out from under his and scooted her chair back, twisting it to get a better view of him. Keeping her knees from bumping his.

"So, talk."

He huffed a breath. "I want to know what you're planning to do once I discharge Clayton?"

Lifting her coffee to her lips, she took her time with the sip. "I already told you. I plan to drive him home to Sundance."

"Well, I took care of that. You can stay in Missoula now." The plea on his face said, 'with me.'

Panic widened her eyes. "Took care of it, how?"

"I've called his father in California. Explained he needed a ride."

"You what?" She jumped to her feet, nearly upending the table. Her bowl careened toward the doctor, but he caught it with one hand. Only a small amount splattered his fingers. Too bad. She wanted it to dump in his lap. "Why would you do that? He's needed in California. You had no right!"

He was wiping his hand of the stew as he shushed her. "Simmer down. He's not coming here. He's calling his sons in Wyoming. One of them will likely come after him."

She plunked back down in the seat she'd vacated and glared. "I already told you I'd be driving him home."

A sympathetic look came over him. "I spoke with Clayton. He doesn't want you to drive him home. I'm his doctor, so I handled it for him."

Tears burned the backs of her eyes, but she let anger push them back. "Handled it, or handled me right out of the picture?"

She pressed her fingers into her eyes, breathed for a few seconds before she looked back up. Lowering her voice, she said, "Listen…Daniel…"

He looked supremely happy she'd used his first name.

"Thank you for watching out for me all these months. For making sure I got fresh air. For buying suppers for me. For the conversation. It meant a lot to me. Kept me hopeful. Grounded. And, thank you for all you've done for Clay."

A muscle twitched in his jaw, his mouth set in a grim line.

"But the truth is, I gave my heart to Clayton Cooper years ago. I never got it back. Even though Clay wants nothing to do with me—" She wanted to say 'no thanks to you,' but that wouldn't be true. It was no thanks to her. "—the truth is, I'm not interested in a relationship with anyone else. I don't have the heart for it. Literally."

The doctor shifted his jaw side to side. Studied her face. Finally, he sighed. "I understand. I don't like it, but I understand. If you ever want to come back to Missoula—"

She scowled.

"—to *work*, you'll always be welcome here. I enjoyed my time with you, Maggie. I care a lot for you. I want you to know that. I hope you'll come back."

Without another word, she rose, gave the doctor a kiss on the cheek, and walked straight back to the telephone booth outside. Peggy had the operator make a collect call to California. She would make sure Cord Cooper knew she would take care of his son.

CHAPTER 27

Clay hadn't felt this low since he'd awoken from the coma. Stuffing what little he had in his small satchel, he pondered which of his brothers would take the time to pick him up.

The door opened.

Clay glanced over his shoulder, saw Peggy, then went back to his task.

"None of your brothers are coming. I called your dad and let him know not to send them."

"You did what?" Clay spouted, straightening as he turned. He growled, then threw down the shirt in his hand. "Why would you do that? How will I get home?"

"I'll drive you. We have Brand's truck, remember?"

He didn't remember. But he didn't want her to drive him anyway. He wanted to be as far away from Margaret Ann as his broken down body could carry him. "No."

"What do you mean, no?"

"I mean, no. I'll figure out another way. You live here. Work here. Have your doctor-friend here."

Peggy huffed an exasperated breath.

She was a stubborn little thing. The last thing he needed was to spend two days in close quarters with her on a drive home.

"Clay…"

"Whatever you're about to say, save it." He finished with the packing and set his duffle by the door. He was ready for his discharge papers. "I'll call Clint."

"He's not available, either."

Clay swung toward her and stuffed his hands on his hips. "What the…? Did you warn him off too?"

She stood, not the least bit scared of his tirade or him. "Yes. Well, Brand did. Felt he'd done enough for this family."

A knock came on the doorjamb, just before Dr. Harris strolled in. Looked like he hadn't slept in days. Clay could relate.

"Here's your discharge papers. Marie will be in to handle the rest. I just wanted to give you a bit of advice before you go." The doctor glanced at Peggy with such longing in his eyes, he wanted to give him a punch rather than a listen.

"Fine. I'm listening."

"You've had a serious injury, Clayton. The likelihood is you won't be the man you used to be. You won't remember as much. You won't get around the same way. Things will frustrate you because either your body or your brain won't cooperate with your own agenda. Be kind to yourself. Take it slow. You'll be a different version of yourself, but you'll do just fine if you allow yourself time to fully heal. Be patient. The paperwork will explain a lot more about head injuries and the aftermath. I'm assuming you got a ride." His eyes landed on Peggy. She remained silent. "Do you have any questions before you head out?"

Oh, he had questions. If he left Peggy behind, would she in fact fall in love with the doctor? Make a life with him? Start a career at St. Patrick's and never come back to Sundance? Or him?

The idea of never seeing Peggy again gave him a fierce headache of a different sort. "No questions."

"That's good. Marie will be right in. Good luck to you." The doctor stuck out his hand. Clay took it and gave it a quick shake.

Marie came through the door and smiled.

The doctor looked to Peggy. "I'll just be down the hall…if you decide to stay…"

"She's not staying," Clay barked, so loudly they all jumped. "She's driving me home."

• • •

Clay stepped around the grill of Brand's truck, viewing its profile with admiration. "When did Brand buy this new toy?"

Peggy grimaced. She knew Clay would have trouble with memories, but this was the truck Clay himself had driven last. The short-term memories were the toughest to recoup, so the doctor had said. Still, it hurt her heart to watch it play out. "Oh, he hasn't had it very long. Pretty snazzy, isn't it?"

"Snazzy?" Clay laughed, and the wonderful sound bathed her in warm fuzzies. His smile remained fixed as he strolled around the truck, stopping to take a closer look at the wheels. "Looks like it's sitting higher." He spoke mostly to himself. Probably figured she didn't know anything about it.

"It's a four by four," she said.

"A what?"

"Four-wheel drive."

He straightened to full height, looking over at her across the bed. "No such thing on stock trucks," he said before running a hand over the two-tone paint job.

"There is now. Too bad it's summer. You'd get a kick out of how well it handles in deep snow."

His head swung up, a surprised smile on his face. "You've driven it?"

"Of course," she said and grinned back. "Maybe we'll get a chance to go off road somewhere on our drive back and I can show you."

"Huh. Maybe." His lip tilted up on one side, and he nodded, looking impressed.

She beamed a little. "We should get going. We have a long trip ahead."

"Gimme the keys. I'll drive."

Peggy unlocked the driver's side and pulled herself in. Then she reached over and tugged the lock knob up on his side. "No, you won't," she said as he opened that door. "No driving for a few months, the doctor said."

"Suggested. There's a difference."

"Well, it won't be happening on this trip. Stuff your suitcase behind the seat where mine is, then we'll be on our way."

He rolled his eyes and did as she said. Compliant Clay was a new phenomena. There was a time she had to use every female wile in her coffer to get her way. Maybe she'd actually enjoy this new Clay. Then again…

Once headed east on Highway 90 on their way to Sundance through Bozeman and Billings, they settled into a peaceful silence. It must have been clear to Clay that she had a handle on driving Brand's truck. Of course, she'd done most of the driving back when Clay rode the rodeo circuit, and that was pulling a trailer.

Three hours passed with little to no conversation. Clay dozed most of the time. She was happy for that. At least they weren't arguing, although that sadly would have been a return to the normalcy of years gone by.

Peggy navigated a blind curve, scanning for pronghorn that were known to leap across the road without warning. Out of nowhere, Clay jerked awake, his hands hitting the dash.

Peggy jumped, holding fast to the steering wheel, though her heart was in her throat. "For Pete's sake, Clay. What was that all about? Scared the life out of me."

"Where are we?"

The road dipped into another turn. She kept her gaze straight ahead. "Just coming up on Bozeman. Are you all right?"

"No, I'm not all right." He scraped a hand through his hair.

She chanced a glance in his direction before clamping her gaze back on the road, then took a double take. The scowl at her, plastered on his face, took her aback. "What's wrong?"

"*What's wrong?* Shall I make a list?"

"Hold on. Before you get into a lecture, what woke you so suddenly?"

"I thought someone was about to hit us."

"Us? Or you?" Maybe he was reliving the blow to his head.

His silence made her glance over again. He fidgeted in the seat. Tried to straighten, twisted slightly, and jammed a palm to the ceiling. Then he dropped his hand and turned toward the windshield again.

"Clay, what is it?"

"The hell, Peggy. For days I've racked my sorry brain for answers on why I'd be in favor of a divorce. Figured it had to be mutual." He turned completely in the seat. She couldn't see his fury, but she could feel the heat rolling off him. "It wasn't, was it? It was you! You asked for a divorce! Demanded it!"

Why did he have to remember this now? "Clay—"

"No! No apologizing, pleading, or cajoling. You were famous for that. That much I remember now. If you didn't get your way, you knew exactly how to wear me down." He rasped both hands down his face and growled into his hands. "You even got me to agree to a divorce. A damn divorce, Peggy!"

This was going to be war. Seeing a truck stop coming up, she took her opportunity. "We need gas, and we need to talk, so I'm pulling off. Hold that thought, will you?"

"See? You're doing it right now. Setting me up for a conversation you have time to think through. Well, I'm not playing that game anymore, hear me?"

In her peripheral vision she saw him rub the left side of his head. Glanced in time to see him grimace.

"Clay, please calm down. This isn't good for your head. Please."

"Don't tell me what to do, Twinkie! We're not married anymore." His gulp resonated in the close quarters. He was breathing hard, like he'd run a foot race up the highway. If he didn't calm down she worried he'd have a stroke. For sure she wouldn't be able to reason with him. He was too far past that.

Her eyes filled; the road blurred. She pressed the back of a hand to her nose.

"Don't give me those tears. I'm not gonna fall for it," he said on a ragged breath.

She kept it together long enough to ease off the highway and pull in near a pump, then looked Clay in the eye. In as calm a voice as she could muster, she said, "Clay. Why don't you go use the men's room. I'll get gas, then we can park and finish this conversation."

She pushed the gear shifter to neutral and turned off the ignition, cringing inside, because Clay hadn't budged. She glanced over. His eyes were on fire, his face beet red. Sweat glistened on his neck and forehead. Finally, without another word, he opened the door and let himself out.

• • •

Clay crashed through the metal door to the restroom, kicking it closed behind him. His breathing was erratic, his head throbbed, his hands trembled. He moved around the small space like a caged cougar. What was wrong with him?

Taking three deep breaths, he worked at settling his mind. Ever since waking from the coma, it had been impossible to order his thoughts. Travel made it ten times worse. The movement of the truck, the onslaught of oncoming traffic, the close quarters with the woman who had him on edge—it all added to the nauseating throb in his head.

He took his time in the restroom, trying to cool himself down. As he washed his trembling hands, he looked up into the scratched mirror and gasped. One look at his ruddy face and sweat-soaked hair, he didn't have to wonder if he'd scared the living daylights out of Peggy. His outburst was enough to send her skidding off the road, yet she'd remained cool as a cucumber.

Had she been that way when she demanded that divorce? Self-composed and calm?

Why had she left him?

What had possessed her to give up on them?

Divorce was not something his family ever considered. Not ever. It got drilled into each of the Cooper sons that if they married, it was for life. The word divorce could never be spoken, it was such a forbidden subject. Yet, his own wife had decided all by herself it was best. And he'd let her.

Fury rose all over again, stoking the heat inside him. She was right, they needed to duke this out. And if she were a man, he'd let his fists do the talking.

Grabbing the edge of the grungy sink, he squeezed, and cringed at the splitting pain in his head. Wouldn't it be better—easier—to let it go? No. Even through the throb, he needed to know why. And he needed to know why he'd never done anything about it in all these years.

Pulling in a final deep breath and holding it in his lungs until he couldn't any longer, he let it burst out. Panted a few breaths. Lightheadedness still plagued him. He dragged his gaze back up to his reflection, misshapen by the warped mirror. It seemed to fit, how distorted he looked. Clayton Cooper, damaged once again. Driving back to a home he'd worked hard to escape, only to be dragged back. Riding in his brother's newer truck because his wouldn't make the trip. And being cared for by the woman who'd divorced his sorry ass.

He didn't belong anywhere, own anything, or have anyone.

So, why bother arguing with Peggy about their past. What did it matter anyway? The ball of anger he instinctively knew he'd lived with for so long shrank away, taking his will to fight back with it. He slipped his hands off the sink, washed them again, and let them drip as he let himself out the door.

Before leaving the restroom, his eyes scanned the area, a habit he'd learned as a smokejumper. *Smokejumper.* Abruptly, one memory after the next slid in of his smokejumping days. No, years. He'd done that for a long time. In Alaska. He'd enjoyed it. It had given him purpose. It was good to grab onto a memory that didn't decimate him for a change.

But as he tugged his mind out of his thoughts and to the here and now, his attention caught on their truck, still parked at the pump.

No Peggy pumping gas. No one in the cab.

He glanced about. Would she have gone into the restaurant? Without him? Not likely.

Panic set in. Sudden and raw.

A man walked by him. Clay grabbed his arm. An angry glare met him but he ignored it. "Have you seen a petite blond woman, 'bout so high?" He brought his hand to his shoulder.

The man yanked his arm away from Clay, then his expression softened. "No. Have you tried inside?"

Clay shook his head and took off for the front door to the trucker's café. He sped through the whole restaurant, looking into each face at every booth. Nothing.

"May I help you?" a waitress asked, pausing as she rang up a bill.

"I'm looking for my…wife. Blond. Petite. In denim pedal pushers and a flowery blouse."

"Don't know, mister. You can look around if you want."

She returned to collecting money, and Clay wandered quickly to the rear of the café. He stood in front of a gal just leaving the restroom in the back. "Is there a blond lady in there?"

Startled at first, the young woman stopped and stared up at him. A slow smile spread across her face, and she fluttered her lashes.

He didn't have time for this. "Well?" He knew he was being rude and could care less.

She huffed a small breath. "No one else in there."

He didn't bother to thank her, just pulled an about face and trolled back through the crowd, slamming through the door back into the heat of the day. He stood outside and searched the station again. Where was she?

"Are you the one looking for the blond woman?" an elderly lady leaning on a cane asked.

He nodded.

"Well, there's one in that big rig." She pointed a gnarly finger. "That man forced her up into the seat and slammed the door in her face." Her nose wrinkled in disgust. "He was not nice."

Clay took off at a run, sprinting past the Peterbilt's grill and around to the driver's side. The driver was just hauling himself up into the rig when Clay grabbed the back of his shirt and yanked him back down.

"What the—" The stocky man let out a string of foul words as he landed on his back between the truck and the pump he'd used. Clay leaned over and fisted the man's shirt, his other fist at the ready if didn't like his answer. "What are you doing with my wife?"

"Your what?"

"Clay, what's going on?" The sound of Peggy's voice from behind froze him. He glanced over a shoulder, and there she stood with a bewildered expression. She glanced at the man on the ground, then raised her gaze back to his with fury behind her eyes.

"What are you doing?" She dashed to him and grabbed at the arm that had a hold of the man's shirt.

"He took you." When the words hit his own ears, he grimaced. Obviously, the driver hadn't taken her. He cursed. This was not going to end well.

"What are you talking about?"

Clay rocked back and came to his feet, reaching down to help the man up. But the man batted his hand away and rolled to his side before wrestling himself upright. "Sorry," Clay mumbled, once he'd glanced in the cab to see a blond woman who was distinctly not Peggy.

"Come on, Clay. Let's go," Peggy said, tugging him away from the scene.

Numbly, he followed Peggy's lead. Their truck was now parked adjacent to the rig. Peggy shoved him in, then she ran around the grill and jumped in the driver's side. They sped away.

"What in the world were you doing?"

Peggy was driving like a mad woman.

"Slow down. You're gonna kill us!"

"*I'm* going to kill us? What were you doing to that poor man? And why?"

His head was spinning, his thoughts flung in every direction. What made him think Peggy had been taken? He frowned, rasped a hand down his face. She was nowhere to be found, that's why. "Where the heck were you?"

"Clay, for crying out loud. I was in the restroom. It took me a little longer because there was a line. What happened?"

He rubbed his face and grappled with the one unassailable truth he'd just learned. The idea of a life without Peggy threw him into a flat panic.

CHAPTER 28

In order to keep Clay from noticing Peggy's shaking hands, she gripped the steering wheel tighter. What had he been thinking, attacking that stranger? If Clay had been at full strength… Peggy didn't want to think of what would have happened. The man was able to rise to his feet and dust himself off. For that, Peggy thanked the Lord.

"Grip that wheel any harder and you'll break it. Or your hands," Clay said. Was that humor in his voice?

"I'm glad you think this is funny."

"Not funny." Clay pushed against the floorboard, sitting straighter in the seat. Out of the corner of her eye, she saw him fist his hands against his thighs. "I thought he took you, Peggy."

She glanced at Clay, sure that confusion and horror comingled in her expression. "Why would you think that?" Forcing her shoulders to relax a little, she tried again. This time lowering her voice by an octave or two. "Start from the beginning."

He heaved a deep breath, sounding exasperated. She knew how he felt.

"I came out of the restroom and you weren't in the truck, pumping gas, or anywhere else. I asked people. Walked through the restaurant."

He paused.

She wanted to prod him, but decided to let him gather his thoughts.

"Then this little old lady came up to me. Told me she saw the trucker push a blonde into his truck and slam the door on her. I figured it had to be you. I snapped."

Her heart quivered in awe. She reached over and grasped his hand. "Thank you. I think. It was sweet."

"Sure, that's me. Sweet."

"Well, you know what I mean. It was an admirable effort."

Red and blue light flashed in her rearview mirror. She groaned.

"What's up?" Clay said, saw where her eyes were focused, then twisted around. "Crap. A sheriff."

"'Fraid so." Peggy pulled over. A deputy sheriff strode up to the window. She rolled it down and peered up with a smile. "Hello, sir. Beautiful day." Yeah, that sounded pretty pathetic.

"Ma'am." He tapped his hat brim. "License, please. This your vehicle?"

"Um. No. But it's his brother's." She nodded toward Clay.

"Then I'll need license *and* registration."

Clay snatched up her purse and handed it to her, then went after the registration in the glove box. Her fingers trembled as she peeled her license out of her wallet. She gave it to the deputy, then handed over the registration Clay found.

The deputy perused the information, then offered it back and bent to look at Clay. "You the man who caused the ruckus at the truck stop?"

"Uh…" Clay started.

"Listen, officer—" Peggy said.

"Deputy."

"Sorry. Deputy. I can explain. You see, Clay here—"

"That's all I needed to know. Follow me, please."

"What? Where?" Peggy said.

"To the station. We'll handle the questions there. Stay close behind." He turned away and strode back to his car. When his vehicle moved around her, light still strobing, she followed.

Clay cursed a blue streak. "They're going to arrest me."

"They are *not* going to arrest you. Let me handle this. As your caregiver."

"My *caregiver*? I'm not disabled. And I'm not a mental case. I'll handle this. Besides, what you said gave me away. It's your fault we're having to do this."

"My fault? Who was the one who assaulted a strange man?"

"*Peggy…*" That was Clay's commanding voice, from long ago. She never won when he used that tone.

She rolled her eyes and shook her head. "Fine. Handle it."

Peggy followed the deputy to Bozeman and pulled into the station beside him. "Well, here goes."

Expecting a bustling station, they instead got a large room with a couple of desks, chairs, a box that looked like a two-way radio, a large chalk board with messy handwriting all over it, and random clothing and jackets hanging from coat trees. There was one door with bold letters: SHERIFF, written across the frosted glass. So not what she expected. But what did she know? She'd never been in a sheriff's office before.

They followed the deputy to the desk in the corner. "Have a seat. We'll wait here for Mr. Flint."

Peggy waited for Clay to 'handle' it.

Clay rubbed his palms against his thighs. "Is that the trucker I...never mind."

"So, you admit you slammed the man to the ground and threatened him."

Clay hopped to his feet, pressed his fingertips to the desk to lean in. "I thought he had my wife. What would you do?"

The deputy looked stunned to be asked that. Peggy was just as stunned. By Clay's passion, his protectiveness. He still had it.

The man pinched the bridge of his nose, then looked up at Clay with tired eyes. "I honestly don't know what I'd do. Why did you think he took your wife?"

"I couldn't find her. Then someone told me that man had forced a blonde into the cab of his truck. I had to move fast."

"Didn't take a good look at the woman first?"

Clay plopped back down. His gaze fell to the floor while he ran a hand down his face. One of her favorite gestures, seeing that large hand slip down that rugged face. It stirred all kinds of good memories in her.

"I understand that's something you would have done, Deputy. Logical, obvious." He looked up and pierced the officer in the eyes, staring a few beats. "That's not where my mind was. I regret if I hurt the man. But I couldn't let him take my wife. Had to stop him."

No one noticed Peggy melting in the seat next to him. He did all that for her? Her heart grew wings and took flight. *Oh, Clay…*

The deputy drew in a breath then blew it out, ruffling the scads of papers he had on his desk. "When Mr. Flint gets here, I'll try to convince him it was a mistake. See if we can get him to drop the charges."

"Thank you, sir. Appreciate it." Clay nodded.

The deputy nodded back.

And that was that. Men knew how to communicate easily. Peggy envied such a simple exchange.

The door to the office slammed open, and the stocky, scowling man entered, his face puffed up in anger. A blond woman trailed meekly behind him.

Clay jumped to his feet and stood facing him.

As they drew near, Peggy noticed greenish bruises on the woman's arms and one on her cheekbone she'd tried to cover with makeup.

By the single-minded march of the man, and the determined look on his face, Peggy knew what he had in mind. Before he could take a swing at Clay, she slipped in front of him.

That didn't stop the crazed man. Not at all. He took hold of her shoulder and shoved her out of his way. She stumbled over Clay's big foot and sailed off to the side. Clay must have leaped after her because the next thing she knew, he had his arm wrapped tight around her waist and somehow made a half-turn before hitting the hardwood floor with her on top. His head thwacked against the wood.

"No! Not your head!" she shrieked.

By then the deputy and sheriff—fresh out of his office—had lunged for the man and flattened him to the ground.

Peggy twisted her attention away from the commotion and centered her gaze back on Clay. He was still solid as an oak, though thin as an aspen. Peggy could feel every rib, every joint, each hipbone. Dark circles showed under his eyes. Even his lips had lost their fullness. She decided then and there, the minute they landed back at Cooper Bar-6, she was going to cook up a storm of bacon, biscuits and gravy, roast beef casserole… She wanted her beefy Clay back.

She sighed to herself. She wanted her Clay back, period.

"Uh…Peggy?"

His deep voice startled her out of her contemplation.

"Are you hurt, ma'am?" came the deputy's voice from above her. "Here, let me help you."

She didn't want to move. Now that most of Clay's memories had returned, when would she get another chance to be this close to him again?

Someone pulled her straight up and off of Clay anyway. Oh, she wanted to slap the intruder for ruining her moment. But she knew Clay would have nudged her off any second regardless.

Flushing, she pressed her palms down her front, then straightened her blouse while she watched the deputy help Clay to his feet.

"Please, let him sit."

"Peggy," Clay said in *that* voice.

The deputy frowned in confusion, looking from her to Clay and back again. She turned away from Clay's glare and faced the second-in-command. "Clay was in a coma for over six months. He woke up a little over a month ago."

The mouths of the sheriff and his deputy dropped open.

"That's right. Shocking, isn't it?" She nodded. "It's one reason why his brain is not processing things quite correctly yet." She walked over to Mr. Flint. The deputy got there first and held one of his arms. "I'm sorry if he hurt you, Mr. Flint, but as you just heard, Clay hasn't been himself."

"Listen, lady, I could give a d—"

Clay launched forward and stopped short of thumping his chest against the other man's. "Watch your mouth around my wife."

"Whoa, whoa, whoa, Mr. Cooper. Hold up now." The sheriff pulled Clay back by one of his arms.

Clay whipped his head toward the man, hand fisted, before seeing who it was and backing down.

Peggy slipped back into the space between Mr. Flint and Clay. "Is this your wife, Mr. Flint?" She gestured toward the other woman.

"What's it to you—"

Clay lunged forward again, but was caught short by the sheriff's steely grip.

"You see, I'm a medical professional. I know old injuries when I see them."

The room went still. The law enforcement men tuned in, as did Clay.

"She has old bruises on her arms and face. You want to explain that to the sheriff here?" Peggy kept her voice even and sweet, but she knew the belligerent man was getting the picture. His face drained of color almost as fast as the blonde's did.

"She's fine." Mr. Flint's gaze flicked to the sheriff.

"We'll see about that," the sheriff said. "In the meantime, are you planning to press charges against Mr. Cooper here? If not, I'm letting him go."

Mr. Flint looked from Clay to the sheriff and back again. If he pressed charges, they would all be there for a long while. Smarter than he looked, he said, "Nah. Let him go. He's frail anyways. He didn't hurt me none."

Clay puffed up over those words, but Peggy took his hand and faced the sheriff. "Can we go now?"

"He needs to sign this form, then you're free to go."

• • •

"It's another hour and a half to Billings. We'll stop there for the night." Their whole day had been wasted by Clay's stunt.

Clay grunted.

"Something on your mind, Mr. Cooper?"

"I hate you driving. I hate that my brain's all mixed up. I hate this dang headache. I hate I don't remember everything about us. I hate…"

"Me."

Clay turned his head toward her.

Peggy shrugged meekly. "I caught what you're not saying."

"I never said that. And it's not true."

"Oh, really? Do you remember how you treated me after a year of marriage, Clay? Then again after not seeing you for over four years?"

He tap, tap, tapped against the armrest. "Okay. You wanna talk? Let's talk."

Silence hummed right along with the engine. "Well?" she said.

"You headed down this particular skunk trail."

"Fine. I'll start then. I loved being married to you, Clay."

He half-choked on a cough.

"I did. Didn't love our life, particularly, but loved you and wanted to be near you."

"Could have fooled me."

"I thought you didn't remember us."

"I do remember, a lot. There are some holes, is all."

She nodded, went on. "After that first blissful year, you began to change."

"I changed? *I changed*? You changed, Twinkie. You didn't want to travel with me anymore. All you wanted to do was get home to Colt."

She stiffened, and inadvertently swerved the truck.

"Whoa. Maybe we should table this discussion until we hit Billings."

Positioning her hands at ten and two on the steering wheel again, she tried to calm the flare of anger.

When she could speak with a steady voice, she said, "Fine. Billings."

It would take her that long to figure a way to tell Clay the real reason she'd left him.

CHAPTER 29

They arrived, grabbed the last room available at the Homestead Park Inn, and beelined it for the corner pub before it closed. Exhaustion pulled at Peggy. She couldn't even imagine how Clay was keeping himself upright in the booth, especially after downing nearly three beers.

"Let's start with what you liked about being married to me," Clay said, a little flippantly.

Peggy eyed the mug in his hand. It brought all the bad memories back. "You might want to slow down. Head injury, remember?"

He swiped his mouth with the back of his hand and laughed. "My body's used to beer. Like yours is to Coca Cola."

"I don't drink that anymore." She took a sip of her coffee as if to put a point on that statement.

He brooded in silence. Took another gulp. "Answer my question, Sunbo."

Peggy warmed at the name. "I was in love with you, Clay." *Still am*, she thought to herself. "I liked everything about being married to you…for the first year." The last part she said nearly under her breath.

He waggled his eyebrows. That made her wince. Beer always did bring out his charm. The problem was, he was such a curmudgeon, it came off as phony…even creepy. This was a Clay she didn't particularly like.

"You want to know my favorite thing about being married to you?" he said with a wicked look in his eyes.

"I already know." She couldn't seem to stop the small smile that crept onto her mouth.

His lips crooked up on one side, making her heart take a flip. "Yeah, you do. That was never our problem, was it?" His smile morphed into a sneer. "Want to tell me what was?"

"You truly don't know?"

"If I did, I don't anymore."

How could she have forgotten that? "I'm sorry. It's true, you may not remember what happened to us."

"Apparently not, since I only remember"—he swallowed hard—"good. Only the good. What happened to us?"

The sincere look on his face broke her heart. He really wanted to know. How could she put it into words without crushing him anew? "Oh, Clay. Maybe it would be best to leave it alone. Why would you want to hurt all over again."

He slapped a palm onto the table, making her jump. "Because I need to know. I thought we were in love, Peggy. I thought we were in it for the long haul. Why'd you bail?"

Sweat popped out at the hollow of her neck. This wasn't a good idea. She shot up an arrow prayer. *Please, Lord, if I have to tell him as he demands, help me to do it in the way you would have me do.*

Closing her eyes, she swallowed, then sipped her coffee and swallowed again, trying to stretch the moment. "How you were feeling was a mystery to me. I didn't know then, and I still don't know. That was part of our problem. You never talked to me."

"What the—"

"Wait." She held up a hand to stop him. "Let me back up. First of all, we were kids, Clay. Straight out of high school. What did we know?"

He settled a little at that, then nodded, so she went on.

"In my mind, we flounced around the country—"

His scowl flipped to a grin in an instant, and a hearty laugh burst from him. "Flounced? Is that what we did? We flounced?" He laughed again.

She chuckled with him. "Teenager, remember?"

The grin still riding his fine-looking face made her pause and watch for a few beats. Age had only enhanced his good looks. She could look at him all day.

"Okay, I get it. Go on."

At least the mood had lightened a bit. "I saw it as a huge adventure. We'd see the great US of A, you'd ride those crazy broncs you loved, I'd watch and beam because my handsome husband was a champion, and all would be well."

"Handsome, huh?" He winked. "Sounds good to me."

"It was. But then…" This conversation was going to batter both their hearts. Her shoulders slumped as the memory infused her.

"But then…?"

"Things changed. You changed. Travel changed. Your friends changed."

Clay sat forward, resting his elbows on the tabletop, linking his fingers. His expression was unreadable. "Want to elaborate?"

"I'll start with travel. We were always on the move. We never got to stay in one place and just enjoy each other. We'd arrive at a new city, you'd slam into duty, you'd ride, come back and beer it up with the boys, then clean up, fall into bed for a few minutes with me, and you were out. Then we were on the road again."

"A few minutes?"

"Out of all I just said, that's what you land on?"

"I took a lot more than a few minutes with you, Margaret."

She grimaced at the formal name. "I know that. You were always a good lover, Clay—gold medal best. As you said, that was never our issue."

"The travel alone can't have made you call the whole thing off."

"No. It was only part of it. It was your friends…"

"Who the heck cares about my friends?"

"They started to do more than give me a two-fingered salute off their cowboy hats."

Clay stiffened. "What. Did. They. Do?" His eyes had grown dark, brows dipping in the middle.

A grown man's reaction. One she knew heart deep he wouldn't have had back then. Should she tell him now? What they had to live through back then was bad enough. If she told him and he didn't believe her, what then? But then, what did it matter? "When you weren't around, I got all kinds of propositions."

"What kind of—Why didn't you tell me?"

"I did!" The coffee cup nearly shot out of her hand. She lowered her voice. "I did tell you, Clay. Time and time again. You didn't listen. Which takes us to our next problem. You stopped listening to me. Or even spending time with me. Your friends and your beer became your top priority. And then there were the buckle bunnies."

"I didn't have anything to do with buckle bunnies, and you know it!"

"They sure had plenty to do with you. I had to watch while they fawned over you, flirted, tried to seduce—you name it, they did it. I'll grant that you were too wrapped up in your good-old-boys club to notice them, but still."

"Now what the heck are you talking about?"

She slumped back into the plastic cushion of the booth seat. "This is old, dirty laundry. Why do you want to look at our marriage with a microscope? It got painful. We grew apart. End of story."

He shook his head. "No, it's not. I need the holes filled in, Peg. The problem is, I don't know if I'm not remembering or I was just that clueless. What aren't you telling me now that I didn't *hear* back then?"

Well, God bless him. He actually sounded grown up. Maybe this was the person Clay had become. It had been over four years since she'd seen him…before the Achilles injury, that is.

Was it possible both of them had grown up enough to discuss this like adults?

"Are you sure you want to know?"

"Yes."

"Your friends…cat-called me and harassed me and threw out all sorts of lewd comments. First about my body. Later about how they could…perform in bed…"

He stiffened.

"They began to follow me, show up when they knew you'd be gone. I had no idea how to stop them. Each day they got a little bolder. They'd brush against me whenever I tried to get around them, trap me in a circle, grope."

Clay looked ready to murder.

She went on. She'd give him the full picture. "I told you. Over and over again. The problem was, often you were too drunk to listen. The more I tried to say, the less you believed a word I said."

Clay squared his shoulders, his mouth grim.

"You stayed out later and later. I tried to stay up, but it seemed so pointless. So I'd go to sleep and wake up the next morning to rumpled sheets on your side of the bed. We only ever interacted when you were feeling frisky. Other than that, I was alone. And I feared what your friends would ultimately do to me. So I went home. Figured you'd never miss me. In fact, I'd convinced myself you would be relieved that I left. When I got back to Sundance, your family insisted I was *their* family and needed to stay with them to wait for rodeo season to end. So I did."

He gulped, his expression changing from anger to understanding. "Because my brother listens."

"Colt just happened to be there." Realizing she'd said that too loud, she lowered her voice. "And, yes. He listens."

"Yeah, listens to you ladies. It's why he can't get them to stop coming around." He scoffed, then frowned, his eyes drifting as he captured a thought. "Or they used to. He's engaged, isn't he?"

Peggy's heart sank a little at the repeated memory loss, but at least it was a change of subject. "Yes, he is. To a cute, feisty little redhead."

He snapped his fingers. "Betsy, that's right. I remember her. Don't see what Colt sees in her, but to each his own, I guess."

Peggy smiled sadly. Last time he'd referred to her as Rylee.

"What happened next?"

It took her a moment to switch gears. "After rodeo let out for the year, you came home. Threw an everlovin' fit over Colt talking to me in the barn, and nearly punched him. If Trevor hadn't been there, you would have."

His mouth twisted, but he remained mute.

"When you kept exploding over Colt's kindness, then accused me of having an affair with him, I'd finally had enough. That was the day I told you I wanted a divorce."

Clay rotated his jaw as if he were chewing his cud. She could read the thoughts filing through his mind, one after the other: *How could she decide that on her own? Why did she want to leave me? If I had known, we could have worked it out.* And he'd be right, about all of it.

Settling back in the vinyl bench seat, she drank her coffee, bent on not saying anything more until he did.

Twice he started to speak but stopped himself and ground his teeth. According to the oversized clock hanging over the door, it took him four long minutes before he spoke again. "So, what you're saying is, I asked for it."

Her mouth gaped. She flutter-blinked to clear her vision, then blinked again in astonishment.

"Never said I was a smart one."

His adorable, sheepish smile had her gushing with laughter.

Yep, that convinced her Clay was all grown up. Made her love him all the more. If he could look at what she'd told him without charging to his own rescue, he'd changed a whole lot. Probably more than she had, and she'd changed so much her mother didn't even recognize her.

But then he slid to the end of the booth, gained his feet, and set his jaw. Was it lip service after all?

"Let's get some sleep," he said. "If we start early, we'll make it home tomorrow."

Home. That sounded good to her. But would Clay let her stay near? She only had one day to figure that out.

She followed him out into the night air, and toward the door labeled #18. The same age she was when she married Clay.

Now that she was all grown up, she knew exactly how to make their marriage work. She'd easily demand more of his time, force him to involve her in decisions, and tell his friends where they could get off. If only…

"Earth to Twinkie." Clay's deep voice yanked her from her dream.

She blinked up at eyes so dark green they looked black. "Did you say something?"

"After you." He was holding the door open to their room and she hadn't even noticed.

"Oh, sorry." She brushed past him and looked around. It was a typical motel room with two twin beds, one nightstand between them, and a dresser under a mirror on one wall. The bathroom door stood open at the far end with fresh towels stacked next to the sink.

Once inside, a vivid memory unfolded in front of her eyes. Clay, carrying her over the threshold of a place similar to this, the train of her white wedding dress dragging along the tattered floor. She hadn't cared one iota what happened to her dress. She had eyes only for her handsome prince. They were broke teenagers back then, but they didn't need luxury, just each other.

They still did, she thought sadly.

CHAPTER 30

"Which bed do you want?" Clay gestured toward the twin beds. He was too big a guy for three beers to make him drunk, but usually after that many he was talkative. Now that Clay had allowed them to talk about their past, she wanted to know more.

"Well, Sunbo? Your choice."

"I'll take the one closest to the bathroom." She gave him her Sunbo smile in hopes it would keep him talking.

"Why'd I know that?" He grinned back. Gad, she'd forgotten how many straight white teeth this man concealed.

"How's the head?"

"Not feeling it."

"Too much beer?"

"Nah. All healed up, is all."

"You think so? That would be good." Now that his tongue was flapping, she had to know. He'd been asking her what had happened to *them*. Well, what had happened to *him*? "Why'd you change, Clay?"

He looked down at himself and frowned. "Nope. Same duds."

"Don't act dumb. You know what I mean."

He trapped her gaze. "You gonna get all serious on me again, Twinkie?"

"That's not going to work either. I want to know. I need to know. And, don't tell me you don't remember. I can tell by the look on your face you do."

He squeezed his eyes shut. The seconds drifted by before he finally reopened them. "Maybe I got a little tired of the same old thing, too," he finally admitted.

"Me?" The thought was like a spear through her heart.

He shook his head. "The road. Gettin' my guts beat to death by the craziest beasts in rodeo. Drunk friends."

"But you got drunk with them."

"Didn't know how to keep them from razzing me 'bout being married. So I drank with 'em."

"You hated being married to me." It wasn't a question. She knew it was true.

"No, on both counts," he said.

No, he didn't hate being married. No, he didn't hate it was me. Soul-twisting relief came over her.

He sighed. "We were too young."

"Do you think, if we were married today, we'd make it?" She believed that, but seeing as how Clay'd run to the other side of the continent rather than try again, she needed to hear this answer above all others.

Clay's eyes widened. He hesitated, thinking or lost in thought, then smiled roguishly and took a step toward her.

She backed one step before he caught her wrist. He tugged her in close and wrapped an arm around her before she thought to protest. "Let me remind you what worked for us."

Clay stole her lips as if he'd never get the chance again, his mouth warm and urgent against hers. The intimacy they'd shared was the most joy she'd ever known. His embrace tightened. She melted seamlessly into him as his hand slid through her hair.

Moans intermingled. Heat swelled. Their lips knew what was wanted and needed. She tasted beer, felt wetness, the scratch of his days' old growth against her tender skin. All of it sent her into a different dimension. A realm only Clay Cooper could create for her.

He slowed the kiss, slipped his palm back from her hair to hold her cheek, then released her lips. Drew back just enough to look her in the eye. Her head tilted back as she locked gazes with him. What she saw in those green orbs were a myriad of emotions; all passion and want and heady pleas.

"I want you."

That was it. All he said. She understood it. Wanted it too. But she wanted so much more.

As much as she yearned to let him take the lead on this, she knew it wasn't right. Things had changed. They'd changed. And they no longer belonged to each other. Legally or otherwise. If they weren't careful, they could come away from this more demolished than ever.

The truth tore a new hole in her.

When he started to lean down to take her lips again, she didn't move a muscle, just stared up at him and stated matter-of-factly. "We're no longer married, Clay."

He stilled. Stared deep into her eyes until he dropped his arm and backed away. He swung around.

Off balance, he steadied himself with one hand on the bed, then regained his equilibrium and strode to the door. "Need some air." Then he was gone into the night.

The strength drained out of her legs. *Lord, please watch over him.* She stared at the shut door, teetering with locked knees to keep from falling until her will slowly returned.

She managed to shower and dry her hair, and was sitting with crisscrossed legs in the middle of the bed, reading the Bible, when Clay returned. Her nightgown was modest, so she didn't bother with a robe.

He came through the door, closed it softly behind him, then stood staring at her. His gaze raked her from flyaway blond wisps down to bare knees. She tugged her hem down.

He frowned, his brows tilted upward in the middle, giving him a look of confusion. He opened his mouth as if to say something, but snapped it shut.

The silence grew awkward. "You okay? Have a nice walk?"

He'd been gone well over an hour.

With the first step toward her, she understood why. He stumbled, then tripped over his big boots, landing face down on the bed. He was out before she got to him. Not one muscle moved as she tugged off his boots, moved his now dented cowboy hat to the end table, then stripped him of his shirt and jeans. This part of their relationship she didn't miss one bit.

Maybe Clay hadn't changed that much after all.

• • •

Before he even opened his eyes, the sunshine hammering his lids stabbed pain through his temples, especially his left one. What had he been thinking, going back out for two more mugs of beer? Not pints either.

But he knew why he'd done it. He'd made a fool of himself with Peggy. He'd wanted her. Desperately. And yet with one statement, she froze him on the spot. 'We're no longer married, stupid.' Of course, she hadn't said *stupid*, but he'd felt it clear down to the marrow. He wasn't dealing with the local harlot, for crying out loud. This was his wife. Ex-wife. The girl who'd been all kinds of innocent when he'd married her.

Part of him had been relieved she wouldn't ride the sheets with anyone out of wedlock—not even him. But oh, the times he remembered in wedlock, the sheer joy of their union. He still wanted her, and he couldn't have her.

Stop it! Fury burned deep, stirring the acid from too much stale yeast in his stomach and sending more pain into his head.

Rage followed. Rage and hurt and defeat. She'd torn out his heart when she left him, and all he had left were daredevil compulsions he could no longer indulge. Peggy believed in God? Well, where was He now? Or was He into stripping people down to bare bones in order to torment them? Clay blew out a tortured breath.

"Oh, good. You're awake. How's your head?" Peggy approached from the bathroom, perfectly put together in a sleeveless sunshine yellow sundress and sandals to match. Long blond wisps had been gathered into a high ponytail and whipped about her face as she bopped around the room gathering clothes. She looked young, and adorable, and irritatingly cheery.

Time to fold up his yearning into a neat little stack and pack it away with his dirty clothes. He'd bury it when they got home. Deep and permanent.

He grumbled his answer back. Rose slowly and took himself off to the shower.

By the time he brushed his teeth, eyeing Peggy's busy reflection in the mirror, he'd concluded there was no point in shaving. He got dressed in jeans and a ratty t-shirt. As he stomped first one then the second boot on, Peggy brought him his hat. "Sorry, it got a little squished when you landed on your face last night."

"Landed on my face?"

"Yep. Passed right out. Thankfully on the bed." She smiled up at him. Looked into his eyes with twinkles in her own as if he hadn't manhandled her last night and demanded her passion. He'd been wanting that kiss, when he'd thought she was still his wife.

If only he could go back there. To those moments when he didn't remember their split.

He tugged and maneuvered his hat back into shape, then stuffed it on his head. "Let's go."

His voice was gruff. His head was splitting. His gut was roiling. The thought of riding in a bouncy truck for another three hundred miles didn't set well. But the sooner they got back to Sundance, the better. He'd be able to figure out a new routine for himself at the ranch. Peggy would be off to Gillette to work as a physiologist— away from him. And he'd finally be able to function as he had before.

Before. The word mellowed in his brain as he gathered his dirty clothes and shoved them in his duffle. What had he done before the head injury? Peggy mentioned an Achilles injury. From rodeoing? No. He didn't think so. Something niggled at the back of his mind. Like he'd already remembered this once…and forgotten again.

He opened the door for her, grabbed the suitcase from her hand, and followed her to the truck, stuffing both cases behind the seat along with his hat.

"Do you want to eat in town before we head out of Billings?" she asked sweetly.

He wasn't sure his stomach could handle food right now, but if he didn't eat, it would only get worse. This was something he remembered well.

"You know you should," she went on. Of course, she'd remember this too.

He ground his teeth, not happy she knew so much about him when he'd yet to connect all the scraps of memories floating around in his head. "Yeah. You know a place?"

"Uh-huh." She brought the truck to life and took them out of the lot and onto the highway toward Wyoming. Just before leaving the city behind, she stopped at a lone restaurant that boasted the last chance for food and the best pancakes in town, all under an unlit neon sign. One word—Diner. Nowhere was the name of the restaurant shown, but Peggy seemed to know it was the place to go.

"You'll love their chicken fried steak and eggs." Another thing she remembered about him. Her grin was so cute, he had to give her a ghost of one back.

Once they were inside and had ordered, the uncomfortable silence nagged at him. "Tell me again who clobbered me."

She looked dubious, but finally produced what he wanted. "Bruce Smith, Martin's brother."

"Why?"

She visibly swallowed, making him wonder what secret she kept. "They'll catch him. You don't need to worry."

He took a sip of his black coffee and winced. Still hot. "You didn't answer my question."

She sighed her acquiescence. "Do you remember smokejumping?"

"Is that what I do for a living? I knew I wasn't ranching."

Peggy's eyebrows shot up. "So you don't remember smokejumping?"

He shook his head, disappointed he didn't remember something that sounded so perfect for him. Or did he? Had he remembered this already?

"Don't worry. It will come. You became a smoke-jumper after we…"

He knew she didn't want to remind him of their divorce. He'd probably wanted to escape Wyoming altogether after they'd split. Just revisiting this past made him want to escape all over again.

"You left for Alaska in late summer, 1957."

His gaze glided around the restaurant, as if the patrons would trigger a memory. They didn't. "How long did I smokejump?"

"Well…" She tapped a finger on her lower lip.

He had no problem remembering those precious lips, all over him. He bit down on his cheek, forcing his thoughts back to smokejumping.

"About four years."

He was stunned. "I was a jumper for four years, and I don't remember any of it?"

"You will. You already did once. Just give it time."

Clay felt the blood leave his face. What more had he forgotten? Again and again. In fact, he couldn't remember the question he'd asked her at the beginning of this conversation. It seemed important. "Promise me something."

A look of resolve came over her, and she brightened. "Anything."

He should have stopped to question her eagerness, but the words came anyway. "When I tell you stuff as it comes, remember it for me…and remind me of it when I forget again."

"Of course."

She looked too pleased to have to do this chore. And before he could force his wounded brain into addressing that concern, a disconcerting thought came to him. In order for her to do that, she'd have to stick real close.

CHAPTER 31

Arid lands flew by as Peggy drove toward Wyoming and the unknown future that awaited them both.

Clay snoozed, his head propped on his hand, his elbow in the crook of the door panel. She couldn't stare all she wanted, but a glance here and there gave her fodder to lock into her own memory banks. He was still the most incredible man she'd ever known. Bigger than life. Worlds above other men.

She thought back to the years Clay was in Alaska, then the months he'd been in a coma. She hadn't dated in college. If she wasn't licking her wounds from Clay, she was grieving her younger brother's death. School was her escape, pure and simple. But, dating Clay's doctor. That had been a true awakening. Dr. Daniel Harris was the epitome of class, attractiveness, and availability. Even better, he'd thought her his equal. The temptation had been real.

But Clay was Samson to Daniel's Aristotle. She'd been around academia so long she'd all but forgotten the appeal of a man who was rugged and strong. Who protected her, was passionate for her, and had been loyal to her. Her man.

Not her man any longer.

Grief filled her again. Should she walk away? Let him find another woman who would never ask for a divorce? Let him live out his days with someone he could trust?

No! He could trust her. She would prove it. She loved him, understood him, would care for him each and every time he tried to wipe himself out. A small smile reached her mouth. Because no matter how much his body betrayed him these days, Clay Cooper would always be a daredevil.

"What's so funny?" Clay's deep voice cut into her musings.

She jumped a little at his voice but didn't let it affect her driving. "Nothing."

"You had a smirk on your face."

"I did? Huh. Just thinking about you and your reckless ways."

Clay adjusted himself to sit up straighter. Ran a hand through his hair and then squeezed two fingers into his eyes. "Reckless, huh? Someone has to do the tough jobs."

A small laugh escaped her. "I wasn't thinking of your jobs, Clay. Yes, someone has to do what you did. Well…maybe not bronc riding. But that's not what I'm talking about. Do you remember your high school days? You and your gang of hoodlums got in trouble all the time."

He lifted his chin. A quick glance told her he was deep in thought. "I do remember a few escapades."

"Escapades? More like shenanigans." She laughed, and it felt good. She had been right there to watch every crazy thing he did—and loved every minute of it. Loved him, no matter what he did.

"Huh. Like what?" he asked.

She chuckled again. "Like jumping out the loft door of the barn into a pitiful little pile of hay…" Her laughter rang out in the cab. "And landing smack dab in the dirt. Nearly broke your tailbone. Remember that?"

She cut him a glance. His smile was widening.

"The worst part was you got them all to follow you. Oh, Clay. Seriously. You can get anyone to follow you anywhere." Including her, though she wouldn't say that now.

Clay rubbed his palms against his thighs, grinning like the wild man he was. "Dad had to take me to the doc the next day. I couldn't move my legs when I woke up."

Her mouth gaped. "What? You never told me that. What did the doctor say?"

"Said I did bust my tailbone.

"What did your dad do?"

Silence reigned for a few tense moments. "Didn't say a word. Dropped me off at home and left for a cattle sale down Cheyenne way. Didn't come home for a week."

Another glance showed her Clay's smile had morphed into a scowl.

"Ah, Clay. It's not what you're thinking."

He ignored her. "The man couldn't be bothered with me. Ever."

"That's not fair." Peggy downshifted, taking a tight corner as she pointed the truck over the Montana border into Wyoming. "Your dad did the best he could with six sons and no mother. I bet he was late to that cattle sale because of your stunt. The fact he didn't chew you out tells me he was used to your antics. What else did you want him to do?"

"Stay around." Clay's voice was harsh. "Make sure his son could walk. Make sure his son didn't need him."

"Maria was there. Your older brothers."

"Not my *parent*."

"No. Not your parent." An epiphany thundered home, and the question was out of her lips before she thought better of it. "Did you do these stunts to get your dad's attention?"

Silence.

Clay sighed, and the sound reverberated off the metal walls of the cab. Peggy knew Clay well. Wondered now about all the F's on his report card when he was smart enough to get A's, all the times he missed the bus home, all the times he pestered the girl in front of him in class so his dad would be called into school, all the times he got into scraps with other boys. He wasn't just a hooligan, after all. *Oh, Clay...*

She waited for an answer. No such luck. She glanced his way, saw his elbow back on the door panel, his thumb rubbing his lower lip. He stared at the changing scenery, more trees in view now.

No sense waiting for an answer. He was going to pass on this one. "We're entering Sheridan. We'll stop for a late lunch. What sounds good?"

He dropped his elbow off the cold metal and pointed ahead. "There's a hamburger stand. That's fine by me."

"We can go into town if you'd rather go inside, get something other than a burger."

"Nah. This is fine. Faster. Only a few more hours and we're home."

A cold chill spiraled down her spine, making her hunger vanish. He was already shifting gears. Would there be time enough to convince him to begin anew?

• • •

Clay jumped to the ground, his boots thudding against the packed dirt and jarring his head. But this time, his headache stemmed from more than a mere landing. Their smokejumper discussion had reopened the door to a world of memories of his life in Alaska. He remembered all of it now. The death of Martin, the newspaper accusations, the blame he endured. It all hit like a sledgehammer to the heart...and consequently, his head. He'd faked that nap to try to recover. No luck. Peggy's brief little walk down memory lane was enjoyable, right up until he remembered Martin flying out the barn's loft door behind him. After that...well, the conversation turned sour on its own.

It seemed all the memories were intact now. Except one. He was missing the actual assault. Hadn't he asked Peggy for more details? Why couldn't he remember her answer?

She rounded the truck just then, keys twirling around one finger, her bright blond ponytail swinging with each step, shining in the sunshine. Her Sunbo smile was in place, warming him soul deep and transporting him back to the burger joint in high school where they ate before football games.

She raised her brows, questioning if he was all right with just her eyes. "A big cheeseburger, french fries, and a chocolate shake sound good?"

"Strawberry for me."

"Ah, so you do remember those days?" she said. "Those were great times. You in your quarterback jersey, and me in my cheerleading outfit, every Friday."

He grinned, thinking about those long legs under that short skirt and that same ponytail swishing around her adorable face. He was grateful for this new reminder of better times.

"Come on, let's get our grub."

"Grub. Yes." He chuckled.

She laughed. "What else do you remember?"

He gave her his best leer. "Not being able to keep my eyes off your legs," he said, swinging an arm around her waist and heading for the window.

Hamburgers in hand, they sat at a picnic table. Same kind as their high school days. Peggy asked, "Do you remember what my favorite thing to do was?"

He grabbed a french fry and dipped it in her chocolate shake, then fed it to her.

"You remember!"

"'Course. Never saw the appeal, but got a kick out of you doing it."

He took an enormous bite of his cheeseburger and grinned around it before he started chewing. Reliving these old times and staring at Peggy, *that* he could do all day. She'd always been a pretty little thing, but now she had a woman's edge to her, of maturity, sophistication, and confidence. He was content to sit here, gazing at her and she at him, in this place where nothing else in the world mattered.

They'd done this often. The memories started piling up inside—Dallas, Reno, Salt Lake. The rodeo circuit had landed them at many a burger joint on the road, where they'd shared each other's company in joyful silence. It felt so…right.

Clay blinked, and reality returned. This wasn't their life now. Peggy wasn't his wife. He wasn't a bronc rider. Life had changed. And not for the better.

He shoved the last of the burger into his mouth. "We should get going." He knew his voice was gruff. Her joy clouded to sadness. He was sorry for that. Never liked causing her pain. But they needed to be reasonable. Life had taken a crucial turn long ago.

When they got back, they'd be going their separate ways.

CHAPTER 32

Three hours later, Peggy found herself eyeing the blasted potholes of the Cooper Bar-6 road in disbelief as she feathered the throttle carefully. It seemed the dang things had gotten bigger, or maybe it was despair that made her bones ache with every bump. Because the vibe coming off Clay since Sheridan was mute anger.

"We're here," she said weakly, rolling to a stop in front of the house.

"Yep. Sure are." He straightened his spine, stretching slightly backwards to loosen the kinks. Without another word he opened the passenger door and gingerly slid out.

That was different than he'd done back at the burger place. "Are you all right? Head hurt?"

"Fine. I'll have Brand drive you home. I'll just get my bag."

She watched as Clay grabbed his duffel from behind the seat, yanked it and his hat out through the small opening, then gave her one last look. His eyes had glossed over and changed color into that toxic swirl of mud and moss and mustard, and a feeling of hopelessness came over her. With a small nod, he slammed the passenger door. Gave a quick wave, turned, and strode to the house. Peggy watched until the door closed behind him, then released the breath she'd been holding. Her hands shook and a rising pressure clogged her throat.

That was it? They'd just spent half a year together, and all he could say was he'd have his brother drive her home? She blinked back tears she would wait to shed. She was tired, discouraged, sad. Even though Clay hadn't been awake for most of the time they'd been together, she'd been there. With him, every spare moment she had. She'd worried over him, washed him, massaged his muscles, worked his Achilles, read to him, prayed for him, and all he could give her was, 'I'll have Brand drive you home?'

Her heart ached in a whole new way. Was this how Clay felt when she'd turned her back on him and their marriage? No. She was sure he felt worse. How could she have done it? Shame on her!

With no movement from the house forthcoming, she let herself out of the truck and went in search of Brand, not sure what kind of reception she'd receive from him. The sooner she got back home to her folk's house, the sooner she could have a good cry in solitude.

A glance at the western sky told her dusk was on the way. Likely Brand was in the barn feeding the animals before supper. She wandered toward it, wanting to blame her lethargy on the long trip, but knowing it was her defeated heart.

Brand was in the far corner, helping Rylee with a rescue horse.

Peggy ambled up to them. "How's the stallion?"

Both jumped, and Rylee let out a startled squawk. "Geez, Peggy, you scared the tar out of us."

The door to the cowpokes' kitchen in the back of the barn swung open. "Hey, hon, can you come in here for a sec'?" Colt's voice drifted through the open door.

"Sure." Rylee turned to Peggy. "Glad you're back safe." Then off she trotted, as fast as her little legs could carry her into the arms of a smiling Colt. When he saw Peggy, he smiled warmly. "Hi, Peg. Welcome back."

Peggy gave a little wave, which was lost to him, seeing as how he'd buried his lips on Rylee's neck. She turned back to Brand. He'd been watching her, she could tell. She looked away, afraid he would see the hurt in her eyes.

"Hey." Brand curled his knuckle under her chin, and turned her face toward him. "What's up?"

"Nothing. Just…just tired, is all."

He tilted his head down, giving her a skeptical look. "That's not all."

She hesitated, remembering how angry Brand had been with her over the phone. Well, she'd brought his brother home. He should be happy with her now. "I need a ride home, is all. Would you mind?" Her voice cracked.

Brand grabbed her into a deep hug, swallowing her up.

The sympathy strangled her, making it impossible to hold back the burning tears. When had this boy crossed over to all man? Tall, muscled, and in absolute tune with a woman's needs. At first she stood stiffly, but soon she snaked her arms around him and squeezed back, pressing her face to his brawny chest, trying hard to stifle the waterworks.

"Ah, Peg. Clay's back to his old self, huh?" He squeezed one last time then leaned back. "That's a good sign, really. It means Clay is going to be all right. And it means he's going to wreak havoc. That's who he is, isn't it? And we want him back, don't we?"

Did she? She wasn't involved in his life anymore. And he wasn't going to let her back in.

Brand chuckled, though it was more in empathy than in humor. "Come on. You look pitiful. I'll drive you home. I just need to make a phone call first." He turned her and started off for the open barn door, keeping his arm tight around her shoulders.

Once he'd delivered her to the truck, he dashed into the house to make his call, then ran back to her.

"Have you eaten?" he asked, eyes agleam.

The burger and shake she'd eaten four and a half hours ago sat like lead in her stomach. "I couldn't eat."

"Hmm. Yes, you can. I have just the place." He grinned with that charming, bone-melting smile of his.

"If you say Higbee's Burger Joint, I'm going to punch you."

He gave her a mock gasp and gawk. "You wouldn't." He grinned again. "Come on, we're wastin' daylight."

Peggy handed Brand his keys and hoisted herself into the passenger seat, still warm from Clay's body. Her strength drained into the cushion, as if seeking the heat's source.

Brand cranked open the driver's side door and looked around the cab. "What did you do, house-keeping in here? Never seen it so clean."

She laughed then, needing to let loose a little tension. "We didn't dirty it up. Thanks for lending it to us, by the way. It drives like a dream."

He beamed. "Glad you like her. She's my baby."

"Until you replace her." Peggy closed her passenger door, gazing through the front windows of the ranch house in hopes of glimpsing Clay. She wondered if she should go back in to say goodbye. But Brand already had the engine running and put her in gear.

"What do you mean, *replace her*?" He sounded horrified.

"With an actual *her*." When he frowned his confusion, she explained. "A woman, silly."

He nearly choked on his next words. "A woman? Never happenin'. I'd find it too hard to choose just one."

"Such a scoundrel," she said on a laugh. Then she wanted to cry. Clay was the scoundrel. To not even say goodbye, after driving for three days…after taking care of him for seven months! Why in the world did she want him so badly? He certainly wasn't worth the agony.

But then, as she pondered the real Clayton Cooper, she thought, yeah. He was worth any amount of effort she could give.

"Going to Higbee's."

"No! Take me home, Brand." She didn't want to be seen in town with Clay's little brother. Not that it would matter, really. She just didn't want to give the people of Sundance the wrong impression. Oh, who was she kidding? All she wanted was to be alone.

Brand reached over and patted her leg. "I can see you need to spew some poisonous thoughts. Talk to me."

She sighed heavily. "I don't have anything to say."

He glanced once at her before refocusing on the road. "This is me, Twinkles. You can talk to me."

A burst of laughter left her lips. "Twinkles? Clay named me Twinkie."

He turned and winked at her. "I'm not Clay."

"No. That's for sure."

"Whoa. What's that supposed to mean?"

"Don't melt down, little brother. It was a compliment. You're too nice to be Clay."

"Huh. So, Clay's been mean on the trip—or since he woke up? Fill me in on that. All I know is he finally woke up in June and thought you were his wife." His mouth was grim as he glanced at her.

Peggy nodded. "I know, I know. Have you forgiven me? I'm not sure Clay has, or ever will.

It's no wonder he doesn't trust me anymore. Between shattering his heart four years ago, and then lying to him about who I was at the hospital, how can he ever trust me again? Heck, I don't trust me."

Brand threw his head back and laughed. "Easy does it, sis. Clay loves you. Always has. He's bound to come around."

"No. He's not. You of all people know who Clay is. Stubborn as a rock. He'll never let me back in. Not ever. I've killed his love for me."

"Well, we'll just have to change his mind, won't we?" He swung a crafty grin at her.

"What are you thinking?"

"See, Clay may be stubborn. And he may be guarding himself. But there is one thing he can't resist."

She shifted. Turned her hip to face Brand and listened intently. "What?"

"You."

The word blanketed her with warmth. Could he be right? Did Clay still want her? Lost in thought, she didn't notice when Brand pulled into Higbee's and parked.

"Wait. No. I don't want anything to eat." She put her hand on Brand's shoulder and pleaded. "Please, no."

He just grinned. "I'm hungry. You wouldn't want to deprive me of sustenance, would you?"

The look on his face was so convincing, she sighed and nodded. "Fine. Let's make it short. Okay?"

"You got it," he said and jumped down out of the truck, coming around to open her door before she even had her hand on the handle. It came to her then. Brand was so good with the ladies because he didn't bulldoze. Nope. He charmed, then waited. Didn't say another word until he got the answer he wanted. Clever man.

Brand opened the door, then guided her by the small of her back into the little hamburger joint. Peggy's stomach rebelled. She didn't want to do this with Brand. If she had to order something, she'd get a salad that she could move around with her fork.

She sat in a booth, the only one open at the moment. The seat squeaked as she moved across the vinyl to the center and picked up the menu.

A warm, hard body moved in next to her and gave her a little shove with his hip, sliding her over a couple of feet. Startled, she looked up into Brand's face. "What are you doing? Sit on your own side."

"We have company," he said with a grin.

Peggy glanced up. "Doc! How are you?"

Her former boss, Dr. Trenton, gave her a professional smile and nodded as he sat across from them. "How are you, Margaret?"

"Good. Fine. Dandy." She cringed. Surely he could see the lie. "How have things been here in Sundance, and in Gillette?" Then she remembered that Dr. Trenton was the one to reveal to Dr. Harris her real relationship with Clay. Had Daniel let on that she'd lied about being married, or had he only absorbed Trenton's information in silence? Her discomfort quadrupled. She waited and watched the doctor's face for clues.

"Well, you probably don't know the latest. Since you were gone in Missoula, for who knew how long, I hired another physiologist for the hospital in Gillette."

"Oh? Who?" She was happy he hadn't mentioned Clay, but astounded he'd replaced her. She'd been hoping to go back to work there. Escape from Clay. Get on with her life. Now what would she do?

"He says he's a good friend of yours."

She frowned in confusion until his words began to sink in. No. He didn't. "Larry."

"Larry Peterson. Yes. Says he went to school with you."

She sighed. "We were study buddies." What was he about? He knew she had that job in Gillette. Dang stinker took it from her. She took a big breath, then jumped in. "I'm happy for Larry, but does this mean I no longer have a job with you?"

He looked apologetic. "Well, yes, it means you don't have the physiologist job at Campbell County Memorial Hospital anymore. I didn't know how long you'd be. Especially after the first month went by and you took the job at St. Patrick's. But you can have a temporary job as my assistant if you'd like. The assistant I have now is pregnant and due any day now. I was planning to ask my former nurse, Ada, to help for a bit. She retired last year. But the job is yours if you want it."

Temporary. Well, she needed any job right now. "I appreciate the work. That will give me time to look for physiology work. Thank you."

Brand patted her back, making her stiffen. She didn't want Dr. Trenton...or anyone else for that matter...thinking she and Brand were a couple. She turned to him as she pulled away from his hand. "Thanks for the comfort, *little brother*," she said. "But, I'll be fine, I'm sure."

Thankfully Brand nodded and dropped his hand back to his lap.

"You can start tomorrow, if you're ready."

"I'm ready."

"Your first task is to bring Clayton in for an examination. His records from Dr. Harris arrived today. They mentioned a job with the smokejumpers based out of the West Yellowstone facility. Apparently, his boss from Alaska called to check on him. Told Dr. Marshall that the job is still his if he wants it. I'd like to go over a few things with him. Check him physically, outline some ground rules before he considers all that travel. Bring him with you tomorrow."

With her? Did Dr. Trenton think she lived with the Coopers? "I'd be glad to go pick him up.

How early we arrive depends on when I can get Clay going."

"He won't fit in your car," Brand said. "It'll rile him. Better come out to the ranch in the morning and leave your teeny weeny tiny little car and take my truck. She's used to a woman drivin' her by now, anyway. She doesn't like it, but she'll deal."

Peggy chuckled. "You're a laugh a minute, Brand. Okay. Thank you. One less thing to fight with Clay over. I'll be there by eight. Be sure to get him up and moving. I'll leave that lovely task to you."

Brand's smile faltered.

She beamed at him to rub it in.

The doctor slid out of the booth and shook Brand's hand. "Isn't it time you come and see me? When *was* your last physical?"

Brand dropped the doctor's hand like it had shocked him and shook his head. "You'll see me when I'm a few breaths away from Heaven's door. No sooner."

The doctor smirked as he shook his head, then strolled away. He turned back just before pushing the door open. "See you in the morning, Margaret."

"Yes, sir, you will."

Once the doctor disappeared, Brand turned to her and slung his arm across the back of the bench seat. "You have a job. You relieved?"

She sucked in a long breath and blew it out. "Not really. I was hoping to do what I was trained for. Now, I'll have to leave the area to find a physiologist job. I don't see myself staying with Dr. Trenton long. Darn Larry anyway. Why did he have to follow me here?"

"Oh, didn't you know?"

"Know what?"

"He's the grandson of Old Man Peterson."

She frowned, unable to recollect a Peterson growing up around here.

"Worst neighbors we've ever had. The ones immediately south of our ranch. Went bankrupt and abandoned their property—and that horse Rylee and Colt rescued. Old Buck. In our barn now."

"Larry? The Larry I went to school with in Ohio? Are you sure?"

Brand nodded. "Old Man Peterson and my dad had been at odds for years before he left the property. I was never privy to that story. You'd have to ask Trevor. All I know is Larry and his older brother's dad took them to Ohio twenty years ago when they were tykes. Rumor has it Charles was in and out of jail. Larry was the straight arrow. Went to school in Cleveland. With you, apparently. Small world, eh?"

"It certainly is. Wow." Peggy's head was swimming with new information, and possible reasons why Larry never told her this little piece of news, when another person sat down across from them.

"Fancy meeting you two here." Colt's old girlfriend, Jenny Renford, plopped herself into the seat across from them, her hair up in the popular hairdo of the day. It looked like a fluffy rat's nest to Peggy. That plus the white lipstick and white nail polish made the poor girl look like she'd been frightened half to death.

Peggy hadn't seen Jenny since Colt broke up with her, years ago. It never stopped her from making a nuisance of herself in Colt's life, until Rylee told her to take a long hike off a short pier.

"So, Peggy. What are you doing with Brand? Thought you'd try out a different brother? Can't blame you there. They're all good looking. Of course nothing like Colt Cooper. How is he, by the way?"

Peggy opened her mouth to put Jenny in her place but stopped short when she saw Brand sneer. She'd never seen that expression on him before.

"You already know, Jenny," Brand said, low and slow. "He's getting married soon, so you can up and find yourself another family to harass now."

Peggy felt the seat cushion behind her indent where Brand's fingers dug in. She stiffened, unsure what to expect next.

Jenny rolled her eyes. "You're so funny. How's Clay? Heard he was back at the ranch. He all well now?"

"How would you know anything about Clay?" It might have been Peggy's imagination, but she thought she saw Jenny blanch. Was she interested in Clay now? Was that it?

It seemed a few seconds clicked by before Jenny waved a hand through the air. "Oh, nothing. I just heard through the grapevine that Clay was in Missoula at some hospital. Heard he got hurt. Hope he's okay."

She stared at Brand then, as if his eyes alone would give her the answers. Brand didn't offer a thing. Interesting.

"Well, is he? Okay?"

"What do you care?"

Peggy didn't know what was going on here, but something was up. She almost started to give Jenny the information about Clay, but held her tongue when she felt Brand's fingers press into her back where Jenny couldn't see. Her eyes landed on Brand. A muscle in his jaw twitched as if he was clenching his teeth. It was clear Brand didn't trust her one bit.

A look of disgust curled Jenny's lips as she swung her gaze to Peggy. "Will you tell me how Clay is? I've been worried."

Why would she be worried? Could Jenny be more to Clay than she knew about? The thought made her seethe with jealousy. She clenched her own jaw and kept quiet.

Jenny tilted her head and glared.

"Clay's just fine," Brand said. "Peggy here's taking real good care of him. Now, go home, Jenny. And stay away."

Jenny looked triumphant. She rose out of the booth, gave them a curt nod, and let herself out of the restaurant.

"What was that all about? And why were you so rude to her? That's not like you."

Brand shook his head. "I may be easygoing, but I won't abide my family being hurt. She tried to hurt Rylee. Cost Clay his Achilles instead." Brand glanced at her meaningfully.

"She's the reason he fell off that horse?"

Brand removed his arm from the seatback and cupped his fist with the opposite hand. "She cut the cinch on Rylee's saddle. Lost Clay the job he was perfect for, that had given him back his self worth after…" He gave her an apologetic look. Yeah. They both knew Peggy had stripped him of that, and so much more.

She wanted to camp on that topic, get it resolved. Find out just how much the whole Cooper clan hated her for what she'd done to Clay. But that was a discussion for another day. "There's something not right about that girl."

"You're the queen of understatement. She's not allowed on the ranch anymore. That's why she tracked us down here. Something's up with her, that's for darned sure. Let me get you home. I've lost my appetite."

CHAPTER 33

C lay wandered out of his bedroom and wobbled on weak legs toward the kitchen. It was already after supper. He'd spent the last several hours face down on his bed in a deep sleep he didn't understand. He'd napped off and on the whole trip home from Billings. It should have been enough, but he guessed his body was still recuperating.

Did it explain his rudeness toward Peggy? No. There was no excuse for that. Now that his mind was clearer, he regretted his behavior. It was the story of his existence. Blow through people, then cry over it later.

It was time for him to grow up and temper himself. Become the person that would make his dad proud rather than disappointed.

He stopped mid-step. He didn't know where that line of thinking had come from just now. Since when had he ever cared what his dad thought of him? The usual fury raced through him, until he stopped himself. Okay, so he knew that statement wasn't true. It was time he was honest with himself. He not only cared about what his dad thought; he craved attention from the man. Peggy was spot on with that one.

He glanced about the living room with fresh eyes, seeing the motives of his youth cast in this new light. But what did it matter? His dad was still gone, and Clay still hated it. Just like he hated the fact he'd up and abandoned Peggy outside after all she'd done to get him home.

The kitchen ahead beckoned with the lingering aroma of supper, but Clay had never felt emptier. He wasn't proud of himself. Problem was, he didn't know where Peggy and he went from here. Part of him didn't think he could ever get past the hurt she'd caused him. Even if the other part of him was brainstorming ways to ask her to dinner...or maybe to go on a horseback ride...

Ultimately, her deception jarred him back to his good senses.

The smell of fried chicken pulled him the rest of the way into the kitchen. Gad, when was the last time he'd eaten anything like that? Rylee was a pretty decent cook, so he was really looking forward to digging into some left overs.

"Hey there, brother." Colt grinned and jumped up from his chair at the kitchen table, and threw his arms around Clay.

Clay patted him once on the back and backed out of his grip.

"How're you feeling? How's the head?"

"I'm right as rain. Where's your bride-to-be?"

"Already went to bed. Wore her out today. She's a trooper, that one." His grin turned downright sappy. "We've begun the hayin'. She works right alongside me. Man, what a prize I got."

Clay gave his brother as much of a smile as he could muster, secretly vowing to shut himself back in his room—alone—after he was done eating. "She is a prize," he said. "Last one in existence. Too bad for the rest of us." He took himself to the refrigerator, opened it, and peered in. "Save me any food?"

"Sure." Colt came up behind Clay and slapped him on the shoulder, then leaned in to look in the fridge with him. He pointed. "Right there is the best darned fried chicken you'll ever taste. There's also—"

"That's enough," Clay interrupted. "I'll gnaw on a couple legs." He pushed back, effectively forcing Colt off him. Colt fetched a plate and handed it to him. Once he had a few legs piled on, he grabbed a napkin and headed out of the kitchen. "Got mail to open. Be in the office. Good to see you," he said over one shoulder.

"Clay?"

Clay stopped, turned half-way.

"Good to have you home. Glad that Achilles of yours seems to be healed. You're walkin' normal."

Clay looked down. He'd forgotten all about the trouble he'd had with that heel. "Yeah. Guess six months lying still in a coma can heal anything."

"What are you talking about? Peggy worked on you daily."

He didn't want a long conversation, so he probably shouldn't ask. But curiosity got the better of him. "What do you mean, 'worked on me?'"

Colt came a few steps into the family room to get closer. "You don't know?"

He hated the games his brothers played with him. "What? Tell me already."

"Peggy worked that Achilles each morning for half an hour. Kept after your muscles so they wouldn't atrophy. Bathed you, read to you, prayed over you. She even brushed your dang teeth for you."

The ground dropped beneath Clay's feet. He ran his tongue over his front teeth as if that would confirm everything Colt said.

"For crying out loud, Clay. Who do you think kept you in good enough shape so you could walk when you woke up?"

Clay hated his brain for missing what should have been obvious. He should have known—known!—that she'd done more than show up in his room for physical therapy once he was awake. He didn't know what to say.

Colt's brows rode low over the tops of his eyes, confusion on his face. "Didn't she tell you she'd been there the whole time? She took a job at the Missoula hospital so she could take care of you. Make decisions for you. Be our eyes and ears. Dad wanted to pay her, but she refused."

"Dad knew?"

"Of course he knew. We all wanted to jump in our trucks and converge on the hospital, but Peggy stopped us. Knew we had ranches to run. Us here. Dad in California. She promised she would take care of you and keep us posted. Wouldn't take a cent. She said the job paid her well enough to live with her old roommate and spend all her time at the hospital. She's a saint, that girl. You ought to be thanking her every way you can."

Clay gaped at Colt.

"How'd you find this out?"

"She called us weekly. Kept us apprised."

"Why didn't she tell me?" Then again, maybe she'd tried. He'd been so furious she had pretended to be his wife, he hadn't listened to anything she'd said beyond that.

"I don't know, Clay. Why didn't she tell you?" Colt's words weren't as condemning as they could have been. No. As usual, his concern showed in every line drawn on his face.

Clay shook his head. Colt had managed to do what no one else could have done. He'd dug deep, exhumed what tender feelings remained in Clay's decaying soul, and then shined a light on them.

"I'll be damned."

"Yeah. You might be."

Clay circled around on stiff legs and headed toward the office. "Got work."

"You have any more questions about the last six months, ask."

Clay shut the door on any more excavating Colt might try to do.

He plopped down into the desk chair, the squeak of the leather grating against his nerves. He was a fool. Why had he never asked Peggy anything about her stay in Missoula? It was only logical someone had to watch over him. He had to know it'd been Peggy. All he cared about was how she'd duped him. He was an idiot. Needed to make it up to her.

Something real began to thaw in his heart. A deep sense of coming home drifted through him just before questions attacked him. Did this mean he forgave her? Was he ready to try again? Did she even want that? Did he?

He stared at the stack of mail Trevor had saved for him on the corner of the desk, then at the plate of chicken legs beckoning him to eat. Neither appealed to him. He had more heavy thinking to do. He did that best on a horse. Maybe he'd check with Rylee about which one needed exercise. Now that he had more facts, he'd go for a ride, watch the sunset, let his mind coast. See what came to him.

Before he could act on that, a folder on the far right corner of the desk caught his eye. A blast of repulsion blew the euphoria right out of him. He knew that folder. He stretched to grab it and laid it down in front of him. Opened it and stared at the document inside.

In the District Court for the third Judicial District within and for Crook County, Wyoming. Margaret Ann Cooper, Plaintiff, versus Clayton William Cooper, defendant. You are hereby summoned...

Skimming down to the bottom of the page, there it was, Peggy's signature, in her perfect, flowery penmanship. Her stamp of approval that this was what she wanted. A document to end his joy, his love, his life...

A dark ache began at his lungs, then spread outward. A red haze colored the edges of his vision, making the paper look like it came from the Prince of Darkness Himself. And maybe it had. Pain gnawed inside, driving the acid up the walls of his stomach. He recognized this agony. It was the same that had nearly killed him when he'd first set eyes on this document.

He leaped to his feet, paced over to the window, and looked west. Glorious pink, orange, yellow, and purple streaks painted the sky, and yet all he saw was gray and loss.

Maybe it was time he was honest with himself. About the divorce.

A knock sounded at the door.

He turned as Brand took a step inside. "How ya feelin'?"

How did he answer that? *Discouraged? Disappointed? Dead?* His little brother would never understand. "What's up?"

"Got some news. Doc Trenton wants to see you. Peggy will pick you up at 8:00 AM. Okay, see you later." Brand ducked out and clicked the door shut behind him.

"Brandon!" Clay hollered. "Get back here."

The door slowly opened. Brand peeked his head back inside. "Gotta go. Have work."

Clay didn't say a word. Didn't have to. He and Trevor were the two brothers who could get Brand to move with only a glare.

"Fine," he said, and let himself into the room. Though he only took one step in.

"Explain."

He sighed. "Doc got your records from Missoula. Wants to see you for a follow-up appointment."

Clay cursed through the next few sentences. "Why can't you drive me?"

"Nope. Can't. Busy. Besides, Peggy's working for Doc at his office now."

"What? Did I miss another chunk of my life? When did that happen?"

"Today. She wanted her job back at the Gillette hospital, but Doc had already given it to her friend from school, Larry Peterson."

Clay's eyes bugged out. "Peterson? The man I met was Larry *Peterson*? Old Man Peterson's son? No. Has to be a grandson. He's too young to be a son."

"Right on the money. Grandson."

"Let me get this straight. While Peggy was gone, taking care of me…" A slice of guilt landed in his gut. Followed by another. According to Colt, Peggy had done more than anyone else would have for him. More than anyone ever had. He swallowed. Continued. "Doc gave away her job to a classmate of hers? Who happens to be the grandson of the neighbor who hates us Coopers?"

"That about sums it up."

"Why would he do that?"

"Geez, Clay. She was gone for well over half a year. She had to quit her job here. Wasn't Doc's fault."

Clay scrubbed a hand down his face. Life was never easy. "I guess. At least he gave her a job with him here. Good of him."

"Yep. Anyway, that's why she's coming to pick you up. Doc asked her to."

Oh. Wasn't her idea. Made sense. "I'll be ready."

"Can I go now?"

"What am I, your dad?"

"Kinda."

"Get outta here." Poor Brand. Clay *had* been like a dad to the twins. Someone had to.

Agh. *Poor Clay* was more like. Clay drummed his fingers on the desk. Far as he could tell, he had three important decisions to make. What to do for a living. Where to live. And if he wanted Peggy with him.

He shoved the divorce folder back to the right corner of the desk. His fingers tingled as they lifted from the paper. Was that what forgiveness would feel like? A weightless, breathless tingling in his heart? Or was he re-experiencing that first brush of poison on his soul?

• • •

The next morning, Peggy rolled into the Bar-6, parked her Valiant next to the familiar pickup truck, then went looking for Brand. She found him mucking out a stall.

"Good morning."

He glanced over a shoulder but kept working. "Mornin' to you, sis. Have you seen Clay yet?"

She closed her eyes and took a deep breath. "No. What kind of mood is he in?"

Brand stopped and turned, resting his hands on the top of the shovel. "Oh, I'd say if he thought he'd get away with it, he'd be in Texas by now. Or Florida."

"What did he say exactly?"

"What, when I told him he had to go to the doc's today? Or that you were picking him up?"

Her heart sank. He didn't want her around. She just knew it. "I don't want to know. Is he ready?"

Brand shrugged. "No idea. I got him up. Should be ready."

She sighed, resigned to do her job. Goodness, why did life around Clay have to be such a roller coaster ride? She was less frenzied during finals week at school.

Letting herself in the back door of the house, she scraped off the bottom of her shoes, decided they were clean enough to wear inside, and started to cross the mud room. "Clay, you in here?" she said, letting her voice pave the way.

"Right here, Sunbo," came the deep voice from the kitchen.

Her jumbled nerves settled a bit. She proceeded through the door into the cheerful yellow kitchen and to another kind of vision: Clay at the kitchen table, holding a piece of bacon between his fingertips. Seeing him gobble down breakfast in his wranglers and denim shirt wasn't the least bit remarkable, and yet her heart soared straight out of her chest. All the more so when he turned his gaze on her and smiled.

She cleared her throat so she could find her voice. "I'm surprised Trevor left any for you."

He swallowed his mouthful, then grinned again. She breathed a sigh of relief.

"How are you this fine morning?" he asked. "Want some breakfast?" He took another bite and crunched while he waited for her answer.

She raised a brow as she examined him. "No thanks. Already ate. I'd love some coffee, though."

"Help yourself." He turned back to his scrambled eggs and overcooked bacon. She smiled at the sudden memory of Trevor's ardor with limp bacon. That was why Trevor had left this bunch of bacon for Clay. Too crispy. She smiled.

Once she'd poured herself a cup of coffee and added milk and sugar, she sat across from Clay and studied his face. He looked serene this morning. What had happened to change him so? Then again, maybe sleeping in your own bed did that for a person. It sure had for her.

She sat quietly, sipping her coffee. "Sleep well?"

"Yup. Like the dead."

That must be it then. "Good. Dr. Trenton is anxious to check you out."

His smile fell off.

Shoot. She should have kept quiet.

"Why does he want to check me over like a brand new calf? I got enough of that to last me a lifetime back in Missoula with *Dr. Harris.*" The doctor's name trundled off his tongue in hostile bitterness.

"Let's see what *Dr. Trenton* has to say. Okay? 'Bout ready?" She smiled sweetly, hoping to reset his mood.

With one last mouthful of eggs, Clay sprang to his feet. "Let's get this over with," he said around the bite.

They both ambled through the mud room, Clay banging into his boots before they let themselves out of the house. Brand stood between her Valiant and his truck, his keys dangling in front of him on one finger. "Take mine."

She glanced meaningfully at her Valiant and laughed. "It's not all that bitty."

Clay eyed her car, then Brand's truck, and guffawed. Before she could protest, he was up in the passenger seat of Brand's truck with the door closed.

"Fine. Thank you, Brand. Have a nice day."

"Day? How long will you be?"

"Not long. I just figured you'd be out on the range by the time we got back."

He bowed with a flourish. "Your chariot awaits."

Down the ranch road she drove, Clay comfortably quiet beside her. The air in the cab was thick with the smells she'd grown accustomed to when they traveled from Missoula. Horse and dirt from his boots, fresh air still lingering in his hair, and Clay. Just Clay. He didn't wear cologne, but whatever he bathed in permeated his skin and clothes. Some sort of pine and spice. Each inhalation reminded her of him and better times.

After a few minutes of breathing him in, she opened her mouth to break the silence, but Clay spoke first. "My next task. Fill these potholes. Don't know why Dad hasn't done that."

Relieved Clay's thoughts hadn't been of them, she joined in. "Brand says the ranch has struggled lately. No money, I guess."

"Doesn't take that much. More labor than anything."

"Think about it, Clay. Your dad and Rebecca and Bronc are in California. You've been in Alaska. I hear one of the former ranch hands is in jail for sabotaging the water supply. Brand has just recently grown up enough to be of any help. Willie and Stogie are getting too old for such a task. Face it, the Bar-6 is radically short-handed."

Out of her peripheral vision, she noticed Clay's gaze on her. After a few uncomfortable seconds, he said, "Been snoopin' into our business?"

Peggy gave a quick glance in his direction and frowned. He was smirking at her. "Oh, you little stinker. Teasing me like that."

"Admit it, Twinkie. You missed our banter."

She licked her lips, wondering how to answer that. Deciding not to, she stopped at the end of the drive and looked both ways before aiming the truck toward town. "How're you feeling, by the way? Dr. Trenton will want to know."

"Good. Only get twinges in my head when I'm too tired now. I think I've remembered most things. Don't know how we'll test that theory, though."

Peggy grimaced at her own absence from his life. "You were in Alaska for quite awhile. Do you have any smokejumping buddies you could talk to? Fill in more gaps?"

"I was closest to Martin. I remember how he died now." His voice had gotten soft, introspective.

"Do you remember the details of that jump?"

"'Fraid so. I can see why his brother blames me."

"It wasn't your fault."

"How would you know? You weren't there." There was censure in his voice...or was it plain ole guilt?

She took a quick look at him. His face was a mask of sadness and regret.

"I know you, Clay. You would put yourself in the mouth of that fire before letting someone die on your watch. I know that for a fact."

Clay's silence made her chance another glimpse. His eyes were on her—solemn but appreciative. "I forced him out that door, Peggy. Martin was no more a smokejumper than I am a crocheter."

She wanted to smile at his cute comparison, but knew this was too somber a topic to do that. "He was a trained smokejumper. From what I heard, you pressed him out to make sure he didn't land in the fire. You tried to save him from that fate."

"And yet, that's exactly where he ended up. I don't blame Bruce for hating me."

"He can hate you all he wants. But kill you? The Montana police are still looking for him, you know. They've teemed up with our sheriff. I don't know if you've heard, but Bruce came back to Sundance and killed his mother."

Clay's head spun in her direction. "He did what? That's not possible. He doted over that woman," he barked. "Where'd you hear that?"

"In town. The sheriff thinks it might have been an accident, but she's dead nonetheless. He's wanted on one count of attempted murder...of you...and one count of manslaughter. He's not a good man, so stop taking his side. You *did not* kill his brother."

"Not on purpose. I should have stopped him from jumping at all. He didn't want to go. I forced him."

Peggy slowed the truck to make the last turn toward town.

"You encouraged him to do his job, and to do it before he'd get hurt. Stop blaming yourself. It seems to me you've done that way too much in your life."

"Nah."

"Yes, you have. You blame yourself for Martin's death. You blame yourself for causing your dad grief. You blame yourself for not being a better father-figure to all your brothers—"

"Wait." He shifted in the seat so he could study her more carefully. Moved closer. "How did you know…?"

"You don't think I watched you try to take care of your siblings? Colt got the glory as the 'old soul' of the family, but you were the one who cared the most. Kept the most watchful eye. None of that got past me. It's one of the reasons I fell in love with you. It's also why your heart shattered when you thought Colt betrayed you with me. It wasn't just me who betrayed you. You thought one of your beloved brothers had too, even though you were dead wrong."

Clay was listening to her. Intently.

She regripped the steering wheel. "And you blame yourself for our divorce."

CHAPTER 34

A hush came over them. So thick, Peggy felt the weight of it against her. She slowed the truck, then pulled over to the wide shoulder and pushed the stick into neutral. She waited while he absorbed the information she'd just lobbed at him. Information it had taken her years to formulate as she'd contemplated every inch of their failed marriage. Now, all she could do was wait to see how Clay absorbed it.

She twisted to the side, pulling her knee up on the seat to watch Clay. He had turned away from her to look out his side window, running his thumb over his bottom lip again and again.

Still she waited. Turned the engine off and waited some more.

Finally, when she thought she'd have to give in and drive them on to the doctor, he spoke. "You're right," he said into the window. "It was my fault. All of it."

"No. Not all of it. It takes two, you know."

He turned his face toward her. Their eyes met and locked. His were dismal, dying. She had to do something to save this poor man. The man she loved more than her next breath.

He rubbed a palm down his thigh to his knee. Set his gaze on nothing in particular out the windshield. "Truth is, I never believed I deserved you. When you came to Sundance High, it was like the sunshine came with you. Before you, my life was colorless. I went through the motions of throwing that football, riding that bronc, climbing that hill, dating that girl. You name it, I did it. It wasn't until you came along, smiled that bright smile, and gave me the time of day that I began to live…to breathe. I couldn't believe it when you became my friend, then my girlfriend. I boasted and beamed and thrived, because Margaret Ann Sassman wanted me."

He stopped, turned his gaze back to her stunned face. "My Sunbeam. Gad, I was proud. And content. Then when you said you'd marry me, I was so happy I thought I'd never feel grief again in this lifetime."

His smile was brilliant, right before it died and a sneer took its place.

She shuddered at his sudden change.

"Then I began the self-destruction. No one did it to me. I did it to myself. To us. I didn't believe I deserved you, and then I made it come true. I saw my rodeo buddies flock to you. Even my brother seemed to take interest. And in my mind you never turned a one of them away. I even began to feel you slip away from me in the bedroom."

Peggy took a breath and held it. It was vital she not interrupt him, though she wanted to defend herself and the beautiful intimacy they'd always shared. But she knew he had to get through this or there would never be any hope for them.

"All lies, of course. I knew that deep down. It was me trying to ruin things so I controlled your leaving instead of the other way around. I figured it would hurt less that way. And as much as I knew divorce was inevitable, instead of nodding my head in agreement when you actually handed me those papers, it felt more like you'd reached inside my chest and yanked out my lungs. I haven't been able to take a full breath since."

"Oh, Clay." Her voice was thick with a barely quelled sob. She reached out to grasp his hand. "Believe it or not, handing you those divorce papers absolutely crushed me. I've been brokenhearted ever since."

He pulled his gaze from hers, dropped it to their connected hands. "Why'd you do it then?"

He asked so softly, she barely heard him.

"Look at me, Clay."

He did. She let him see the pain in her eyes. The agony she fought daily to hide so that no one else knew what she lived with. "I was young. Stupid. Still thinking like the teenage girl I was. I honestly thought that if I handed you divorce papers…you would…you would rip them up right in front of me and take me in your arms and love me again. That was my fantasy. I didn't want a divorce, Clay. I wanted to shock you out of the way you were treating me." She took another choppy breath. "Imagine my surprise when you read those first few lines so carefully, when you looked up at me with such excruciating pain in your eyes, and then nodded. You didn't say another word. Just turned toward the house with the papers in one hand. I wanted to scream at you. Make you do what I'd prayed so hard you would do."

His nostrils flared. "What does that say about God, Peggy? That He doesn't answer prayers? He didn't answer mine either."

She let her eyes drift shut and pleaded to God for the right answer.

It came.

She opened her eyes, pinned him with her gaze, and told Clay the truth as best she could express it. "God answers the prayers of the faithful, Clay. Every time. Sometimes our prayers are in line with what He wants for us, so the answer is an immediate yes. Sometimes they reveal the naiveté of a teenage girl, and the answer is no. And sometimes the answer is wait, maybe for years." Peggy rubbed the ache in her heart with trembling hands and looked into the very depths of who Clay was. She beseeched him. Pled with him. To understand her actions back then. To unblock the love she knew he had bottled up. To try again.

As he stared back at her, she watched the emotions swirl around in his eyes. But as she watched, the hopefulness she first saw began to slip into distrust and despondency. Had it gone too far, this chasm of theirs? Would they not be able to pull the edges back together so they could mend?

She wouldn't give up. She couldn't. What would she have left if she did?

Clay pulled his lips in and bit down. "We have a lot to think about," he finally said. "Doc is waiting."

And just like that, hope tried to shatter. But she wouldn't let it.

"You're right." Her voice was taut, barely audible. She turned back in the seat and started the truck back up. It was hard to take the next few breaths with her constricted lungs, but she was determined to be strong. Clay'd had years of feeling betrayed. He needed time. It was okay. They'd be okay.

The rest of the trip to Dr. Trenton's office was strained. She'd forced herself to discuss menial things in order to keep them talking and had nearly run out of topics when she pulled into the parking lot.

Clay popped out of the truck and looked back at her. "Coming?"

She smiled and hoped it didn't look too shattered. "I'll be right there."

His brows pulled together in a confused frown, but he nodded, stuffed his hat on, and banged the door shut.

She watched until he was inside and then dropped her forehead to the steering wheel. What she wanted to do was cry. What she did do was pray. "*Lord, I come to you humbly, I come to you broken. Forgive me for lying, for manipulating events according to my will.*" The divorce papers back then, the lie she'd lived in the Missoula hospital now. How she wanted to crawl into a hole. If ever there was a slow learner…

"*I'm so sorry, Lord. Please align my heart with Yours. I yearn for Clay. I want to make a family with him; I want us to make you proud. That is my desire. Show me clearly if you want something else. Amen.*"

By the time Peggy let herself in the door, Clay was being called to the back by a very pregnant nurse. He eyed the nurse and raised his brows, then turned his head toward Peggy as he rose. "You coming?"

Surprised at the invitation, she nodded once and followed.

The nurse ushered them both into the exam room and patted the new examination table.

Clay frowned at her. "What do you want me to do with that?"

"You can sit on the end for now, let your legs dangle. Well, they're so long you can probably rest your feet on the floor. Whatever's most comfortable."

Clay went to the padded table and leaned-sat on the end.

"Are you Peggy Cooper?" the nurse asked.

"I am."

"Nice to meet you. I'm Sandy Prickett. This is my last day. I hear you're taking my place."

"Oh! When is your baby due?"

"Overdue." Sandy blew out an exasperated sigh. "I'm so glad Dr. Trenton found you. It's darn near impossible for me to stay on my feet these days."

A pang of jealousy tapped Peggy's heart at the thought of a newborn. She wondered how many children she and Clay would have had by now, if it hadn't been for her foolishness—and his insecurity. At least now she knew she didn't have to shoulder the full burden of guilt for their failed relationship.

"Oh, wait a minute." The nurse looked down at Clay's medical records. "Your last name is Cooper. I should've realized. You two are married. Any little ones in your future?" She looked from Clay to Peggy and back again with a bright smile on her face.

"We're not—" Peggy began.

"Down the road, I'm sure," Clay said over the top of Peggy's words.

The nurse clapped and smiled some more. "That's wonderful. You're a handsome couple. Good luck to you. The doctor will be in shortly."

With that, the nurse waddled out. As soon as the door closed, Peggy turned and faced Clay. "Down the road? Want to explain that?" She couldn't help the small tilt up of her lips, but worked extra hard not to beam and burst into song.

The look on Clay's face gave nothing away. He blinked. Studied her. Blinked some more. He'd just parted his lips when the door clicked open and in came the doctor. This had to be the mother of all bad timing.

Peggy sighed and turned to greet the doctor.

"How are we today?" Dr. Trenton approached with Clay's records in his hand. He reached out a hand, and Clay met it with a shake.

"Were you planning to stay today, Peggy? Sandy is here, and since tomorrow is Friday, you can start Monday if you'd like."

"That would be perfect, Doctor. That way I can drive Clay home."

"Well, let me take a look. It might be we'll let him drive."

Clay lit up at that statement, though Peggy felt utterly deflated at the prospect of him not needing her anymore.

For the next twenty minutes the doctor poked, prodded, cuffed, and tested reflexes. He took his time checking Clay's eyes and asking him pointed questions. Finally he asked, "How's the Achilles? Dr. Harris sent

X-rays of it upon my request. But how's he walking?" He looked to Peggy for the answer.

"Perfectly, Dr. Trenton. I think some of it has to do with him not even remembering he should limp. When he woke up from the coma, he didn't remember the injury. It's amazing what the body can do when our brains don't get in the way." She leaned forward as if confiding a secret. "Of course, I did work my magic on it all those months, so it should be better than ever." She rolled her eyes at the mock praise she'd given herself.

"You tease. But you know your stuff, Peggy. I'm sure Clayton is far better for it." The doctor looked to Clay. "You probably don't realize what a gift you were given having Peggy with you all those months. Without her working your muscles daily, you would have had a much harder time of it. Maybe even lost mobility permanently. Believe me, I've seen it happen."

Clay glanced at her, a look of awe registering on his face. "Guess I haven't stopped long enough to give it thought. She is pretty amazing." His eyes softened, and one side of his mouth quirked up.

Butterflies started fluttering around in her stomach. The man could still give her butterflies! She smiled at how far they'd come.

"Well, Clayton," the doctor started. "You're cleared for light work." He pointed a finger in his face. "Light work. I mean it. No risk taking. No heavy lifting. Otherwise, you can do as you please."

"Can I fly?"

"Oh, I forgot you own a plane. Sure. But you must promise me if you feel light-headed or get confused, you'll land and come to see me."

Clay thrust his hand out again. "You bet I will. Thank you, Doc."

The doctor shook his hand, then held it for another split second longer. "As far as driving, I hear you've been offered a job as a traveling instructor with the smokejumpers. It will mean a lot of travel by car, I'm told. Even if you decide to fly instead, as long as you take it easy and don't travel too much at one time, you should be good to go. If your vision gets fuzzy, stop right away. Of course, it goes without saying, if anything changes in the way you're feeling, come see me. If you're not in town, give me a call and I can likely recommend someone in that area."

Peggy sat stunned through the doctor's speech. She felt Clay's sheepish gaze glance off her briefly, then return back to the doctor. Suddenly she was the one who felt faint.

"I'll do that," Clay said. "Thanks."

The doctor said his goodbyes and exited the room. "Hang on a minute. I'll be right back," Clay said to Peggy, then followed the doctor.

When he returned, he grabbed up his hat and pushed it on his head.

"What was that all about?"

Clay grinned. "Nothing. Just had a question. Come on." He made a beeline for the door. Peggy stumbled after him, through the two doors he opened for her. He tugged open the passenger door of the pickup and gestured her inside.

She balked. "But I—"

"No. You heard the doctor, Sunbo. He says I can drive now. And you can be sure that's just what I'm gonna do."

She clambered into the seat on nerveless legs. He slammed the door and tootled around the pickup to the driver's side. He slid in with a big smile on his perfect mug, readjusted the seat, then reached out his hand for the keys.

She plopped them in his palm, feeling a smile form on her own face. When Clay was happy, she was happy.

Peggy watched Clay's driving carefully, but he didn't miss a gear. Miles passed. He still had that contagious smile riding his face. "Happy now?" she asked.

"Happy."

She tried to keep from asking, but her mouth didn't heed her brain. "Want to tell me what the whole 'traveling the country training smokejumpers' was all about?"

He groaned. "You knew this was coming."

"I knew they might have you train. Not travel to train."

"Apparently." He didn't look any happier about it than she felt.

"How long have you known?"

"Since I went to West Yellowstone."

"Is that why you went there? I thought it was to avoid physical therapy on your Achilles."

"You think I would have driven there in the dead of winter to avoid you?"

"Not me—Wait. You went there to avoid me?" She'd tried to keep the hurt from her voice but hadn't quite accomplished it.

Without looking at her, he reached a hand over and patted her on the thigh. "Not you. Just the torture you caused."

"Oh, ha ha. So you remember that now?"

"Like I told you before. I remember everything. Except the assault."

"You don't remember Bruce clobbering you?"

"Pretty sure I didn't see it coming."

"Makes sense." She was avoiding the main issue. Afraid of what he'd say. What if he took the job and never saw her again. What if that's what he truly wanted? Would that be all right with her if it made him happy?

"I can hear your wheels crankin' over there, Sunbo. What's up?"

She flinched at his perfect guess.

He chuckled. "Spit it out."

"No."

"What do you mean, no? No, you're not thinking of anything, which we both know isn't true. Or no, you don't want to tell me."

"Oh, Clay…" She felt tears gathering at the backs of her eyes. He was going to leave her, and there was nothing she could do about it.

What would it take to get him to let some of the love swirling and teeming at his banks flow toward her again?

He tapped the steering wheel with his finger. "You need to know if I want you in my life."

She slapped both hands to her face then rubbed. "My gosh. You never were a subtle man."

"Beating around the bush is a waste of precious time." Clay found the same widening in the road Peggy had used on the way into town and pulled over. He killed the engine and cranked down his window. "Open your window so we can get some breeze."

She did as he asked, then held her breath.

"Look at me, Peggy."

Again, she obeyed, trying to hide her worry behind her professional face.

"I'm glad to have gotten the all-clear from Doc. I'm going home to pack."

Her heart flipped then dipped.

"Then I'm flying to West Yellowstone tomorrow to see about this new job. It's time I get back to work."

She swallowed, trying to bring some moisture back to her mouth. "Just seeing about it?"

"It's a done deal, if I want it. Unless I decide to ranch, I don't really have a choice, do I? Smokejumping is too risky for this old man now." He laughed, though there was no humor in it. "Never thought I'd hear myself say that."

"Do you want this job?"

"It'll be lonely."

Her heart brightened, hope filling her. "Yes. Lonely."

"Would you like to come with me?"

Now her heart sped so hard she got light-headed. Did he mean just tomorrow? Or forever? "Tomorrow?"

"Sure. You haven't flown with me yet." A contemplative look crossed his face. "Have you ever flown?"

She shook her head, nervous to think about flying. Especially in a small plane. But for Clay, she'd tackle anything. "Never been. I'd love to go."

"It's settled then. Pack for an overnight. We'll stay at Harper's, then fly back the next day." He grinned, looking positively euphoric. Most pilots got excited about flying, so she wouldn't take it personal. He probably just wanted company.

"I'll pick you up at 7:00 AM."

"Okay."

Clay turned over the engine with a flourish and took them back to the Bar-6, whistling Johnny Cash's "*Oh Lonesome Me*" as he drove. She couldn't remember the last time he'd whistled happily.

Maybe her life was ready to bust its banks and venture into an undetermined future.

CHAPTER 35

The next morning Clay pulled up to Peggy's folks' house and watched her practically skip down the walkway toward him. She was cute as a bug with her white pedal-pushers, frilly white and blue blouse, and sandals to match. The sleeves of her navy sweater were tied around her neck. Her silky blond hair was high on her head in a thick ponytail that tossed about with every step and swing of her hips. She looked more like she was heading to the marina for a sail rather than a flight, but he didn't care what she wore, just that she'd agreed to come with him.

He let himself out of Brand's pickup and gave the fender a little pat, grateful he didn't have to drive his clunker to the airfield in Gillette. Hustling around the front grill, he got to the passenger door just before Peggy. He opened it, darn near bouncing on his toes with pure glee. "Good morning, Sunbo. Sleep well?"

She nodded. "You're in a good mood today."

"Nothing better than flying." *With your best girl*, he wanted to add but didn't. He couldn't wait to introduce Peggy to flying, one love to the other.

After stashing her overnight case behind the seat and helping her slide in, he shut her door and hummed to himself on his way back to his side of the truck. Yes, he loved Peggy. Gad, he loved her. And yes, her commitment to him during his coma showed she was in it for the long haul this time. They were just kids before. As adults, they stood more than a good chance of making it.

Yep. He was ready. If she wanted another chance, he was willing to give her one.

That decided, his hum turned into another whistled Johnny Cash tune as he pulled out of her neighborhood and onto the highway toward Gillette.

They relaxed into each other's company, chatting amiably about his first time in the cockpit, her first day in Anatomy Lab. They were catching up, like two friends on a date. He warmed to the idea. He purposely kept the conversation light, keeping his big gun of an idea under wraps until they got back tomorrow.

An hour later, he aimed the pickup toward the hangar where his Piper Comanche was stored. His pulse sped. "Here we are." He rubbed his hands together and grinned toward her. She looked nervous. He almost giggled. She'd get over it once they were in the air.

They piled out of the truck, luggage in his hands, and headed to the hangar's side door. With a shoulder, Clay flipped on the lights. The fluorescents flickered and buzzed and stretched into bright bars of white light overhead. He breathed in the smell of rubber, grease, and stale air, and shivered with anticipation. Forgetting all about Peggy, he strolled up to his baby, dropped the bags next to her sleek bronze and white body, then caressed the wing as he made a sweep around her tail and back to the propeller. Six passengers could fit in her fuselage pretty as you please, with room to spare.

When the warmth of Peggy's body drew near, he turned his head to grin like a crazed jester. "Well, what d'ya think?"

"It's beautiful, Clay."

"She…She's beautiful."

"Are planes always females?"

He chuckled. "Planes, cars, trucks, motorcycles, boats… You get the idea."

She smiled back and nodded.

"Wait here." Clay strode over to the hangar's double-wide overhead door.

Once the door was unlocked, he rolled it up to let in the morning sunshine. On his way back to the plane he grinned at Peggy, feeling lighter than he had in years. He was about to fly to Montana with his girl, and his future never looked brighter. For the first time since that fateful day over four years ago, minus his short stint with amnesia, he didn't feel like he had a hole in his heart. It was filling by the minute, with hope, and love, and possibilities.

He slowed to a stop, swung his gaze from the plane before him to the beautiful woman standing next to her. The one who owned his heart. A profound truth came to him as he stared into her sky blue eyes. He didn't give one whit what he did for a living as long as his girl was by his side.

That was a genuine first for him.

Giving her a heart-felt smile, he tore his eyes from hers and forced his legs into motion. While Peggy looked on, Clay recircled the aircraft, kneeling, ducking, and climbing to systematically click down his safety checklist. The engine's cotter keys were firmly seated. The ailerons and flaps moved effortlessly. The landing gear tire pressure was perfect. The fuel tank was full, and no oil leaks were evident. He cleaned the windows, tossed in the luggage, pulled the chocks off the tires, and helped Peggy up the skid-proof ramp on the wing to the door. After sliding across to his seat, he gestured for her to pull the door shut hard behind her.

"Are you going to start *her* up right here in the hangar?" She bit the side of her lip, her eyes wide and blinking. She looked so cute trying not to look terrified, he had to laugh.

"Very good question. Usually no. We use a tow bar to maneuver the aircraft in and out of cramped spaces. But this hangar is large, and we have it all to ourselves right now. We can roll from here. The crew will close it up later."

She nodded with those big eyes of hers, clearly only partially convinced.

He shrugged with a laugh. Having already called in his flight plan before picking up Peggy, he was good to go. He pulled on his headset, inserted the key, opened the small window to his left, and hollered, "Clear," then turned the engine over. It roared to life before he closed the small window. The sound of the prop spun joy right through him.

He looked over at Peggy with a grin. "Ready?"

She looked ready to hyperventilate, but graced him with a nod anyway.

He laughed and let off the brakes, using the pedals to taxi his baby out of the hangar and onto the runway.

He spoke to the tower—or more like radio operator in this small airport. "Niner-Zero-Two-Eight Papa, ready for takeoff".

"Two-Eight Papa, you're cleared for takeoff on runway 16/34," the radio rasped over the airways. The radio operator continued with weather information while Clay taxied to the far end of the runway. He pressed hard on the left toe-brake pedal, throttling up to bring them around. He set the flaps, then dipped his head and smiled into Peggy's face. "You ready?"

She bit down on her bottom lip with a smile leaking over the top. Nodded.

"Okay. Here we go."

Clay's feet were well planted on the brake and rudder combination, his toes pressing against the brakes while he pushed the throttle all the way in. The propeller sped and the plane rocked under the pressure of being held back until it was time. Then with a wide grin and a flush of exhilaration, he let off the brakes and the plane gained speed down the runway. He controlled the rudder with his feet. The speedometer reached 70...80 mph. He eased back on the yoke. The Comanche glided off the runway, smooth as silk.

Peggy gave a little squeak, then covered her mouth, her eyes wide. Clay grinned at her as he continued to climb up and over the thousand feet they needed to fly over the city. He tugged the lever to raise the landing gear and lowered the flaps. It was easy flying from that point on.

He glanced at his passenger every so often to make sure she was doing fine as he circled to climb higher. Peggy yawned once to pop her ears, but otherwise she grinned like a little girl on Christmas morning. He banked toward Montana. Peggy clung to the armrest with her left hand and leaned hard toward the window to take in the beautiful sight of farm and ranchland in neat little squares of green, brown, and gold. Rows of crops and bales of hay coated the countryside, houses dotted the landscape, and rivers weaved throughout.

Pulling his headset off his right ear, he caught Peggy's eye. "You okay?" he said, raising his voice over the engine roar.

She nodded and smiled. Sunbeam indeed. He reached over, squeezed her forearm, and beamed back at her. He couldn't remember being happier. Even when they'd been married, the constant tension of travel, crazed broncs, tight purses, and rowdy buddies kept him and Peggy from truly enjoying each other. Today, they would do nothing but enjoy each other.

They were silent the rest of the way to West Yellowstone as they both enjoyed the view from seven thousand feet up. The flight only took them an hour. Peggy was amazed. "We're already here?" she yelled toward him as Clay circled the small airport next to the National Park.

"Doesn't take long," he said and flashed her a lopsided grin.

She nodded.

They landed flawlessly, and Clay whooped as he taxied to a space near the Yellowstone Aviation building. He parked and shut the plane down, then pried Peggy's hand off the armrest and laughed. "Sure you're okay?"

"Think so." Her own laugh was glorious, full of relief and joy.

"Let's get on out." He nudged her shoulder until she rose and stepped out onto the wing. He followed, locking the door and sliding to the ground behind her. After he retrieved their luggage from the rear of the fuselage, he blocked the wheels, closed out the flight plan, and the two headed for their ride at the front entrance.

Pete palmed off his cowboy hat and waved it once in the air as he walked toward them.

Clay offered his hand. "Hiya, Pete. How was the drive from Harper's?"

"A bit toasty, but it weren't no trouble at all." Pete grasped Clay's hand with genuine affection. He then turned to Peggy with a squint and furrowed brow. "You're looking paler than a ghost cat. Did ya have a good flight?"

"It was...I don't know how to describe it. Have you ever flown before, Pete?"

"Well, if ya count when I slipped off the barn couple years ago after the earthquake when I was tryin' to fix her, but she had too many holes and I got kinda tangled up and—"

"So. Not in a plane." Clay chuckled.

"Nope. Never been in a plane. There was that time I had to cut off the top of a pine for Mabel to put up a Christmas tree one year, and got a mite too high and tried ta step down on a branch and 'lo and behold', it weren't there and—"

"Got the old truck, Pete?" Clay said over the top of him.

"Right over yonder." He pointed. "So, Clay, 'bout that airplane ride. You gonna take me up?"

Clay followed, overnight bags hitched to each side. "Someday, Pete, someday."

They arrived at the old clunker truck and piled in.

"Think you could drop me by the smokejumper base for a few minutes?" Clay said. "Won't take me long. It's why we're here."

"What? And miss out on Mable's fresh pie?" Pete waggled his eyebrows. "You owe me."

• • •

True to his word, it only took Clay ten minutes to greet Commander Wallace, sign the employment papers, and get his schedule. It was surreal, walking the hallway, knowing he'd been assaulted there but remembering none of it. He acknowledged a few staffers with a nod on his way back out the door, unsure if he should feel embarrassed or proud. Did they know? Did it matter?

As soon as he stepped back outside and breathed fresh air, his discomfort vanished. There Peggy sat, in the center of the bench seat, looking the worse for wear under Pete's watch. Clay chuckled.

He unfolded the paper in his hand and read the details of his first assignment. Lead trainer. Five-week rookie course. Redding, California. Starting in ten days.

He stood planted in place, his legs heavy with the reality and tempo of this new life. He glanced back up at Peggy through the windshield.

She wouldn't like this, and neither did he. No way could they get their relationship figured out in time.

But seeing as how it couldn't be helped, he set his shoulders and vaulted back into the truck.

She looked over and rolled her eyes. He laughed and swung his arm around her, unsettled by the length of his assignment. Still, he pulled her in and hoped for the best. "You talk Peggy's ears off, Pete?"

Pete looked abashed for about two seconds, then resumed babbling wildly into the windshield as he backed up the truck and headed for Harper Ranch. First West Yellowstone slid into the rearview mirror, then Lake Hebgen. Clay and Peggy listened in bemused silence. Finally Clay tugged Peggy closer to his side.

She looked up at him with a question on her face.

He shrugged and whispered, "Pete's a little wild with that shifting. Thought I'd keep you out of harm's way."

She smiled softly. "Thank you."

They gazed into each other's eyes for what seemed like the better part of the trip, and Clay felt the weight he'd carried for years shift to a different sort. Could he simply have a conversation with her about his new job responsibilities and location? Or would she see this as another obstacle she was too life-worn to face?

"Miss Peggy, you two been married long?" Pete asked.

Peggy's eyebrows shot up.

Clay cringed. Whoops. He'd never had the chance to tell anyone at Harper's—other than Roy, who in turn had told only Clint—that they were divorced. Then again, maybe now he didn't have to. He fidgeted. Or, well, seeing as how he didn't want to tell them anything at all, he waited to see what Peggy would do.

She looked to him for answers. He just gave her a closed-mouth grin.

"Uh…" Peggy turned toward Pete. "We got married in the summer of '55."

True. When she turned back to Clay, she shrugged and he chuckled.

"No young'uns yet?"

Clay thought he'd better field this one. "Not yet."

"They're a lotta fun. You've met baby Molly, Clint and Jessica's kid. Cutest little punk ever."

Yeah, she was pretty cute. Clay let himself imagine Peggy, married to him again, waddling around with a big belly and a baby on the way. The idea warmed him clear to his toes.

"Roy's home this time, but not Mary. She's up at her old cabin packing up a few more of her things." Pete said. "Roy plans to head up tomorrow to fetch her. He'll be mighty glad to see you two, though."

Roy. Clay grimaced. Would he bring up the divorce? He glanced at Peggy, wondering if she was thinking the same thing, but her expression gave nothing away.

Pete pulled up in front of the two-story ranch house and turned off the engine. Clint and Roy banged out of the house as if in a race to greet them.

"How are you, Clay?" Clint roared, leading with his hand. The two shook. "You look fully recovered. Peggy here must be taking good care of you." Clint pulled her in for a bear hug.

"Yep. She's pretty amazing."

Roy stepped forward for his turn, one eyebrow raised. "Good to see you, Clay…Peggy." His lips pressed into a questioning smile.

Clay nodded, trying to order an explanation in his mind but thankfully Roy dropped the subject.

Jessica appeared at the top of the porch stairs, her eighteen month old in her arms. The little girl's brown locks framed her munchkin face, and a blue-and-white checkered dress wrapped around her chubby body. A matching bow held back the curls on top of her head.

Clint climbed the stairs back up to his wife and gave her a kiss on the top of the head. "Put her down, little one. Let them see what she can do now."

"Oh no. You want to chase after her?"

He chuckled and grinned. "Sure. Besides, Uncle Pete is here now."

"Okay, smarty pants. Here goes." Jessica set the little waif down, and off she went. No grass growing under this little tyke's feet. She toddled to the edge of the stairs and started to step down.

"Whoops. No stairs yet, squirt," Clint said, snatching her off the top stair and into his arms.

"Told you so." Jessica snorted then laughed.

"Yeah, you're not her momma for nothin'." He gave Jessica a big fat kiss on the mouth.

Clay envied their easy interaction. They seemed able to tease and criticize without giving offense, because with every glance and smile, Clay could tell they adored each other.

He couldn't remember the last time he'd let love flow naturally. Toward anyone. When he was married, he and Peggy fought all the time. It seemed Peggy had always been bent on making him dig for how she was feeling. Was that just her youth or were they truly not suited for one another? The truth of that possibility scratched at his mind.

The front door opened again with a burst of energy, and Mabel beckoned with one hand, the other on her round hip. "You gonna bring them in here or not? Food's turnin' to icicles."

Roy and Clint laughed. Molly wiggled in Clint's arms until he let her down, and she toddled up to Mabel and clung to her legs. Mabel's smile transformed her from the irascible, no-nonsense cook to a melted puddle of goo in Molly's hands. The woman was made to be a grandmother. Clay's soul ached dully, a hint of anger burrowed into the center. His mother would never get to see any of his little ones.

The dark thought hovered over him until the day's activities took on a life of their own. The bustle culminated in Mabel and Jessica's roast, carrots, and potato dinner—one of the best meals he'd ever eaten. His full stomach managed to calm him some, but the boisterous cowpokes, Molly's squealing, and the conversations to his right, left, and across the table made him jittery. His brain couldn't contain it all. Thankfully, Peggy noticed him grinding his back molars.

She stroked his arm while she studied his face. After a minute or two, she turned to Jessica. "Do you mind if we call it a night? Clay's brain still gets a little taxed after a long day, and he has to fly us out of here tomorrow."

"Oh. No. Of course not. We have the master bedroom and bath upstairs ready for you. Roy likes to sleep downstairs when Mary's not here, and Clint and

I…well, you already know about our place down by the stream."

Peggy smiled with genuine relief, though Clay saw through to her apprehension. One bed for the two of them. "Thank you for putting us up tonight."

"Our pleasure," Jessica said, cleaning up Molly and tugging her out of her high chair. "It's time for us to go too, honey." She gave Clint a wink.

He was on his feet and clearing dishes before another word was uttered.

"Come on, Sunbo. Time for bed." Clay likewise winked to his faux bride.

"Hold on a minute. Sunbo?" Clint halted his progress with the stack of plates in his hands, a question in his smile.

Clay and Peggy glanced at each other and grinned. He nodded for her to take the lead. "When Clay first woke up, he had a hard time formulating words. Even simple ones. He tried to call me by his nickname for me, Sunbeam. It came out Sunbo. He's called me that ever since." She turned back to him and grinned.

Her smile suffused him in warmth.

"Ah. I see." Clint's clear-eyed expression proved that the man *did see*. He was no fool. He saw the love that had begun to flow between Clay and Peggy again.

"I can tuck Clay into bed and be right down to help with the dishes. I insist," Peggy said.

Jessica and Mabel both looked horrified.

"Oh no you won't, little miss," Mabel said.

"But—"

"But, nothin'. You go be with that good lookin' man 'a yers. Now go. Shoo." Mabel chased them out of the kitchen with her dishtowel.

Nothing to do but make the best of it. Clay's frisky inner self was cheering, while the rational one—the one concerned with Peggy's feelings and sensibilities— wanted to reassure her he'd be sleeping on the floor. It was Roy's house, after all, and they would be in his bedroom.

They both turned toward the stairs, Clay following Peggy up, and the rest of the world disappeared from view. Just the act of following his wife upstairs at the end of an evening gave Clay's heart a renewed rhythm of hope.

CHAPTER 36

When the door closed behind Clay, Peggy twirled around to face him. The mischief in his eyes made her giddy. She had enjoyed every minute of this day with a tender, selfless, attentive Clay, the adult version of the one she'd married. She wasn't sure what he had in mind for tonight, but she was pretty sure he'd show the self-restraint of the man he was now. Part of her regretted that, but the sensible Peggy knew it was for the best.

"It's okay, Sunbo. We'll enjoy each other tonight and go back to the way things were tomorrow."

Her mouth flew open, and she gasped. Strike that. Had she been that far off base?

"You should see your face." He threw his head back and let out a roar of laughter. Oh, but it was good to hear that sound. Not to mention what it was like to watch him laugh. The man was magnificent. She'd forgotten the good times, buried as they were under the heartbreaks of the past.

Clay tugged her into his arms and tucked her head under his chin. His arms held her snugly. It felt different than it ever had, but oh so good. So right.

"I just want to hold you tonight. Would that be okay with you?" he spoke into her hair.

Peggy pulled back within the circle of his arms and looked up. "Do you think that's wise?"

He chuckled. "Probably not. But since when have we ever been wise when it comes to us?"

So true, so true. She tightened her arms around him. Stole the moment to snuggle her face back into his chest, close her eyes, and breathe him in. True contentment filtered through her body, saturated her mind, touched her heart, filled her soul. *Oh Clay...* "Yes," she said. "I want you to hold me all night."

She took herself off to the bathroom and returned in her modest nightie. She chuckled to herself at how Clay tried his hardest not to stare before he slipped by her to use the facilities.

When he returned, she was already under the sheets, waiting.

Though she knew he usually slept in the buff, a quick peek told her he'd left his underwear on. He slipped in next to her. When he drew in close, he bent down to give her a quick kiss on the lips, then rotated her to her other side. Pulling her back up against him, he held her close. His breath caressed her ear before she felt the kiss on the tender skin under it. "Go to sleep, Twinkie. We have an early flight."

Her heart fluttered, every inch of her body feeling electrified until she finally inhaled a contented breath and relaxed. "Goodnight, Hot Dog."

He chuckled. Clay pulled in a long sniff of her hair and sighed. "Goodnight, Sunbo. Sleep well."

• • •

Morning light brightened the room, coaxing Clay out of the kind of deep sleep he'd only experienced beside his wife. *Wife*. Was that something he wanted to do again? Risk again? At times he was absolutely sure, and others...

"Morning." Peggy turned to face him. She ran her hand down his jaw, his beard rasping against her palm.

A pang of longing hit him. This was how they used to awaken, before he'd chosen the dang broncs or his friends over her. What a fool he'd been.

"How'd you sleep?" she asked softly.

"Better than I have since the six-month coma."

"Oh, ha ha. Not very funny." She tried to look stern, but couldn't quite keep her mouth from tilting up at the corners.

"Kinda was."

Her cheeriness mellowed as she stared into his eyes, hers as blue as the clear Montana sky at the break of dawn. She opened her mouth as if to say something, but closed it and turned over to scoot out of the bed. "Time to get dressed and head out."

He could think of a dozen ways to start this day, none of them being this.

She scurried to her overnight case, grabbed it up, and headed for the bathroom. "I won't be long. I know you're in a hurry."

"I'm not in that much of a—" But the door shut before he could finish his debate.

He sat up and swung his legs out, sitting on the edge of the bed. It was for the best. The last thing he wanted was to give her the wrong impression when he hadn't fully decided if his heart could handle another round of 'love and risk.' The old wounds had nearly filled, and that was Peggy's doing, but that was all he was ready to admit to.

Peggy exited the bathroom, looking adorable in her cut-off jeans and sunshine blouse. He tried not to notice, and followed her lead in starting the day.

They trundled down the stairs toward the aroma of bacon. Clay's stomach rumbled audibly as he stepped around the corner to see Mabel at the stove.

"Where're Clint and the gang? The cowhands?" Clay asked her.

"The cowboys'll be here after they do the feedin'. I suspect Clint and Jessica aren't all put together yet, I imagine. Takes a mite longer with that little rascal of theirs."

Clay chuckled. Yeah, he figured kids took time. Not that he was averse.

Clay pulled one of the bench seats out and gestured for Peggy to sit. Once she did, he tugged them back in and started in on the breakfast Mabel set before them.

Peggy placed a hand lightly on his thigh. "I'd like to say grace first."

He nodded, surprised he wanted that, too.

"Why don't you do it, as the man of the table?" she said, then grinned.

He couldn't deny her anything when she gave him the sunbeam smile. "Not sure what to do, but I'll give it a try."

She hitched a shoulder. "Just say any thankful thing."

He nodded, then bowed his head. "Lord. Thank you for this food. Thank you for Mabel fixin' it. See us home safely. Amen."

Peggy smiled and shook her head.

"What?"

She didn't look up at him, just forked a bite of egg and said, "Like a pro," and began eating.

He grinned, genuinely happy he'd pleased her.

After breakfast, the two said their goodbyes and went in search of Pete. He already had the old truck aimed in the right direction and grinned when he saw them approach.

"Enjoy your visit?" Pete asked.

"Yup," Clay said.

"Very much," Peggy said at the same time, turning to him with a laugh.

The drive was much like it was the day before, with Pete jabbering, and Clay and Peggy chuckling over how obliviously entertaining he was. When they reached the airport, the commander of the smokejumping base strolled out to meet Clay at the plane.

"Go ahead and get in, Peg. I'll be there in a minute." He handed her the key, then turned back to Commander Wallace. "Everything in place for Redding?"

"It looks like they'd like you to begin sooner than we thought."

Clay frowned, suspicious of the sheepish look his new boss was giving him. "And that would be?"

"In three days. But not Redding. You'll still move around but you start in Missoula. To train Hotshots. They're putting a rush on your group. Your commander in Alaska thinks you're the man for the job. And it's a benefit you're a rancher. If you're still there in the off season that crew puts up hay."

Clay nearly dropped his teeth. In three days he was supposed to have all of his things packed up and ready for his first five-week stint and get himself to Missoula on top of it? But training Hotshots had been a dream of his. They were the special fire units who worked the most complex terrain in the nation. His time as a Hotshot had been too dang short before becoming a smokejumper. He loved those guys—their work ethic, their skill set, their physical conditioning.

He'd kept under wraps the answer Dr. Trenton gave him to his final question at the end of Thursday's appointment. Yes, his Achilles was in good enough shape to smokejump again. He'd been mulling what that meant in the long run, but the more thought he gave to it, the more he realized Peggy was his focus now. He'd meant it when he decided he'd do anything as long as she was by his side. And if he went back to smokejumping, he would only force her to live in constant fear of his death. That wasn't what he wanted for her…or him, anymore.

But to train Hotshots. Now that was something he could sink his teeth into…because hotshot trainers often joined their crews at basecamp. He could still be close to the action, but not too close.

"It's been an unusually dry summer. Everywhere." Commander Wallace squinted at the horizon. "The fires are out of control. We need more smokejumpers and Hotshots. Lots more."

Clay rolled his jaw to the side to keep from smiling too broadly.

Wallace narrowed his eyes at Clay. "And, no, you're not going to join the Hotshots at basecamp like trainers often do. You're too valuable on the front end of the training pipeline."

Clay rocked back on his heels, surprised...but strangely unperturbed. This was surreal. He truly didn't care what he did next, as long as Peggy was in the picture. "I understand, sir."

The Commander gave him a pleased smack on the shoulder, then turned and strode off.

After circling and checking his Comanche, Clay opened the door to find Peggy already buckled in. He chuckled at her diligence, and nervousness. Facing her with his hands on her seatback, he stretched his leg to his side, gave her a quick kiss on the mouth, then crawled over her and into his seat.

"'Off we go into the wild blue yonder...'" he sang.

"'Climbing high into the sun...'" she sang back.

He grinned, unable to take his eyes off her smile. If he knew they'd make it this time, he'd ask her to marry him right here and now, and never look back.

That was the question. Would they make it? He needed a test...a big one. Maybe that would satisfy his apprehension.

Peggy seemed better...more at ease as they flew back to Wyoming. Puffy cumulus clouds dotted the cerulean blue sky. The temperature was high, but once they approached ten thousand feet, the air flowing into the cabin was cool and soothing. Here he was, flying his own plane with his girl at his side. Clay couldn't think of a more perfect moment.

Maybe he could borrow a vehicle to use at each job site, freeing them to fly instead of drive to the different training centers. *Them*. He smiled.

She tilted her head toward him. "What's the smile for?" she shouted over the engine and wind noise.

He took her hand in his and squeezed, looked her in the eye, and let the simmering exultation he felt in his chest show on his face. She smiled back, a look of understanding in her eyes.

This time, when they landed at the Gillette-Campbell County Airport, Clay didn't have to peel Peggy's hands off the armrests. It helped that the sizzling 97-degree heat outside was magnified in the cabin. They exited as quickly as possible.

One of the hangar crewman approached with a two-fingered salute to the temple.

Clay returned the greeting. "Hey, Bill. Can you gas her up for me...check her out? I have to fly out of here on Monday."

Peggy's head jerked his direction. He winced, hoping to communicate that an explanation would follow shortly, then patted her shoulder and slid his hand down to guide her by the small of her back toward Brand's pickup, parked next to the hangar.

"Will do," Bill said to his back.

Clay waved a hand over his head in answer. He looked at Peggy. "Let's get you home."

She glanced at him again, confusion knitting her brows over her wide eyes. So beautiful, yet so unsure.

"It's gonna be all right," he said, and opened her door.

Clay pressed their bags behind her and closed her door. She stared at him, waiting. He wasn't sure what to say at this point. He wanted her with him. Exactly how that would happen, he had yet to figure out.

They drove in silence back to her house.

When he turned onto her street, she finally spoke. "I really enjoyed the last two days, Clay. Or was it just twenty-four hours?" She laughed. "To think we went all the way to Montana, stayed the night, and came all the way back to Wyoming is amazing. And the views! I love flying!"

A tension inside him he hadn't known was there loosened. "Glad you like it. It's important to me."

She shifted her body around to face him, a frown robbing him of her smile. "What's going on here, Clay? What are we doing?"

Her house came into view. As he stopped the truck in front of the house, he remembered how often they'd done this very thing when they were in high school. "What d'you mean?"

"Don't play coy with me, Clayton William Cooper! Are we dancing around something, or was this a goodbye trip?" Her voice broke as she heard her own words.

Goodbye? Never again. He sucked in a dry breath, trying his best to order his thoughts. With one arm on the seat back, the other dangling over the steering wheel, he faced her. "What do you want it to be, Peg?"

Her face clouded over. "That's not fair. You tell me."

"I don't know what you want."

She bounced once in a huff, her hands fisted, her lips puckered. "Are you joking? Haven't I taken care of you for the last eight or nine months now?

"Yeah. You've been there for me."

"No! You don't get it. It was like a few seconds to you. But the coma was six long, grueling months for me, Clay." Her eyes glassed over. She gulped a couple of times. "You've never had to sit day after day, holding the hand of someone you care about and praying they come back to you."

He watched her vacillate between seething and tearing up, trying to put himself in her shoes. And then, he did. "True enough. I didn't have the chance to do that for Martin. Instead he landed square in a fire while my buddies held me back, and we watched him burn."

Her eyebrows flew up to nearly her hairline.

Clay faced the windshield again, and gripped the steering wheel hard. "I would have loved to talk to him, hold his hand, read to him. I would have even prayed for him if I'd had the chance."

"Oh, Clay." She grasped his hand and held it so tight he thought she'd break bones.

Yeah, he knew it had been a cheap shot. But, by golly, he'd suffered loss too. And Martin didn't get the chance to open his eyes again.

"I'm so sorry, Clay." She clenched her eyes shut and pulled in a ragged breath. "So, so sorry."

"Come with me."

It was as if he'd slapped her. Her eyes popped back open, and her face showed the shock.

"What does that even mean?" she whispered, her eyes pleading.

"It means…it means if you show up at the ranch at 7:00 AM Monday morning, I'll take you with me."

"If I—*What? Where?*"

"Missoula."

Peggy's seat may as well have turned to lava. She bounced, her gaze bobbing from the dash to him, to the lawn outside, and back to him. She cranked her window down. "It's hot in here."

He watched, but didn't say more. She needed a moment to wrap her head around what he'd proposed.

And what had he proposed, exactly? For her to live in Missoula *with him*? They weren't married anymore. That presented a challenge of its own, but those were details he could figure out later. Right now, he needed to know if she was willing to go anywhere with him, any way she could. "I forgive you, Peggy. I'm willing to give you another chance. If you want another try, this is how we do it."

She went stock still, except for the unhinging of her jaw. Beads of sweat slid down her beautiful skin from her temples to her chin. She didn't breathe. She just…sat there.

He'd seen this before—Peggy, motionless on the outside, quivering with outrage on the inside. Adjusting his grip on the steering wheel, he steeled himself for a verbal lashing, wondering what he should have said differently.

But then she made a sudden change. Instead of looking like she was ready to blow, the air about her calmed. By the time she spoke, her face showed no emotion at all. His gut warned him this was even worse.

"Let me get this straight. You forgive me. And if I want another chance with us, I'm to come to you on Monday morning. At the ranch. To fly with you to Missoula. And, if I want another try, this is the only way I'll get it. Does that sound about right?"

"Yes." He frowned as he thought through how those words must have sounded to her. "Well, no. It didn't come out exactly right." Panic and confusion hit him so hard, he felt light-headed. Blinking, then blinking more, and then more, he gulped in a breath. Then tried to gain another, but it didn't come. *Are my lungs blocked?*

"It didn't…come out right." He panted. "What I meant was…" But his body wasn't cooperating. He couldn't find the right words, didn't have enough breath to say them. He tried to breathe harder.

"Clay." Peggy scooted to him, patted him on the cheek. "Clay, can you hear me?"

Her voice echoed to him from the end of a long tunnel, and though she was shouting, he barely heard her.

Nothing around him made sense, other than Peggy scrambling to grab her purse off the floor, tearing it open, and searching for something inside. She found what she wanted and scrabbled back to his side. "Here. Breathe into this."

She held an opened brown paper bag in front of his mouth.

He pushed it away.

"No. Don't." She forced it to his lips and shouted. "Breathe!"

He sucked in a deep breath. Then another. With each breath in and out, blowing the paper bag up then sucking it flat over and over again, he soon had his breathing back under control.

She pulled the bag away and studied his face. "You okay now?"

He nodded. "Think so."

"Panic attack."

At his confused look, she said it again. "That was a panic attack. Not unusual after what you've been through. It might happen again. Here, you keep this bag. If you feel that light-headed, out-of-control, dying sort of feeling again, breathe into the bag. Okay?"

She described what he'd felt perfectly. He gave her a half-smile and a sheepish thanks. "You should go in. I'm fine now, but it's hotter than Hades in here. Probably part of my problem."

"Probably." Her smile waivered, reminding him they'd left things unsettled.

"Listen. I know I didn't say it right, but—"

She placed her index finger over his lips. "Don't say anything more. It's my fault for not remembering your brain isn't always going to function right. Let's cover this again. You said to be at the ranch on Monday at 7:00 AM to fly to Missoula. Why?" She stared into his eyes, worry for him clear, but needing to know where he was taking her.

"My first assignment is at the Smokejumper Training Center there. I want you to come with me. Be with me." The look on her face nearly sent him into another panic attack. Would she want to come with him? Trust him enough? Or was she done with him?

Before he could give her more details to make her decision easier, she spoke first. "I have a lot to think about and pray about. So, I'll see you." She turned away from him then and let herself out of the truck.

"Let me get that for you," he said, starting to open his door when she grabbed her case.

"No. I got it. You should get home. Rest. Bye, Clay. Thank you for the enjoyable airplane ride and time with you. I loved every minute." Her eyes connected to his for a few heartbeats.

Just as she started to slam the door, he called out her name.

She held the door in one hand, her suitcase in the other. "Yes?"

"Pack for several weeks."

She didn't say a thing, just stared as her wheels turned. Finally, she slammed the door and gave him a small wave.

He watched as she took herself up the walkway, into the house, and out of his life. Or so it seemed. She hadn't told him her plans. But then, he hadn't been clear about his either.

Was she gone for good? Or would she show up on his doorstep on Monday morning?

CHAPTER 37

After a restless weekend that ended in a fitful night of sleep, Clay wandered the kitchen alone for an hour before Trevor trekked through the mudroom and joined him.

"What are you doing here?" Clay asked. "You're usually gone before sun-up."

"Came to say goodbye to you."

Clay stared at his older brother. No guilt trip. No disapproval. No list of chores Trevor had to shoulder because Clay was deserting again. Just brotherly connection. Clay didn't know what to say. He resumed his pacing, and Trevor took a seat at the kitchen table.

After several minutes, Trevor spoke up. "Eat something. Or don't. Just sit the heck down."

"I'm heading out soon." He hoped that would distract Trev from getting on his case, but he knew his older brother would slam him into a chair if he kept annoying him.

Clay stopped and looked out the kitchen window for the dozenth time. It was 7:40 AM on Monday morning. No Peggy. He'd told her 7:00 AM. And he'd been pacing ever since *late* changed to *not coming*. What should he do now? His old pickup was packed with as much gear and clothes as would fit in the Comanche assuming Peggy packed double, which he knew any woman would. Man, but he wished to see the absurd pile of suitcases she was sure to bring. Right now.

"She's not coming."

Clay cocked his head so he could see Trevor over his shoulder. "How did you know?"

"Didn't. A man only wears that expression when a woman lets him down." Trevor rose from his chair and, with one stride, stood at the window next to him. He slapped Clay on the back of the shoulder, then turned him. Trev pulled him in for a hug. Clay awkwardly squeezed back, trying to recall the last time Trev had hugged him.

That would be a never.

Trevor released him, and they stepped back from one another.

Clay noted the worry lines etched into his brother's face. "I'm sorry you won't have my help. I know you're short-handed."

Trevor's mouth was grim. "Can't be helped. You were never meant for ranch work. We both know it."

"Still, I'm sorry it's going to pile more on you."

Trev tilted his lips up on one side. "Take care, brother. Glad you found a job you can do." Clay nodded, gave a smile back, then stood there by the sink as he watched his oldest brother and the Bar-6's greatest asset saunter out of the room and on out the back door.

Clay glanced at the clock—7:50 AM. He needed to leave. As it was, he'd have to change his flight plan. Why hadn't she come? Should he call her? No. She'd made her choice.

He staggered to his old beater truck and headed for Gillette. One last hope entered his mind. Maybe Peggy, realizing she was late, went straight to the airport. Clay gunned the accelerator on the old Ford.

Fifty-six minutes later, Clay pulled into the airport, his nerves spun out in all directions. No sign of a Valiant. No sign of Peggy. His heart bottomed out in his stomach. He entered the hangar, numbly, lifting the hangar door and circling the plane by rote. His gaze settled on the airport office building.

Still no sign of a beautiful blonde waiting for him. No sign of his future. The only future he wanted now. The only future that meant anything to him.

Deciding he had to at least try, he half-strode, half-jogged toward the solo building, entering through the back door.

"Hey there, Clay. You're late," Bill said. "I've got your flight plan here. What do you want to change it to?"

Clay perused the station. Black and white linoleum floor with nobody on it but him. Folding chairs set up around the perimeter of the room with nobody in them. The radio on the table by the door, with no one on it. Bill behind the counter. His office behind him. No Peggy.

He turned back to Bill. "Seen anyone this AM?"

"Nope. Just me. No one's flyin' today. Not so far. I might go up in the Cherokee if no one comes in by noon."

Clay nodded, sick to his stomach. Maybe he should call her.

The telephone on the desk behind Bill began ringing as if deciding for him. Bill took his time swiveling in his chair and leaning back to reach for the receiver, sloth-like. Clay clenched his fists to keep from shouting at the man to answer it already. He wanted him to get this call out of the way so he could call Peggy.

Finally, Bill answered it. "Hello, Campbell County Airport—What? Now? Yeah, he's right here. Surprised you caught him. Okay, okay. Hold your horses." Bill looked confused, but he stuffed the telephone receiver into his chest. "This call's for you. Your brother."

Hope bloomed inside Clay. She must be at the ranch. Something had delayed her. He almost leapt over the counter, but ran around it instead. Clay sat on the edge of the desk and grabbed the receiver. "Clay here."

"Clay! We need you up in the air. Now!" Colt's voice was frantic.

"Slow down. Start from the beginning."

"There's a fire on the ranch. It started in the hay fields out back. We're diggin' trenches and trying our best to keep it from the barn and house, but it's headin' fast toward the cabin and the entire east side of the ranch. We're gonna lose the cattle and all our hay if we don't stop it."

"I'll go up right now and take Bill. He can fly in case I need to jump out with my gear."

"*What?* No! We just want you to see how extensive it is. You're not going to jump out of that damn little plane of yours!"

"If need be, I'll—"

"No!" Colt stopped him. "It's worse than you think."

"What do you mean?"

"Peggy's missing. We know who took her."

Clay jumped to his feet, pulling the phone off the desk along with a slew of papers. It clanged hard to the floor. The cord stretched tight, the receiver still to Clay's ear. "What are you talking about? Someone *took* Peggy? Why? Who? How do you know?"

"Sheriff thinks she was on her way here, we figure 'bout 8:00 this morning. Her car was T-boned by Bruce Smith, or someone in Bruce's car, right outside our main gate on the highway."

Clay swore, scrubbing a hand down his face. He'd just missed it. If only he'd waited…

"Bruce totaled both cars. No one's out there now, just the two cars in the ditch. Don't know how they got out. We had the sheriff out investigating when we saw the fire. Get your plane, Clay. Fly over. Then get on your radio to report back. We'll have the shortwave set to channel 7."

"I'll do it, but only if you promise me you'll look for Peggy. Find her, Colt!"

"We'll do our best."

Clay yanked the phone back up to the desk by its cord and slammed the receiver down. *This can't be happening.* Why hadn't he told Peggy how much he loved her. That he wanted her for his wife. That he'd never let her leave him again.

He was such a coward!

Well, he wouldn't be anymore. "Bill, close up shop. We have to go up in my plane."

"You got it, boss."

Clay had never been Bill's boss in any capacity, but he respected Clay. Even if Bill didn't agree with what Clay intended, Clay knew he'd follow orders.

Clay sprinted to his plane and crab-crawled to the back to pull his smokejumping gear out of the tail section and into the space behind the front seats. As routine, he'd already checked his equipment thoroughly, including his helmet, which sat on top.

He poked his head back out in time to see Bill running from the office toward him. "You still have that fire retardant you keep for runway emergencies?" Clay hollered.

"Yep."

"Get it. I'll go through the checklist and get suited up." Bill circled back around while Clay pulled on his fire-retardant jumpsuit. It had a built-in parachute made for tight quarters in the cockpit, but he intended to be ready for anything today.

Bill retrieved the retardant cans and hoisted them, and himself, into the plane. He pointed at the windsock.

Clay checked the sock and nodded his agreement, taxiing for take off.

Bill looked worried. "You flown from the right seat before? You want I should take her up?"

"Done both. When we get in the air, you can take over while I search the area."

Bill nodded, and Clay throttled them up into the air.

A furious plume of caramel smoke writhed to the west. Within minutes, Clay reached the Cooper spread. "Okay, Bill, circle us around."

Bill banked to the right to give Clay the best view. The fire had started near the barn, but with the prevailing wind and two firetrucks from Sundance barreling down the ranch road, Clay knew the real threat lay not to the house and barn structures, but to the baled hayfields due east. Sure enough, Bill's fly-by confirmed the blaze's hungry path.

Clay winced at the damage—and the acres upon acres of fuel ahead. All of Montana and Wyoming were tinderboxes. He wanted to scream. A simple cigarette butt could have started all of this. His vision darkened at the sheer horror of it. Then sunlight flashed off the metal roof of the little cabin in the pines that his grandfather built.

He chopped his hand toward it. "Fly us to those pines. We may have to drop some retardant on the cabin."

Bill slowed the airspeed and dropped his altitude over the forest area that surrounded the cabin. The south line of the fire was headed right for the forest. Clay growled deep in his throat. "The flames will be there in less than thirty minutes. Sooner if the wind builds. Take us closer."

Now only five hundred feet above the tips of the pines, Clay got a detailed look of the cabin's roof—and thought he was seeing things. "Lower. I think I see people."

"What? Are they crazy? Do you usually get squatters in that cabin?"

"No. Never. I have a bad feeling about this." He thought of Peggy and that twisted bastard, Bruce Smith.

The cabin was a heck of a hike from the car wreck, but it was possible they'd covered the distance…

"I can drop another hundred feet, Clay, but we shouldn't get closer."

As if in answer, a gust of wind pushed them into a violent updraft. Clay hung onto his seat and pursed his lips, exhaling under pressure against the G-force. The Comanche straightened out. He peered out the window again. He'd gone lower himself. Search and rescue demanded it. But he couldn't hold Bill to the same standard.

"Do you want me to take the controls for now?" Clay asked.

"Do you mind?"

Clay took the wheel in hand, feet on the pedals. He banked hard and dipped the nose.

Treetops loomed ahead. Bill gasped, shoving his palms against the cockpit roof. "Too close, too close! Pull up!"

"Relax. I'm going to bank your way. Tell me what you see."

A glance at Bill told Clay he had to make this run count. His co-pilot's nerves were about to break, and Clay was going to need him later for more daring feats than this.

"I see…Wait a minute. I see two men. One's dragging a woman along. Oh, sh——! Clay. I'm pretty sure that's Peggy. Let me fly. You look."

Clay's hands began to shake, rage building as rapidly as the wildfire. Bill took over and banked right, giving Clay the next view. Just as they passed overhead, all three people on the porch looked up, affording Clay a perfect view of their faces.

"Pull up, Bill," Clay growled. "I've got to jump. But first take me to the forest edge. If I can drop the retardant there, it should shunt the fire away from the forest line and miss the cabin altogether. I can deal with the fire better in the field."

"Roger."

Clay nodded. "Try not to breathe until after I shove the can out the door. Got it?"

Bill nodded wordlessly and banked for the forest edge while Clay donned his helmet, pulled down the screen, and positioned himself at the door. "We're nearly there, in 3-2-1-now!"

Clay popped the retardant lid, then opened the Comanche's door, battling the wind. He wrestled the container of rust-colored chemicals onto the wing, eyed the landscape below, and shoved the can off with his foot. A fan of red spread across the azure sky. Bill circled as they watched the show under them. The barrel smashed into the ground in an eruption of color. One more pass confirmed effective placement of the retardant.

Clay slammed the door of the Comanche shut, lifted the helmet screen from his face, and turned to Bill. "Take us to fifteen hundred feet."

"Clay, you're not serious about jumping, are you?"

"Up, Bill. As fast as possible."

Bill bit down on his upper lip but pushed the throttle in and circled them up.

When the altimeter read fifteen hundred feet, Clay turned once more to Bill. "Once I've jumped, get on the radio—channel 7. Have Colt tell the sheriff that Peggy and two perps are at the cabin, that the fire is headed due east, and that I'm on the ground. Have them send one of the trucks out. Got it?"

"Got it." Bill's glance was wide-eyed but deadly serious. "Be careful, Clay."

Clay dipped his head and hinged the shield back over his face. He wrenched the door back open. The wind roared against him. He lowered himself to the traction strip on the wing, bracing against door and fuselage, straining to stay upright and balanced. White smoke mushroomed from a red hot fringe of fire far below. Clay took a steadying breath, said a little prayer, and dove headfirst into the open air.

CHAPTER 38

Clay plummeted toward earth, arms and legs extended to catch the force of wind against him, the material of his jumpsuit flapping like hummingbird wings. Immediately, he pulled his ripcord and thanked the Lord the chute opened as it should. It whipped and thrashed before it caught air and opened with a *wump,* seizing him at his back and shoulders with a hard jerk.

If the situation hadn't been so dire, Clay would have smiled at the rush of sheer joy he felt. He loved this. All smokejumpers did. The thrill of the unknown, the squall against your body, the uncertainty of how you'd land, and the battle against the toughest opponent nature wielded—fire.

It was a hard man's occupation, and he'd missed it. But after spending time with a woman who leaned on God instead of her own abilities to get through life, he knew he should do the same. *"Lord, help me land well. Help me find and save Peggy."*

Feeling a sudden surge of strength, he pulled his legs together, knees slightly bent, and glimpsed the wildfire one last time. Then he hit the ground. Pain jolted through his skull. His heel hit hard, the sting in his bones quickly spreading to a burn. In spite of it all, he flawlessly tucked one shoulder into the *parachute landing fall and roll* that was so natural for him.

Leaping to his feet, he unhooked the chute, rolled it into a ball, and ran toward the lodgepole pines. They were less than a hundred feet away. He couldn't have landed a better jump if he'd practiced for weeks.

Chucking the chute behind a large pine, Clay sprinted for the cabin, intent on outracing the flames to his left. He ducked into the forest where the retardant had hit, patting himself on the back for a perfect shot. The red chemicals had spread farther than he'd estimated, successfully diverting the fire to the southeast. He'd have to find a way to redistribute the stream water to the fields next. But Peggy came first. Maybe he wasn't capable of loving her correctly, but he sure as shootin' could protect her effectively.

As he neared the cabin, he dropped speed. Although the little structure was no longer in the path of the fire, it wouldn't take the blaze long to circle around the forest and close in from an easterly direction. He needed to work fast.

Slowing, he eased toward the back wall, trying to keep his firefighting gear from clanking and banging too much. For now he tossed his helmet down and crouched as he slowly crept under the window at the back, then made his way to the south side. Peering around the corner, he was surprised to see the lean-to smashed—the offending large branch lying nearby. It looked to have happened some time ago. The scene slammed home the fact that he'd been gone a long time.

He didn't live here anymore. He really didn't belong here anymore. And, for the first time, that was okay. Instead of running away from his home because love had died, he wanted to run toward the life he was meant to live. The clarity of the moment pulsed through him—and sharpened his focus on the obstacle ahead.

He'd dealt with criminals to save victims before. He'd do it again. Only this time, the life he saved would save his too.

He picked his way through the rubble of the collapsed lean-to and stopped just shy of the corner where the porch connected to the house. He pivoted carefully for a peek. No sign of Peggy or Bruce Smith. A man he didn't recognize, wearing a New York Yankees ball cap, stood on the far side of the porch. Had he been hired to help Bruce take Peggy, then start the fire? Seemed foolish to start a fire only to hide where they could be burned out. Of course, the westerly wind today could have fouled up even the most well-devised plan.

The ball cap man watched the slow encroach of gray smoke curling around the cabin with increasingly fidgety movements. He turned toward the cabin door.

Clay ducked back.

"Smith!" The ball cap man coughed. "It's smoky out here. Fire must be close."

"Quit worrying, Renford. We set it by the house. That has to be half mile or so away. It'll take awhile. Come in here and get us something to eat."

Renford? That was Colt's ex-girlfriend's last name. But Jenny didn't have a brother, and she hadn't married. Clay wanted to growl his confusion and frustration.

"Hold up. Smoke's too thick for the fire to be far away. I'm gonna check."

Good. *Come on out here and check, you nitwit.* Clay's fury rose. Bruce Smith he could almost understand. But this guy? He readied himself.

Renford clopped down the steps, then turned the corner at a jog. Clay lashed out, caught him in the crook of his elbow from behind, and dragged him back to cover. Renford bucked and heaved, arms flailing, heels digging. But Clay had already locked the choke hold with his opposite arm. He maintained tight pressure against the man's carotids until Renford went limp. For one dreadful moment, Clay contemplated taking Renford out altogether. But a new gust of smoke burned his nose and brought him back to his senses. He was no murderer, and Peggy was still inside.

Clay hauled Renford off in the direction of least danger, and tied him to a lodgepole pine at the back edge of the clearing ten yards away, then trotted back to the cabin. He crossed the distance to his previous position at a low hunch and rocked forward to peer at the porch. There was his nemesis, his back to him as he paced away, gazing around. "Davis! Where in Hades are you? Renford? It's time for us to leave her and go. Give Clayton Cooper a taste of what it's like to lose a loved one in a fire. For cryin' out loud, where'd you go off to?"

They plan to leave her to the fire to get back at me? He figured her kidnapping was payback for Martin, but Bruce wanted her to die the same horrific way? Clay might deserve it, but she sure as hell didn't. His fury threatened to spiral out of control, but he lashed it down. *Keep calm. It's the only way you can save her.*

The storm inside him quieted. But only briefly, because as soon as Bruce Smith turned in profile, a lightning strike of remembered pain flashed inside Clay's skull. Recalling the lava hot sting of the crowbar, he felt his stomach turn violently. He staggered back into the safety of the cabin's shadow and leaned hard against the wall boards. That man had tried to *kill* him. Somehow the reality of the attack only now sank in.

Clay gulped a breath, quivering as the blinding white panic leeched away to reveal dark blotches of color that slowly resolved into ponderosa pines. A hot breeze chafed Clay's cheek, followed by a curl of choking smoke. The winds had shifted. He was running out of time. Tucking his nose into his sleeve, he peered around the corner in time to see smoke pouring onto the porch.

Bruce stiffened. "What the—?"

He slowly stepped down the porch steps and tiptoed toward the south end and then quickly peeked around the shattered lean-to. When he turned back, Clay was waiting for him.

"You!"

"Yes, me." Clay leaped forward and tackled Smith to the ground. The man was only two-thirds his size. This would be easy. He punched Bruce in the nose, the cheek bone, the jaw. He could do this all day and not break a sweat. But when he coughed on smoke again, an icy chill sliced up his spine. He didn't have all day. "Did you hurt her?" he barked, cinching Bruce's shirt tighter at the neck with his left hand and cocking his bloody right fist for another go.

If she was dead, so help him, Clay was going to bash Bruce Smith's skull against a rock and leave *him* for the fire.

Clay's fist wavered. No, that wasn't who he was. Not how he was trained, and certainly not what Peggy would want.

Without wasting another moment, Clay jumped off of Smith, hauled him to his feet, and pushed him forward. Bruce stumbled once, then used his lowered position to twirl around and slam his shoulder into Clay's legs. They both went down. Clay's head hit the ground hard. Pain jolted through his brain. White smoke swirled as Clay raised a hand to protect his head, giving his opponent the advantage. As Bruce swung his arm to catch Clay across the jaw, Clay grabbed his fist, bent his knee, and threw him off.

The force of his fury and the added adrenaline sent Smith into the porch boards. Clay was on top on him then, ready to finish him off. But a vision of Peggy blazed through his mind. He had too much at stake. Peggy would never forgive him if he killed a man, and rightfully so. Besides, he wasn't that man anymore. The one who was willing to do reckless things without considering the cost. The cost had been too great in the past. He wouldn't make that mistake again.

"You killed my brother," Smith shouted, not realizing Clay had already decided to spare him.

Straddling the man, looking down into his angry, bloodied face, a revelation was born. He hadn't killed Martin. Martin had chosen the wrong path, just as Clay had done many times before. Life was full of wrong paths taken by heedless, ill-equipped souls who needed their God to direct their paths. For the first time, Clay understood why Peggy drew so close to God. He loved His Creation—enough to guide them if only they'd lean on Him.

"You're wrong." And he was. "I tried to save your brother." And he had. A peace that could only be sent from the Almighty filled him as he stared into the face of evil.

All at once the fury and guilt left him. He jumped off Smith and strapped him to a tree adjacent to Renford's. Clay couldn't be sure they'd continue to be safe, but Peggy was all that mattered now.

He raced back to the cabin, leaping up the porch steps and sliding into the open doorway. "Peggy!" She sat with her chin on her chest. His chest tightened in fear. "No! Don't be dead."

His eyes dropped to her arms, pulled behind her. Restrained. Her feet, too. As he leapt forward, terror overtook him.

He dropped to his knees, wincing at the pain. "Peggy! You have to be alive! Sunbo!" He took her face in his hands, gently slapped one cheek, then the other. She moaned.

She was alive, thank God. Looked like she'd been drugged. Her head lulled, her eyes cracked open. She blinked, studied him as if he were a complete stranger. Those pale blue eyes scanned his jumpsuit and packs. "Who? Clay?" She slurred, but knew who he was. *Thank you, Lord.*

Relief engulfed him. He leaned in, his lips grazing her nose, cheeks, forehead, chin, then finally her lips. An explosion of crazed emotions—love and relief—surged from his lips to hers. The kiss was brief but it tore through him, filling the last of the holes in his heart. He leaned back, baffled and exhilarated.

She looked as shell-shocked as he was.

"A-are you all right?" he asked. "Did they hurt you? Damn, Peggy, I thought I'd lost you. Don't know what I'd do if I—"

He clenched his jaw, eyes burning, chest tightening. No, he couldn't break down. Not now. He dove for the safety of his training, checking her limbs, her face, untying the knots around her legs and hands. But still the pressure inside him climbed. Desperate, he pulled her close and buried his face in her golden hair, breathing her in until he got control of the emotions on his face. Then he had her up in his arms and out the door. "We've got to get out of here."

"Clay, put me down. I'm fine. I can walk."

"We have to hurry, Peggy. Can you run?"

Peggy flexed her legs, then nodded.

He set her down on her feet. They hustled across the porch. "The fire is closing in. I still need to save the hay and cattle."

The smoke had formed a wall around the cabin and them. She grabbed his hand. "Let me help."

Clay opened and shut his mouth, wishing with all his might he could take her somewhere safe. But she was right. "We have to get to the stream before we're blocked from it. Come on." He closed his fingers around hers and ran to the back of the cabin to retrieve his helmet, then steered them south.

Clay weaved in and out of the trees, Peggy right on his heels, holding tight to his hand. The forest underbrush whipped at his pantlegs, tinder dry. One tickle of flames here, and they'd lose the cabin and that entire section of trees. But if he could save the hay and the cattle, he will have won. Otherwise Cooper Ranch was doomed to go under. And the legacy his father had sacrificed so much time and blood and treasure for would soon belong to the bank.

They broke free of the trees and hit wide open prairie, dotted with hay bales for as far as the eye could see. Beyond that, cattle roamed clear to Devils Tower.

Behind him, the smoke snaked low to the ground, so thick Clay couldn't see the main house or barn, only the flaming front skimming across the dry stubble and igniting each hay bale into an inferno. "Come on!"

He took off for the stream, running at full speed across the hay field toward higher elevation as fast as the extra pounds of pack supplies allowed. Peggy pounded after him, right at his heels. Then a memory tumbled in: Peggy Sassman, female track star in the hundred-yard dash at Sundance High School, years of '54-'55. Hallelujah, she could probably outrun him. His heart swelled. As did the wall of fire. But he didn't veer off. Couldn't. They had to reach the stream and divert it to the field.

Peggy stumbled once, but her grip on him kept her upright. His legs felt like concrete pylons. They were both gasping, running out of steam. "Keep going.

Have to beat it," was all he could eke out through the fire in his lungs.

A siren reached his ears, then the rumbling of a large vehicle. A look over his shoulder showed the firetruck heading across a hay field behind them. Oh! And two cars. The sheriff and Fire Chief. All three vehicles plowed over the rough terrain toward the cabin. Smith and Renford would soon get their judgment. They weren't his problem anymore.

The stream was close. Clay only needed to board up the check dam and open the irrigation flood gates upstream of it to shunt water into the fields. It was a system based on gravity that would only take hours to flood the burning hay fields.

Peggy's hand slipped out of his. He grasped at the empty air, feeling his own strength suddenly cut in half. "Come on, babe." The stitch in his ribs twisted in. "Only a bit farther. You can do it."

In the next breath, she was sprinting even with him.

If he'd had any extra energy, he would have laughed with sheer joy. Instead, he blinked back the black edges of his vision in search of the check dam. There! He cut across the last fifty yards to the stream's edge and staggered to a stop, chest heaving, heel burning, and every muscle in his body straining against the weight of his gear.

Out of the corner of his eye, he saw Peggy hunch over, her hands on her knees, her breath sawing in and out of her.

Clay tried to estimate how far the check dam was from here. About an eighth of a mile, he figured. He looked to Peggy. "You don't have to follow me downstream. Stay here, close to the water."

"I'll go…" she said, still sucking air.

Clay nearly denied her, but if she were with him, he could protect her. So he pulled Peggy up onto the stream bank with him and sprinted toward the check dam with Peggy hot on his heels.

Coming abreast of the first flood gate, he yanked the folding shovel out of his thigh pocket, locked it open, and banged the metal gate all the way up. On to the next gate he ran—and the next and the next. His eyes burned from the fire now off to their right, blazing through one bale after another. If only they hadn't been so shorthanded, these bales would have long since been cleared off the field.

Once the gates were open as far down as the check dam, Clay climbed it and twisted on the valve, diverting a full head of water from the stream through the head gate and on to the smaller gates. Water gushed into the field, like a hound after a fox. It rolled over and devoured flames relentlessly, heading across the field toward the ranch house and barn. Clay heaved a sigh of relief.

Now to stop the eastbound blaze behind them.

"Come on." He gestured to Peggy.

She caught the urgency in his eyes and nodded. They ran back the way they came.

Clay scanned the eastern fire front, marking the wind direction. He knew every bump and dip of these fields. Hauling the baler twice a summer for a decade in his childhood had burned the topography in his mind. A fire was a living, breathing thing, and he could think like it, know exactly where it wanted to go. With a glance at Peggy to catch her attention, he pointed toward a gentle slope in the field below. "We're going to build a fire break there. Ready?"

Peggy wiped sweat off her chin and nodded again, wide-eyed but determined.

His heart swelled. Before the goofy grin on his face gave him away, he swung around and headed down. Peggy's footsteps crunched over the several inches-high stubble of cut grass immediately behind him.

A gust of hot wind from the south nearly blasted Clay off his feet. That wasn't the direction of the prevailing wind. He analyzed the live edge at a glance, groaning inside. The fire had grown hot enough to make its own weather. A swirling mass of caramel and white smoke plumed, flames roared, furnace heat scorched. The devil had turned its head to stare them down.

Clay spun to find Peggy, only to have her sprint past him, already on a new trajectory to avoid the wind.

That's my girl.

He caught up and beckoned her to a different area. His heart pulsed in his temples. The sensation was nothing new, but the cramp in his heart was. Why did he bring Peggy out here? If anything happened to her...

But it was too late for regret. All that remained was work, furious, exhausting work. He adjusted his trajectory one more time to outflank the new fire path and skidded on his knees, pack thrown down and zippers open before he came to a stop.

"Here." Clay tossed her his fireproof jacket, a pair of gloves, and his shovel. She stuffed herself into the jacket, then hitched the gloves onto each hand while he donned his own gloves and picked up his flat-nosed pick.

He looked at her, hard, gauging her ability.

"Tell me what to do." Her jaw was set.

Gad, he loved her, so deeply it hurt. He gulped and wrestled his thoughts back to survival. "Start shoveling here. Deep enough to get the dry layer off. We don't have time for more."

She shoved the jacket sleeves up so her hands showed and yanked the shovel upright. "How wide?"

Clay swiveled to take in the full length of the intended break. "Ideally it'd be three feet, but since there's only two of us, make a one-foot scrape and head toward me fast as you can. Got it?"

"Got it." Peggy's voice rang clear. Even swimming in his jacket like a kid playing dress-up in her daddy's clothes, she carried herself with strength.

He stared his fill of her one last time as he pulled off his helmet, tightened the band inside, and plopped it on her head, visor down.

Clay jogged halfway across, dropped equipment, then jogged the rest of the way. He began to scrape against hay stubble and dry ground as fast as his arms could function. It had been months since he'd used these muscles. A burn started in his biceps, then his forearms and upper back and neck. Soon, each impact of pick hitting earth made his head throb.

He looked up to check on Peggy. She'd come a surprisingly long way, her row clean and uniform. Impressive.

Back to his own work, he plowed away until they met near the middle, each breathing so hard they couldn't speak for a full minute.

A diesel thrum vibrated through the ground into Clay's boots, then a shrill siren blipped from immediately behind. Clay turned in time to see a fireman hop out of the rear-facing seat of the fire engine.

Engine crews had their shortcomings with wildland fires, but right now, Clay was fully prepared to kiss the entire crew and the Mack truck's grill. The fire officer jogged toward Clay while the nozzleman, lineman, and driver disembarked.

"The cabin's unharmed. You diverted the fire from the forest with that stunt of yours from the plane." He shook his head, a look of disbelief on his face.

Clay merely shrugged, glanced at the encroaching fire front behind them, and faced forward again. "You found the men I tied up? They're the ones who kidnapped Peggy."

"Sheriff has them."

Peggy stepped to Clay's side and hauled off her helmet. Her eyes met Clay's eyes. They shared a brief, grim smile.

"I want you back from this line, Sunbo."

She looked on the verge of arguing, but shrugged out of the jacket and handed it and the helmet to him instead. Her gloved hand lingered on top of his. No words were exchanged. None were needed.

The nozzleman jogged past Clay, the fire hose uncoiling behind him, water streaming from a leaky gasket in the nozzle.

"How much water you got left in that pumper?" Clay yelled while stuffing himself into the fireproof jacket.

"Enough to keep the back burn contained on this side."

Clay raised his fist to acknowledge the help, then bent to pick up the drip torch he'd set down on the fire break. Sweltering smoke blew in like a cruel fog, stinging Clay's eyes and scorching his throat. No doubt about it, the wind was funneling the fire right toward them. Flames crested the nearest swell in the terrain, red hot tongues flashing to lick up the fuel ahead.

Time to dance with the devil.

He looked one last time at Peggy. "Back!" he yelled.

She obeyed immediately. *Good girl.*

He returned his attention to the drip torch in his hand. He prepped it, lit it, and faced the enemy ahead.

CHAPTER 39

Peggy seemed to freeze in place as she watched the love of her life jog off toward danger. This was something she should be used to by now with him, but somehow his hellbent fearlessness disturbed her more now that she was older. Of course, this wasn't about him being reckless. This was about keeping the ranch from going under, keeping his family secure, keeping all these lives on the field safe. It was a good reason to run toward danger. And, for the first time ever, pride swelled in her for what Clay had achieved in his life, and what a difference he'd made. Peace followed. A peace that only the Creator could finish in her. She understood now. It wasn't a mistake that Clay was who he was. God had made him this way. For such a time as this.

The aggressively bold son had always been destined to one day save the ranch from physical destruction.

Peggy bent to work alongside the rest of the fire crew, silently and relentlessly extending the fire break. They worked for what felt like hours, until at last they could take a breather. Peggy swayed on her feet a little, dehydrated, overheated, and exhausted as she was. She leaned against her shovel and wiped her face and neck with her sleeve, then glanced down the line to see the rest of the crew doing the same. The air was still polluted with embers and acrid smoke, but she could finally make out the swell of hills beside her again.

Clay burst through the cloud of white and crested the hill at a jog, yanking off his gloves and stuffing them in a thigh pocket by rote. She nearly melted with relief. When he reached her, he trapped her in his gaze, never wavering as he grabbed the fingers of her too-large gloves and stripped them off in one pull. He stuffed the gloves in another of his pockets, then took her shovel and his pick in one hand and grasped her hand in the other. His hand was rough with grit, his grip gentle despite its strength.

Clay glanced around, then nodded. They had accomplished all they could here. Peggy about burst with a heady sense of satisfaction. So this was what Clay felt out here...

He and Peggy boarded the firetruck along with half the crew and skirted the flooding fields back to the main hub of the ranch. At last, the firetruck came to a dusty stop in front of the ranch house. Clay helped Peggy down before he thanked the crew and sent them on their way.

Turning for the house, Peggy ran her tongue over the sandpaper grit on her teeth. A glass of water never sounded so good.

Rylee was out the back door to greet them before she and Clay even made it halfway up the walk. "Peggy! You're okay. I'm so happy those men didn't have the chance to hurt you." Rylee looked her over carefully, then grabbed her up in a bear hug.

"I'm fine. Just tired. And sore from the accident."

Clay stopped dead, and turned her toward him. "Geez, Peggy. I forgot all about the accident. And here we had you working like you were a bonafide line cutter."

"I'm fine, Clay. Just sore, like I said. I was perfectly capable of opening my mouth if I didn't think I was okay." She smiled up at him.

His smile turned lopsided.

"Come on. I'm hungry." She dragged him by the hand into the house via the mud room.

"Colt wants to see you, Clay," Rylee said. "I'll take care of Peggy."

Clay opened his mouth as if to object.

"I promise to take good care of her."

"Go," Peggy said. "I'm fine. Truly. Go." She shooed him off, then followed Rylee into the house.

"That guy is crazy about you." Rylee held the door open for Peggy.

"Do you think so?" She shook her head, not quite sure she should believe it. "Sometimes I think so. Other times I think I killed his love permanently."

"He was scared, Peggy. Colt said Clay didn't want to fly over to evaluate the fire. He only wanted to find you. Colt pressed him, otherwise he would have let the ranch go and concentrated on finding you only."

She held deathly still, only blinking. "He did?" She mulled that piece of information round and round. No. He was just worried, like he would be for anyone in trouble.

That truth sank in like too much weight on a bobber. Clay had always been the first person to jump in the river to save someone from the current; to pull a person from a burning building, long before he became a professional firefighter; to distract a bull or bronc so a buddy could escape; to ride a horse no one was sure about. She'd been so wrong to believe he'd only ever been heedlessly irresponsible.

Clay was always there for everyone. No wonder he felt so betrayed by a father who never made time for him, unless it was to reprimand him. Or by brothers who thought so little of him as a team player, as a husband. Or by being blamed for the death of a friend he'd tried to save.

But, she mustn't forget the ultimate betrayal: her decision to divorce him because she'd been too selfish, too short-sighted, and much too young.

Peggy groaned loudly and viciously.

"What's wrong? Are you all right?" Rylee peered into her face, brows furrowed.

"No. I'm not all right. I'm a fool, Rylee. A complete and utter fool. I once belonged to the most amazing man in the world, and I threw him away." She stared at her left hand, where her wedding ring used to sit. "And I don't know how to get him back."

• • •

"You wanted me?" Clay asked Colt as he strode up next to him. Colt sat on the far corral fence, facing the devastation. He lifted his chin in greeting and patted the rail. "Take a load off."

Clay climbed up to join him.

Colt studied his features, then pressed his lips into a closed-mouth smile.

"What?"

Colt shrugged, but his eyes shimmered. He tugged at his nose, trying to pass off the emotion as a case of smoke exposure.

Clay knew better, and a piece of his soul that had broken away long ago snapped back into place. He swallowed and nodded back at Colt, respect bleeding between the two. They stared out at the mess that was water and mud and burnt hay and soot and one more attack on the Coopers.

Clay took in as much of the ranch as he could see. His main concern now was the water still flowing in from the stream. It usually took a few days to flow all the way to the western pasture, but since all he wanted was to douse the fire, he'd shut the gates soon. For now he desperately needed to let his body wind down from the hard work and adrenaline.

The westerly wind calmed, fluttering warm air against Clay's skin, lulling him into a stupor. At last, the irrigation water burbled down a gentle slope, past the main camp and toward the west pasture where the majority of their cattle roamed. He sighed.

"Time to turn off the diversion valves, close the flood gates," Colt said.

"I see that. I'll need a few of the crew."

"Take Brand, Eddie, and Sam." Colt tilted his head to look at Clay. "Will that be enough?"

"Yeah, sure."

Colt patted Clay on the shoulder. "Good job, today. We couldn't have saved the ranch without you. You know that, don't you?"

Clay's gaze left the fields for his brother. Colt looked tired, wet, muddy, but relieved. They'd all worked hard to save the ranch. "Didn't do it alone."

Colt slammed a shoulder into Clay, nearly knocking him off the fence. "Hey! Watch it."

"I told you *not* to jump out of that dang plane. You could have killed yourself."

Clay laughed then.

Colt frowned like he was missing something.

"I did this for a living for four and a half years, big brother. Into far worse situations. Bigger fires. More hazardous terrains. Riskier jumps. This was a *stroll down the lane*."

Colt laughed. "Don't you mean a *walk in the park*?"

"Nah." Then they both laughed, enjoying each other like they had as kids.

"Did the sheriff lock up Bruce and whoever that Renford man was?" He swung his gaze back to Colt. "Who was that guy, anyway? Related to Jenny?"

Colt slapped the side of his thigh. "Ah-ha! Yes. So, that's who he is. That's Jenny's cousin. Never met him, but knew of him. That sonovabitch! He probably helped Jenny to get back at me. Sheriff never got it out of Renford and Smith how they knew each other, though. I'll let him know what I know about him. Maybe that'll help with the investigation. For now, he's got 'em locked up. They're guilty. Peggy can identify them both."

"They set the fire," Clay said softly.

"Assume so."

"Don't have to assume so. They did it. I heard them talking about it. Bruce's motive was to get back at me for the death of his brother. Make me suffer a similar loss and take out the ranch all at the same time. I'll need to head in and tell the sheriff what I know. As long as they have them locked up, it can wait until tomorrow. I'm beat."

"Yeah, me too."

Clay scrubbed a dirty hand across his chin. "Tell me. How long have you lived with a saboteur? Sheriff needs to get to the bottom of this pretty dang soon, don't you think?"

"I'm too tired to think."

Clay grunted agreement, then jumped down from the fence. Faced Colt. "I need your help with something."

Colt's brows nearly hit his hairline. "You don't say. What is it you think I can help *you* with?"

Clay regarded him a moment. "You don't think I can draw from you?"

"You're the tough brother."

Clay's smile was weak, matching his remaining strength. His face crackled with the dried soot and sweat. "You're the gentleman."

"Ah, you need my help with Peggy." Colt grimaced. "What did you do this time?"

"It's not so much *this time* as the time before."

Colt arched his eyebrows.

"I have some rodeo *friends* who need a Cooper class on how to be gentlemen."

Colt regarded Clay. "With our fists?"

Clay smacked a fist into his palm. "You got the idea."

"Then, yes. Gentleman 101 coming up," Colt said with a grin back and a pat on the shoulder. He let his hand linger. "Now tell me. What are you planning to do about Peggy?"

Clay's gut clenched. He kept his gaze on the field. He still didn't want to talk to Colt—of all people—about Peggy. "Don't know what you mean."

"Sure you do. You gonna marry her again?"

Clay swung his gaze back to Colt. "Why the heck would you think that?"

"Because you love her. Have since you were in high school."

Clay combed his fingers through his damp hair, letting his mind wander to his school days with the most beautiful girl at Sundance High.

Colt rubbed at the sweat on his cheek with a shoulder. "Look. I nearly lost my opportunity with Rylee because I wouldn't speak up. Don't goof up like I did. You know she's worth it."

"Yeah, she's worth it. The question is, am I? Maybe she'll tell me to get lost. Do I take that risk?"

Colt scrubbed his palms up and down his thighs. "This from a guy who jumped out of planes into fires for a living." He threw his head back and laughed. "Risk is your middle name."

Clay heaved a sigh, feeling the slump of his shoulders. Did he have the strength to do this again? But Colt was right. He'd never stopped loving Peggy.

Colt turned toward Clay, clamped a hand on his shoulder. "Listen to me. I know we haven't always gotten along. But you know I love you, don't you, brother?"

Clay let the statement settle in, testing it for truth, and nodded.

"You've always had a good heart, Clay. Problem is, your heart is so stinkin' swollen with the love you've held back for years, it's probably 'bout ready to burst." Colt gestured toward the water rushing through the field in front of them. "Learn from what you did to save the ranch from that fire. Break open the flood gates. Let your love flow again."

CHAPTER 40

C lay stumbled, trying to twist his boot at the correct angle for the boot tree. After closing the flood gates and shutting off the diversion valves, he'd fallen in beside Trevor, who was riding through the flooded field with his dog, Dash. Trev's face looked gray and drawn, and his gaze swept the ruined fields with an air of refrained anguish. Clay, barely able to stay upright on his noodle legs, joined Trevor's silent vigil and knew what *he* knew.

The ranch was saved for now, but not for long.

Yes, Clay's efforts had won the day, but the weight on Trevor's shoulders pressed firmly onto his own. And for the first time since waking from his coma, Clay wondered at the fact he no longer desired attention or accolades or admiration. In fact, right now, all he wanted was supper, a shower, and to hit the hay…a softer, less combustible hay.

Just as he removed his last boot, he heard a shuffling of stockinged feet against the floorboards behind him. He turned, and the image that met his bloodshot eyes was nothing less than blinding splendor. Peggy stood at the open door, her hair illuminated by the kitchen light behind her, making it look like golden silk. The simple sundress she wore with yellow and white squares, gathered at her chest and nipping in at her tiny waist, reminded him of their early days, before their marriage, when Peggy was young and innocent and oh, so enticing. Thin straps rested on her shoulders. Bobby socks drew his attention to her tiny feet. He desperately wanted to take her in his arms and make her his again. Colt was right. He was still in love with this woman. So much so he ached.

It was time to take a risk.

And it was time to let her know it.

"You look…" he began, but couldn't quite get the words past the sudden lump of emotion caught in his parched throat. He waited as he swallowed, trying to clear a space for his voice. The day's smoke certainly didn't help. "You're incredible. Stunning."

She looked down at herself. "It's Rylee's. You like it?" she said, then blushed.

"More than like it, Sunbo." One side of Clay's mouth came up in a smile. She was such a temptress. Her look of innocence had always drawn him right into her sphere. He was entangled there for sure—and this time, he had no intention of cutting himself free. He grinned at the thought.

"What are you smiling about?" She grinned right back at him, and a new warmth began to surround them. A cocoon of love and contentment and relief. Another thing his brother had been right about. He'd kept his love bottled up until his heart couldn't contain it anymore. Now that he knew he had been the one holding it back, he mentally cranked open the gates and felt the love leap and bound and rush toward Peggy.

"Give me a few minutes to shower so you can stand me."

She chuckled. "Do you think I haven't smelled worse on you?"

He thought of all the times he'd rolled through manure on the rodeo circuit, and a sheepish grin caught his lips.

Peggy threw her head back and laughed.

The sound soothed his soul and awakened in him a fervent gratitude for the God who'd taught others to love him when he wasn't loveable.

It was time he put his faith in something bigger than himself. He'd suffered long enough trying to handle life alone. *Please, God, restore us. Give us a another chance to get it right this time,* he said in his head, knowing full well that God heard every prayer that was voiced, whether aloud or silently.

A peace beyond any he'd ever known washed over him and over him.

Peggy took a step toward him, and he grimaced. "Seriously, Twinkie. You don't want to get any closer." He smirked, and she laughed again.

In the next moment she threw her arms around his neck and fixed her lips on his. All other thoughts and concerns went up in smoke. He wrapped his arms around her sweet little frame and assaulted her mouth with a passion born of a free-flowing heart.

The back door flew open, crashing against the wall of the mud room, and snapping them out of the passion they'd wrapped themselves in.

"Whoa, whoa, whoa." Brand drew to a fast halt just inside the door. "What's this?" Then he laughed and moved in to close the door. "It's about time you two figured out who you belong to." He laughed again as he rammed his heel onto the wooden tree and yanked off his boot.

"Mind your own business, little brother," Clay said, letting go of Peggy, but keeping her snared by the love pouring from him into her big, blue eyes. They gleamed with joy, glistened with happiness. He was sure his reflected the same. "I'm going to shower, then I want to show you something."

She smiled her sunbeam smile and nodded, coming forward to hug him.

An index finger to her forehead stopped her. "Hold that thought, sweetheart. Until I'm clean."

"Okay." If a smile could light up the world, hers did. It was sure enough lighting up his.

• • •

"Glad that smell is gone. Whew." Brand opened the fridge to retrieve a jar of strawberry jam.

"Oh, you think the smell is gone, eh?" Peggy smeared peanut butter on the slices of bread she'd flopped onto the countertop. "You know what they say about skunks don't you?"

Brand whipped upright and gave her a mock look of offense. "That they can't smell their own stink? You saying I'm a skunk, Miss Peggy Sassman?"

"Peggy *Cooper*, if you don't mind. I haven't been Sassman for half a decade." She smacked him on the top of his head, then grabbed the strawberry jam from his hand.

Shutting the refrigerator door, Brand schooled his face into a somber expression.

"What are your intentions toward Clay?"

Though his face showed no signs of humor, Peggy laughed. He had to be joking. "Ah, Brand. You're so funny." She swished a hand through the air.

"I'm not joshing, Peg. I want to know. You can't play with him like that. That kiss? He takes all that seriously. It'll break him apart if you throw him away again."

Peggy's smile dropped to the floor. She swallowed. "Brand. Look at me."

He fixed his stony gaze on her.

"I won't. I didn't want to the first time."

Brand's face showed such relief, she felt bad for causing his worry.

"You two look terribly serious." Clay said, re-entering the kitchen.

Peggy took him in. All cleaned up in fresh Wranglers and a button-up Carhartt rolled at the sleeves, his hair wet and combed straight back. His face was pink from the elements, and his clean shaven cheeks showed every blessed dip and crease of his handsome features.

Oh, but he cleaned up well...and fast. "Don't you look delicious," her mouth said without her permission. Her fingers came up to mask the gasp that came next.

Clay's eyes glinted. "Come here and find out for yourself."

He held out a hand, and without hesitation, she slipped hers into it. He tugged her into his arms, and his smell of soap, and musk, and Clay reached her before his lips did. Somewhere in the background,

Peggy heard Brand scoff and bound out of the room, but all she thought was, *never let me go*.

She parted her lips to deepen the kiss, and he took everything she offered. Soon, he pulled back enough to linger in a barely-there touch for a moment before he broke the contact. "I've missed that," he muttered. "I've missed you in my arms. It's where you belong, Sunbo."

His eyes searched hers. One arm remained locked around her while the other hand came up to cup her cheek. He brushed the silk of her hair back from her face, his palm caressing her jawline over and over again. His eyes softened, hope and fear swirling together. "Don't ever leave me again." It wasn't a question. It was a statement, a fear-driven demand, and she felt it reach her soul.

"Never." Because it was true.

He smiled tenderly at her, glanced at the sandwiches behind her, and tipped his head toward the living room door. "Come on. We'll eat later. That something I wanted to show you is in the office." He took her hand and led her there. With the door shut behind them, he strode to the massive mahogany desk, opened a drawer, and pulled out a folder.

"Sit down, Peggy." He gestured at the chair in front of the desk.

Her stomach flipped. Nothing good ever came from that request. She stayed rooted in place.

"It's okay." He gestured again.

"What is it, Clay? You're scaring me."

He grinned, though it didn't reach his eyes. In fact, he looked as nervous as she felt. What did he want to tell her?

When she finally relented and sat on the very edge of the chair, he sat behind the desk. The leather squeaked under his weight. Clay sat forward a bit. "That assignment I got for Monday? It's a job training Hotshots—for now—in Missoula, at the smokejumper base."

Her breath hitched. Oh. He was going to move. Her heart bottomed out in her stomach. "I see." Her voice squeaked, sounding as strained as the chair had.

"I'm to be there at 0700 hours day after tomorrow. I'll have to fly, or I won't make it in time."

"Oh?" She must sound so weak to him. She cleared her throat.

"Peggy, I…" He stood, as if he couldn't be still and say what he needed to say. Now she was downright petrified.

He came around the desk to squat before her, so he was looking up into her face. "You can be a physical therapist anywhere. While we're in Missoula, you can work at St. Patrick's Hospital." He chuckled. "Or maybe find another hospital, Dr. Harris free."

His expression sobered. "When I'm transferred from Missoula, you can find a new hospital to work in, there. Wherever *there* is. Peggy, I want you to come with me."

He'd said this before. What did 'come with me' mean? She couldn't speak, her mind scrambling around to make sense out of what he'd just said. "You mean, fly with you there? How will I get home?" She was so confused.

He chuckled, then grinned. "Either I'm not saying this right, or you're not paying attention. No. I don't want you to go home."

"So. I will fly with you there. And stay? How long?"

He shook his head and groaned. He shot up to full height and tugged on her hand to bring her to her feet with him.

What was he doing? He turned them and sat in her chair, then brought her to his lap to hold her. "You looked like you might scamper away. Now that I have you trapped…" He grinned, but then wrapped his arms around her and pulled her close, tucking her head under his chin.

She hadn't felt this cherished since he woke at the hospital and thought they were still married. She basked in his closeness. Found herself snuggling in.

"Do I have your full attention now?"

She nodded, her face rubbing up and down against his shirt. His scent filled her nostrils. She could feel her heart swell with love and life. *Please, Lord, let him be asking what I think he's asking.*

Instead of continuing their conversation, he seemed to settle into the chair and mold her to him. They sat there and just breathed. And listened to each other's accelerated heartbeats.

After a few minutes, Clay cleared his throat and sat them up straighter. Peggy whisked her head back to look at him.

Nerves seemed to flare up in him again, which started hers too. What was he trying to say?

"What if," he began. Thought some more, then started again. He ran one hand down the side of his thigh before he slipped it around her waist again. "How would you feel about a person who promised to do something but didn't do it?"

Confused, Peggy kicked her head back farther so she could see his eyes. Her brows scrunched. "Uh…I wouldn't like it. When someone promises something, they should keep their word."

Clay sighed. Seemed to think it over some more. "What if it was an oversight? They meant to do it, but due to…life circumstances, didn't get it done."

"Life circumstances? Like what?" She wanted to demand he get to the point, but somehow she knew playing along was the only way she'd get to hear the conclusion.

"Difficulties. Hurdles…" His voice dropped to a whisper. "Sadness."

She stilled her impulse to ask him to explain. "Well…that would be different."

"Would you forgive that person?"

She shifted a bit on his lap to get a better look at his face. As she studied him, trying to decipher where he was going with this, she thought about how to answer. Finally, the answer came. Obvious in its simplicity. "Of course, I would forgive him. Jesus forgives us. I should do the same. Especially if they ask for forgiveness."

He licked his lips. "Please forgive me."

Now she was really puzzled. Except this had to be about their past. "Forgive you for what exactly? I'm the one who hurt us. I'm the one who asked for a divorce."

"Hold on a minute. Can you grab that folder?"

Peggy looked where Clay was pointing. The folder he'd taken out and set on the desk when they'd first come in. She leaned over to grab it while he held her hips to keep her from falling off his lap. When she brought it back, she looked up at him. "What is this?"

"Open it."

She opened it and, after seeing the title, jerked her hand away, sure she'd felt a sting. "Why are you showing me this?" Her eyes filled as she scanned the document: *In the District Court for the third Judicial District within and for Crook County, Wyoming. Margaret Ann Cooper, Plaintiff, versus Clayton William Cooper, Defendant. You are hereby summoned...*

She must have read the contemptible thing two hundred times while away at school. It had kept her from running back to him.

"It's okay, sweetheart," Clay said, wiping away tears on her cheeks with the pad of his thumb, ones she hadn't realized had fallen. "I'm not trying to torture you. Look at the bottom."

"What? Why?" she asked. What was he trying to do?

"Just...look."

She forced her gaze down and stared at her signature, the flowery scrawl she used in high school. "I see that. My signature." She slumped on his lap, feeling the last of her energy drain out of her. Was this her punishment? If so, she couldn't blame him for rubbing it in her face.

He stroked her bare skin where her sundress had ridden up a little. His touch felt so good, so right.

"And?" he said with a tad of humor thrown in.

"And?" She looked closer. Yes, there was her signature. But...not... "Wait a minute. What am I looking at?" She picked up the document to look closer. "This is the original. Where's your signature?"

He chuckled at her wide-eyed expression. "Where indeed?"

She gasped and stared into his eyes. They were filled with joy and mirth. "Clayton Cooper! You never signed this. Never sent it in." She was half-mad at him for being so negligent until the truth of it dawned. "That means...that means we're..."

"Still married," he finished for her.

"Oh my God!" she said, then jerked her head back, looking up at the ceiling. "Sorry, God."

Clay caught her cheek with his palm and turned her face toward him, calming her. She held her breath and listened clear down to her soul.

"Once we became one, I never wanted us to be apart. I lived too many years without you. I don't ever want to do that again." He brushed away tears that were sliding down her cheeks faster now, though she remained silent.

"Forgive me for not being the husband I should have been back then. My heart always belonged to you. It never questioned who it should love. Only how it would love. And, clearly, I wasn't much good at how to love. Though I don't deserve it—don't deserve you—I want all the days before me to be with you. I want every single memory to be made...and kept...with you. I want to watch you carry my children. I want you to be my wife. I want you."

Peggy's skin buzzed with the vibration of her rushing blood. Clay inhaled under her touch, his shirt tightening across his chest, his heart pounding against her fingertips. He wasn't finished. Her entire world spiraled into the silence between them.

He closed his eyes, then reopened them. "God has given me another chance, Sunbo. Will you?"

Unable to pull in a breath to answer, she stayed glued to his eyes, seeing the hope and love and fear in them. She gripped the material of his shirt in her hand and nodded.

He grinned for all he was worth. "Margaret Ann Cooper, would you do me the honor of being my wife again…still. For life?"

Her ceaseless longing, regret, guilt, shame—Clay had vanquished them all in a single, impossible act of love. She opened her mouth to recite a speech as beautiful and heartfelt as his. "Clayton William Cooper…Yes!" she said, and laughed at what came out. Not elegant. But *the* answer. The *only* answer. "I will go anywhere with you."

Peggy grabbed both sides of his face, and on his lips planted a fierce, wild kiss.

Finally, after many glorious seconds, Clay leaned out of the kiss. His eyes were glazed with a passion matching hers. "Shall we go tell the others?"

She grinned, mischievously. "Can it wait until morning, *Mr. Cooper?*"

Clay shot to his feet so fast, Peggy nearly slipped out of his arms. He tightened his grip on her and dashed out the office door and on up the staircase. "It certainly can wait, *Mrs. Cooper*, it certainly can."

Clay opened the door to his bedroom, carried her over the threshold, and dove into the flood waters of love unbound.

Did you enjoy Clay and Peggy's story? I hope so!

Would you take a moment to leave a review and rating? It doesn't have to be lengthy. Just a sentence or two to share what you liked about the book.

Use this link: https://www.amazon.com/gp/product/B07Y2 HLCWZ

Thank you for reading *Let Your Love Flow Again*, and for leaving a review!

• • •

Do you want to be one of the first to know when Book Four comes available? Join my newsletter.

TO JOIN MY NEWSLETTER and receive a FREE book, leave a message at any one of these links:

www.janithhooper.com

Facebook: www.facebook.com/groups/janithhooper

Email: janithhooper@gmail.com

AUTHOR'S NOTE

A MESSAGE ABOUT FLYING

I was very young (only 17) when I started my flying lessons. At the time, my dad owned Rainbow Aviation at the Sutter County Airport in Yuba City, California. What an adventure it was for me, as a teenager, learning how to fly. My dad owned five airplanes at the time that were available for flying lessons or charters. The Piper Comanche featured in this book was my father's personal airplane. The Cherokees, the Mooney, and the Citabria (an aerobatic aircraft—oh so fun) were the work-horses. It was an interesting time in my life. I learned a lot about the art of flying, which I did my best to bring to life for you in this book.

I hope you enjoyed reading *Let Your Love Flow Again*. Stay tuned for the next installment of the Cooper family's Life Without Breath series, as sapphire-eyed Hunter, the veterinarian, takes center stage.

ABOUT THE AUTHOR

Janith Hooper grew up on a ranch in northern California. Ranch and farm life is what she knows, romance what she adores, and western romance what she loves to write. Janith lives with her husband of forty-six years in Oakdale, California—Cowboy Capital of the World. She has four grown sons, three daughters-in-love, and five grandchildren. After raising her four sons, God directed her path to write novels. A Quaking Heart is her debut trilogy (Harper Ranch Series). Three books in her next series (Cooper Bar-6 Ranch series—A Breath Without Life Novels) are now available.

Now fourteen years into this writing journey, Janith still treasures every joyous moment of writing with God for you, her beloved readers.

Visit her website: www.janithhooper.com

Facebook: www.facebook.com/groups/janithhooper

Email: janithhooper@gmail.com

Made in the USA
Coppell, TX
23 July 2023